I0601648

THE BEAUTIFUL CLUB

A NOVEL

DAVID W. FREDERIKSEN

simply francis publishing company
North Carolina

Copyright © 2025 David W. Frederiksen.   All Rights Reserved.

No part of this publication may be reproduced, stored in a retrieval system or transmitted, in any form or by any means-electronic, mechanical, photocopying, recording, or otherwise without the prior written permission from the publisher, except for the inclusions of brief quotations in a review.

All brand, product, and place names used in this book that are trademarks or service marks, registered trademarks, or trade names are the exclusive intellectual property of their respective holders and are mentioned here as a matter of fair and nominative use. To avoid confusion, *simply francis publishing company* publishes books solely and is not affiliated with the holder of any mark mentioned in this book.

This is a work of fiction. Any references to historical events, real people, or real places are used fictitiously. Other names, characters, places, and events are products of the author's imagination, and any resemblance to actual events or places or persons, living or dead, is entirely coincidental.

NO AI TRAINING: Without in any way limiting the author's [and publisher's] exclusive rights under copyright, any use of this publication to "train" generative artificial intelligence (AI) technologies to generate text is expressly prohibited. The author reserves all rights to license uses of this work for generative AI training and development of machine learning language models.

Library of Congress Control Number: 2025919857
ISBN: 978-1-63062-081-3 (paperback)
ISBN: 978-1-63062-082-0 (e-book)
Printed in the United States of America
Cover and Interior Design: Christy King Meares

For information about this title or to order books and/or electronic media, contact the publisher:

simply francis publishing company
P.O. Box 329, Wrightsville Beach, NC 28480
www.simplyfrancispublishing.com
simplyfrancispublishing@gmail.com

DEDICATION

To my beloved wife, Julie Lane, who said, *Then write.* To Miss O, Zozo, and Evie, thanks for the best job in the world—being your Dad.

It is hard not to desire things that are beautiful and attractive.

The Buddha

CHAPTER 1

SATURDAY, AUGUST 19, 1989

Some thought the place smelled like a broken sewer pipe. Dewey Cellars did not. Occasionally he'd escaped the dominant smell of Charleston, South Carolina, as he moved clothes, groceries, and a bulky computer up to the fourth floor of St. Philip Street dormitory at the college. The smell had been there back in the spring when Dewey interviewed, and he remembered it long before that, in the early 70s, when he visited the Holy City as a young boy.

The odor came in waves and was especially pungent on hot, August days like the one now before Dewey and hundreds of other incoming freshmen heaving and hoisting suitcases and storage containers up the stairwell. Dung dropped by large, sweaty draft horses tugging tourists in Antebellum-style carriages through surrounding streets reminded Dewey of the terrible stench. As did the green bottle flies that followed ecstatically, perching themselves almost pridefully on the brown, textured patties of half-digested hay.

Dewey knew from years past that escaping the city's peculiar fetor meant ducking into places like King Street's Omni Hotel, which smelled like coffee and linen, or immersing oneself in the barrage of sweet and savory aromas near the waterfront—rich, seasoned sauces; freshly-baked bread; pizza from a wood-fired oven; and the piney scent of juniper from a bottle of gin. Even a few of the city's clothiers and haberdasheries offered respite, with scents of leather, sandalwood, and bay rum.

Still, the odor persisted. It blanketed the old, seaside city, swirling low amid cobblestones and soaring high above church steeples. Only recently had Dewey been able to put his finger on the smell, only recently in his eighteen years had he found the words to describe it—it was the smell of decadence and decay.

St. Philip Street dormitory—informally called New Dorm because of its recent construction—had opened its doors for the first time that morning. New underclassmen waited anxiously with their parents in nearby parking lots to enter the stucco and sheetrock building at the corner of St. Philip and Calhoun streets.

New Dorm rose six stories high, a big clay-colored thumb with slender, tinted windows at regular intervals, a lobby with a shellacked brick floor and two elevators. Built adjacent to the historic Francis Marion Hotel, the dorm lacked the style and elegance of its regal neighbor—and for good reason. Within months, the place would be nearly trashed, elevator walls smudged with tomato sauce from late night pizza, dirt from intramurals, sand from the beach, and occasional body fluids. The elevator's nubby brown carpet sponged up countless spills and splashes from red and yellow Solo cups full of Pabst and Budweiser beer.

Dewey's fourth-floor room was part of a four-person suite with a common area, a shared bathroom and bedrooms branching off either side. Each bedroom had two beds, two built-in wardrobes, and desks with shelves. A sliver of window looked out onto a courtyard corridor, which was composed of bricks, tabby concrete, and red crepe myrtles.

Dewey walked into the right-side bedroom. Sitting on one of the beds was his new roommate. He was short with dark, curly hair that was thinning, and he was picking a pimple on his face.

"How's it hanging, dude," he said, extending his hand. "I'm Alex."

"I'm Dewey. Good to meet you." Although hesitant about Alex's greeting, Dewey shook his hand.

Alex wore a red Polo shirt, khaki Bermudas and a brown braided belt that formed a half-hitch knot at his side. Furry, black leg hair spilled over Alex's white crew socks, as the soles of his shoes brushed the floor.

"How about those stairs?" said Alex.

An elevator fuse had blown on the men's side of the dorm, forcing students and their parents to take the stairwell.

"Yeah, unfortunate, especially when it's so hot." Dewey's shirt dripped with sweat.

"Hell, yeah, it's hot. It must be a hundred damn degrees. I could almost feel it when we crossed the state line." Alex wiped his forehead, then flapped his shirt to try and cool himself.

Dewey heard footsteps behind him. There were Alex's parents, both out of breath, arms full of clothes, a stereo and several cartons of juice boxes. Alex's father was of medium height with black, curly hair and a big belly and fuzzy beard. He wore a gray, athletic tee-shirt with NYU written on it, jeans and dark brown Birkenstock sandals. His mother was short and busty with strong arms and dark eyes. She wore khaki shorts and a white, sleeveless linen blouse with images of small birds embroidered on it. "That's the last of it, dear," she said, squatting to ground a carton of juice boxes. She eventually rose, cleared her throat and addressed Dewey. "I'm Frieda Bocker, and this is my husband, Stuart. You must be Alex's roommate."

"Yes, I'm Dewey Cellars." He gave them each a quick handshake.

"You okay, son?" asked Stuart, looking down at Alex on the bed.

"Yeah, I guess," said Alex, searching for another pimple.

"What's *that* supposed to mean? Either you feel good about this or you don't?" Stuart had one hand in the air, one at his side.

"Well, let's just remember, this school thing wasn't my idea." Alex stopped picking his face and pointed at Stuart.

"If you'd just put a little more time into this decision, you might be where you really want to be. Planning, Alex, planning." Stuart sighed, resting his hands on his hips.

"Oh, yeah? And just exactly where is that?" Alex briefly came off his bed, then sat back down.

Frieda raised her arms as if to separate them. "Everyone just settle down. We just got here, and we've probably already traumatized poor Dewey. Just everyone cool it."

Dewey stopped hanging up his clothes, turned around and glanced at Frieda. "It's okay. Really, I barely heard anything with all the traffic outside."

In truth, Dewey had heard the whole exchange; he admired how Alex had asserted himself in front of his father, something Dewey could never imagine doing.

Frieda and Stuart helped Alex sort through his things, eventually creating an ant hill in one corner of the room. At the top, among other things, was a blender still in the box, a pair of white Reebok high-tops and a plastic bottle of Sea Breeze astringent. From time to time, something would topple down, only to have Frieda or Stuart retrieve it and, with an exhausted sigh, put it back in the pile.

"So, are you from around here, Dewey?" asked Frieda, who had begun making Alex's bed.

"No, I'm from Ohio, but we lived in the South a long, long time ago—Charlotte area." Dewey lowered a shirt he was hanging up and gazed out the window.

"How nice. So, you're no foreigner to this place." Frieda reached across Alex's bed to catch a corner with a fitted sheet. "We're from Raleigh. Moved there twenty years ago from New York."

Stuart, who had returned from exploring the common room, then spoke. "How long's it take you?" He paused and looked at Dewey. "To get from Ohio?"

"About ten hours, but we split it up," said Dewey. "Stopped halfway in Asheville for the night."

"Hmm," mumbled Stuart.

"We absolutely love Asheville. Don't we, Stuart?" said Frieda.

Stuart looked out the window again. From where he stood, Dewey could only see the letters N and U in Stuart's shirt. For a moment he wondered what Stuart wore to the office and court. Was he a flashy, fancy-dressing attorney or a plain-dressed public defender?

"Yeah, the mountains are great," said Dewey. "I went to summer camp not far from there."

"Are your parents in the lobby or nearby? We'd love to meet them." Frieda continued smoothing out the wrinkles on Alex's white bed sheets, until finally his bed looked like a big block of ice.

"No, they headed back already." They would have been well into their return trip, thought Dewey, driving north and west along I-26 to Columbia to Greenville then Knoxville and Lexington and, finally, Cincinnati.

"Next time," said Frieda, with a reassuring smile.

"Sure."

The Bockers smelled earthy and sweet, and reminded Dewey of the smell of a farmer's market he visited as a child on Saturday mornings. Alex's family was loud, often hijacking each other's sentences and, in times of disagreement, swatting the air. They communicated in ways that left contrails of emotion in the air, the three of them seemingly encapsulated in a strange shroud of vapor.

After helping situate Alex's things, Frieda and Stuart came to sit on either side of him on the bed.

"It's a nice suite, and your room is great," said Frieda. "And, look, you have a view."

"All you can see is that crappy courtyard," said Alex, squinting at the bright sun coming through the window.

"But this is where you landed. You should be so happy." Frieda swung her arm around her son and pulled him close.

"I know, I know, and I'll try to make the best of it. But, you know …"

"No negatives. Only positives, my little radish." Frieda looked up and smiled at Dewey, who had resumed hanging up his clothes while thinking how perfect—with Alex's red, angry face—Frieda's pet name was for her son. "How did you end up here, Dewey?"

Dewey said the first thing that came to mind. "Pre-med." Then, quickly, behind it, with a dowdy-looking polo shirt in his hand: "They've got a strong pre-med program here."

Dewey looked over at all three Bockers on the bed, well-knowing this wasn't the truth. He had not chosen the college for its pre-med program, academics, campus life, or even its nearby beaches, but for something else.

It had begun the previous spring when his parents drove him from Ohio for a campus tour. That day, the afternoon sun was warm, as twisted live oak branches swayed in the wind, and bright sun poked through quivering palm fronds onto George Street in front of Porter's Lodge, the formal entrance to the college, and Cistern Yard, the campus green, known simply as the Yard.

As the tour concluded, Dewey watched students cross back and forth over George Street. Suddenly, four young men, roughly his same age, appeared before him riding bikes in a diamond-shaped formation. Dewey could not tell from which direction they came. It was as if the air had spawned them, or maybe they'd just always been there.

Mesmerized, he followed them with his eyes. The lead rider, lean and muscular with a broad chest and narrow waist, pedaled effortlessly, casually leaning back in his seat. His blue eyes and wavy blond hair stood out against the dusty radiance of nearby brick buildings. High, chiseled cheekbones and an aquiline nose made his face look like something lifted from a Roman bust. An easy smile and caramel-color tan made him look like he'd just walked off the beach.

He wore a blue Oxford cloth button-down, white linen shorts and white bucks, no socks. The afternoon sun and heat seemed to have little effect on him or the cobblestone path ahead. Angel Boy—the name Dewey quickly gave the mysterious figure—was someone with the whole world in the palm of his hand, thought Dewey.

The attraction was magnetic, pointing every filament of Dewey's being in Angel Boy's direction, a pull so strong, fierce and fabulous that he felt every bone tug and every blood cell tremble with delight. Eventually, Angel Boy and his pack glided to a stop on the other side of George Street in front of a group of coiffed co-eds. Here, this tan, beautiful club of people smiled, spoke and laughed. They hugged and high-fived, toned arms moving and mingling with desire.

Back home was different, he thought, and though he'd had some success in high school, he still felt inadequate—never good or handsome enough, never a steady girlfriend, always feeling painfully out-of-step with his classmates. So, when the college acceptance letter arrived at the house later that spring on the bleakest and grayest of Ohio days—and with Dewey having endured yet another unremarkable year in high school—he knew exactly what he wanted. He wanted to be like Angel Boy. He would go in search of him, certain they would meet, talk and laugh, and become friends. Angel Boy would introduce Dewey to beautiful people like himself, and gradually, over time, Dewey would become beautiful, too.

"Medicine would make a great career." Frieda's sudden affirmation drove Angel Boy and the beautiful club from Dewey's thoughts. "Good doctors are always needed."

Then Frieda and Stuart stood up and moved away from Alex, leaving two crater-like impressions in the bed.

"Where's a good place to eat?" Stuart turned and looked out the window.

"There's some restaurants down in the Market," said Dewey.

"Can we walk?"

"Yes, sir."

"Would you like to join us, Dewey?" asked Frieda. "Like a welcome celebration."

"Sure. And as far as restaurants, I'd recommend Magnolia's or Carolina's. Maybe even Poogan's Porch."

"We'll check into our hotel and be back around dinner," said Frieda. "You boys behave." They walked to the door and exited, the smell of vegetables and leafy greens following in their wake.

Instantly the room felt bigger and lighter, Dewey noticed. And Alex seemed more relaxed, even taking time to look out the window without squinting. "They do have some cool-ass buildings around here. Maybe it won't be so bad after all."

Dewey felt the room settle. "So, your parents carried all your stuff?"

"Yep, every last fucking bit," said Alex.

Like his clothes, blender, and Reeboks, Frieda and Stuart seemed to have picked him up off the couch and simply transported him here, thought Dewey.

Dewey's things lay neatly on his bed—two large, beige Hartmann suitcases and a garment bag, a small Christian Dior Dopp kit his mother had given him at graduation, a bulky computer with a dark screen and a pair of Adidas running shoes. He had decided to pack light, though he was beginning to think he'd packed too light.

His parents had arrived early that day to ensure a quick and hassle-free move-in. They'd all stayed at a bed-and-breakfast on The Battery the night before. Dewey recalled his mother, a bon vivant with a trust fund, saying, *Come, Dewey, have oysters Rockefeller and enjoy the garden,* followed by her characteristic cackle, while Dewey's father reached for a book on theology in his briefcase, quietly settling into a chair in a corner of the room. At move-in, while his mother milled about the dorm lobby, Dewey and his dad carried his things up the four flights of stairs to his room.

They'd been saying their good-byes since the evening of Dewey's high school graduation, when as class vice-president, Dewey mounted the podium on a still-cool, Midwestern June evening for a short speech—at one point, the wind blew off his mortar board and he felt stupid. That had been three months ago. A quick *Bye, Mom, bye, Dad*, was now all he had to offer in the loud, busy lobby, with Dewey looking down at their reflection on the shiny, shellacked floor. They turned and disappeared.

Alex looked across at Dewey from the window and grinned. "Hey, dude, what did the penis say to the condom?"

"Dunno," Dewey replied.

"Cover me, I'm going in!" Alex laughed.

"Nice," Dewey said, unsure how to respond.

"Plenty more where that came from." Alex sat down on his bed again and started picking his face.

After taking a break and drinking juice boxes in the common room, Dewey and Alex finished unpacking. Alex put his stereo on his footlocker, stacking his CDs beside it. On top of the stack lay a CD cover featuring a monkey with a halo. Another cover showed a thin, pale woman with a shaved head clutching her blue tank top. The last cover featured a man's eyes and forehead on its top half, while the bottom half showed two scruffy bison.

The images captivated Dewey. He wanted to hold the CDs and look at them more closely, but he didn't want Alex to think he hadn't seen them before. In high school, Dewey mostly listened to *American Top 40*, except when he played soccer with the varsity team, and they cranked up music from bands with names like Creedence Clearwater

Revival, Roxy Music, and The Smiths. For the first time in his new environment, Dewey felt out of place, as the CDs piled higher and higher.

Then Alex began unpacking his clothes: shirts, chinos, jeans, wool sweaters, sports coats, and dress pants. J.Crew and Polo. Like the CDs, Dewey wanted to touch them. Alex opened a box and pulled out a new pair of leather boots, white tissue paper still stuck deep inside the toe boxes. When Alex wasn't looking, Dewey grabbed the box and put it up to his face to get a whiff of animal hide. It made him think of luxurious things. Then Dewey turned and looked at the clothes in his wardrobe. They were drab in comparison—mostly old jeans and sweatshirts, and on the upper end hand-me-downs from his father from Brooks Brothers that made him look old and dowdy. It had always been this way—Dewey not feeling like he knew who he was, either chasing after this or that or simply accepting what was passed down to him.

As Alex opened another suitcase the size of a treasure chest, Dewey realized how out of place he felt in his new environment.

With the setting sun reaching finger-like into the courtyard, Alex and Dewey prepared for dinner with Alex's parents. Together, they rode the elevator to the lobby with a long-haired boy wearing jeans and a tee-shirt that read Husker Du, and a girl in khaki shorts and dark blouse with *Blessed* written on it in rhinestones.

"Where y'all headed?" said Alex, as the elevator doors closed.

"To a kegger," said the Husker Du fan.

"To an SCA welcome party," said the girl.

"SCA?" said Alex.

"Yeah, Student Christian Association." Her face was heavy with make-up, her blonde hair pulled into an updo. A small gold cross dangled from her neck.

Dewey thought of the girls from his childhood at nearby Kiawah

Island. They were slender, tan and freckled, with blonde or auburn hair. They had soft, gently sloping noses, and smelled of Coppertone and afternoon naps. Camisoles hid their tiny breasts. At night, they'd sit by the bonfire, small glowing cannonballs of arms, legs and ass.

"Y'all off to walk around?" said the girl with an accent that made Dewey think of barbeque and beauty pageants.

"Nope, going to catch dinner with the parents, then off to the freshman mixer at the Stern Center," said Alex.

Then the elevator door landed with a loud thud and opened. Alex and Dewey stepped off onto the lobby floor.

"Later days, better lays, y'all," said Alex, looking behind him at the other two.

"Good one," said the Husker Du fan, laughing aloud.

The girl, unamused, looked down at the floor.

Dewey looked back and gave her a slight wave.

The building's side exit lay directly ahead, revealing the courtyard, where Alex's parents stood waiting. From a distance, Frieda looked like a sweet potato and Stuart like a stalk of celery, thought Dewey. Behind them, Calhoun Street burst with color from speeding cars. Which one was Angel Boy in?

* * *

Poogan's Porch sat on Queen Street between Meeting and King streets. The two-story Victorian home had been converted into a restaurant in 1976, the same year Dewey turned six. He had dined there occasionally when his family drove in from Kiawah and he was happy to be back.

Alex's parents had reserved a table for four overlooking the second-story balcony. The room was spacious and grand with high ceilings and shiny, hardwood floors, easily four or five times the size of Dewey and Alex's dorm room. Miniature palms planted in giant clay urns occupied each corner. Plaster walls painted mustard yellow revealed spider web-like cracks, while thick, glossy white crown molding gave the room a tight, finished look. White, cotton tablecloths draped each table, with vases of swamp sunflower and sweet pepperbush at their center. Dewey thought the space smelled clean and fresh except when the city's stench infiltrated.

They ordered drinks—white wine for Frieda, draft beer for Stuart, sweet tea for Alex, and for Dewey a Shirley Temple. Frieda wore a white sleeveless linen shirt and sat directly across from Dewey. Stuart, who sat next to Frieda, stroked his wild, untamed beard, while looking intermittently at the menu. Alex, who sat next to Dewey, looked around the room cautiously while resting a finger on his lower face.

"So, you said you visited Charleston when you were younger?" asked Frieda, tipping her menu to see more of Dewey.

"Yeah," said Dewey, "we mostly stayed at Kiawah, but we'd come into town for lunch or dinner occasionally. The town was pretty dingy back then."

"You mean unsafe?"

"Not exactly, just kind of rough-looking, like if you walked off in the wrong direction, you could get mugged."

"Any chance we'll get mugged tonight?"

Dewey could tell she was teasing. "Nope, you're safe. Some of the alleys can be a little dark and scary, but otherwise you're fine."

Dewey remembered how on one vacation he'd gotten lost downtown. He was ten years old and just familiar enough with the city to make his way around. He ended up on The Battery just down from Rainbow Row, where he felt a sudden mix of sun and heat overwhelm him. He became dizzy and panicked, and only with help from an unknown passer-by made his way back to the restaurant in the market where his parents ate lunch.

"We're tough, you know, being from New York." Frieda suddenly took on a real New York accent, puffed out her chest and laughed.

Alex looked across the table at his mother with disdain. "Why do you always say that, Mom? It's so stupid. You and dad haven't lived in New York since I was born."

Frieda leaned in hard over the table like she might pounce. "Once a New Yorker, always a New Yorker."

"Well, we're in Charleston now," said Alex. "I mean, *I'm* in Charleston."

"Yes, you are." Frieda had relaxed from her near pounce and come back into her seat. "So, what are you boys up to tonight?"

"We thought we'd check out the freshman mixer," said Dewey.

A waitress cruised by with a tray brimming with entrees—shrimp and grits, fried flounder, rice, and a bucket of oysters. Dewey could smell salt, black pepper, dry mustard, lemon, and butter.

"Yeah, I read about that. I think they said it was at a place called the Stern Center." Frieda bumped around in her big black purse searching for the orientation brochure.

"Should be pretty cool," said Alex.

"Yeah, I'm excited," said Dewey. "Wonder how many people will be there?"

"Maybe we can even get drunk." Alex lowered his head close to the table and snickered.

"Less drinking, more studying," said Stuart from behind his menu.

"Yeah, right," said Alex, sarcastically.

"Maspik!" Stuart shouted, without warning.

Dewey, sitting directly across from Stuart, could feel the weight of the unknown word by the force of Stuart's breath.

"Yes, Dad," said Alex, sounding ashamed.

A waitress passed by and refilled their water glasses, big chunks of ice clinking and clanking as water from the pitcher poured into the glass's empty spaces. The air conditioning kicked on, causing Frieda to pull her sweater up around her shoulders. Later, Dewey would be sure to ask Alex the meaning of what his dad had said.

Dewey looked around for something to take his mind off the tension at the table. He spotted a curious-looking man sitting alone at a corner table wearing a striped tie and blue blazer. Dewey tried guessing his age. The man had a boyish face with bushy eyebrows and eyes like small black marbles. He had slight shoulders and a pear-shaped body. When he lifted his glass, his hand revealed a soft, supple-looking palm. They weren't working man's hands, thought Dewey. They were a doctor's or lawyer's hands. Hands that held fine ink pens. Hands that signed important documents about important things. Hands that probably purchased beautiful artwork—seascapes, country pastures and small cafes after dark. Dewey had seen such hands when he went antiquing with his mother or to the bank to watch her sign financial papers.

The sporty tie and blazer made Dewey think the man lived somewhere downtown. Maybe a hidden, sleepy side street off The Battery, where gas lamps flickered, and horse drawn carriages careened. Dewey decided he was probably not from across either the Cooper or Ashley rivers, as there seemed nothing suburban, in look or manner, about him.

His interest piqued, Dewey decided he would excuse himself to go to the bathroom to get a closer look, cutting a path to the stranger as inconspicuously as possible. As he got closer, however, Dewey accidentally brushed the man's table with his hip. The table shook. The man looked up.

"Sorry," said Dewey. "I was headed to the restroom."

"Well, next time watch where you're going," said the man. While firm, he was not mean or rude. In fact, Dewey felt as if the man might have actually welcomed the interruption.

"I'm new to the college," said Dewey. "I'm with my roommate's parents—over there." Dewey pointed at the Bockers, all of whom had a hand in the air gesturing about something. "Again, so sorry for bumping you."

"I accept your apology—you say you're new to the college?"

Dewey tried pretending he didn't hear the man, but something inside made him decide to turn around. "Yes, sir," he said, "I moved into the dorm this morning."

"There are so many of you running around nowadays that I'm beginning to think you might just take over the whole city."

The man swiped his napkin from his lap, waving it like a matador before wiping his mouth. His disparaging words had landed as if said from the other side of a fence or gate, thought Dewey, just like the city's wrought iron gates and the passers-by who looked through them with envy and intrigue. Dewey suddenly felt like one of these passers-by, an outsider, just like he felt looking at Alex's wall of CDs.

"Here, take this if you need anything," said the stranger, proffering his business card.

Dewey could tell from a distance it was heavy card stock, with the man's name and phone number embossed on it. He took it and rolled his fingers over it, *Joseph Hermes Lyman, MD*, it read.

"Thank you, I'll remember this," said Dewey. "I've got to get back to my table."

"Maybe I'll see you around town," said the man.

Dewey gave up going to the bathroom and walked back to the Bockers. He looked back once more at Dr. Lyman who had just dug a fork into his baked flounder. The image reminded Dewey of an entry on the bottom-dwelling fish from a set of high school encyclopedias his mother once bought him. It explained how the fish used camouflage to capture prey and hide from predators.

Back at the table, Alex, Frieda and Stuart were eating. "Your food arrived, Dewey," said Frieda. "We were getting worried." "Sorry, there was a line at the bathroom," said Dewey. "They were so slow."

Frieda gave an easy smile, as she had so many times before that day and dug her fork into a big plate of pasta and red sauce.

"Eat up, Dewey," she said, "You and my little radish have to get to that freshman mixer."

CHAPTER 2

Dewey and Alex left Poogan's Porch and headed out into the warm night back toward the college along King Street. Lower King Street, where they walked, was less busy and commercial than Upper King. It was quiet and calm, with homes that were not mansions, but still grand, and real families that lived in them. From Dewey's observations, they were well-heeled working people with kids who went to school and on weekends packed the back of an old Chevy Suburban or beat-up Range Rover and headed to a second home at Sullivan's Island or Folly Beach. To outsiders, they probably lived quite extraordinarily, but to anyone from Charleston, they probably lived quite ordinarily.

Alex and Dewey walked quickly, sweat visible on their shirts, occasionally stumbling on a raised crack or bump in the sidewalk. A men's clothing store Dewey had known from years past eventually came into view. He became excited, as he slowed his pace and indicated for Alex to stop.

"Look at all those cool clothes," said Dewey.

Through the storefront window, Dewey could see a seemingly endless array of blazers, button down shirts, wool pants, cashmere sweaters and fine socks in a variety of colors carefully folded in cubbies or immaculately hung from metal floor racks. In the center of the floor, on a raised platform, a six-foot mannequin made of foam plastic displayed a gray turtleneck sweater, red corduroy trousers and a Burberry trench coat. The mannequin gazed past Dewey and Alex, beyond the storefront window, toward a distant horizon. Like Angel Boy, he immediately captivated Dewey's attention.

"Those clothes are for fags," said Alex.

"*What?*" said Dewey, incredulous.

"I mean, nobody really wears that shit. Maybe if you're old or fake or super gay or something. I mean, who buys that shit, anyway?"

Dewey conjured images of the models in the store's catalog, a copy of which he'd once snagged and taken back with him to Ohio and kept in secret, only to thumb through when he felt depressed or unattractive. He always wished he could jump into the catalog, and suddenly he'd be sitting in a plush, private garden with flagstone pavers and a running fountain, or in a bright, sunny foyer wearing a cashmere crewneck sweater with someone pretty at his side.

"They're just clothes. And you've gotta admit that they're pretty cool. Right?"

"Nope, not for me, too bodacious." Alex pointed to the mannequin in the center of the floor. "Check out that guy, he's just Mr. Perfect, isn't he? I could never look that good, and he's a fucking dummy."

Dewey's heart sank. The mannequin was perfect in his mind. "Well, I think he's a stud. There's a reason he's up there. He could get any girl he wanted."

"Do you hear what you're saying, dude? He's not even fucking real."

"I know. I mean, I know he's not. Still, just look at him. If he were real, he'd have it all." Dewey maintained his stare as if spellbound.

"Let's just go, okay? This is getting weird." Alex nodded in the direction of Upper King.

Dewey kicked himself. There would be no way of ever explaining Angel Boy to Alex. He, himself, didn't even have words to describe the attraction. For a moment, he felt like a dummy.

Dewey and Alex passed a row of antique stores. One of them featured a vintage ceramic Dalmatian in repose surrounded by a sterling silver tea set, and fine blue and white bone china plates with flower and leaf motifs. The spotted pooch's pointy snout drifted slightly upward and looked like it could have once guarded an English manor.

"My mom was into this kind of stuff," said Dewey, pausing in front of the store. "I remember she once bought a butler's table at this very store, and we drove it all the way back to Ohio strapped to the top of the car. Another time, in Upstate New York, she stumbled on an old bunk ladder from Ft. Ticonderoga, and we got stopped at the Canadian border by Customs for suspicious activity."

"I wouldn't give you two cents for all that junk," said Alex, leaning in for a closer look. "It's just a bunch of old stuff."

Dewey liked it because it *was* old. He'd grown up in a house full of old stuff—stoic family portraits and framed, tattered documents with whimsical signatures. On large canvases above the fireplace he'd seen hunters, dressed in red jackets and black riding helmets, trotting across the drab, gray English countryside.

"Okay, so what kind of stuff do you like?" asked Dewey, sincerely.

"La-Z-Boys with leg rests and cup holders for beer," said Alex, stretching out his arms.

"So, you drink, then?"

"Doesn't everyone?"

Dewey bristled over the fact that Alex liked La-Z-Boys. It reminded him of his grandfather, a temperamental, obese man with diabetes who loved his La-Z-Boy. As a child, Dewey watched his grandfather—wearing boxers and a robe, with TV's *Solid Gold* blaring in the background—plunge back into the chair's puffy Naugahyde, violently expelling an odor of sweat and motor oil.

Dewey and Alex eventually reached George Street and headed toward the Yard. Long since filled in with dirt and a layer of grass, the cistern—a huge, oval-shaped structure nine feet deep—had served for almost a century to collect rainwater. Now, however, it only collected students and sunbathers.

Surrounding the cistern were some of the college's oldest and most iconic buildings—Randolph Hall, Towell Library, and Porter's Lodge. Randolph Hall, with its portico and pillars, had served as the college's main academic building for most of the school's early history. Towell Library—Randolph Hall's quiet, studious sibling—had once been filled with books and maps, until modern times found the two-story structure converted into an admissions office. Welcoming generations of students into the Yard through arches and wrought iron gates was Porter's Lodge. The three ancient structures, all oxblood red, lived within a stone's throw of one another on an acre or more of lush Bermuda grass, herringbone brick paths, and giant live oak trees.

"This makes me remember the day I interviewed here," said Dewey, stopping on the brick sidewalk just outside Porter's Lodge.

"What did that all entail?" asked Alex, who had also come to a stop.

"Well, first there was a tour by this upperclassman who was a biology major, then I interviewed with this admissions woman." Dewey peered through the arch of the Lodge and pointed to Towell Library, where the interview had taken place. "It feels just like yesterday, but it also feels so long ago. I think I can even remember what everybody was wearing."

"Go for it."

"The tour guide wore khakis, a white Oxford and blue jean jacket. Curly hair. The admissions counselor wore a long, ankle-length dress, turtleneck sweater and some kind of matching cropped jacket. Short wedge haircut."

Alex reared his head back, astonished. "Damn, you really remember shit, don't you?"

"Yeah, I've always been like that."

"Did they ask a shitload of questions at the interview?"

"Not really. I was surprised, honestly. I remember going on and on about my horrible SAT scores, and the admissions woman just looked at me like I was from another planet. In her mind I guess it was no big deal. She said I could apply early-decision, and they'd let me know."

Alex pursed his lips to one side. "I bet you were an easy in."

"What makes you think that?" Deep down, Dewey knew what Alex was going to say. He had done very well academically. Almost any small college would have happily admitted him early-decision.

"Because you just look like the type who would do good in school. Good grades and everything. You're probably good at just about everything."

It was nice to say, thought Dewey, especially this early in their friendship. But it was hard for Dewey to receive such glowing affirmation, for he didn't think of himself this way. In fact, he felt mostly the opposite—as someone just smart and good-looking enough to get by, but whose self-esteem was fragile.

Night was beginning to fall on the Yard. Exterior lighting from all three buildings had come on, in addition to smaller ones along the brick paths. Dewey was reluctant to say anything more about his interview and the moments that had produced Angel Boy.

"I got a brochure in the mail," said Alex. "It had cool pictures of the beach and people sailing, so I just randomly applied. Could have cared less. I take that back—all I cared about was the ratio."

"What ratio?" said Dewey.

"The girl-guy ratio. A guy from my high school who went here said it was like 12 to 1," said Alex. "If you can't get laid here, you can't get laid anywhere."

"I suppose." Dewey thought back to the handful of girls he'd dated in high school.

"'You *suppose?*' What are you, some kind of homo? The girls here are incredible, and the good thing is, from what I can tell, most of them don't even know it. Speaking of hot chicks, which way is the mixer?"

Dewey briefly gazed at the top of Porter's Lodge. Chiseled there was ΓΝΩΘΙ ΣΑΨΤΟΝ, Greek for "Know Thyself." He remembered the tour guide pointing it out, explaining how at commencement graduates passed underneath the Lodge one final time. Sensing Alex's impatience and hoping to lighten the mood, Dewey pointed across the street and spoke. "I think the hot chicks are that way."

Not far from them a sandwich board read, *Freshman Mixer, 8-10pm, Stern Student Center*, with an arrow pointing to a modern-looking building made of brick and glass. Together, Alex and Dewey crossed over George Street to the Stern Center. Dewey gave Porter's Lodge one last look, thinking how funny it was that this ancient structure was his only real witness to Angel Boy's existence.

With the Stern Center now in front of them, Alex and Dewey followed a long row of tiki torches leading to a terraced brick patio and grass courtyard behind the building. They entered through wrought iron gates that soon gave way to long, tablecloth-covered banquet tables with food and drinks. Welcome posters featuring the college's mascot, Clyde the Cougar, stood on tripods, while the real thing, dressed in a school basketball uniform, handed out furry high-fives.

A rock band played on a makeshift stage, its blond, skittish front man belting out a ballad about a girl with pearls in her hair. A few college admissions counselors in maroon-colored polo shirts circulated through the crowd, greeting students and answering questions.

"That band is totally rad," said Alex. "And look at all these people."

"Let's walk around," said Dewey, feeling a bit overwhelmed. The music was raw and scratchy, he thought, not like on the radio. He thought again of the stack of CDs on Alex's footlocker.

The night was hot with an occasional breeze, stirring nearby Confederate jasmine that smelled like sweet perfume. Dewey breathed deep, trying to manage his anxiety over the large crowd assembled. He recognized a few faces from earlier in the day, residents from New Dorm who he'd seen march off wildly without direction looking for somewhere to eat. Dewey recalled thinking how a little part of him wanted to go with them. Others that he didn't recognize talked along the outskirts of the courtyard.

"I'm going pre-med," said a girl with brown hair from Hilton Head.

"I want to go into international business," said a thin boy from Kentucky.

"I'm majoring in getting fucked up," said a thick-necked boy in surf shorts and flip flops wearing an *I Love New Jersey* tee-shirt.

Dewey, having separated from Alex, weaved through the large crowd, casually dropping in on different groups of co-eds. In the first, he noticed the boys wore clunky, white gym shoes, and the girls white, slip-on Keds sneakers. "I just can't wait to hit the beach. It'll definitely be different from the lake," said one of them dressed in a short-sleeve cotton shirt with a fake polo on it. He wore a glitzy, high school graduation ring with a big red gemstone and miniature cross emblazoned on one side. It made Dewey think of a big red cough drop. A girl wearing a white ruffled blouse and blue jean shorts asked aloud, "Hey, they got SCA here?"

Making his way further into the courtyard, Dewey briefly settled in behind another group of kids, some wearing linen shirts and colorful fleece anoraks. Dewey heard them talking about boarding school and summers abroad in Spain, Italy, and France. About drinking beer and coffee in small cafes. About partying their asses off and smuggling contraband through Customs. Dewey couldn't help but notice their smooth, buttery complexions, straight teeth and thick hair.

In a more remote area of the courtyard, where jasmine vines crept over a nearby wall and a small garden fountain bubbled softly, half a dozen kids dressed in madras and khaki talked casually as if they'd known each other their whole lives. When Dewey approached, they looked him up and down with critical eyes, before resuming their conversation. "We have that little place on Wadmalaw, you know," said a petite girl with straight blonde hair wearing Guess jeans. "But daddy said we may have to sell it. It would be a shame." A boy next to her in white bucks looked at his watch. "Gotta run," he said, "Maybe I'll see some of y'all later at the yacht club." Dewey hoped the boy would acknowledge him as he passed, but he only looked through him, while calling out to a boy in Nantucket red pants across the way, "Legare, is that you?"

Dewey, feeling dejected, stopped in the middle of the grass courtyard, free of any group, and looked around. He tried imagining what life would be like on campus after Alex's parents had left and Clyde the Cougar had been returned to some small storage closet in the Stern Center rec room. Knowing Angel Boy and his entourage would surely make things better, he thought. It would make every day at the college perfect. It would make his old self and old home forgotten things.

Dewey suddenly spied Alex standing on the edge of the brick patio talking and laughing with a small group of people. He looked happy.

For a moment, Dewey even imagined him with a beer in his hand, just a normal college kid. Whether he wanted to be in Charleston or not, Alex might just do okay, he thought.

"Hey, man," said Dewey, having made his way to Alex.

"Dude, where'd you go?" said Alex.

"I was just floating around checking things out."

"Pretty cool mixer, huh?"

"Yeah, not bad." Deep down, however, Dewey felt the event was a little contrived, with admissions counselors—one of whom Dewey thought he recognized from his interview back in the spring—hovering close by.

"Meet anyone new? I'm sure they were all over you."

"Nah, just kinda took notes." Dewey appreciated Alex's confidence in him but still couldn't understand why.

"Notes? Already? Told ya you were a fuckin' genius! Notes at a freshman mixer. That's a first!" Alex laughed heartily, as though he might have to steady his beer.

"You ready to head out?" Dewey looked in the direction of the wrought iron gate where they'd entered.

"Yeah, I'm good." Alex stretched his arms and looked up at the sky, layered thick with fading bands of pink and blue. As Dewey and Alex turned to walk out of the grass courtyard behind the Stern Center, a tall, black man in a maroon shirt extended his hand. "Y'all having a good time?" he said.

"Sure, it was great," said Dewey, surprised by the man's sudden appearance. "We were just heading out."

"I'm Lucious Seabrook."

"I'm Dewey—Dewey Cellars." Dewey guessed the man was in his twenties. He shook his hand, noticing how strangely pale, almost white, his palm was. "This is my roommate, Alex Bocker."

"Nice to meet you, Alex. Y'all settled in?" said Lucious. "Any problems? I assume you're in New Dorm."

"Big problem," said Alex. "Damn elevator's broke, and we had to take the stairs today. Thought they called it New Dorm, not Broke Dorm."

"I heard about that," said Lucious. "Sorry. Apparently, it was some kind of circuit problem. We knew we'd be cutting it close finishing up construction. It's beautiful, though, isn't it?"

"Yeah, pretty nice," said Dewey, looking off in the distance at a row of Antebellum rooflines. Truthfully, the only part of the dorm that Dewey really liked was the courtyard corridor beneath his room. He brought his gaze back to Lucious. "By the way, I think I recognize you."

Lucious brought his thin, delicate hand to his chin. "Yeah, if I'm not mistaken, I think you interviewed here last spring. You were with your parents, right? Ohio, maybe?"

"Yeah, you're right. Good memory. You're in admissions, then? Towell Library?"

"You guessed it. For about two years now," said Lucious. "I travel a good bit around the country recruiting kids. Mostly the Southeast, but I do occasionally get up to the Midwest and New England."

Lucious' job description made Dewey think again about his own path to the college—how strange it sounded to hear of actually having to *recruit* someone to come to college. Angel Boy's sighting had been so powerful and overwhelming, almost magical—it was in and of itself a kind of recruitment. Dewey had given little consideration to anything else—academics, campus life, even the beach. None of the campus literature had really appealed to him, except for pictures of the Yard, with its live oaks, Spanish moss, and ancient edifices.

For a moment, he wondered if there might be something wrong with him. How could he have chosen a place solely on a face? How could he have bet his whole future on a glimpse of someone he'd never met?

Despite Lucious looking familiar, Dewey couldn't remember if he'd actually seen him or not that pivotal spring day. It had been unusually warm, with heat mirages in the street and fuzzy light through oak trees, not to mention countless families and students shuffling in and out of Towell Library.

"Well, welcome to the college, Dewey," said Lucious. "I hope it's everything you wished for and more."

"Thanks, glad to be here," said Dewey. "I hope to see you around campus."

Alex and Dewey pushed open the wrought iron gate to the Stern Center patio, waved one final goodbye to Lucious and headed out into the night. They cut through the Yard back to New Dorm, a place now full of motion, blaring music, and late-night pizza deliveries.

CHAPTER 3

The white envelope stuck halfway out under their dorm room door. On the front was written, *Alex B. and Dewey C., New Dorm, Rm. 403.*

"What's this?" said Alex, bringing it to eye-level.

"Probably more orientation literature," said Dewey. "They've printed half a forest."

Alex opened it and read it aloud: "You are cordially invited to participate in the Interfraternity Council Fall Rush." Alex looked confused. "What's it mean?"

"I think it's a fraternity thing," said Dewey. "Basically, you go around to all the fraternities and see if you like any, and if any of them like you, then they ask you to join. It's called rush."

Dewey knew about fraternities because of a family friend who'd joined one at a small university back home. The boy, partially blind since birth, had given Dewey a red corduroy hat monogrammed with his fraternity's letters on it. Unfortunately, during the transfer of the hat to Dewey, the boy misjudged the distance, and the hat fell to the ground, soiling it. Dewey never forgot the image of the boy, nearly on his knees, frantically trying to scoop it up to protect it.

With the invite still in hand, Alex looked at Dewey. "You gonna to do it?"

"You mean *rush?* Not really my thing," said Dewey. "But feel free."

"Yeah, maybe I will," said Alex, stroking a red pustule on his chin. "What kinds of questions do they ask?"

"The usual—where you're from, what you like to do, how you see yourself fitting in."

"How do they decide who gets in?" Alex raised his eyebrows.

"They vote on you." Dewey couldn't resist looking Alex up and down. Would the brothers find favor in him? Could he possibly get a bid?

"What do you mean *vote*," said Alex. "Like an election?"

"Yah, pretty much. It's called a bid, and if you get one and accept, then you're a pledge."

"That doesn't sound too bad." Alex rubbed his hands on his thighs.

"Nah, it's pretty painless. And it's a good way to meet people."

"Do you live at the fraternity house, if they accept you?"

"Probably not, at least initially. That's more for brothers."

Alex held the invitation, reading it again and again, until he finally laid it on his desk.

Dewey changed the subject quickly, fearing further discussion might get Alex's hopes up. "Hey, let's listen to some music. How about some of your CDs?"

"Sure." Alex grabbed the CD with a man's eyes, forehead, and two scruffy bison. It read, *Life's Rich Pageant.* The sound was hard-driving and layered, with occasional pianos, organs, and accordions. The songs lacked the typical, teeny-bop quality of Top 40, thought Dewey, and included inward-looking lyrics about life and nature. The songs took Dewey to another place, a place where he felt cool, where anything was possible.

The music played as Alex and Dewey readied for bed. Their new wardrobes smelled of wood chips and Elmer's glue. Dewey inhaled, making him think of the pine needle-covered trails of his youth at summer camp. It was a pleasant smell. Dewey looked at the clothes in his wardrobe. Most were from high school, except for a few jeans and shirts he'd bought months prior. Growing up, he'd shopped at Brooks Brothers—two trips annually, Easter and Christmas, with his father—and had adopted a style of gingham check, pinstripe, cuffed trousers, blue blazers and winter coats with endless layers, zippers and hidden pockets.

Now, however, his clothes looked drab, colorless and old. Even Alex—with his pimples, white crew socks and baggy Bermudas—seemed more stylish. If only he could dress like the mannequin in the men's store on King Street, he thought.

Alex grabbed his Dopp kit and headed for the bathroom. He emerged a short while later wrapped in a towel from the waist down, his pasty, white chest and back covered apishly with patches of thick, black hair. "I'm gonna do it. I'm gonna rush."

"Sounds like a plan," said Dewey. "But why?"

"I don't know. I just felt I need something to do. I feel like I never do anything."

"Are you sure you want to do it first semester? It'll be busy enough as it is and, if you get in, pledging takes up lots of time."

"Yeah, I can do it. I mean, fuck it, what have I got to lose?" Alex rested his hands on his waist and looked out the window, which was cracked open, inviting the smell of the marsh. He suddenly dropped his towel and, bare ass showing, slipped his legs, then arms, into his white, monogrammed pajamas.

Dewey was taken aback by Alex's lack of modesty. He thought for sure Alex would be one of those roommates who would scurry around after showering to hide his nakedness. The kind of roommate prone to turning off lights and locking bathroom doors—but no. Alex was, instead, a short, hairy body in full view of the world. In this way they weren't that different, he thought. As Dewey got ready to shower, he looked back at Alex, fully clothed in his pajamas, reclining on his bed. He couldn't help but imagine poor Alex with zits and white crew socks going from frat to frat begging for a bid. Chances were slim, thought Dewey, but better he found out now.

Dewey stepped out of the bathroom after showering and walked back into the bedroom, where Alex twitched and quivered in his sleep. He pulled a tee-shirt and sweatpants from a drawer in his wardrobe, then walked to the window. In the moonlight, a pretty girl in a yellow sundress with cherry blossom petals on it smoked a cigarette under a crepe myrtle. She flicked her cigarette, the orange glowing ash drifting to the ground and disappearing.

Leaning over to extinguish it seconds later, she dragged it over the crushed oyster shells, revealing her small breasts. Dewey inched closer for a better view, clutching the window with his hand—he knew there was more. He'd seen more in a stash of *Playboys* he'd found wrapped in a garbage bag in a wooded park across the street back home. Pressing his body up against the window, he wanted to see more.

Then, just as quick, she was upright, again heading for the dorm's side entrance, meaning she'd be more or less underneath Dewey in a few seconds. He watched as she disappeared. He sighed. He could almost smell her. Then, a sudden whiff of Ligustrum. He hoped some day they would meet, she would find him handsome like Angel Boy, and they would fall in love. But maybe these were just figments of his imagination, he thought. It had been such a full day—move-in, meeting the Bockers, Poogan's and the freshman mixer. Nonetheless, in this moment he felt something beautiful, serene and content, a feeling he feared might be gone forever the next day.

CHAPTER 4

Dewey awoke the next morning for the first day of class. Staring unenthusiastically into his wardrobe, he finally pulled a pair of poplin khakis and a white, short-sleeve polo shirt off the rack. It was the easiest, most basic thing to wear, he thought, though he wished he'd had more options after seeing all of Alex's clothes. Dewey wondered what Alex would wear the first day but, from the looks of it, it wasn't going to matter, as Alex had twice slept through his alarm.

"Alex, hey, man, you gotta get up," said Dewey, slipping on his white polo shirt. "Your alarm has already gone off a couple times."

"Yeah, yeah, it's only the first day, and it's so warm here under my blankets," said Alex, rolling over. "I don't want to go anywhere."

"Okay, but just remember what your dad said. By the way, *What did your dad say?*" Dewey, gathering his books and putting them in his backpack, recalled the uncomfortable moment Stuart had shouted at Alex at Poogan's Porch.

"When?" said Alex, calling out from underneath his covers.

"At Poogan's. Remember? When he yelled at you?" Dewey had walked to the bathroom to brush his teeth and comb his hair.

"Oh, that. It's some Hebrew bullshit. It means *Enough!* Who wants to know?"

"Just curious. He sounded so harsh. Anyway, I've got to go. Biology starts in twenty minutes, and it's over in Physician's Auditorium." Dewey said a final goodbye and took off toward the elevator. In the main lobby, dozens of co-eds swarmed the area with books and schedules in hand.

Dewey walked the short distance from New Dorm to Physician's Auditorium for his first class. The sun was up, but George and St. Philip streets still seemed sleepy, as if, like Alex, trying to deny the bright yellow reality above. Physician's Auditorium eventually came into view, a sprawling, brick building with arches and a breezeway nestled among trees and Spanish moss situated the next block over from the Yard. Giant, slate gray tin eaves hung down over the sides of the structure, giving the home to all pre-med majors a sense of foreboding.

The pungent, vinegary smell of formaldehyde greeted Dewey as he entered the building. It was a smell he recalled from high school biology, when he and a lab partner once dissected a fetal pig. He remembered sitting in front of the pig every day for a month, his hands a slimy mix of dead skin and intestines. Dewey looked down at the lobby floor, which was mostly white with black and brown specks. A row of wooden display cases directly in front of him featured certificates and plaques noting recent student awards and accolades. Just then, Dewey started feeling anxious, just like the night before at the freshman mixer. He felt dizzy, in his mind's eye the lobby suddenly expanding, then shrinking, at increasing speed. He leaned against a wall to steady himself before heading to class.

Dewey's classroom was spacious with tiered seating, the optics of which—the steep, angular decline into the pit—only made him feel dizzier and more anxious. It reminded him of home, when as a boy he'd watch baseball at Riverfront Stadium. From the dark, cavernous entrance where hundreds of fans entered the stadium at once, third base seemed just an arm's length away. Dewey stepped down into the middle of the tiered seating and took a seat, the room filling fast.

Front and center in the pit was a short man with a long, tanned face wearing khakis, a collared shirt, madras bow tie, and white lab coat. A pair of reading glasses dangled wildly around his neck. Dewey guessed he was in his 60s.

"All living things are uniquely beautiful, including you," said the man. "I'm Dr. Herman Freeport, your professor. Please turn to chapter one in your text."

Looking up from his textbook, Dewey just happened to spy the girl from Gaston in the front row, the one he and Alex had met on the dorm elevator.

"Linnaeus," Dr. Freeport continued, "was the father of taxonomy. He divided and classified the animal kingdom according to various characteristics. Dolphins and giraffes are both animals, but you may have noticed they possess substantial differences." Dewey and a few others chuckled, as Dr. Freeport grinned, exposing his perfectly white teeth. "The important thing is to respect all living creatures for what they are, even if they happen to be an African, horned toad." With that, Dr. Freeport pulled a picture out from behind the podium of a palm-sized, slimy, green frog with spikes on its back. The class laughed again.

Dewey fanned through the textbook's pages. Taxonomy and classification topped the table of contents. The bulk of the book showed complex biological charts and diagrams, pictures of all the continents, and animals of all shapes and sizes. The back offered a seemingly endless list of Latin-derived terms and references, a handful of which Dewey knew, having taken honor's biology back in high school.

"Now, when we classify something, we mean to discriminate it from something else," said Dr. Freeport. "Naturally, then, living things with shared characteristics begin to fall into groups, and, eventually, even smaller groups, until, finally, we arrive at a species name. This is most often demonstrated graphically as a hierarchy."

Using a small, black remote control, Dr. Freeport activated the drop-down screen behind him, where a few seconds later an image of a great white shark appeared. Underneath was written *Carcharodon carcharias*. Dr. Freeport put his glasses on and gazed up at the upper rows. "Don't get caught swimming with one of these, dah'lin." Then he smiled and continued lecturing on Linnaeus.

Dewey stared inquisitively at the screen, as did some of the other students. The shark was massive, its white belly flashing outward, a burst of flesh, muscle and teeth, a singular species, a freak of nature. Dewey thought of Angel Boy. He continued staring at the screen, thoughts of Latin and Linnaeus floating in his head. One random thought after another, then the smell of tea olive and sun, and clouds sweeping fast overhead; then in the front of his mind, *Angelus Puer*. Silently he repeated it over and over, almost obsessively, until he started chuckling. Angel Boy, unbeknownst to anyone in the room but Dewey, had entered the world of Linnaean classification.

"There are so many marvelous, beautiful things in the natural world, and I encourage you to experience them all but don't get bit." Dr. Freeport—smiling, big bow tie—glanced at the screen behind him, the great white hovering overhead.

Dr. Freeport looked small, frail and vulnerable in comparison to the predator above, thought Dewey, like he could be vanquished at any second.

It had been almost fifty minutes. Dr. Freeport shuffled a big sheaf of notes on his podium, retracted the screen behind him and spoke. "Read chapter one and be prepared for a quiz Wednesday. Thank you." With that, he turned and disappeared through a tiny door at the side of the pit.

Homo professorus, chuckled Dewey, while checking his schedule to confirm his next class: English 101, Maybank Hall.

Maybank Hall—like the Stern Center and Physician's Auditorium—had been built in recent decades and was located behind

Randolph Hall in a section of campus with boxwoods, bike racks, and black, wrought iron benches. It was a two-story, clay-colored, stucco structure with two-dozen classrooms that tried hard to compliment the rest of the campus architecture. Through salt-caked, opaque windows on the back of Maybank overlooking St. Philip Street, New Dorm's main entrance was visible.

Dewey walked the short distance to Maybank. Upperclassmen carrying blue, gray, and brown backpacks stood shoulder to shoulder on the stoop smoking and talking about the new semester and the previous night's parties. Dewey watched from a few feet away, when a girl called his name.

"Hey, was that you in biology just a few minutes ago?" said the girl. "I thought I recognized you. I'm Mary Pate Hackney—we met on the elevator." She wore blue jean shorts and a white tee-shirt with rhinestones on it shaped like the state of South Carolina. A big, green palmetto tree grew out of the middle. She had on the same gold cross necklace as the other night.

"Oh, hey, I remember you," said Dewey. "Yeah, that was me. biology's my first class." Dewey backed away from Maybank and headed in Mary Pate's direction near one of the bike racks.

"So how was the mixer at the Stern Center?" Mary Pate cradled her books in her arms.

"It was okay. A little lame with the mascot there, but we met some pretty cool people." Dewey leaned against the bike rack. The sun shone on the back of Randolph Hall, and Dewey caught some of its warmth on his face. "How about your SCA meeting? Where do y'all meet anyway?"

"We met over at Buist dorm. I think we brought some people over." Mary Pate shifted her books from one side to the other, rolling them across her breasts.

"*Over?*" Dewey tightened his backpack straps.

Mary Pate looked at Dewey and smiled softly. "Over to the Lord."

"So, exactly how do you know when that happens?"

"When they stand up and accept Jesus as their personal savior. Others take a while, but you can tell in the way they start talking about God. You and Alex are always welcome to come."

"Thanks, I'll let you know." Dewey wanted to be nice to Mary Pate, but he wasn't much interested in hearing anymore. He'd grown up in the church and had mixed feelings about God. He changed the subject. "Do you have class in Maybank?"

"No, I'm headed to Simons Fine Arts Center for a drawing course," said Mary Pate.

"Cool. Well, I guess I'll see you back at the dorm."

"Yeah, sure." Mary Pate started down a brick path toward St. Philip Street. As she did, she turned around and yelled back at Dewey. "What's your roommate's name again?"

"Alex," said Dewey. "Alex Bocker."

* * *

Dewey's watch read almost ten o'clock. When Maybank's doors suddenly swung open, the group of upperclassmen talking and smoking on Maybank's stoop twitched like a giant herd of buffalo as they turned and entered the building. Dewey followed close behind, until he stood in the middle of the crowded lobby, which he noticed smelled like a mix of mildew, Brut aftershave and strawberry-scented shampoo.

Dewey shuffled through a crowd of students wearing tie-dyes, sundresses, and Oxford cloth shirts before quickly climbing a staircase to locate his classroom which was at the end of the hall. He took a seat amid a dozen other students and casually looked out the windows through a row of palm trees to see New Dorm in the distance.

A tall, thin man with gray, feathered hair entered. He wore light green, polyester slacks and a yellow, wide-collared shirt with a green and blue tartan plaid tie. "I'm Dr. Berrygood. And this is British Romantic Poetry. I hope you're in the right place."

Dewey first noticed Dr. Berrygood's voice, slightly nasal with a noticeable rise and fall that could pass as patronizing.

Dr. Berrygood quickly took attendance, with students nodding their heads when he called their name aloud. Then he sat on the edge of his desk and, folding one arm underneath the other, looked out through the windows in the back of the class while stroking his upper lip. "So, class, what is Romantic poetry?"

"Love, love, love …," came a voice in the back of the room. Dewey turned around to see the thick-necked, New Jersey surfer from the freshman mixer.

"Not exactly, but I'll give you an extra point or two on your first quiz because there is some of that. Romantic poetry does, at moments, concern itself with love, but more broadly it has to do with taking inspiration from nature and celebrating man's inner emotional life."

"Whoa, sounds like serious stuff," said the Jersey surfer, pumping his fist in the air over the extra points he'd just won.

Dewey had read the works of various Romantic poets in high school—Wordsworth, Coleridge and Byron. He loved the rich, imaginative language and intense feelings. He loved to hear them read aloud.

"'When I Have Fears That I May Cease to Be,'" said Dr. Berrygood, "We'll start there. John Keats wrote this poem in 1818. What do you think?"

His question sent Dewey and the others scrambling through their texts for a page number. After a few seconds, Dr. Berrygood spoke again, "How about you?"

Dewey looked up to see Dr. Berrygood staring straight at him. "I think it's probably about someone reflecting on something—mortality, maybe?" said Dewey.

"Very good," said Dr. Berrygood. "And your name?"

"Dewey Cellars."

"Dewey Cellars from …" Dr. Berrygood stopped and waited.

"… from Ohio."

Dr. Berrygood glanced at his roster to confirm Dewey's name, then looked back up. "Well, Dewey Cellars from Ohio, do you reflect on things often?"

"Not really. I mean, maybe. I guess right now I'm pretty busy with life."

"And what about life has you busy?" Dr. Berrygood's patronizing tone was suddenly on full display.

"Well, college definitely, and meeting new people. And going places around town." Dewey wanted to say more but didn't.

Dr. Berrygood ceased stroking his upper lip with his finger. "You freshmen always seem to be chasing something. So impulsive, so ready to be somewhere."

Dewey looked down at the floor. It was the same as Physician Auditorium's—white with black and brown specks. He felt anxious and queasy.

Dr. Berrygood began again with his patronizing tone. "Well, Dewey Cellars, wherever you're going, let's hope you get there in one piece." He paused before addressing the whole class. "For those of you still looking for the poem, try the table of contents or, if you lack the effort, which, I suppose, as freshmen, you might, just turn to page 312."

Dewey turned to the assigned page to find Keats' poem, along with the poet's portrait. The dusty, reddish-brown image captured Keats at a desk looking up from a book, chin in the palm of his hand, as if caught by surprise. He liked how the light hit his face and torso, as if to suggest the muse had just visited. His features were soft and delicate, his nose noble-looking, thought Dewey, just like Angel Boy's.

Dr. Berrygood started reading the poem aloud and, much to Dewey's surprise, his patronizing tone all but disappeared. He read each line with as much intention and sincerity as Dewey had ever heard, one line flowing lyrically to the next, just as the poet would have wanted. His body joyfully vibrated with each line, as the palm trees outside gently beat against the windows, and warm sunlight flooded the room.

As Dr. Berrygood delivered the poem's last line, the Jersey surfer reached for his backpack, jostling the zipper and giving rise to other classroom commotion. Dewey thought he heard him mutter something under his breath about waves and catching a ride to Folly Beach. Minutes passed, and the sunlight that had once flooded the room had disappeared, covered up by high, lofty clouds in the sky. Dewey felt a certain melancholy descend on the room.

"'Of the wide world I stand alone, and think/Till love and fame to nothingness do sink,'" said Dr. Berrygood, slamming his text shut in an exaggerated way. "Quiz Wednesday. See you then."

The hallway outside filled fast with students, including many from the front-stoop herd. Dewey exited the classroom and joined them, trying to blend in, but it was difficult, if not impossible—he was, after all, just a freshman in plain clothes with few friends and little to no experience at anything. He wished his backpack was cooler—a brand name one and slightly faded from the sun—so it didn't look so new like the one he now wore, yet another sign of being a freshman.

Once out of Maybank, Dewey headed toward the Yard through the back of Randolph Hall, until he eventually crossed George Street. His next class was Freshman Seminar, which was held in the Education Center, a three-story, brick building next to Craig Residence Hall on the far end of St. Philip Street toward Wentworth

Street. Marked by a traffic intersection, the vicinity was also home to the school cafeteria, a few faculty and administrative offices, and the George Street parking deck.

Dewey entered the building and climbed the stairs to the second floor. He entered a classroom, where a dozen or so students were seated facing a podium and chalkboard. He took a seat in the back of the class. After a few minutes, a tall, skinny woman with long black hair in sunglasses and a long-brimmed straw hat walked in. She sat her tote bag on the podium, took off her glasses and turned toward the class. When she did, her face revealed high cheekbones, dark eyes, and a kind, gentle smile. "How's everybody today?" she asked.

The class groaned collectively, acknowledging her inquiry.

"I can see you're all freshmen—right?" she continued, laughing vigorously at her phrasing, at which point her hat tumbled to the ground. "I mean, of course you're all freshmen. Who else would you be? I'm Dr. DuGow." She picked up her hat. "Anyone here *not* from around here?"

Dewey and some others raised their hands.

Dr. DuGow looked at an Asian girl in jeans and a white tee-shirt in the front row. "Where are you from?" she asked.

"Just up the road in Goose Creek. Born here. Dad was military." The girl dragged a yellow, No. 2 pencil with a heart-shaped eraser along the spirals of her notebook, making a zippy sound. Dewey detected a sense of shame in her voice because she didn't have a more glamorous birth story.

"Well, at least you're close to home for laundry and things like that." Dr. DuGow smiled, as if somehow, she too, might know the score. The Asian girl looked back with a fake smile.

Next, Dr. DuGow spoke to a girl in an equestrian-print turtleneck with elbow-length sleeves and black, tapered pants. "And how about you?"

"Broad Street, but I've been away at school. New Hampshire." The girl twisted her skinny legs into a figure eight and crossed her arms, as if she might be cold. To those unfamiliar, Broad Street might as well have been on the moon, but to Dewey, who had walked along the celebrated thoroughfare on many a vacation with his parents, the historic street meant pedigree, money and beauty.

Gradually, over the next few minutes, other students raised their hands and volunteered where they were from—Virginia, Florida, Vermont, Massachusetts, even Bermuda.

"So, how's everybody settling in?" asked Dr. DuGow. "Getting around campus okay? Everyone get their student ID?"

Dewey pulled his ID from his pocket and held it in the palm of his hand. In a thumbnail photo taken just the day before at the bursar's office, wild, curly hair and blue eyes sat atop broad shoulders from years of high school wrestling. Smiling and wearing a white tee-shirt with the name of his old summer camp across the front, he looked happy and content next to his name printed in big, bold letters— PAULDING DEWEY CELLARS—with his birthdate and social security number stamped beneath. He slipped it back in his pocket, his curly hair and broad shoulders disappearing into darkness, lint and loose change.

Settling in behind the podium, Dr. DuGow pulled a large packet of papers from her tote bag. "I've put together a series of readings for the semester. You can find this packet at the bookstore, unless, of course, you can't find the bookstore. That would be a problem." She laughed hysterically, again almost doubling over.

"Do we have to read all these?" complained a girl sitting a few seats from Dewey.

"Yes, I'm afraid so, and there'll be quizzes, too, with a comprehensive exam at the end." Dr. DuGow leaned on the podium and smiled, her thin, strong arms out in front bracing her upper body.

She paused, as if waiting for further objections from the class.

She was attractive, thought Dewey, especially her eyes which, though dark, seemed lighter because of her energy and enthusiasm.

"You're in a big world now," she continued. "You have assignments and responsibilities. And people are even going to have different opinions from yours."

The girl a few seats away from Dewey who'd complained about the packet rolled her eyes.

A boy in faded blue jeans, duck boots and a flannel shirt with a logo on it suddenly spoke. "You mean like Yankees?"

"What do you mean?" said Dr. DuGow, raising a brow. A few students began to chuckle.

"I mean having different opinions—that's all those Yankees seem to have." The boy smirked, digging the heel of one of his duck boots into the floor, scuffing it.

"Yes, I suppose even Yankees," Dr. DuGow responded, amused by the boy's quaint point of view. "But that war's been over for a long time."

The boy sank further in his seat like he might be falling into a hole. "Well, where I'm from, that war still lives on."

"And where are you from …," she began. "And I don't seem to have your name."

"Darryl Hinshaw," said the boy, barely raising a brow.

"Right, then, Mr. Hinshaw. So, exactly, where are you from?"

"Place called Little Delos."

"Yes, well, I'm sure Delos is quite beautiful. You know it's a Greek Island—right? I mean, not where you're from but in the real world. Not that you're not in the real world." Dr. DuGow began to laugh, again realizing her phrasing. "I mean, it's far away in the Aegean Sea."

"Didn't know that, Dr. Doo-Gow," said Darryl, mocking her last name.

Dr. DuGow's temperament changed, and she lost her smile. "It's good to know you, Darryl," she said. "I look forward to hearing your and everyone else's opinions in a fair and equal manner." Her tone was less familiar and more professional; she'd gone from happy mentor to serious academic in the span of a couple of subjects and verbs. Meanwhile, Darryl stretched out both legs and seemed to fall further back into his hole.

Grabbing her packet of readings, Dr. DuGow waved it in the air for all to see. From where Dewey sat, he could see some of the article titles—*Sex and Sexuality; Me, You and Multiculturalism; Searching for the Essential Self.* They were not unfamiliar titles, at least the words behind them. Dewey had heard them passed around in high school and on public radio. He'd also seen them on book spines on shelves in his dad's office.

"Don't forget these packets, people," she said. Her smile from before had returned.

Dr. DuGow then went around the room learning everyone's name and something about them. A very nervous boy briefly forgot his name. A girl named Rainbow said she'd spent her summer as a ranch hand in Colorado. Dewey's introduction was short.

"I'm Dewey Cellars from Ohio," he said, thinking how ordinary and dull he sounded. Angel Boy would have sounded cooler.

"Dewey, what do you like to do?" asked Dr. DuGow.

"I'm big into running," said Dewey.

"From what?" She smiled kindly. "It's a joke. I mean, not your running, but my asking."

"When I run, I don't think I'm running from anything."

"Well, then, let me put that a different way. What are you running to? What is it you want out of this experience called college?"

Dewey straightened up in his seat, and with his right hand felt for his college ID in his pocket. Nervously, he traced over its clear vinyl sleeve trying to think of something to say. Finally, he spoke. "Pre-med. I'm here for the pre-med program. So, I guess that means being a doctor."

"Well, that's admirable," said Dr. DuGow in a way that led Dewey to believe she didn't quite believe him. "While I have you, how far do you run, exactly? And where?"

"A couple miles a day. Around here. I like running down King to The Battery," said Dewey.

Before Dewey could say anything more, Dr. Dugow interrupted him.

"Oh, yes, I know just where you're talking about. Lower King is my favorite part, too," she said before pausing, as if giving Dewey the chance to expand, but he did not. "Good knowing you, Dewey, and keep running."

Dr. DuGow smiled, then lifted her head in search of the next student. After a few more introductions, she thanked the class for their participation. Then, in a loud, crackly voice she transitioned topics: "Okay, class, what does tolerance mean?"

"It means accepting someone who's different from you," said the girl from Bermuda, who had a round, tan face that reminded Dewey of the Kiawah girls.

"Yes, that's correct," said Dr. DuGow. "And sometimes that's hard. Sometimes it's a lot more complex than we think."

Dewey and the others looked critically at one another as if testing Dr. DuGow's advice. It was, in fact, so easy to judge someone without even knowing them, he thought.

"So, here's your first assignment. Befriend someone you've never met before. Just walk right up and introduce yourself." Dr. DuGow extended her hand as if to demonstrate.

"Creepy," said the boy from Florida. The class laughed.

It was a bold assignment. Dewey's mind quickly jumped to Angel

Boy. This was the perfect excuse to try and meet him. But how? Where in Charleston was he?

Dr. DuGow raised her thick packet of readings in the air a final time. "Buy your packet, people, and go meet someone new. See you next time."

Dewey descended the stairs quickly and walked out onto St. Philip Street. He breathed deeply, taking in the smell of live oak leaves by the curb, light brown and desiccating in the end-of-summer sun. He looked at New Dorm in the distance, the big, clay-colored structure prominent against radiant blue skies; it was growing on him, not quite as offensive as he originally thought. Then he thought about the rest of his day—run, eat, study and watch Alex get ready for rush.

* * *

Fraternity row was on Wentworth Street—a series of old, three-story homes made of brick or wood, some dating to before the Civil War, with wide front porches where frat boys in khakis lounged about. Curious about the row and this section of town, Dewey decided to walk the short distance around the corner from Craig Hall to Wentworth Street before heading back to the dorm. On the edge of fraternity row next to a bike store, he stopped and stared at the frat houses and the large, wooden Greek letters on their exterior. Together, these houses, just a few feet separating them, formed a wall, with narrow alleys in between leading to a giant gravel parking lot in the back.

Dewey admired the houses' ornateness: wood molding and trim, brackets under the eaves, Greek-inspired porch columns and occasional stained-glass windows. The houses were mostly painted blue, yellow or white, each one its own little fiefdom.

From the sidewalk, Dewey imagined what rush might look like— a couple hundred recruits with *Hello, my name is* nametags walking up to each house's dimly-lit, creaky front porch and introducing themselves. It would be like a factory, with each recruit trying to fit a mold and the brotherhood watching closely for quality control.

Yet for Dewey there was also something very attractive and satisfying about fraternity row—it offered a certain order that dorm life lacked. There was identity and belonging. Young men voted into these houses knew, for the most part, what they wanted—booze, sex, and popularity.

He walked closer, before crossing the street and standing in the front yard of Grace Church, a cathedral-sized church opposite fraternity row with a giant steeple and multiple, ornate arches with corridors leading to small fountains, grassy areas and shade-filled spaces. The front lawn was bright green and cut very short. A sign read, *11 a.m. Holy Eucharist.*

"Whatcha' lookin' at, douchebag?" said a loud, husky voice from across the street. Dewey looked up to see a frat boy leaning over a porch rail pointing at him. The boy laughed, then quickly retreated, but not before Dewey could flip him off.

Dewey gazed at the green grass beneath him. He was on church property, a place of mixed feelings. His father had served a half dozen parishes by the time Dewey was eighteen. Coming and going was a way of life. And so was being welcomed and told good-bye—or worse: like the frat boys across the street, parishioners could be a rude bunch, saying mean, disparaging things, as the moving trucks pulled up.

Dewey had seen enough of fraternity row and from his interaction moments before had a pretty good idea how the evening might go. Maybe he could bring Alex up to speed when he got back to the dorm. He turned and headed toward Coming Street, a busy, one-way street parallel to St. Philip Street on the campus' west side. It was home to sorority row, Student Health, the back of Physician's Auditorium and a wide brick path—the Green Way—which led to the back of Randolph Hall. Shade trees, parking meters and tall streetlamps lined the street.

Dewey noticed a distinct smell—a combination of rotten eggs, ammonia, and decomposing marine life—known as *pluff* mud. He took a deep breath and held it in.

Once on the way out to Sullivan's Island, Dewey's father couldn't stop talking about the smell. "It smells like sewage. How could anyone ever live here?"

For the rest of the trip, Dewey put his head out the window in defiance, imagining his face caked with pluff mud.

CHAPTER 5

Back at the dorm, Dewey walked in to find Alex organizing his desk. A coffee mug labeled JMU held pens and pencils, while a worn baseball with a New York Mets insignia on it occupied the opposite corner. In between was a small, metal framed picture of Frieda and Stuart, both dressed in gloves, wool hats, and puffy coats with ski tags dangling off them, as if they'd just come off the slopes. Stuart had a big smile, his left arm raised victoriously.

"What's up, dude?" said Alex, hearing Dewey come in. "How'd your first day go?"

"Pretty good. All my professors seem pretty cool," said Dewey. "How about you?"

"Yeah, same here. Just a butt load of reading."

"Your favorite activity, huh?"

"Yeah, I guess. I don't mind reading stuff that's interesting like spy novels and stuff, but all that English and poetry crap just isn't me."

Dewey dared not mention Dr. Berrygood's class and the passage from Keats. "So, where are most of your classes?"

"Up near Craig in the Ed Center," said Alex. "Did you know Craig Hall was all female?"

"No, I didn't," said Dewey.

"Dude, how could you miss it?" said Alex. "All those hot chicks hanging out near the entrance?"

Dewey wondered how he could have missed such a sight. Did he just not notice? Was he distracted? Anything to change the subject. "So, what's on your agenda this afternoon?"

"I'll probably nap, then start getting ready for rush," said Alex.

"Oh yeah, I forgot to mention I checked out fraternity row on the way back from class," said Dewey.

"Well, what's it like?"

"Pretty much what you'd expect. A row of old houses with Greek letters on them."

"Were any members hanging out?" said Alex.

"You mean brothers?"

"Yeah, brothers."

"No," said Dewey, choosing not to mention the boy on the porch who had called him a douchebag.

"Yeah, well, I guess things will probably pick up later this afternoon," said Alex. "We have to be in front of the Stern Center at seven o'clock."

"We?"

"Yeah, I was hoping you'd go, just for the first night." For the first time since they met, Dewey sensed fear in Alex but also sincerity.

"Why would you want me to tag along?" Dewey rested his hands on his waist only to discover a threadbare place in his khakis.

"Because I figured you'd know what you were doing," said Alex.

Dewey looked at Alex with surprise, while putting a hand over the tattered place in his pants. "What makes you think I'd know what I was doing?"

"You're nice and you look the part," said Alex.

Dewey didn't press Alex on the full meaning of what he'd just said. "Okay, I'll go with you but just tonight."

"Thanks, man. I swear I'll fucking pay you back." Alex smiled at Dewey, then looked out into the courtyard where a girl on a bike road by.

For the rest of the afternoon, they continued setting up their new room. Alex hung a few wall posters, and Dewey set up his computer. As he connected its different wires and cables, he recalled how anxious and inadequate he'd felt just a few weeks before about not having a computer. The freshman orientation packet said there would be some computers in the library, but Dewey had already imagined duking it out with the college's 7,000 other students for a screen and keyboard with a paper due the next day. He'd shared this anxiety with his parents, whereupon they immediately went out and bought Dewey a computer, including a two-day crash course from a man in the office supply business. "You'll do fine in college, Dewey," he said repeatedly. "Just remember, you can always reboot."

With the last cable plugged in and Alex looking over his shoulder, Dewey flipped the switch. He could hear the computer groan, as a fan inside the machine started whirring. Small, orange numbers and characters blinked on a dark screen for a long time, leaving Dewey thinking he might need to reboot.

"Beef stroke-me-off at the cafeteria tonight," said Alex. "Interested?"

"Sure, why not." said Dewey. "This computer thing may take a while."

Alex and Dewey grabbed their meal cards and headed for the elevator. When the heavy, tired-looking elevator doors opened, two girls stepped out and, laughing, raced down the hall.

"What are you waiting for?" said Alex, who had already stepped on the elevator.

"Do you smell that?" said Dewey.

"Smell what?"

"First crush."

"What the hell are you talking about? Now get in here."

"Their hair, it smelled so good," said Dewey, stepping on, as he watched the two girls find their room. "Vidal Sassoon, or maybe Wella Balsam or Prell. I just always associate that kind of stuff with my first crush."

Alex pressed a button, and the elevator doors quickly closed. "Who was your first crush?"

"Abby Bowling. Fourth grade." Dewey tried remembering what she looked like. Amazing hair and smooth, tan skin. Big blue eyes that when she looked at Dewey made him think they'd be together forever. Until the big ice cream social in the park where they had agreed to meet, and Dewey saw Abby from afar walking with her parents. She waved to him, but that was all, as her parents—wearing loafers, corduroy and disapproving looks—headed for shade trees to talk with the parents of other children Dewey didn't know.

"I never had a first crush," said Alex. "I guess the closest thing I ever had was fingering a drunk girl at a party in eighth grade. Her hair did smell amazing, though."

The elevator doors opened onto the lobby floor, and Alex and Dewey walked out the main entrance of New Dorm toward the cafeteria on the far end of St. Philip Street.

"How do you think tonight will go?" said Alex, walking faster than usual.

"I don't know," said Dewey. "I've never been to one of these things. It can't be too bad, right?"

"Do you think there'll be a lot of guys there?" Alex put his hands in his pockets.

"Probably." Dewey swung his arms in giant circles, like an athlete warming up before a competition.

They passed the Simons Center, eventually crossing over St. Philip Street toward the Yard. New faces coasted up and down the busy sidewalks, many now more familiar to Dewey through brief lobby encounters and elevator rides. As they walked, the late afternoon heat persisted with occasional pockets of cool air that Dewey thought smelled like strawberry and tea olive. The sky was blue and hazy, as Dewey and Alex reached the cafeteria and stood in line with other students.

"What do you think's holding things up?" said Alex, raising himself on the balls of his feet to try and see over the other students' heads.

"Not sure," responded Dewey. "But if they don't open those doors soon, there's going to be a riot. Everyone is hungry. I'm hungry."

"Me, too," said Alex. "Hunger will drive you crazy."

* * *

A few hours after dinner, Alex and Dewey had come to stand in front of the Stern Center, a modern, three-story, brick building named in honor of one of the college's former presidents. A plaque with Stern's stocky bust in bas-relief greeted visitors at the main entrance, an area which dozens of rushees now dominated. Many wore khaki or seersucker shorts, white Oxford button-downs and white bucks or gray running shoes. Still, others wore plain-front khakis, polo shirts, and flip-flops. They gathered in small groups, chatting and laughing as they awaited the official start of rush.

Polo and *Drakkar Noir* cologne hung heavy in the humid, early-evening air, as Alex and Dewey joined one of the small groups that had just been signaled to start walking toward Wentworth Street and fraternity row.

The one who had given the signal, a young man in a blue polo shirt, khakis and flip-flops with a name tag that read *Greek Council Rep.*, led the group slowly around the corner onto Coming Street, while spouting facts about Greek life, "Twenty-five percent of students belong to a fraternity or sorority. Fraternity and sorority members participate in a wide variety of service projects. Student Government is almost all Greek."

He paused and looked back at the busy swarm of dapper young men behind him. "And we're some of the best-looking people on campus!"

Alex ignored him, instead looking around, seeming to enjoy the short walk to fraternity row, having not yet explored Coming or Wentworth streets. Alex's dark hair and dark-colored eyes stood out, noticed Dewey, as he looked past black wrought iron gates up to rooflines of Antebellum homes against the backdrop of a setting sun. Dewey thought he almost looked happy.

Fraternity row appeared on the horizon. Dozens of brothers stood on front porches welcoming rushees. Some looked like they wanted to be there, while others looked like they'd just put their beer down and been picked up on the curb.

"Can y'all huddle up over here?" said the Greek rep. They were on the sidewalk in front of fraternity row. "Bring it in, boys, bring it in. Remember, be a *stud*! Take it from me!" Grinning, he gave two thumbs-up, almost as if he were on some kind of game show but the giant ball of men before him were mostly silent. One boy worked quickly to tuck his shirt tail in before entering the houses. "Just kiddin', guys," said the Greek rep. "Where's your fucking humor?" Then he divided the group in half and pointed them to various houses.

"What was that?" said Alex.

"Head game," said Dewey.

"Thought that shit ended in high school."

"It's just on a whole different level here."

"What house we headed to?" Alex stretched out his arm to confirm the direction they were going.

"Kappa Tau," said Dewey.

Alex and Dewey's small group bottlenecked at Kappa Tau's front porch, as brothers and rushees shook hands. It was hot, and for a second Dewey thought about going back to the dorm, but he didn't want to abandon Alex.

"How y'all doing tonight?" said one of the Kappas. Alex and Dewey nodded and smiled, and continued into the house.

Once inside the foyer, Dewey saw an old staircase leading up to the house's second and third floors. It was creaky and needed painting.

In the parlor with twelve-foot-high ceilings, Dewey smelled Pine-Sol on the hardwood floors. A cobweb occupied a far corner of the room, its silky threads gently undulating. Overall, the house was clean, thought Dewey, the kind of clean accomplished when parents call from out of town saying they're minutes away from home. A green carpet remnant, two old sofas, three used La-Z-Boys, and some collapsible chairs rounded out the downstairs' furnishings.

Above the fireplace mantle was a large, framed composite with headshots of all the brothers. In the center of the picture was the Kappa Tau crest—a shield with an all-seeing eye, daggers and a calla lily. In the picture, each brother wore a white Oxford, red tie and blue blazer. Dewey and Alex inched forward for a closer look.

"That sure is a lot of dudes," said Alex.

"Yeah, pretty impressive, all those faces," said Dewey. He doubted he'd ever be accepted in such a place, as he gazed at the clear complexions, bright white smiles, and blue blazers. He glanced at Alex and couldn't help noticing how red and angry his acne was. Dewey had watched him scrub it hours earlier, both hands scrubbing nearly every inch of his skin, hoping with each cycle, he might see a reflection without blemish.

Suddenly, the lights in the front parlor dimmed, as two brothers wheeled a slide projector to the back of the room.

"Welcome to Kappa House," said a mysterious voice, as the Kappa crest appeared on the wall. "At this point, everything's new.

You're free, maybe freer than you've ever been. And you're in Charleston. Which almost always spells trouble."

Behind the projector, ruckus applause and laughter erupted, as fuzzy, broad-shouldered forms shoved and high-fived each other, their motion whipping up clouds of microscopic particles in front of the projector.

"So, what will you make of your time in the Holy City and, potentially, here at Kappa House?" said the voice. "Just so you know, Kappa Tau's the only house on the row with *real* Charleston roots, founded just before the Civil War a couple blocks from here. Back then, all the founding fathers seemed to be headed for bible school. They all wanted to be ministers. Times have changed. But I guess you could say this is still our little slice of heaven, and we're all little devils!"

The fuzzy, broad-shouldered forms behind the projector started up again. "Gettem', Rad," said one of them, slurring his words. "Good ole boys is here!"

"Shut him the fuck up," said another one of the fuzzy forms, looking over his shoulder.

The mysterious voice at the back spoke again. "What he meant to say is there's lots of personality at Kappa House, and we hope you consider us, as we consider you."

Dewey thought the voice sounded closer now, seeming to have inched out from behind the projector.

As the voice grew stronger, the smell of lemon and honeysuckle passed through an open window, and the day's last rays passed by, bathing the parlor in yellow-orange hues that eventually illuminated the face behind the mysterious voice. Dewey couldn't believe his eyes, as he looked back and forth between the face now before him and the composite of the myriad rows of bright smiles and blue blazers above the mantle. In the second-to-last row toward the end, Dewey spied the face attached to the voice, and he had a name: Radford L. Gaillard

III, Rush Chairman. To friends, he was simply "Rad." To Dewey, he was Angel Boy.

Dewey's spirit soared with excitement. On one level, it was believable that Angel Boy—good looking, popular, and charismatic—was in a frat, thought Dewey, but on another it was not. Back when Dewey saw him gliding down George Street with his entourage in tow, he seemed to materialize out of nowhere, as if not from this world, let alone a fraternity. But perhaps it was precisely this ethereal quality that now put him center stage in front of his fraternal peers.

"What did you see back there?" asked Alex, noting Dewey's hasty look back at the mantle.

"Nothing. Just wanted to look at that picture again," said Dewey, trying to contain both his excitement and disbelief.

"What do you think?" said Alex, fishing for feedback on the night so far.

"About what?"

"About the Kappas."

"Oh, right. Seem like good guys. All in all, I guess it's better than the freshman mixer."

"Good point," said Alex. "Do you want to stay for the rest?"

"Yeah, I'm okay with it." Dewey didn't move a single muscle. It was a sign, an omen, that he and Radford were meant to meet. Then he remembered Dr. DuGow's assignment to introduce himself to someone he'd never met. Maybe this was his chance.

Dewey, Alex, and the other rushees watched, as one of the Kappas flipped through slides showing brothers partying, bar-hopping or hammering nails at a service project. One slide featured a handful of brothers in a wheelbarrow race. In slides with large groups of brothers where there were girls and alcohol involved, the fuzzy forms behind the slide projector erupted with hoots and catcalls. Finally, the last slide came and went, leaving a lighted box of nothing on the parlor wall.

"Hope it was everything you expected and more, fellas," said Rad, standing in front of the rushees, as someone switched on the lights. "Good luck getting to know the rest of the houses." By now, Rad was just a few feet away, and Dewey began to think of him as he'd been back in the spring pedaling with his pals down George Street—handsome, carefree and much-admired, a product of the ancient, pedigreed and aromatic world around him known as Charleston, bound by dank dwellings, unrelenting heat and uncommon beauty. So close now and within reach. Just a simple handshake and, "Hey."

"You ready?" said Alex. "You act like you've been in a trance the last few minutes."

"Yeah, I'm ready. We can go," said Dewey.

With Dewey leading the way, the two of them stood up and made way to the front of the room, where Rad stood with his hands on his hips, smiling. As Dewey and Alex passed him, Dewey paused and looked over. "Thanks for putting all this on," he said.

"Sure, man, nothing to it," said Rad.

Dewey tried introducing himself, but by that time Rad had lifted his gaze to look and wave at the crowd of fuzzy forms behind the slide projector. With Alex prodding him, Dewey cruised past Rad without saying anything more, before turning toward the foyer and front door.

"Dammit," said Dewey, frustrated over having missed the opportunity to introduce himself. Then he thought about how he might have appeared before Rad—was he cool, or did he come across as weird? After all, he was the only one to approach Rad after the slide show. What if he looked lame? What if he looked like Alex?

Dewey and Alex made it to the foyer, edging their way around the group amassed there. Through the open front door, Dewey spotted the Greek rep that had led all of the rushees from the Stern Center to fraternity row. He noticed how his hair, parted and swept to one side, was the same as it had been when they'd begun the march to frat row hours before. How enviable, thought Dewey.

Night had fallen on Wentworth Street, as Alex and Dewey departed Kappa House and the rest of rush. Light shone from the windows of the frat houses into the darkness, so they looked like giant, glowing pumpkins. It was late August, almost September, the height of hurricane season. Soon, fall's cool temperatures would arrive, and the Lowcountry would begin to hibernate in hues of gray, brown and red. The sun would turn cold and sharp, and the pungent smell of pluff mud would be muted until late March, rolling in only occasionally with onshore winds on winter's warmest days.

* * *

Returning from rush, Dewey and Alex cut through the Yard, slipping under Porter's Lodge. The arched entryway was dank and moldy, and reminded Dewey of a cave. It also made him feel transported back in time, his having read somewhere that the college was one of the nation's oldest and that its founders included three signers of the Declaration of Independence. He imagined these esteemed gentlemen sitting in nearby Randolph Hall wearing powdered wigs and breeches while smoking small, porcelain tobacco pipes. Through Randolph Hall's oozing, hand blown window panes, he envisioned them sitting fireside raising genteel fists in heated debate about the country's fate—tea, taxes, and revolution. Then, full of rum or Madeira, they would head out into the night much like he and Alex had done, and amble across bumpy cobblestone to lavish homes with everything from fine china to chamber pots.

"It's hot as balls in this city," said Alex, eventually stopping to sit on one of the Yard's wrought iron benches.

"Yeah, back home it would get so hot we'd sometimes head to the river to a park where a bunch of us hung out. The place was shaped like a serpentine," said Dewey, who had joined him on the bench. "Any place to catch a breeze."

"Is that where you were born?" asked Alex.

"Yeah, but we moved around a lot after that."

"Where to?" Alex looked at the lights along the brick pathway that had suddenly come on.

"Charlotte, then back to Cincy, then back South again." Dewey turned his head as if following his family's moves across the country.

"Why'd you move so much?"

"My dad."

"What business was he in?"

"He worked for the church."

"No shit?" Alex released his hands from beneath his thighs.

"What did he do?"

"He's a priest."

"No, shit, your dad's a priest? Really?"

"Yup."

"No, shit. So, how'd *you* get here? Did your dad screw a nun?"

Dewey and Alex laughed aloud, shattering the surrounding quiet. "In our church, priests can marry," said Dewey.

"Did you like growing up a preacher's kid?" said Alex.

"It was okay. It had its advantages," said Dewey, "but it also had its downsides."

"How so?" said Alex.

"People judge you pretty fast, especially when you're new to a church. And there's the pressure of always being perfect." Dewey looked at the ground and swung his feet. A row of hostas behind him rustled in the wind.

"So, when do you think they'll give out bids?" said Alex.

The neat part in his hair had disappeared, and the heat and

humidity had made his face red and puffy.

"Probably within a week," said Dewey, "after they review everyone."

"They probably won't even remember me," said Alex.

"Why do you say that?"

"Because no one fuckin' remembers me."

Dewey waited for Alex to say more, while looking out at the Yard's manicured centipede grass, which had begun catching the evening dew.

"Even my own parents almost forgot me coming here," he said, chuckling. "And before that in high school I missed a ton of days. Some days I wouldn't go at all. I wouldn't even get up. The whole thing just bit the big one."

Dewey thought about his own high school and kids like Alex who weren't popular, except maybe as study partners before final exams, if they were smart, or as the occasional free ride home after school, if they had a car. Fresh in his mind from just a few months ago, he remembered the jean jackets they wore, decorated with small lapel pins with clever sayings, peace signs and rainbows. They performed in plays and musicals, and volunteered in the principal's office and library.

"I thought college would be different but after tonight I don't know," confessed Alex. "Seems like a lot of the same shit. Just a big popularity contest."

"I wouldn't worry too much about it," said Dewey, looking like he might also have reservations. "Everything's just so new right now you can't really tell what's real or not. In a way, it's kind of like a dream."

"Maybe you're right." Alex gazed out into the Yard.

They sat in silence a little longer, until Alex yawned and said they should go. As they got up and began walking, Dewey looked back over his shoulder. The Yard, in all its grandeur and beauty, was truly the grande dame of all campus spots, and now with him and Alex almost beyond her walls, she could finally rest her head.

* * *

That night, Dewey dreamed he was walking down a dark, paved road on nearby John's Island, a place he remembered from his youth on the drive out to Kiawah. Eventually, he came across a middle school with a tetherball court out front. The bright yellow ball shone in the darkness, as Dewey grabbed and hurled it counterclockwise, until the rope suspending it wrapped fully around the pole. Dewey watched the ball slowly unwind, his attention caught in its sweeping, mesmerizing orbit.

Behind the school lay a dirt path leading to a small patch of land surrounded by tidal creeks and marsh grass. Dewey followed it, until he came to a place with a large bonfire that lit up the night sky, where dozens of tanned, lean-bodied people gathered laughing, shouting and listening to reggae. Above, long ribbons of pink and red clouds crisscrossed the night sky, as cicadas screamed all around. Dewey smelled wet burlap and the ocean. Then a tall, thin black woman suddenly appeared before him.

"Come to join da party?" she said.

"I'm not sure," said Dewey. "Who are you?"

"I's Desirée."

"I'm Dewey. What *is* this place?"

A warm breeze rolled across the marsh, engulfing them.

"It's a celebra-shun," said Desirée, looking out onto the revelers.

"What kind of celebration?"

"A par-dee for duh young and boo-tiful. Do it once a year. Lucky for you stumbling on to it."

"But who are they and how did they get here?"

"Dayz from every walk of life, but mostly uppah crust. Doc-tuhs, law-yuhz and such. They dream dis up, jus' like you. You mus' be one of dem."

"But how? I'm not even from here. I don't know any of these people."

Two men in green, knee-high boots wearing khakis and bright red flannel shirts pulled the burlap off an open fire revealing a mountain of steaming oysters. A giant plume of smoke arose, as the men used thick, canvas gloves to hoist the oysters onto a banquet table, at which moment the revelers began approaching.

"Come eat 'til your heart's duh-zire!" shouted one of the red-breasted men, whereupon Desirée broke into laughter, before looking back at Dewey.

"Day sayz people out here have dis expeer-ence back on dee mainland that lead dem here. *Mus-teer-e-uhz* experience. Say, you don't have no *mus-teer-e-uhz* experience, does you?"

Dewey could only think of Angel Boy. It was like he'd been put under a spell that day on George Street. He looked at the revelers, as firelight played on their faces, then at Desirée. "I can't say if I've had any mysterious experiences."

"Well, Lawdy, if you doesn't know now, maybe later. But I'd say jus' lookin' at you, you may well have had one. Maybe sump-tin. Or maybe nuttin' at all."

Then, just as quickly as they had appeared, Desirée, the revelers and the bonfire disappeared from Dewey's mind, and he awoke. Alex, tangled in bed linens, reminded Dewey he was back in his room. A dove cooed in the courtyard. The vivid dream and Desirée's advice felt so real that Dewey checked his legs for bug bites and scratches.

CHAPTER 6

For a few minutes, Dewey watched the sun rise through the bedroom window before getting up and going into the common room. He grabbed a juice box, sat down and turned on the morning news, where a bow-tied weatherman delivered the forecast: "Absolute scorcher today with temperatures in the upper 90s," he said. "Could you ask for anything more?" A live picture of the Cooper River Bridge with a slow trickle of cars on it showed in the background. That's when Dewey heard a knock at the door.

He opened it to see one of the fuzzy, broad-shouldered Kappas from the night of rush standing in front of him in khakis, a white Oxford, blue blazer and red tie, just like in the composite. "I'm looking for Dewey Cellars."

"That's me," said Dewey, still in his pajamas.

The Kappa handed Dewey a small, white envelope embossed at the corner with the letters *K* and *T*. "Congrats, Dewey. You got a bid. You have till Wednesday to accept."

"Thank you," said Dewey. "This is pretty cool. Is there one for Alex?"

"Who?"

"Little short guy with thin, black hair from Raleigh. He's my roommate. We were together the night of rush."

"Can't say I remember him. There's only one envelope, and it's for you."

Dewey stood for a moment, half expecting another Kappa to

arrive at the door saying there'd been some confusion and hand over Alex's bid. But no such Kappa materialized. Whereas before he'd been wary of fraternity life, Dewey now seemed to be embracing it. He was excited about it. Instead of doing Alex a favor, it was Alex who'd unwittingly done him a favor and, in doing so, quite possibly changed his life. But the bid only made things more difficult. How would he keep it from Alex? He looked down at the envelope in his hand, the raised letters *K* and *T* casting a slight shadow over the rest of the envelope. He would figure something out.

"Hey, before you go," said Dewey to the Kappa. "That guy Radford. What year's he in, and where's he from?"

"Rad's a senior, he's from Charleston. Been here all his life," said the Kappa, backing into the hallway. "Definitely a guy you want to know but keep some distance."

The Kappa said something else, but Dewey had stopped listening, stuck instead on the former's warning. What was *wrong* with Radford? Had he done something? Why the cautionary advice?

"Perfect," said the Kappa.

It was the first word Dewey recalled hearing from the Kappa in what seemed several minutes, and it startled him. Had the Kappa somehow read his mind, he thought. After all, Radford and perfection had—since that spring day on George Street—become virtually synonymous in Dewey's head.

"Excuse me? Perfect *what?*" responded Dewey.

"For beer," said the Kappa. "Perfect night for a *beer.* Maybe a six-pack. I'm headed back to the house. Don't forget about the bid."

"Cool, thanks, I'll let you know."

With that, the Kappa reverted back to his fuzzy form and faded into the hallway.

Dewey sat back down, realizing he'd still been holding Alex's juice box the whole time. He began to feel bad for Alex and guilty. He turned on the TV, where the same weatherman as before was giving the forecast. "Hot with strong thunderstorms this afternoon," he said. "And there's a tropical disturbance off the African coast we'll need to watch."

Between the previous night's dream and the Kappa Tau's bid, college life was quickly getting more complex, thought Dewey. Moreover, how would he tell Alex that he didn't get a bid? Something like this might destroy him, he thought. Then again, it might act to gird him up a bit and give him some perspective.

After a few minutes, Dewey decided he wouldn't tell Alex. He'd let him find out on his own. Or maybe Alex would just forget the whole thing. Doubtful though, he thought. He'd probably have to face Alex at some point, but for now Dewey was okay with his decision, for the preceding moments had somehow clarified his course. Alex would always be there, but Radford and the beautiful club might not.

"Is it Friday yet?" said Alex, walking groggily from the bedroom into the common room wearing blue, gingham boxer shorts.

Alex's sudden appearance caught Dewey off guard. His heart raced; his face warmed. Dewey picked up the bid envelope from the couch and slid it under his thigh.

"Nope, it's only Tuesday," said Dewey, trying to remain nonchalant. "Day four since move-in."

"You gotta be shittin' me—feels like we've been here forever." Alex grabbed his crotch and yawned. "By the way, who was at the door?"

"Just some drunk dude," said Dewey. "He had the wrong room."

It was the first time he'd lied to Alex since they met. Like news of the bid, Dewey had mixed emotions about this untruth. The lie came easily. Dewey felt guilty as he wondered if Alex had caught on, but he hesitated to confess.

"We'll probably start to see a lot of that around here," said Alex.

"A lot of what?" Dewey's mind was still stuck on the lie.

"You know, people in the dorm getting fucked up and trying to find their way back home."

"Yeah, I guess so."

"Just be sure to wake me when it's a hot, drunk chic who knocks." Alex turned and headed back into the bedroom. "I'm gonna shower and get to class. Can't be late for this one."

As Alex disappeared into the bedroom, Dewey reached for the bid envelope under his thigh. It was mashed and sweaty, but the *K* and *T* had endured. Dewey rubbed his thumb across the letters. They felt sure and sturdy. In them he felt Kappa Tau's order and attraction, their customs and traditions. And he sensed a clear route to Radford.

Dewey put on jeans, a shirt and shoes, and quietly slipped out of the room before Alex finished showering. He headed down St. Philip Street toward the cafeteria, along the way passing the Simons Center. Slowing for a minute, he looked into the brick building's massive, smoked-glass windows. Inside, large, painted canvases featured sea life. Seagulls, whales and corals hung on one stretch of wall, while in the visitor breezeway, a papier mâché ballerina with bright red lipstick pirouetted. Further down were portraits of dour-looking men with poofy, rainbow-colored, powdered wigs and high, stiff collars. A curvy naked figure lying atop the grassy cistern eating grapes was the subject of still another composition. Other canvases depicted Lowcountry landscapes with marsh grass and shallow pools reflecting the sky above, browns, greens, grays, and blues melting together to form a slow, still, impenetrable paradise.

When Dewey reached the last smoked-glass window, he noticed a palm-sized sticker at the bottom of the pane featuring the bust of a man with a wide forehead, black curly hair, deep-set eyes and puffy, almost over-exaggerated, lips. The left side of the sticker read, *André the Giant Has a Posse.* On the right, it read, *7'4" and 520 LB.* Dewey knew famed wrestler André the Giant from TV, but his appearance here seemed strange. It wasn't exactly art, he thought, but somehow it did fit in with the rest of what he'd seen—the marine life, the dour-looking men, and the naked figure atop the cistern.

Dewey walked on, eventually reaching and entering the cafeteria, where he grabbed a brown, plastic tray and worked his way down the hot line for a scoop full of scrambled eggs and a bagel. He sat down and pulled out his syllabus for Freshman Seminar. So far, it was his favorite class.

The reading list was extensive. Articles plucked from publications like *Psychology Today*, *The New Yorker*, and the *Journal of Human Sexuality* had been collated and stapled into a large packet. The first entry in the packet's table of contents read, "You, Me and the Other." Another read, "My Best Black Friend." Still another read, "Gender in the Modern Era." Dewey found the titles both interesting and familiar. Back in high school his English teacher, a tall, thin man with dark hair who'd graduated from Harvard, would require similar reading. The titles also made Dewey think how his father had used his sermons to advance social justice and how he'd witnessed firsthand the effects of the women's liberation movement with a mother who'd chosen to break out of her privileged upbringing, take a 9-to-5 job and hike part of the Appalachian Trail.

And then there was Tyrone and Malik from elementary school, bussed by court order from Charlotte's inner city to the leafy suburbs, where Dewey lived. He remembered how different they were. How they spoke and smelled. Even the way they healed—from childhood injuries that left dark, enigmatic scars along their arms—stood in contrast to his own wounds, faint and tidily stitched.

Dewey finished breakfast and walked his tray to the tub of soaking dishes near a window into the kitchen. A black hand reached for his tray and pulled it in. He looked through the small window to see a middle-aged black woman looking back and smiling at him. Her name tag read Iris, and there was something very familiar about her. "Thank you," he said, handing her his tray.

"You welcome," said the woman, who was wearing an apron and hairnet.

Outside, the line to the cafeteria filled fast. The campus bustled with backpacks, mostly strapped to freshmen like him with class schedules and campus maps in hand. Dewey headed to Craig and climbed the stairs to Freshman Seminar. Dr. DuGow was settling her long-brimmed hat into a chair. She plopped the stapled packet of readings on the lectern and thumbed through it.

"Good morning, class," she said with a big laugh like the first day of class. "How's the first week going?"

"The beer is good," said the no-neck surfer.

"I'm totally lost," said the Asian girl.

"Busy," called out a voice in the front row where Dewey had taken his seat.

Dr. DuGow wore an ankle-length dress with small flower petals on it and three Bangle bracelets on her wrist. "So, how's your first assignment coming?" she asked.

Some students pulled out notebooks with a page full of words. Others looked away and hid their heads. Dewey had a single paragraph he'd hastily composed while watching the weather back at the dorm. He had chosen to describe Radford.

"Anyone meet someone new or different?" Dr. DuGow continued.

"I met a girl with dreadlocks," said a boy wearing white, clunky athletic shoes.

"What did you think?" said Dr. DuGow.

"Do they ever wash their hair?"

"I can assure you they do."

"No shit," said the boy.

Dr. DuGow seemed unbothered by his language.

"Who does that anyway?" said the girl who had spoken before.

"She may just like it or maybe it's a custom where she comes from," said Dr. DuGow. The room filled with silence.

"I'll go, next" said Dewey. "There was this guy at rush the other night who looked interesting. Apparently, he's from here, and people just flock to him." Dewey knew he was in risky territory. How much should he say about Angel Boy and what would those around him think?

"Elaborate, please," said Dr. DuGow.

"He just has that one-in-a-million thing—girls, popularity, just everything." A few students perked up when they heard this. Dewey meant to convey something deeper, something more aesthetic about Angel Boy, but he feared it would be lost on his peers. Worse yet, they might make fun of him or call him gay. They might misunderstand or take it the wrong way.

"Did you find out his name?" said Dr. DuGow.

"No," said Dewey, reluctant to give away Radford's identity.

"All those pretty boys are alike," said the no-neck surfer.

"What do you mean?" said Dr. DuGow, sharply.

"They run the show and tag anything that moves because they can."

"Well, first off, you've grouped them altogether, and that's a problem."

"They all look the same to me."

"But you forget they're individuals, too." Dr. DuGow quickly focused her attention on the packet. "Which brings us to our first assigned reading. For those who have them, could you please get your packet?"

Several students, including Dewey, reached into their book bags and produced it. The first article, "You, Me and the Other" talked about finding the "real self." In a text box on the side of the page were several questions—*What makes us who we are? Are we the same person from one moment to the next?*

Dr. DuGow went to the chalkboard and drew a giant circle. On the outside of the circle in roughly 30-degree arcs, she wrote: *Favorite Book, Favorite Food, Favorite Music, Personal Motto, Birth Order,* and *A Skill You Are Proud Of.* In the middle of the circle was written, *Three Adjectives that Describe You.* "This is a Personal Identity Wheel. It's not super-scientific but rather something to get you thinking about who you are."

Dewey copied the wheel in his notebook underneath his paragraph about Rad. He chuckled at the personal motto prompt. "Seize the Day," he thought. Or maybe, "Keep Your Feet on the Ground and Keep Reaching for the Stars." But in reality, Dewey didn't have a personal motto, which disturbed him.

Dr. DuGow completed the wheel using fictitious examples. "So, there you have it," she said. "A finished wheel, which, using your own answers, should begin to tell you something about yourself. Let's aim to have these completed by next week."

The class seemed genuinely intrigued by the assignment, as it was clearly beyond more traditional courses like math or English. There was something magical about the Identity Wheel, thought Dewey. You could fill it in any way you wanted, and no one would know if you were telling the truth or not.

Dewey stared at a piece of white notebook paper, when he noticed a group of small, squiggly lines float across his line of vision. Not some kind of imperfection on the page but, rather, something originating in the eye. It mostly happened when he looked up at a bright blue sky or lighted background. The lines would appear and seconds later disappear, briefly distorting his vision. He'd noticed the mysterious phenomenon over the summer but thought nothing of it. But the squiggly lines were becoming a nuisance. Maybe he would go to Student Health to get it checked out. Maybe he would try to find a doctor in Charleston.

Dr. DuGow dismissed the class, her characteristic nervous laugh punctuating the moment. Dewey exited the building onto St. Philips Street, where he happened to bump into Mary Pate.

"Big plans this weekend, Dewey?" she said.

"Not really," said Dewey.

"How about the roommate?"

"I'm not sure what he's up to. He'll probably just hang out at the dorm and listen to music."

"Maybe I'll see you out."

"Sure. Maybe." Dewey said goodbye and headed to New Dorm. Tomorrow he would have to answer the Kappas about the bid.

Passing Simons Center, he looked down at André. He looked happier, thought Dewey, as the early afternoon sun struck his face.

CHAPTER 7

Dewey awoke early the next morning and decided to go jogging. Kappa House was on his mind, so much so that he decided to stick the bid envelope in his pocket. He took the elevator to the first floor and exited through the corridor onto Calhoun Street. He turned onto St. Philip Street, ran past the back side of Maybank Hall, past Simons Center and turned right onto George Street, passing Porter's Lodge and the cafeteria. He thought briefly of Iris, the cafeteria worker, before making a left onto Coming Street, then Logan Street, and finally Tradd Street. In a few minutes he was on The Battery.

Charleston's Battery consisted of a long seawall and promenade at the southernmost tip of the city's peninsula, where the Ashley and Cooper rivers met to create Charleston's harbor. Paved roads running one way in each direction with a generous median full of oleander in between boasted slow-motoring tourists, runners and Sunday strollers.

Across from The Battery sat White Point Garden, a grassy, six-acre park with ancient, gnarled oak trees and a gazebo—a place known for afternoon picnics and marriage proposals. The garden's idyllic grounds also featured a variety of defunct mortars and cannons from the Civil War, several commemorative statues, and views of nearby Fort Sumter and Sullivan's Island lighthouse.

The harbor was placid, as Dewey set out along the promenade. He had walked it many times as a child, stopping along the way to straddle the park's cannons, while making funny faces into his father's camera.

He remembered how hot the cannons' matte black surface could get on a sunny day and how thankful he was to be wearing jeans. The battle scenes he imagined taking place may have been small on history, but they were always big on smoke and fire, and always ended with a Union victory and, eventually, a fried oyster supper in the Market.

Dewey, having picked up the pace again, marveled at The Battery's long row of stately, impeccably kept mansions facing the harbor. Some dated back to the early 1800s and were made of brick or wood in a variety of colors, and almost all possessed the characteristic creeping fig leaf somewhere on their exterior.

The Battery had a kind of tragic beauty to it, he thought. With its palms and balmy breezes, it was one of the city's dreamiest spots, but Dewey knew deep down that its ambiance, its mansions—its fifth-and-sixth-generation Range Rover-driving residents—could never have existed without slavery.

Yet here he was in the very lap of it, bathing in it and quickly forgetting the city's one-time fervor for human bondage in exchange for its material abundance, whimsical architecture and spectacular views. Here at this very spot during childhood was planted, perhaps, the seed that would finally and only be fully expressed on a college visit one spring day in front of Porter's Lodge. But how could someone choose a place or thing based on beauty alone, he thought, especially something as crucial as college? Shouldn't there have been some academic consideration? At least a quick review of campus literature? A paragraph or two in a college guidebook? None of that for Dewey—only the pleasing symmetry and visage of a stranger on a bike amid dappled sunlight and unrelenting heat, and a madness in the air that overwhelmed the senses and defied all logic.

His pace quickened, thoughts of the bid intensifying with every stride, as he raced along the promenade into a hazy, cloud-stacked horizon.

Heading back to New Dorm along East Bay Street, with its green trash cans and red recycling bins, Dewey smelled stale beer and wet cigarettes. He thought about the people behind these guilty pleasures—married couples, lovers and one-night stands spilling out onto the city's streets at closing time.

At the corner of East Bay and Broad streets, he passed the Old Exchange Building, with its octagonal cupola and Venetian windows. Further on, The Vendue and Magnolia's restaurants looked stunned and sleepy in the morning light, soon to rise off their haute haunches and prepare for the next wave of discerning palettes.

A mile now from New Dorm, Dewey turned left onto Market Street, encountering a series of one-story, open-air stalls made of bricks spanning several blocks comprising the city's old Market. Some had dark green, almost black, louvered blinds to help shield the sun, while other stalls offered unobstructed views to the sidewalk shops on either side of the Market.

Vendors had begun pulling out their wares from beat-up minivans and sea-salt-eaten station wagons onto old, wood display tables. A black man in a white cassock and brown fez unloaded wood carvings showing the African continent and a group of shackled men, women and children. A short, plump woman in blue jeans and a pink shirt carefully laid out rows of sand dollars with hand-painted lighthouses on them. A wrinkle-faced black woman in a red, cable-knit sweater, long green skirt and droopy, blue hat leaned coiled baskets against a wall at the entrance to one of the sheds. She sat down and began weaving together a handful of sweetgrass.

Dewey briefly slowed his pace, making his way to the Market's front entrance on Meeting Street, marked by a two-story, mustard-colored structure with columns topped with a pediment decorated with images of bull and sheep skulls, and two flights of stairs on either side with elaborate iron work. He was in awe of the ancient-looking edifice. How magnificent it was in the morning light, he thought, so effortlessly grand and beautiful.

Dewey closed his eyes and inhaled the Market's sweet stench—body sweat, cigarettes, food scraps, pluff mud, sugar, spice, horse dung, bubble gum, coffee, leather and—as far back as he could remember—sewage. A carriage full of tourists clip-clopped by. Dewey felt the sun on his face, his brain tingle, and his heart pound.

He looked down Meeting Street at Hyman's, where his mother always ordered she-crab soup, and his dad complained how the air conditioning was too cold. Then down at Marianne's, where, in its dimly lit interior, she always ordered French onion soup. Just beyond was Wentworth Street, where fraternity row seemed to call. Memories from the night of rush filled his head—the long line of brothers in Oxford shirts, red ties and blue blazers above the mantle and the slide show of beautiful, laughing people. Dewey tried imagining himself as one of them. He remembered the tall, boisterous Greek rep who'd led them from the Stern Center to fraternity row, how clean and well-dressed he'd been, despite the hard time he gave them, and how under the veil of darkness, he'd lifted his hand, dispersing, as if by magic, everyone into different houses.

Dewey realized he'd likely never meet Rad unless he accepted the bid. They had no classes together, no mutual friends and very little in common—Rad, for all Dewey knew, might never have even heard of a place called *Ohio*. He wondered if coming to the college had been a mistake, as he replayed that spring day in front of Porter's Lodge over and over again in his mind.

Dewey turned toward the Omni Hotel across the street, with its green awnings, small balconies and dainty mannequins. The next left was Hasell Street, and after that Wentworth—home to Kappa House. Sprinting now as if chasing something, he felt an unshackling, a sloughing off of his old self.

His last few strides seemed effortless, as oak leaves and sunlight gave way to the bigger-than-life *K* and *T* on the front of the light green, three-story house that Dewey and Alex had visited just a few days before. He stepped onto the porch, but there was no welcome line— no handshakes, no commotion and no jockeying for position. There was only Dewey, half naked in running shoes and shorts, and sweating.

He pulled the bid envelope from his pocket. It was moist and crumpled, as it had been when he hid it under his thigh back at the dorm, but his name was still legible. Still catching his breath, he held it up, as if to confirm that he was indeed the recipient. His face could not hide that particular feeling of knowing what can be taken back and what can't.

Dewey knocked on the door.

After a pause, footsteps approached. A lemon-scented breeze drifted over the porch.

A brother in khakis and sandals opened the door.

"I accept," said Dewey in a voice that he did not recognize as his own.

* * *

Dewey returned from his run and Kappa House to find Alex still sleeping. He looked over at his desk chair to find his clothes from the day before draped over it. A drawer full of shirts and shorts lay part way open. He went to the bathroom, and with an outstretched arm in front of him braced himself against the wall over the commode and began to pee. He had closed the door but not yet turned on the light. A knock came at the front door. Dewey heard Alex shuffle through the common room, and recognized the visitor's voice, surprised when they asked for him by name.

"No, Dewey's not here right now," said Alex, "but he'll probably be back soon. I think he's out running."

"Shoot," said the visitor in a twangy voice. "Well, just tell him Mary Pate dropped by."

Dewey was surprised, even a little excited, to hear it was Mary Pate. Why had she dropped by? He tried remembering when he last saw or spoke to her; it was outside Craig, just after Freshman Seminar.

"Didn't we meet on the elevator?" said Alex.

"Yeah, I met y'all the night of move-in," she said. "My name is Mary Pate Hackney."

"Cool. I'm Alex."

"Yeah, I know, I saw Dewey at Maybank the other day and couldn't remember your name. He told me again."

"You want to come in?"

"Sure."

"So, how's your first week of classes?"

Dewey heard Alex's voice perk up.

"They're okay," said Mary Pate. "You know, just finding where stuff is. How about y'all?"

"Well, I was late to my first class, so that bit the big one. Can't speak for Dew, but he seems like he's doing okay—he gets up early and goes running, so that's annoying."

Having taken a seat on the commode, Dewey listened carefully, chuckling at how Alex had framed his early morning athletics.

"So, how was the freshman mixer?" said Mary Pate.

"There were a lot of people, but it was kind of lame," said Alex. "But we got to meet Clyde."

"Who?" Dewey thought he heard Mary Pate laugh.

"The school mascot, the cougar."

"Never knew we had one."

"Me neither, but apparently he's official."

Alex sounded cheerful, one of only a handful of times Dewey had heard him sound like that since they'd arrived. Dewey was glad to hear

Mary Pate and Alex getting along.

"Dewey says you're from the big city of Raleigh." Mary Pate's voice rose sharply.

"Yeah, born there, but my family's originally from New York," said Alex. "Raleigh's alright, I guess."

"Was your high school cool?"

"Yeah, but not for me."

"What do you mean?" Dewey heard Mary Pate's voice dip.

"Well, I wasn't popular or smart like, well, Dewey. I was just kind of there, floating from group to group, pissed off, with the occasional fight."

"Pissed off about what?"

"Ya know, I don't even really know. Wait, I take that back. I was mad at pimples, mad at not being able to get my hair the way I wanted it, tired of pretty girls dissing me, and I hated every Southern hick fucker football player there was." Dewey listened to the silence that followed.

After a minute or two, Alex spoke again. "Want a juice box?"

"Sure," said Mary Pate.

Dewey heard Alex shuffle over to the kitchenette counter to the cardboard crate of juice boxes that Frieda and Stuart had hauled up during move-in. "Here," he said.

"Shit," said Mary Pate, "it shot into my face. Stupid straw."

"Don't worry. It happens."

Dewey heard them laugh.

"Do you know your major?" said Alex.

"Probably business administration," said Mary Pate. "How about you?"

"Pre-med, maybe. By the way, how was SCA the other night?"

"It was pretty big, and everyone seemed on fire for Jesus." Dewey noticed Mary Pate was speaking faster. "You can come, if you want.

We'll be having some picnics and service projects this year."

"Do they let Jews in?"

"So, you're not Christian?"

"No."

"You didn't grow up going to church?"

"Nope again."

"There were a few like you back home. I suppose you could come, but you'd have to be someone else. I mean, you'd have to disguise yourself."

"I'll get back to you."

Dewey could hear it—the way Alex's voice fell, his heart falling with it. He imagined Alex sitting hunched over in front of Mary Pate, his black leg hair spilling over his white crew socks against the backdrop of honking cars and shouting students.

"Just remember we're open to everyone," said Mary Pate. "Well, I guess I'd better go. Tell Dew I dropped by. Also, I'm having some people over to my room tonight if y'all want to come."

"Jews allowed?" said Alex.

"You're just being funny now," said Mary Pate.

Dewey heard them get up, and the door open and close. He decided to stay in the bathroom until he heard Alex leave. Finally, Dewey heard the door open and close again. The fire exit door clanged. Dewey put his shoes on and headed out. The TV was on. "Some real scorchers ahead. Be sure to exercise caution," said the weatherman.

CHAPTER 8

The sign outside the Stern Center read *Hot Dog Eating Contest, Winner Gets $100*. Dewey and a group of students had lined up next to the sign waiting for the doors to open. At the front of the line stood the no-neck surfer from the freshman mixer who was also in Dewey's biology and Freshman Seminar classes.

It was a beautiful day, the same one that had earlier found Dewey down at The Battery jogging, and, though still technically summer, he knew the signs of fall in Charleston were beginning to show—shadows of church steeples stretched out long and cold across city streets; empty seats on horse-drawn carriages; and the occasional scent of tea olive.

The Stern Center's front doors suddenly swung open, surprising everyone, not the least of which was Theodore Stern, the building's namesake, whose chiseled face and smile on a nearby cast bronze plaque seemed to Dewey to swell with delight.

The college admissions counselor who Dewey and Alex had met at the freshman mixer stood with a hand on each door as if announcing a store grand opening. He wore a blue, seersucker suit and a madras bow tie. He was lean and muscular with shiny, black skin.

Lucious had graduated from a military college across town. As he looked out onto the long line of students, Dewey imagined him marching men around a parade deck in perfect cadence and shining his shoes until he could see his reflection.

"Ready to eat some dawgs?" said Lucious. "Come here, you!" He pointed to the no-neck surfer. "What's your name?"

"Trey Fontaine."

"Well, Trey, get over here and hold this door." Trey shuffled over to Lucious and held the door with his foot. "Okay, come on in, y'all," he said to the waiting crowd.

The long line of students broke ranks and flooded the Stern Center lobby, the same place where Dewey and Alex had come the night of rush. Signs directed contestants and onlookers upstairs to a large, open room, where Clyde the Cougar frolicked amid banquet tables holding giant platters of hot dogs stacked like pyramids. Dewey watched Clyde sweep at one of the platters with a big, furry paw, pretending to grab and eat a hot dog, only to have his fingers stumble in the final moments trying to find his mouth. A huge picture window overlooking George Street invited in trees and sunlight.

"Okay, y'all, find a table and sit," Lucious told the crowd. He'd taken off his suit jacket, revealing splotches of sweat under his armpits. It was mid-morning and already seventy-eight degrees.

Trey, having satisfied his door-holding duty, entered the room last and, recognized Dewey. "Hey, dude, what brings you out?" he said.

"Had to get away from the dorm, and I saw the contest sign," said Dewey. "I haven't been over here since the night of rush."

"*You* rushed?" Trey pointed to the floor as if to confirm both of them were talking about the same place. He wore a Billabong graphic tee-shirt with an image of an old Volkswagen bus and a setting sun. His hair was long on top and swept to the side, with one side of his head buzz cut.

"Yeah, I went as a favor to my roommate. He practically begged me."

"Why?"

"He didn't want to go alone, I guess." Dewey looked down at the place on the floor where Trey had pointed.

"Well, that's fucking stupid," said Trey. "I mean, like I said in Dr. Doogie's class, it's just a bunch of bullshit. Pretty boys and bullshit."

"You mean Dr. Dugow?"

"Yeah, however you pronounce it."

"How about you? What brought you out here?"

"I dunno. I was slamming beers with my buddies last night and one of them mentioned this would be an easy hundred bucks. Said he thought I had what it takes."

"So, you're going to compete?"

"Damn right."

Trey turned his attention to Lucious who, holding his hands above his head, began to speak. "Everyone of y'all should have a plate of hot dogs in front of you," he said. "If you finish that one, raise your hand, and we'll get you another." Then he pulled a whistle from his pocket and blew it. The room erupted in motion with hands, mouths and hot dogs.

Trey immediately shoved two hot dogs in his mouth. Halfway through the pork and bun platter, he shouted, "Go Cougars!"

"You're such a weenie," shouted someone from across the room.

"You're a dickhead," said another, who Dewey could only see from behind.

Dewey watched as Lucious circulated around the room, including stopping to give Trey an encouraging pat on the back. A girl at Trey's table looked like she was about to pass out, as a flaccid, half-torn hot dog hung from her mouth, her plate full of tattered bits and pieces that looked like fish bait. Trey glanced and smirked at her, before diving back into his pyramid of dogs.

Lucious finally made his way over to Dewey. "You ain't playing?" he said.

"Nah, just observing. Saw the sign, and it looked kind of crazy," said Dewey, leaning back in his chair. "You do this every semester?"

"Yeah, it's an ice-breaker kind of thing. Gets the kids talking."

"Cool."

"Sure you don't want to jump in on the fun?" Lucious raised a hopeful eyebrow.

"No, I think I'm good, but thanks anyway."

"Suit yourself. Let me know if there's anything I can do." Lucious continued snaking his way back and forth between banquet tables among the ferocious horde of hot dog eaters.

Dewey was taken aback by Lucious' casualness. Was he just another ruckus freshman or was he the dutiful admissions counselor?

Several minutes had passed and the contestants, drooling and laughing, pushed back more hot dogs. Most looked like they'd lost count of how many hot dogs they'd eaten. They appeared as if in some kind of trance. Finally, Trey and another freshman were the only ones who remained. Lucious had moved both of them to the same table opposite one another, as they battled for the last dogs. The room gathered around, taking sides.

"C'mon, Trey, stuff it back!" said a boy in a bright green polo shirt. "Don't be a pussy!"

Trey's face looked red and strained, as beads of sweat rolled down his forehead. Meanwhile, his hot dog-eating foe, a thin boy in jeans with dark hair and glasses, was in only slightly better shape.

Then it happened—at first just a trickle, which Trey tried cupping with his hand. Then his mouth opened just barely, as bits of chewed hotdog began falling out. He brought his forearm to his head and leaned forward, as if he might rest slumped over on the table. A loud gurgling noise from somewhere deep in his bowels came next, then a violent thrust forward and back, accompanied by red-colored vomit spewing from his mouth. The soupy mixture of half-eaten hot dogs and gastric juice splashed on the table, but not before Lucious reached across and raised Trey's arm victoriously in the air.

"We have a winner, y'all!" Lucious waved an envelope marked *$100* in the air, as everyone squeamishly stepped away from the table.

"Hell, yeah!" said a guy in a blue, pin-striped shirt.

Gradually, everyone began to leave. Trey's hotdog-eating foe looked glum as he stood up, his once-thin belly now noticeably extended. "Way to go, dude," he said, extending a congratulatory handshake to Trey, as the latter's vomit rolled off the table.

Lucious hovered over Trey like a coach over an injured player. He'd undone his madras bow tie, a strap of fabric hanging limp around his neck. "What an inspiration, Trey!" he said. "They'll be talking about this till their senior year!"

Dewey had moved from his seat near the large picture window closer to Trey and Lucious. He noticed Trey's face had returned to its normal color, and he'd stopped sweating. Where chunks of spewed hot dog once emanated, words gradually began to form.

"I'm totally stoked about those hundred bucks, dude, but right now I think I need to go to Student Health," said Trey.

"That's probably a good idea," said Dewey, trying not to spoil Trey's win. He looked at Lucious.

"Okay, I'll take him," said Lucious, looking down at Trey. "Maybe they can give you some Pepto or something."

"I'll take anything," said Trey, barely lifting his head off the table. "I feel like shit."

"Mind if I come?" said Dewey.

"Fine by me," said Lucious. "And I think I speak for the both of us." Lucious looked down at Trey, then back at Dewey. With help from Dewey, Lucious lifted Trey from the table and walked him downstairs. As the three of them exited the building, a chiseled Ted Stern happily looked on.

* * *

Student Health occupied a narrow, three-story brick house with dark green shutters and a gable roof near the corner of George and Coming streets, within easy walking distance of the Stern Center. Only the first story was occupied, however, with the upper two stories dark and abandoned-looking and windows caked with sea salt, similar to the windows on the backside of Maybank. The house had two porches, one at ground-level and another above it, both supported by columns running the full length of the house.

With Lucious and Dewey helping hold him up, Trey rambled up Student Health's front porch steps. His dry heaving had intensified, as they shuffled over creaky porch boards and approached the front door.

"Easy, Trey, almost there," said Lucious.

"You're the one who fuckin' did this to me, dude," said Trey, looking at Lucious vengefully.

Dewey opened the front door, and together the three of them squeezed through. A woman of medium height with dark brown hair and a kind smile greeted them, her arms folded as if she'd been preparing for this.

"Well, gentlemen, this looks serious," she said, smiling at Lucious like she knew him.

"A casualty, of sorts," said Dewey. "A casualty of hot dogs."

"Did you put on that silly hot dog eating contest again, Lucious?" Dropping her arms, the woman reached out for Trey. "Poor kids."

"Yeah, you know, we do it each new semester," said Lucious. "Gets them talking."

"Well, let's get him into an exam room and have a look. Probably just indigestion."

Dewey and Lucious followed the woman down a short hallway into a room that looked like it had once been a kitchen, with a long white countertop and a series of drawers next to a boarded-up space the size of a dishwasher. "I'll take it from here, boys," she said, shooing them away.

Dewey and Lucious returned to the lobby and sat down. "Thanks for helping out with Trey," said Lucious.

"No problem," said Dewey. "He's in two of my classes, so I know how he can be." Dewey looked at Lucious, then at the carpet. He noticed it was old and tattered; in some places it had become so threadbare that the floorboards showed.

"Oh? And exactly how is that?" said Lucious, sitting back in his chair and relaxing.

"A loudmouth. Big loudmouth. Apparently, he heard about Charleston from friends back in Jersey who go here. They're all big surfers."

A large, gilt-framed oil painting of a Lowcountry marsh with green, brown, and blue hues hung on the wall opposite them; in the painting's foreground, a pool of water reflected the infinite blue above. It reminded Dewey of his dream about Desirée and the revelers.

"Those boys are a long way from home," said Lucious.

"For sure," said Dewey.

"So, how do you like your classes?"

"Good so far."

"What's your favorite?"

"I'd have to say Freshman Seminar, Dr. DuGow's class."

"She still got that laugh?" Lucious looked over with a big grin.

"So, you know her?"

"Kind of. A long time ago, she visited my high school as part of a bridge program for academically gifted students. She spoke to our class about career stuff. She's a trip."

"That's right. I keep forgetting you're from here. So, why'd you go to the military college across town and not here?"

"I had an uncle in the Army. He suggested it. And I lived close by, and they gave me a scholarship."

"What did you study?"

"Math and French."

"Parlez-vous?"

"Un peu."

A girl with blonde hair wearing white cotton shorts and a shirt with big silver, gold and blue sorority letters on it walked out of another exam room. She carried a large backpack whose weight had the effect of stretching the front of her shirt, making her breasts into two peaks. She sipped on a tall fountain drink that Dewey recognized from the Stern Center cafe. Dewey could smell her perfume, a mix of geranium, jasmine and vanilla. It reminded him of an old girlfriend at summer camp who wore Fendi, and how he'd held his nose close to her neck at evening campfires.

Reaching the door, the girl turned and looked back at Dewey. Rather, Dewey noticed she seemed to look past him like he wasn't even there. He lowered his head and looked down at the carpet, as she passed him. The Kiawah girl had come and gone.

A sudden commotion made Dewey and Lucious look down the hallway. There, Trey stood with one hand on his hip and the other on his forehead. The nurse who had walked him back, the one who acted like she knew Lucious, had a hand on Trey's shoulder. "He's going to make it," she said, gently guiding him toward Lucious and Dewey.

"Thanks," said Lucious, winking at her. "You did it again."

The woman walked them to the door and said good-bye.

"Alright, fellas," said Lucious, looking at Dewey and Trey in the hot afternoon lull. "Lick your wounds, and let's get you back where you came from."

CHAPTER 9

A wave of cool air enveloped Dewey, as he entered New Dorm's lobby. Waving good-bye to Trey and Lucious, he stepped onto the elevator. It groaned as it climbed to the fourth floor, where he found Alex in the room watching TV.

"Where ya' been?" he said.

"Just out walking around," said Dewey. "Went down to the Stern Center."

"Anything big going on?"

"Nah, just this crazy hot dog-eating contest. Fun to watch."

"Well, you'll never guess who dropped by?" said Alex, excited.

"Let me guess, Clyde the Cougar." Dewey lifted his hands in the shape of two big paws.

"Not even close. Try Mary Pate."

"Mary Pate Hackney?" Dewey tried looking surprised.

"Yeah, I guess that's her. She dropped by a half hour ago. Wants us to come over tonight. Her roommate and a couple other people are having a party."

"What floor are they on?"

"Third, I think." Alex pointed downward.

"Yeah, that sounds cool." Dewey took a seat on the other end of the couch. "So, what did she have to say?"

"The usual. Said how y'all were in the same biology class, and we talked a little about meeting on the elevator the other night. And, can you believe it, she tried pitching me on SCA."

"Oh Jesus Christ. Sorry, didn't mean it like that. Did she say how their event went?"

"Yeah, she said it was great. They were all *fired* up." Alex waved his fingers to mimic burning flames. "Then I dropped the bomb I was Jewish. You should have seen it. Totally threw her."

Dewey remembered the Kagans back home, and how he and his family once joined them for a Seder meal. He remembered most of all their daughter, Mercedes, and her beautiful olive skin, and how the meal they shared that night quickly moved from dining room to TV room when news of the Ronald Reagan assassination attempt broke, leaving the rest of the evening a mix of Dan Rather, matzo balls and a gray-suited, secret service man with an Uzi submachine gun hovering over the president.

"So, I guess SCA's off your list then?" asked Dewey.

"Maybe." Alex chuckled as he picked a pimple on his chin. A few minutes passed. "Do you think Mary Pate's hot?"

Dewey envisioned Mary Pate, overlaying her face and body atop the image he had in his head of a Kiawah girl. No match, he thought, wincing at his shallowness, but to be nice he answered affirmatively.

"Yeah, I'd say she's hot. How about you?"

"Yeah, same here. I like her hair and make-up," said Alex. "Seems sort of innocent, you know, with the Jesus thing and all." He paused, leaning over the arm of the couch to look out the bedroom window, where the sun was setting and a girl with long, wavy hair wearing high-heeled Chelsea boots walked by on the sidewalk. "What makes a chic hot, anyway?"

"Looks," said Dewey.

"That's what I say—tits and ass." Alex grinned with delight.

"Not quite what I meant. I just meant that's always the first thing you notice. You almost can't help it."

"So, what exactly makes someone beautiful?"

Dewey thought for a minute. "It's the arrangement of the eyes, nose and lips. High cheekbones, a good smile and smooth complexion." Dewey stopped abruptly, a list of countless other attributes rolling like a film strip in his head.

"You're a regular Mary-fuckin'-Kay, but I agree, it's definitely the face." Alex looked at the smooth, white ceiling above, just months-old and flawless.

"And the body. Not too long a trunk, and the arms and legs not too long either." Dewey's voice became more vigorous.

"Goddamn, who thinks about this stuff?"

"In art class, one of the first things you learn is ideal proportion. Beauty is really just a ratio, a matter of mathematics."

"How so?"

"Well, turns out the magic number is 1.6, meaning if you compare the measurements of two body parts—say the mouth and the nose, the width of the mouth should be about 1.6 times the width of the nose. It's called the golden ratio. They say that's what makes someone, quote, *attractive.*"

Alex got up and reached for a juice box, stretching his short arms and small hands for the upper shelf. "So, beauty comes down to millimeters?"

"Maybe not that extreme." Dewey drew a contradictory look on his face. "But beauty's got to be more than that—I mean, there's things about people that are beautiful that just aren't quantifiable. It's more than just looks—it's something they might say or do, or how they make you feel. Right?"

Alex sucked on his juice box, as Dewey got up from the couch and walked to the other side of the common room. He could hear Calhoun Street beginning to fill with rush hour traffic. The light outside was fuzzy and gold-tinted.

"Take this city, for example. There's so much beauty here. Can you say exactly what makes it that way?" said Dewey.

"Lots of people say they like the old architecture," said Alex, holding his juice box straw with his teeth like a toothpick.

"I agree. Even as a child, I found this place magical—the columns, gates and porches were almost surreal," Dewey said, feeling his pulse quicken.

Alex took the straw from his mouth and held it up like a wand. "And since you brought it up I just have to say there's so many damn good-looking people around here," he said. "I mean, I'm not gay, but if I looked like some of the guys on campus, I'd just fuck any and everything in sight. I'd keep a list of every type of girl and try to fuck three a day."

Dewey, who was gradually getting used to Alex's vulgarity, came to a stop and looked down at Alex on the couch. "Yeah, I got to admit, there are some pretty unreal-looking dudes here, and they probably do get all the girls." Dewey stared at the TV, half-expecting Angel Boy and his pals to appear from the corner of the screen, and he could point to them.

Dewey began again. "Remember when we were talking about how we chose the college?"

"Yeah, I remember. You came for pre-med. Right?" said Alex.

"Yeah, I guess you could say that," said Dewey, "but there's something, someone, else."

"What do you mean?"

"Well, it's going to sound really weird, but when I was interviewing here, we went for a campus tour, and I saw these guys, these really cool-looking guys, biking down George Street. And I just knew that whoever they were, I wanted to be like them."

"Have you seen them since?" Alex looked out the window.

"No, not the whole bunch, but I did see the main guy, I think."

"Where?"

"During rush at Kappa House."

"At rush?"

"Yeah, it was total luck. Remember that big picture of all the brothers over the mantle? Well, he was one of them."

"Well, what's his name?"

"Radford, and he's rush chairman. Funny, huh?"

"I'll say. Where's he from?"

"Here in Charleston, from what I understand."

"How can you be sure? Maybe he's just like one of us."

Dewey stared at the fuzzy, golden light in the bedroom. "No, he's not like us. He's not like anyone."

"Pretty crazy." With his palm, Alex crushed his juice box and lobbed it at the waste can. It made a loud thud when it landed. "Bet you won't be seeing him again, huh? I mean, we haven't exactly heard back from anyone from rush. No bids, I guess."

Dewey felt his stomach drop and his face redden, as he scrambled for something to say, confident that Alex still knew nothing. "Well, no big deal. Maybe I'll catch up with him somewhere on campus."

"Yeah, maybe."

Dewey tried moving the conversation along. "Why don't we go explore the library. It's one place we still haven't been."

Alex, who had sunk lower into the couch, stared at the waste can and waved his straw back and forth in his hand like a pendulum. "Why not? I'm sure it's just *full* of beautiful people."

* * *

Robert Scott Small Library stood directly across from Maybank Hall. Like Maybank, it was a newer building, but its architecture seemed grander and more formal, making it more reminiscent of Randolph Hall. Its façade featured a series of imposing arches and marble staircases on both sides. A long, spacious porch complemented the building's front entrance, while huge windows loomed in the background revealing countless rows of bookshelves and the tops of students' heads, as they roamed the library floor. Boxwoods and palmettos ran along the front of the building, softening its clay-colored, stucco exterior.

With sunglasses on and campus maps in hand, Dewey and Alex entered the building looking more like tourists who'd taken a wrong turn than college students looking for a place to study. Dewey noticed a musty smell. Not a stench like outside, but the smell of old books that had not been opened in a very long time. It was a comforting smell reminiscent of home, originating from his mother's many stacks of old family books and other documents going back more than a hundred years. It was the first time he felt at ease in his new environment.

"Hello," whispered a short, red-headed man at the reference desk who was putting books on a cart.

Dewey and Alex nodded and smiled at him, before heading for a stairway leading to the building's upper and lower floors. They chose to head to the upper floor, climbing the stairs and eventually setting their backpacks down at one of the long, brown study tables. Unzipping their backpacks, they pulled out their textbooks.

"I guess I'll dive into some biology," said Dewey.

"Is it hard?" said Alex, looking around at the endless rows of books.

"Not yet, but we're still in chapter one."

"I don't think I've even cracked a single book since we got here." Alex reached cautiously into his backpack like a snake might jump out, eventually pulling out a book on economics that was still shrink-wrapped from the bookstore. He laid it on the table and got up. "I think I'll take a walk around," he said, disappearing into the stacks.

Dewey opened his textbook and skimmed chapter one, trying to remember where Dr. Freeport had left off. The whole week had been about taxonomic hierarchy. For a moment, Dewey considered the hierarchy of his own life, with Radford and his pedaling fellows topping the pyramid, followed closely by his professors, Dr. Lyman, then Alex, Mary Pate, and Lucious, then the fuzzy, broad-shouldered Kappas and, finally, at the bottom of the pyramid, Trey, whose hot dog-eating antics had already become epic at New Dorm. Linnaeus and Dr. Freeport were right, thought Dewey, there was, in fact, a natural order to things—the only nagging question left: Where was *he* in this hierarchy?

He returned to his textbook, where after reading a paragraph on single-celled organisms he noticed again the dot-and-squiggly-line configuration obstructing the vision in his right eye. In most instances, it passed unobtrusively, similar to a gentle snowfall, occasionally altering the letters, numbers and images in its path. Other times, it seemed to attach itself to everything he looked at, regardless of how hard his eye tried outrunning it. It had become a nuisance. While he had a moment, he figured he'd try to find a doctor to look at it, so he headed back downstairs to the lobby to the reference desk in search of a Yellow Pages.

At the reference desk, Dewey grabbed the attention of the short, red-headed man who had welcomed him and Alex, and asked for a Yellow Pages. The man nodded, reached under the desk and produced one. Dewey took it to a nearby study carrel and flipped through it, trying to think what an eye doctor was called and how to spell it.

He found the heading *ophthalmologist* and looked at the names listed beneath. His eyes and finger stopped abruptly at the name *Lyman*. Where had he seen that name before, he thought. Then he remembered. He reached into his wallet and pulled out the business card he'd gotten from the mysterious man at Poogan's. *Dr. Joseph Hermes Lyman, Ophthalmologist* read the card in firm but delicate font.

What a coincidence, he thought, as a strange yet warm feeling came over him.

At that moment, the dots and squiggly lines careened across the page. Dewey decided he would call Dr. Lyman's office when he got back to the dorm. He closed the Yellow Pages and put them back on the reference desk's white-and-brown-speckled counter. The red-headed man smiled, as if he might ask how Dewey was doing or if he needed anything further. Maybe tell him a joke or let him know college life was going to be okay in the way parents with college kids do. But for some unknown reason that made Dewey hate himself, he disengaged, leaving the pale, bespectacled man looking rejected. Dewey turned and climbed back up the stairs, where he found Alex back at the table with a pile of books.

"Where'd you go?" said Alex.

"Just to look up a phone number. This squiggly thing in my eye keeps bothering me, and I need to get it checked out," said Dewey. "How about you?"

"I came across these books about horror films. You should check out some of these masks."

"Oh, yeah?"

"Yeah, take a look." Alex opened one of the books and pointed to a scaly figure with scales and blood on its face.

"Pretty ghoulish. They look like they're from the old horror movies that used to come on real early Saturday morning. Remember those?" Dewey's face lit up with excitement.

"Yeah, I remember—back in the days before cable. I loved *The Mummy* and *Swamp Thing*."

"True story," said Dewey, "I once knew this kid whose bedroom was full of horror masks. He'd actually make them with this plaster stuff. Weird thing is, he was partially blind. Went to college and everything, majored in accounting, I think, but I always remember thinking how strange it was for someone half-blind to be so fascinated with something he couldn't see."

"Yeah, pretty fucked up, man," said Alex. "Why do you think he was like that?"

"Maybe he just liked masks. Or maybe the masks did something for him. Made him feel he could be someone else and make him forget he was blind."

"It would bite not being able to see who you really were. I mean, like when you looked in the mirror. You'd just be totally blind to who you were." Alex gazed at the table in front of him, where the overhead lighting had produced a shiny reflection of his pimply face.

"Something like that." Dewey suddenly felt bad about lying to Alex about the bid. He had been so vulnerable in the moments before. "So, you going to check those books out?"

"Sure thing. They'll keep me busy on study breaks."

"Since when did you start studying?" Dewey smirked.

Alex scowled. "Take off, hoser!"

Dewey looked in the direction of the stairs. In the open slits between the steps, he saw glimpses of the pale, red-headed librarian passing back and forth with armfuls of books. Alex and Dewey zipped up their backpacks and headed for the stairs. As Dewey descended the last step onto the lobby floor near the reference desk, he caught another whiff of mustiness.

"Find everything you need?" said the librarian, who had stopped ferrying books back and forth to give Alex and Dewey his full attention.

"Yeah, pretty much," said Alex. The man took Alex's ID card and scanned the books.

"These will be due on Thursday, September 21. So, about a month from now," said the librarian.

Dewey could see the man's face in full now—a kind, thoughtful face with small, orange freckles.

"You guys take it easy," said the man, handing Alex his pile of horror books.

"I'll take it any way I can get it," said Alex, grinning and shoving the books in his backpack.

Alex and Dewey turned and walked out. It was almost dusk.

"Did you have to be such a smart ass?" said Dewey. "He seemed like a nice guy."

"He'll get over it." Alex looked over the porch railing down onto Maybank's front stoop, where in recent days Dewey had watched the Maybank herd congregate before class. "Trust me, he won't remember our faces anyway."

CHAPTER 10

Alex and Dewey decided to skip dinner and get ready for Mary Pate's party. A basket of clean laundry sat on Alex's bed, as a giant shard of light from the window passed between their beds. Dewey noticed the sun seemed lower in the sky.

"Hey, why don't you jump in the shower first," said Dewey. "I've got to call that doctor about this eye thing."

"Good deal," said Alex, reaching for his Dopp kit.

Dewey pulled Dr. Lyman's business card from his desk drawer and reached for the phone. He dialed the number, fully expecting to leave a message, as it was after hours. Much to his surprise, someone answered.

"Hello," said a man.

"Yes, I'd like to make an appointment with Dr. Lyman," said Dewey, strangely feeling the need to straighten his posture.

"This is Dr. Lyman speaking. Is your condition an emergency?"

"No, sir. I've just got this dot and squiggly line thing in my eye that floats around, and I just wanted to get it checked out."

"Does it hurt?"

"No, sir, it just gets in the way of things, especially when I look into the light."

"Okay, can you come to my office Monday morning?"

"Well, I have class at ten o'clock. Could I see you before then?"

"Yes, I can see you at nine. My office is on East Bay Street."

"Yes, I have your address."

With just a few seconds remaining, Dewey felt the urge to mention their chance meeting at Poogan's Porch the week before. But maybe that might be too familiar, he thought. Then again, it might facilitate a better visit. Dewey had watched his dad do this. His dad would try to find a connection—a mutual friend, a recollected event, a name drop—with someone to try and advance his cause, any cause. Dewey disdained this habit but, just like his father, he proceeded anyway in an attempt to connect with Dr. Lyman.

"Excuse me, sir, but didn't we meet at Poogan's Porch?"

"I'm quite sure I've *never* met you," said Dr. Lyman.

"But I have your business card. You gave it to me and told me if I needed anything to call you."

"I did no such thing. I can assure you!"

"My apologies. I must have you confused with someone else. I've met so many new people since coming here."

"Perhaps so. See you Monday morning. Good day." The phone clicked, as the voice on the other end ceased just as abruptly as it had begun.

Dewey put the phone down and anxiously looked out the window. He craned his neck in the direction of East Bay Street, as if Dr. Lyman's office might somehow magically come into view.

Just then, Alex walked out of the bathroom with a towel around his waist. "Shower's all yours," he said. "Did you get a hold of the doctor?"

"Yeah, but it's got to be one of the strangest calls I've ever had," said Dewey.

"How so?" Alex sat on the edge of his bed and dried his hair. Dewey thought he looked like a wet rat.

"Well, for one, I wasn't expecting anyone to pick up, and two, when I asked him if he remembered me from Poogan's Porch, he said no. But how does that explain this?" Dewey held Dr. Lyman's business card in mid-air.

Alex stopped drying his hair and looked up, confused. "You met *him* at Poogan's Porch?"

"Yeah, when I went to the bathroom. Remember? I was gone for a while, and you guys said you started worrying."

"I sort of remember." Alex furrowed his brow, as if trying to recall the events of that night. "Well, what did he say?"

"Not much. I'd accidentally bumped into his table and was apologizing. He told me his name, and we chatted. Then he gave me his business card and said if I ever needed anything to call him. I swear it happened."

"I believe you, but do you think he'd really remember something like that?"

"I don't know. On the phone he sounded kind of stern, almost defensive."

"Like a prick?" Alex went back to drying his hair. "Just kidding. But it does sound weird. By the way, what are you wearing to Mary Pate's tonight?"

"My usual. An Oxford and some khakis. Nothing special." Dewey put Dr. Lyman's business card back in the drawer and opened his wardrobe. "How about you?"

"Dunno." Alex opened his wardrobe and began throwing clothes on his bed: chino, khaki and moleskin pants, Bermuda shorts, long- and short-sleeve polo shirts, pink, mint-green and blue Oxfords and a handful of braided, leather belts. At the bottom of his wardrobe was a long row of shoes: leather sandals, white bucks, penny loafers, camp moccasins, and New Balance running shoes.

The ease with which Alex pulled out so many clothes and in such a wide variety made Dewey feel jealous. He marveled at the pile of clothes, as if it were a mountain of gold.

"I think I'll go with Bermudas and a red J. Crew polo. And I think

I'll wear sandals," said Alex. "It's muggy as fuck out there."

Dewey nodded, still mesmerized by Alex's mountain of gold. If only he could have clothes like that, maybe even just borrow some, especially now that he'd decided to pledge Kappa House, he'd be so much cooler and stylish, he thought.

"I'm going to jump in the shower real quick," said Dewey. "Then we'll head to Mary Pate's. Cool?"

"Yeah, that'll work," said Alex.

Dewey undressed in the bathroom and jumped in the shower. Warm water ran over his head and shoulders, and down his back. For a few minutes he stood completely still like some rained-on garden statue. He looked at his reflection in the shower mirror—5' 9" and 175lbs.

Overall, he liked his body. Throughout high school, girls on the soccer team had admired and joked about his legs. They were the most muscular part of his body, resulting from years of track, soccer and ice hockey. The ability to run quickly, however, had not been guaranteed, as his legs were bowed and necessitated metal leg braces. He had eventually become fast, though, one of the fastest at his school. His knees and elbows were scraped from falls, and a giant keloid ran across his left knee cap. Dewey's Scandinavian skin tanned well—reddish-brown May through August.

Dewey pushed his wet hair off his forehead and gradually moved both hands to his testicles. He cupped them tightly against his body, feeling their warmth. He felt strange being naked and showering so far from home in a place he would live the next four years with people he barely knew.

It had been a long, anxious week, full of new people and places. And as he had so many times before at home under such anxious circumstances, he released one hand from his wet, warm testicles and wrapped it around his penis. The other he lowered to the base of his penis. Closing his eyes, he stroked. Slow at first, then faster, until the divine friction transported him to a place of past girlfriends, topless sunbathers, and stashed Playboys.

Climaxing, Dewey felt his breath quicken like it might be his last, and he no longer felt the water splashing on his back. All his anxiety went away. Only the smell of ammonia, strawberry-scented shampoo, and small, milky-white puddles in the shower drain were left. Gradually, thoughts of past girlfriends, topless sunbathers, and stashed Playboys faded. Then Dewey could feel the water pelt his back again and he felt at peace. He turned the shower off and reached for a towel.

"Hurry up, Dew, we've got fifteen minutes before we have to be at Mary Pate's," Alex called out from the bedroom.

Dewey quickly dried off, put on deodorant and splashed his neck and face with the cologne his father gave him. He opened the bathroom door, hot steam billowing out around him. Alex stood dressed next to the window looking out onto Calhoun Street.

"I'll be just a minute," said Dewey, wrapped in a towel. He looked at Alex. Amazing how he could be transformed by clothes, he thought. And just as he'd promised: Bermudas, red J. Crew polo and sandals.

Dewey opened his wardrobe to see clothes for someone middle-aged. He felt ashamed, as he inched the wardrobe doors closer in to prevent Alex from seeing its fuddy-duddy contents. If only he had clothes like Alex's. Dewey grabbed a pair of his dad's gabardine trousers, a red gingham short-sleeve shirt, a brown leather belt and camp mocs. He gave a quick look in the mirror and rolled his eyes—more shame and disappointment. "Okay, I'm ready."

"Snazzy pants," said Alex.

"Screw you," said Dewey.

"What you wanna say is, Fuck You. Screw you is something *good* kids who want to be *bad* say."

"Thanks for the pointer." It was the only moment so far that Dewey felt Alex had power over him. "Let's take the stairs. She's just one floor below."

"You win, snazzy pants," said Alex, chuckling.

A red, glowing exit sign pointed the way to the same stairs they had trekked up just a few days before during move-in. Disappearing into the stairwell, they continued talking, until their voices, distorted by the echoing, almost sounded like one.

* * *

Mary Pate answered the door wearing a short black skirt with star-shaped rhinestones along the hem and a white crop top exposing her belly.

"Hey, y'all," she said. "Glad you made it. C'mon in!"

"Thanks," said Alex, stepping in front of Dewey.

"How y'all doing?" said Mary Pate.

"Good," said Dewey, looking over Alex's shoulder.

"Me, too," said Alex, inching up on his toes, smiling.

"Don't worry, Alex, I haven't forgotten you," said Mary Pate, recognizing his need to be seen. "Now let me introduce you to some folks." Mary Pate gently reached for Dewey's shoulder and pointed to a half-dozen people in the common area sitting and talking. "This is Lamar from Dillon, Ginger from Orangeburg, and Brian from Greenville."

"That'd be Greenville, *South* Carolina," said Brian, butting in.

"We all know that, Brian," said Mary Pate matter-of-factly. "And over there is Linus from here on the peninsula and his cousin James. Cynthia from Boston is over there too."

Muffled *heys* arose from the group, as Alex and Dewey smiled and nodded in return. In the background a loud mix of pop and country music blared. Dewey surmised at least a few of them were from SCA, Ginger and Brian especially, as they seemed to have a certain zealous quality about them, just like Mary Pate.

Dewey sat on the floor, while Alex leaned against the wall. The sudden newness of Mary Pate's room, though laid out almost exactly the same as his and Alex's, felt completely new to Dewey. Mary Pate, who had taken a seat across the room near the kitchenette, eventually gestured at him to come sit by her. Dewey obliged, snaking his way across the small but crowded room, until he was by her side. "Did Alex tell you I dropped by?" she said, holding a red Solo cup.

"Yeah," said Dewey, "I guess I was out running."

"Yeah, he said you were," said Mary Pate. "I was just curious to see your room, so I dropped by."

"Well, what do you think?"

"Pretty much the same as mine."

They both laughed.

On one of the walls Dewey noticed a white porcelain crucifix with Jesus looking up at the sky. Quaint, he thought.

"So, how are classes going?" she said.

"They're okay," said Dewey. "Biology's going to be tough. I think the professor is just being nice to us right now."

"Totally." Mary Pate raised her cup in the air as if to second his observation.

"So, how'd you meet all these people?"

"Some live here at the dorm, some from class and some from SCA. Speaking of, when are you coming out, *preacher's kid?*"

"Probably not anytime soon." Dewey didn't recall telling Mary Pate about his father being a preacher. Maybe Alex had mentioned it when she dropped by.

"Why not?"

"Can you keep a secret?"

"What about?"

"I rushed and got a bid. I accepted."

"*You* rushed?" said Mary Pate, taken aback.

"Yeah. Why'd you say it like that?" Dewey drew his head back.

"I just didn't think you were the frat boy type."

"What do you mean?"

"Because you're not exactly a pretty boy." Mary Pate looked Dewey up and down.

"You're saying I'm ugly?" Dewey looked down at his dowdy trousers one waist size too big and his red gingham short-sleeve shirt with its wide, uncomplimentary cut. He was ashamed. Why couldn't Mary Pate envision him in the Kappa composite with Radford and the others? A burning flash of anxiety washed over him, and a lump formed in his throat.

"I didn't mean it that way. I just meant you're different."

Dewey felt as if he'd gotten the wind knocked out of him. "Different how?"

"Because deep down, you seem like a really nice guy. Not a jerk, not someone trying to be something he's not."

"You hardly know me, Mary Pate. I feel I sometimes hardly know myself." He began feeling impatient with her, even angry.

She stood up to get more Coke from the kitchenette. "I've just got this feeling, and I'd just hate to see you run off with those sinner boys."

What Dewey wanted to say was that he didn't really care about Kappa House. It was all just a means to an end, and in his mind the end was befriending Angel Boy. But how could he ever expect anyone wearing a cheap skirt with rhinestones to understand that?

The voices on the other side of the room had grown louder, as Dewey listened in.

"So, who's your roommate?" said Ginger, looking at Alex who had come to sit on the floor.

"His name is Dewey. He's from Ohio," said Alex.

"Do y'all get along?" said Lamar.

"Yeah, pretty much. He's interesting. Sure likes to run. We rushed together the other night, so I guess that makes us friends."

"Rush is so fake," said a girl who had not been introduced.

Alex shrugged his shoulders. "I did it just 'cause I was curious. And Dewey was just along for the ride."

"Did y'all get in?" said Brian, his eyebrows arched and hopeful.

"Nope. Said we'd get an invite by Wednesday if we made it, and neither of us got one, so, you know." Alex ran a hand over the brown, nubby carpet in front of him. "So, who gives out bids at SCA?"

"We're not that kind of club," said the girl who had not been introduced. "Jesus accepts everyone."

Alex laughed, but the girl did not.

Dewey felt sorry for Alex.

"Do you have a personal relationship with Jesus Christ?" asked the girl.

"You could say I do, but I'm no carpenter." Alex chuckled, as the others looked perplexed. "You know, as in, like, the bumper sticker?" Still, they looked perplexed. "What I'm saying is I'm Jewish, just like Jesus, but I'm not very handy with a hammer, as in carpentry, which is what they say Jesus did for a job. It's supposed to be funny, as in *ha-ha*."

"Yeah, well, we don't think of Jesus as Jewish," said Ginger. "He's really a Chrisitan."

"But his parents were Jewish, which would make him Jewish, too. It's the whole Messiah thing that makes him Christian."

Ginger looked at him unfazed and played with her side ponytail, occasionally grabbing long individual strands of hair and depositing them in a nearby waste can. "Yeah, well, so we have different opinions."

Alex looked at her in disbelief. "Y'all need to take a chill pill, maybe read some history." Alex stretched out his legs, as if pushing the others away. Then he laughed and lifted his fists in front of him in a pose reminiscent of a turn-of-the century boxer. "Well, I know one thing, I sure didn't come here to fight or get converted, so let's change the subject."

Dewey, who had lost track of Mary Pate, turned to find her standing above him, her cup of Coke refilled. "It's so loud out here. Wanna go to my bedroom?"

"Sure," said Dewey, shifting his attention away from Alex and the others.

Together they walked into Mary Pate's bedroom, which had the same layout as Alex and Dewey's shared bedroom, with two beds, two desks and two wardrobes. A narrow window in the room looked out onto the same courtyard with red crepe myrtles but from a different direction. Busy Calhoun Street still bustled close by. Mary Pate's bed was neatly made, with a patchwork quilt at the foot of it. Her desk was clean, with pens, pencils and Post-it pads well organized in a black, wire-mesh desk caddy with a Woolworth's sales sticker on it. On a shelf above her desk in a black frame was a picture of Mary Pate with what Dewey guessed was her family—her mother, father, big brother and little sister. Her mother stood out in particular, thought Dewey, slender with good posture, her chin lifted noticeably high. She wore a white, starched blouse with an embroidered collar and a camel-colored, knee-length skirt; her hair was pulled back into a low, tight bun. Mary Pate's father smiled kindly, revealing a missing tooth. He wore a stained red and black polyester golf tee and khakis. They were pictured against a backdrop not of Lowcountry marsh but of sand, scrub, and tall pines.

"So, who gave you the bid?" said Mary Pate.

"Kappa Tau," said Dewey.

"They're not so bad."

"How do you know?"

"Because my cousin's a Kappa."

"Really? What's his name?"

"Radford Gaillard."

"*Your* cousin is Radford?"

"Yes, our mothers are sisters, I mean, were sisters. It's a long story."

Dewey couldn't believe what he'd just heard. How could Mary Pate be related to Radford? Impossible, he thought, but he wanted to know more. How, though, without sounding weird or giving his story away? "So, did y'all grow up together or something?"

"We were close as little kids, but our mothers got into a big argument, and we didn't see each other for a long time." Mary Pate looked down at the carpet, as if she'd dropped something.

"So, that means your family—Radford's family—is from Charleston?"

"Yeah, that's us. But after the big argument, we got run out of town, but I don't remember a lot of it because I, *we*, were so young. I do remember some legal papers and the fact we were very poor after that."

"Poor?"

"Yeah, Radford's mother apparently high-tailed it to the lawyer's office and did something with the family money, so my mother couldn't touch it. Made her mad as hell, but what could she do?"

"She never tried getting her fair share back?" Dewey looked at Mary Pate as if she might respond with a perfectly good answer.

"With what, exactly?"

"Sorry, I wasn't trying to pry." Dewey noticed Mary Pate's poofy hair had begun to sag, some strands completely unloosed and running down her neck. The sun was setting, and through the window a pink and blue cluster of clouds rested on the horizon.

"Shit happens. Besides, I don't mind being a poor country mouse." Mary Pate looked at Dewey and smiled in a way that made him feel as if she somehow might be reading his mind.

"So, how'd you end up at the college?" said Dewey.

"It's close to home, and I'm on scholarship," said Mary Pate.

Dewey felt this might be the case, considering the twang, rhinestones and denim.

"Not exactly a scholarship," she said. "It's this trust thing."

"What do you mean?"

"Well, my great-grandfather, a Confederate general, went here and left the school a bunch of money saying that all his future kin—like me and Radford—could go here free."

"You mean all his *descendants*," said Dewey.

"What?"

"Future kin. Another word for that is descendants."

"Yeah, I was thinking that." Mary Pate tilted her cup back for one last gulp of Coke.

"So, that means Radford's here on that trust thing, too?"

"Yup, *his* great-grandfather is *my* great-grandfather," she said, sing-songy.

"Wow, I had no idea. Not that it makes any difference." Dewey looked out the window; the pink and blue clouds had disappeared, and the courtyard lamplights had come on.

"Why would it make a difference?"

"No, I didn't mean it that way. Just forget that part."

Mary Pate sat silently with an empty cup in her hand. "Would you like to meet Radford? It might help with pledging."

At first, the offer overwhelmed Dewey. Up to that point, he'd treated Radford and Kappa House as separate entities but somehow still connected, one encapsulated in the other like a Russian nesting doll. "Sure, I'd love, I mean like, to meet him."

"Good deal," said Mary Pate, smiling, "but only because I like you. I'll set something up."

In Dewey's mind, Mary Pate's place had suddenly and dramatically shifted, moving her near the top of his hierarchy.

Alex, meanwhile, had remained in the same place in the hierarchy, as had Lucious, the Kappas, and Trey.

At that moment, Mary Pate reached her hand across the bed and put it on Dewey's knee. He had seen it coming from the corner of his eye, part of him wanting her to come close but part of him not wanting her to. Once her hand dropped, however, Dewey could not deny feeling something about someone he had absolutely no attraction to, someone who in his mind wasn't beautiful.

Without warning, Alex blazed into the bedroom. "Who wants pizza?" he said. "Let's do Sharky's!"

"I want some," said Mary Pate.

"Awesome!" Alex, oblivious to the moment unfolding before him, turned and sped out of the room to call Sharky's Pizza parlor on King Street.

Mary Pate, her hand still unmoved, looked at Dewey. Then gradually, almost reluctantly, he put his hand on top of hers. Their hands did not cup easily. Dewey noticed hers were small and coarse, like a child who spent a lot of time on a rope swing. His were soft on top of hers, except for a scar from a fishhook. In this way their attraction was not as opposites but as two people both on the outside trying to break in.

After a few minutes, their hands uncoupled, as the country song playing in the common room came to a crescendo.

"Do me a favor?" said Dewey.

"Sure," she said.

"Promise not to tell Alex about the bid, okay?"

"I promise."

"Thanks."

They walked out of the bedroom, as Dewey turned to look at the picture of Mary Pate's family. It was a sweet picture, he thought, even with her sad story of how they lost nearly everything because of an argument, then were exiled to a small rural town full of sand and scrub. No wonder Mary Pate's mother held her chin so high.

When the pizza arrived, everyone passed Alex a few bucks, while the delivery guy stood in the hall, hidden and faceless. "Thanks, dude," he said, then he vanished as Alex took the pizza.

The girl who'd said rush was fake stood up and blessed the pepperoni pizza. Within minutes, it was gone.

"I'm going to head out," said Dewey to the group.

"But we're just getting started," said Alex.

"Then you can stay, but I'm tired."

"Nah, I'll leave with you. That's cool."

Dewey signaled his departure to Mary Pate, who had returned to the kitchenette. She gestured back at him to wait.

"It's been nice," she said. "Thanks for coming."

"Great get-together," said Dewey. "Thanks."

Mary Pate looked like she wanted more than just a goodbye, her body gently drifting toward him, but at the last minute something held her back.

Dewey and Alex walked into the hall, which had become busy with students going back and forth between floors. Someone had punched a hole in one of the walls, while scuff marks dotted another. A half-eaten slice of pizza sat near the stairwell exit. Dewey still couldn't believe Mary Pate was Radford's cousin and that she'd offered to arrange an introduction. A dream come true. Never did he think the path to Radford would be through a girl with an up-do and rhinestones, but it was shaping up that way, and Dewey was more than happy to oblige. If he could leverage Mary Pate just enough to get to

Radford, then he would have accomplished what he came for. Of course, he'd have to endure Mary Pate's advances, but in his mind, it was worth it. Anything was worth it for Angel Boy.

"Let's take the elevator," said Alex. His voice broke Dewey's concentration.

"Okay, you win," said Dewey. "Maybe we can catch a ride if we're lucky. Somebody here has to be on their way up."

* * *

Dewey and Alex stepped off the elevator onto the fourth floor, when Dewey spied another white envelope underneath the door. With Alex right behind him, Dewey panicked. From the looks of it, it was something from Kappa House. He couldn't let Alex see it. He slowed his pace, then quickly moved in front of Alex to obscure his view. He needed an excuse. "Shit!" he exclaimed.

"What?" said Alex.

"I think I forgot my key at Mary Pate's. Can you go back down and look?"

"Sure."

"Thanks."

Alex turned and hopped back on the elevator. Dewey rushed to the door and knelt down to pick up the envelope. It had the same feel as the first one, including the embossed letters in the corner. But this time Dewey was not gentle opening it; rather, he ripped it open. It read:

Welcome to the Kappa Tau Fall 1989 pledge class.
Please meet at the KT House on Sun., Aug. 27, at 7pm for the
start of pledge education.

Sincerely, Kappa Tau

At the bottom of the letter was a crest featuring a shield with an all-seeing eye, daggers, and a calla lily. Dewey was exhilarated. But concealment was quickly becoming a chore. The pursuit of Kappa Tau was almost like having another roommate. For now, it would have to remain a silent roommate, however, lest Alex find out.

He put the envelope in his coat pocket and reached for his key, and was about to unlock the door when he recalled the errand he'd sent Alex on. Dewey heard the elevator chirp and Alex's clumsy footsteps head his way.

"Nobody could find your key," said Alex.

"I know," said Dewey, "it's been here in my back pocket all along. Sorry."

"No prob."

Dewey pulled the key from his pocket and opened the door. Once in the room, Dewey asked to grab one of Alex's juice boxes. Of the original forty-eight at the week's beginning, only six remained.

"Sure, you can have one," said Alex. "I can't believe we've gone through them so fast."

Dewey grabbed one and sat on his bed. It was late, and he was tired. "Yeah, juice boxes are so addictive," he said. "Suck them dry and crush them." Dewey fake-crushed the juice box in his hand, careful not to over-exaggerate and send juice spewing all over the room.

"What did you think of Mary Pate's?" said Alex.

"Pretty cool," said Dewey. "I'd never seen most of those people."

"Me neither. So, what was the deal with you and Mary Pate in the bedroom?"

"Nothing. Just talking." Dewey looked at the floor, then out the window.

"I think she digs you, man."

"Nah. She was just telling me how she got to the college. Turns out she's got a full ride."

"As in scholarship? How?" Alex moved closer to Dewey.

"Something to do with her great-great grandfather. But don't say anything, okay."

"I promise. Also, and this may sound weird, but I have a confession. I think Mary Pate's totally hot!"

Alex opened his wardrobe to grab his pajamas, and the same mountain of clothes from hours before spilled out. And same as before, Dewey marveled at them, as he felt the awkward shape of the envelope stuffed inside his pocket.

That's when it occurred to him. What if he borrowed some of Alex's clothes for the pledge meeting? It would surely make him more fashionable and more like the guys in the composite. He might fit in better and be more likable. And with so many clothes, Alex wouldn't miss a thing.

"Do you think she'd go out with me?" asked Alex, mopping up his clothes and shoving them back into his wardrobe.

"I think she said she had a boyfriend," said Dewey. He felt bad for lying but knew Mary Pate wouldn't go out with him for the same reason Kappa Tau didn't give him a bid—no mutual attraction.

"So what? Tons of girls have boyfriends," said Alex.

"Yeah, but I don't think she's the cheating type," said Dewey.

"How's it cheating if you just ask someone for coffee?"

"Because it leads to places."

"Stop being a dick. Not everyone can be Mr. Cool."

"Who's Mr. Cool?"

"You, dickhead."

Dewey looked up from Alex's pile of clothes, surprised and confused. "I've never been Mr. Cool."

"Well, you are. Everyone likes you, including Mary Pate."

"Who's everyone, exactly? I haven't been here long enough for anyone to like me."

"Well, you look a lot more likeable than me."

"You're perfectly fine, Alex." Dewey felt bad for saying this because he knew Alex would have a harder time making friends.

"So says you," said Alex, "with your wing back chairs and Civil War ladders. I'm not dumb, but I am who I am, and I'm asking Mary Pate out!"

"Okay, okay," said Dewey, looking to make peace. He finished his juice box and lobbed it underhand into the waste basket, then changed into his tartan plaid pajamas and pulled back his bed covers.

Alex changed into his white linen pajamas with blue piping and the monogram *AJB* on the breast pocket. Dewey lay awake for hours, unable to fall asleep. He thought about Alex's words about being Mr. Cool, and if there was any truth to them. With the first pledge education meeting the next night, he had a feeling he was about to find out.

CHAPTER 11

Dewey stood outside Grace Church close to where a frat boy from across the street had hurled an insult at him. It was Sunday, exactly one week since he'd arrived. Going to church, he hoped, might fend off any potential homesickness.

The Gothic-style building, with its pointed arches, vaulted ceilings and intricate stained-glass windows, occupied almost a whole block. The church was flanked by small grassy areas, a breezeway and, to the rear, a parish hall.

A black-and-white checkerboard walkway greeted parishioners who entered the church through heavy, wooden doors. Atop the church, a towering, ornate spire overlooked the city. Dewey would later read in the service bulletin how the church had, over the century, endured war, earthquakes and hurricanes.

Entering the narthex, Dewey smelled oak and spray starch. It was the eight o'clock service, and only a few dozen parishioners, most in their 30s, had showed up. They were attractive, stylish and fit—straight out of the catalog from the men's clothing store on King Street.

He entered a pew in the back. A couple seated there looked at him curiously, nodded and smiled. Dewey wore khakis, a collared shirt, blue tie and a hand-me-down, V-neck sweater.

Teenage acolytes dressed in white albs appeared from one side of the altar and began lighting candles. Dewey thought they looked slightly disheveled, like they'd had a long day surfing or sailing the day before. Eventually, they sank into the carved choir stalls on either side of the altar, exchanging smirks and funny faces while casually swinging their white, braided cinctures hoping to make the service go faster. Dewey looked on, amused, remembering what it was like growing up in the church and the duties bestowed upon clergy offspring.

In his memory, the fun times at church had been running and roaming long faintly lit hallways that seemed mysterious and never-ending, and feasting on snacks and treats in the parish hall. Until at a certain age he and his church pals had worn out every hallway and sampled every snack, and, suddenly, the fun of church seemed to disappear like a thief in the night. At this point Dewey began to learn the realities of the church—petty vestry squabbles, fundraising pressures and the constant grooming of parishioners likely to leave the church in their will. From this point on, church was, for Dewey, a business wrapped in theater.

With a bell signaling the start of the service, the crucifer, a boy in brown Sperry boat shoes, shuffled by, leading the choir and clergy in a procession. The priest, who was at the very end of the procession, was a short, plump man with gray hair so shiny that it looked shellacked. He wore a white alb and sky-blue stole with gold embroidery. A white clergy collar wrapped around his neck. His vestments reminded Dewey of his father's own, pulled from a cloaking room containing a colorful trove of albs, cassocks, surplices, and stoles. Dewey watched his father vest up nearly every Sunday, virtually transforming him into another person. It reminded him of Alex's wardrobe and how he planned to borrow from it for the evening's pledge education meeting.

After the procession reached the altar, the congregation sat down, and the priest said an opening prayer. Two parishioners then read from the Old and New Testament—Dewey vaguely knew the passages—after which the priest came down into the nave to read the

Gospel. He returned to the pulpit for the sermon. "What if God was one of us?" he began.

Dewey noticed the congregation looked unfazed by his introduction, as if, perhaps, God wasn't one of them unless, of course, God happened to be from Charleston.

From his periphery, he saw the woman from the couple next to him scoot toward him. "Are you new to Grace?" she whispered.

"Yes, ma'am," whispered Dewey. "I'm at the college. A freshman."

The woman, a petite brunette, wore a white blouse and blue seersucker jacket and skirt. Around one wrist bangle bracelets dangled, around the other a bracelet with three small silhouette charms—one boy and two girls—with birthdates engraved in a wispy font.

"We just love college students," she said, her voice sweet and sincere, but also distant. "Remind me to get you some information on our Canterbury Club. It's for people like you."

She smiled and scooted back down the pew next to her husband, who wore a white Oxford shirt, blue blazer, Nantucket red trousers, and tasseled loafers—no socks. Dewey envied them, as he imagined waving to them from the other side of a wrought iron gate.

Dewey's thoughts momentarily drifted to Alex's wardrobe and what he would borrow. He liked Alex's Khaki chino pants, and red and blue striped short-sleeve Polo shirt made of Egyptian cotton—its weave soft as silk. As for shoes, Dewey imagined Alex's leather, ankle-high cap toe boots. Narrow at the toe, they made the foot look long and athletic. But not on Alex. Because he was so short and his jeans often so long, the boots endured an avalanche of denim that covered the boot's stitching and finer features, until what was left of them to see made them look off the rack. Instead of a braided belt, Dewey considered wearing one of Alex's more traditional-looking belts, a solid strap of dark leather with a matte-gray belt buckle.

But just how and when to execute the borrowing? Maybe at dinner, he thought, when Alex was at the cafeteria. Dewey would plan to disappear that afternoon, returning only to sneak back in the room and get the garments.

Bringing his attention back to the altar, Dewey realized he'd missed most of the second half of the service. He looked at the couple next to him and to his surprise found them standing impatiently, waiting to exit the pew so they could receive communion. Embarrassed, Dewey got up and quickly walked the length of the nave, where he knelt at the altar.

"The body of Christ, the bread of heaven," said the priest, handing Dewey a small bread wafer. A chalice bearer quickly followed with, "The blood of Christ, the cup of salvation."

Dewey turned from the altar and walked back to his pew. The organ groaned, signaling the closing hymn. He watched the priest draw a white linen napkin from behind the altar and place it over the chalice. One acolyte resumed his position as crucifer, as another extinguished candles. The choir and clergy rose, gradually forming a line in the direction of the narthex.

The pretty couple next to Dewey quickly exited the pew, as if trying to beat the long procession out the front door. Dewey fell in behind them. As he approached the open doors, fraternity row came into view and, much to his great surprise, so did Mary Pate who seemed to be coming from the direction of Kappa House. Dewey paused and stepped into the shadows of the doorway in case she might look his way. Why would she be at Kappa House, he thought, as he watched her race toward King Street.

* * *

Alex was still asleep when Dewey arrived back at the dorm from church. The blinds were pulled. Alex considered shaking the bed or yelling loudly to be funny but chose not to. Dewey went back out to the common room and sat down. For a moment, he thought about creeping back into the room to explore Alex's wardrobe. After all, Alex slept like a log and with the blinds closed, the room would be dark. But then there'd be the commotion of finding the clothes he'd picked out in his mind which could wake him. Better to wait.

The phone rang. "Dew?" said a female voice.

"This is him," said Dewey.

"Hey, it's Mary Pate."

"Hey, how's it going?" Dewey was shocked to hear her voice.

After all, he thought he'd just seen her headed for King Street just a short while ago. Strange she should call so suddenly and without the least bit sensation of distraction or breathlessness.

"It's okay," said Mary Pate. "I just got back from church."

"Me, too."

"I thought preacher's kids ran from the church."

"They do, but sometimes they come back. Me, I just do drop-ins. How was SCA?" He hoped this question might provide some clues to her sudden appearance in front of fraternity row.

"Yeah, we met over at Buist this morning. Praise Jesus. Anyway, I was calling to see if you wanted to go to the cafeteria."

Dewey didn't know whether to believe Mary Pate about her whereabouts or not. At the start, she had seemed like someone he could trust, but now he wasn't so sure. "Yeah, lunch at the cafeteria sounds good. Meet you in the lobby in a few."

"Does Alex want to go?" she said.

"Nah, he's still sleeping."

"Oh, yeah, I forgot, he doesn't go to church. Where do they go again?"

Mary Pate's words stung. The Kagans from back home flashed in

Dewey's mind; they'd been so kind and hospitable at the seder. "It's called a synagogue, Mary Pate. Jewish people worship at a synagogue."

"Oh, yeah." She paused. "Well, meet you in the lobby in a few, okay?"

Dewey thought about saying something mean about SCA. And he also thought about saying something mean about Mary Pate. It was the first time he'd been angry with her.

"Yeah, sure, meet you in the lobby."

Before he left, Dewey adjusted the thermostat to keep the room from getting too cold. On a scrap piece of paper, he wrote: *Went to cafeteria with Mary Pate. Maybe see you there? Dewey.*

In the lobby from around the corner came Mary Pate in a tee-shirt with *Charleston* written across it and denim cut-off shorts. Dewey faked a smile. Together, they walked outside into the corridor past the red crepe myrtles and crossed over to St. Philip Street.

"Let's go through the Yard," said Mary Pate, pointing toward Randolph Hall.

"Suits me," said Dewey, curtly. He decided on a new subject to distract from their earlier exchange. "Strange to think about your great-grandfather or whoever walking this campus, maybe even these same paths, don't you think?"

"Who?" said Mary Pate, looking confused.

"Your ancestor—you know, the one you were telling me about. The one who left all that money for you and Radford to go here free."

"Oh, yeah. I mean, well, I don't think about it too much to tell you the truth."

"You'd think someone like that would have a plaque running around here somewhere. What did you say his name was?"

"It was something French and hard to say. You know, one of those names." Mary Pate seemed to be scouring the building entranceways they passed.

"Try me. I took French in high school."

Mary Pate adjusted her white, frilly elastic band with rhinestones that held her ponytail. "Are you *always* like this?"

They crossed over St. Philip Street onto a wide herringbone brick path that led to the Yard.

"Let's sit on the grass for a minute," said Mary Pate, pointing to the cistern. "It's so peaceful here. Almost like a dream."

The sun was directly overhead, and the grass felt warm on Dewey's legs. He glanced in the direction of George Street.

"How'd you end up here, anyways?" said Mary Pate, lying back on the grass and squinting up at the sky.

"We used to vacation here, and one of my dad's friends told him there was a college here, and that we might want to look at it. That was last spring." Dewey looked at the long, dueling shadows under Porter's Lodge.

"So, are you saying you decided to go here pretty much sight unseen?"

"Well, yeah, pretty much. I mean, I was familiar with the area, so I kinda knew what I was getting into, but I'd never actually seen this place until we toured it."

"I almost can't believe that." Mary Pate plucked a blade of grass and put it in her mouth. "I think you're lying."

"Lying about what?"

"About why you came here."

"Nope, nothing. Just wanted to get out of the cold and away from people who were so damn square."

Dewey stood up from where he'd been leaning against the edge of the cistern. Mary Pate stretched out on the grass, her long blonde hair spread out in a hundred different directions like Medusa.

"So, you still want to meet Radford?" she said, raising her hand to keep the sun out of her eyes.

"Sure. I assumed you already had something in the works."

"I do. I'm just making sure." Mary Pate sat up, leaned on her elbows, and looked out into the Yard. "Okay, how about next Thursday? We both have class at Maybank and could come here right afterwards. Cool?"

"Sounds good," said Dewey. "Thanks."

Clouds suddenly rolled over the Yard. Dewey looked up against their white fluffiness only to see the same group of small, dots and squiggly lines passing across his field of vision. He looked at Mary Pate and found the squiggly lines there, too, which distorted her face. He blinked hard to try and make them go away.

"Okay, then, here at Porter's Lodge next Thursday at noon," she said, pointing to the ancient structure, with its stucco sides and green shutters. "So, changing subjects for a minute, how many guys do you think will actually come to your pledge meeting tonight?"

"No idea. Depends on how many bids they gave out."

Dewey wanted to avoid talking about the fraternity at all costs, so he wouldn't have to explain that his bid had been a fluke. He'd done it for Alex, whom he barely knew, because he felt sorry for him.

"Just be careful, Dewey."

"What do you mean?"

"Radford's just a different kind of soul."

"Go on."

"When we'd visit each other growing up, he always wanted to play in the marsh. He said it made him feel free. I think he was a kid who lived in his own world."

"As in, *not all there?*"

"Kind of." The blade of grass dipped up and down as Mary Pate spoke. "Only certain people were allowed in."

"What happened?" Dewey crossed his arms and with his toe

gently kicked the bricks beneath him.

"He cut his family off and started hanging out with these boys. Something was strange about them, and no one knew exactly where they came from. But they were definitely *Charleston* boys."

"How so?"

"Because they had that look—you know, good hair, pretty face, right clothes. It's like they were real, but they weren't."

Radford's entourage from back in the spring flashed in Dewey's mind. There was, indeed, a strange quality about them, he thought, if, in fact, Mary Pate and he were talking about the same boys. Still, they seemed real enough for Dewey—real enough to make him pick up and move more than 500 miles away.

The clouds parted, and the sun appeared. A gust of wind rattled nearby cast iron plants. A young couple holding hands passed in front of the cistern on their way to the cafeteria.

"They're cute," said Mary Pate, smiling at Dewey. "Kind of like us." She took the white frilly elastic band from her ponytail and slung it at Dewey who dropped it. Dewey thought of the red fraternity hat and how his blind friend had frantically tried to scoop it up to protect it.

"Yeah, cute." Dewey tried thinking of something else to say to keep Mary Pate from saying anything more. "I think he's on the basketball team," said Dewey, pointing to the boy, "and I've seen her walking around at Physician's Auditorium."

The couple crossed underneath Porter's Lodge over George Street and disappeared into the line of people in front of the cafeteria, as Dewey and Mary Pate followed close behind.

CHAPTER 12

In darkness, Dewey stepped onto the porch of Kappa House and extended his hand. A brother grabbed it and looked at him. "You're that douchebag from across the street at the church the other day," he said. "I was just kidding. Promise."

"Don't worry about it," said Dewey.

"Thanks, dude, congrats on being a pledge."

"Glad to be here." Dewey tried freeing his hand as quickly as possible, as the brother, a beer in his hand, looked like he might tumble over.

Dewey stepped through the foyer into the parlor. He glanced at the fraternity composite. Radford hadn't moved—still in the second-to-last row toward the end, a smirk on his face.

The parlor was the same as it had been the night of rush—three rows of chairs lined up in front of a projector screen. With windows open, the smell of sun-baked wood and nutmeg from nearby Confederate Jasmine permeated the room. Dressed in khaki chino pants, a red and blue striped, Egyptian cotton Polo shirt, cap toe boots and a solid strap of dark leather with a matte-gray belt buckle, Dewey felt like he was finally beginning to fit in.

"Alright, gentlemen, take a seat," said a brother dressed in white pants and a blue fleece anorak. "Welcome to Kappa House. And congratulations on being selected as a pledge. Unfortunately, our head pledge educator, Radford, can't be here tonight, but he sends his congrats."

"Dammit," said Dewey under his breath. He'd gone through all the trouble and risk of secretly borrowing Alex's clothes. He'd hid in Maybank all afternoon, then returned to the room at dinner and opened Alex's wardrobe. Dewey recalled how it smelled like Frieda and Stuart, as he frantically pushed aside hangers, and plowed through drawers looking for clothes. But the real trick would be getting the clothes back in the wardrobe without Alex knowing.

"Okay, on with the show," said the brother. "As a Kappa pledge, you'll be expected to know our history and code of conduct, and in a couple days you'll be getting a big brother."

The projector clicked, and an image of a shield with an all-seeing eye, daggers and a calla lily filled the screen.

"Let's start with the crest," said the brother. "The calla lily represents youth. The dagger is the guardian of youth. The eye at the bottom means God is watching and so is everybody else, so don't fuck up. Honor, accountability and loyalty—get it? Good."

The brother turned and grabbed a pile of small booklets from the table. "Here, pass these around." He thumbed through the pages and chuckled. "These are your pledge books. Memorize this shit. You'll need it for initiation. Oh, yeah, there's some areas in here where you'll need a volunteer coordinator's signature."

The projector clicked again, producing an old, sepia-toned photo of a dozen men in suits and ties with waistcoats and short haircuts.

"These are our Founders. You can read about them in your book. It's interesting to note almost half of them became ministers."

For a moment, Dewey thought he heard *monsters* instead of ministers. He chuckled, as he thought of his dad and the priest from earlier in the day. Something about the church made Dewey feel like he was being swallowed by a big, ugly monster, only to be spit out, with the clergy family packing its possessions and leaving overnight, the only farewell from a neighbor who didn't even go to church.

"Pledge pins, please," barked the brother in the fleece anorak, as he reached into the darkness behind the screen. Sounds of scuffling ensued until his hands re-emerged holding a large brown box. "One of these marks you as ours." The brother opened it and picked up one of the twelve smaller boxes within. Each of them contained a black, oval-shaped pin with an all-seeing eye, daggers and a calla lily etched on it. He passed them out.

Dewey held the pledge pin in his palm. For something so small, it's meaning was heavy. A switch inside had flipped. It was the opposite of how he'd felt the first day of class at Physician's Auditorium, when he walked in tight-throated, anxious and alone. He'd been short of breath, and his vision seemed distorted. Objects were first big, then small, then big again like something out of *Alice in Wonderland*.

The brother stepped in front of the screen again, as a slide titled Campus Service Project appeared.

"Part of pledging will be to volunteer on campus," he said. "You need thirty hours. Lots of guys have worked in the library or mail room. Just find something."

Dewey started thinking where he might volunteer. He liked exercising, so maybe the gym. He also liked history, so maybe the history department. Then he thought of the short, red-headed man at the library; he could always ask him for a job.

"Pledge meetings are weekly on Sunday nights," continued the brother. "Don't miss them. Okay, you guys are free to go."

Chairs scuffed the floors as Dewey and the rest of the pledges rose to their feet. The Kappa crest reappeared on the screen. While a few pledges mingled, Dewey wasted no time heading for the door, as he knew he had to get Alex's clothes back in his wardrobe.

He cut through the Yard and entered New Dorm through the courtyard. When he opened the door to his room, Alex was asleep.

Dewey laid his pledge pin on his desk and quietly slipped out of Alex's clothes. He gently opened Alex's closet and shoved them in, sure to hide them at the bottom of the pile. Dewey got into bed and looked out the window. Light from nearby lamp poles played in the courtyard under the crepe myrtles. Angel Boy was close.

CHAPTER 13

Dewey awoke the next morning and stayed in bed a few extra minutes to be sure the coast was clear after having snuck in the night before still wearing Alex's clothes. As Alex wasn't hovering over him, Dewey figured he must not have discovered anything missing or out of place. In fact, if Dewey were to get up and look in Alex's wardrobe at that very moment, he figured he'd probably see the same mountain of clothes that had been there since move-in. But there was no time for that—he was due at Dr. Lyman's office within the hour.

The walk from the dorm to Dr. Lyman's office on East Bay Street took just a few minutes. It was a straight shot, with the only intersections being King and Calhoun, and a little further down, Meeting and Calhoun. In between was Marion Square, a six-acre park with a bronze statue of Southern statesman John C. Calhoun.

Dr. Lyman's practice occupied the lower half of an Antebellum mansion on East Bay Street. The stuccoed brick house was dingy-looking but still breathtaking in its grandeur, Dewey noticed, possessing two large, semi-circular balconies one atop the other supported by fluted columns facing East Bay. Double covered piazzas ran the length of the house, while a pierced brick privacy wall skirted along the house's outermost edge. With the Cooper River just a few blocks away, Dewey could smell the pluff mud.

An engraved, bronze plate bearing Dr. Lyman's name hung on the front door. Dewey opened it and walked into the lobby. It was small, with only a few chairs and, in one corner, a giant, green monstera plant with leaves three times the size of Dewey's hand. Throughout the office, artwork abounded, mostly fine charcoal sketches of Charleston and the Lowcountry. One sketch featured the Market in the early 1900s—a row of cavernous, wooden vegetable bins, a black woman with a headwrap balancing a large woven basket on her head, and a mother in a long dress grabbing her small, playful child by the arm.

Another sketch showed a local church, its steeple thrust high into an afternoon sky full of light, billowing clouds and small birds gliding on warm sea air. Another image showed a black man on a farm, his strong arms guiding the plow through fertile soil, as he leaned forward into his work. In the last one, a long, sandy stretch of land pushed out into a salt marsh with tidal creeks and craggy trees full of brilliant blues, greens and browns. Dewey squinted hard hoping he'd find Desirée and the revelers.

He stepped up to a small sliding glass window with a middle-aged woman in a white blouse and gray skirt sitting behind it making notes on a piece of paper. "Your name, please?" she said, looking up over her reading glasses.

"Dewey Cellars. I spoke with Dr. Lyman on Friday. He said to come on Monday at nine."

"Okay, take a seat."

A few minutes passed when the woman called Dewey's name. He walked into a hallway off the main lobby, which also included a variety of sketches on the wall. A nurse greeted Dewey and showed him to an exam room, where he hopped up on an exam table. Soon, Dewey heard feet shuffling outside the door. A knock followed, and the exam room door opened. Dr. Lyman walked in holding a paper chart. Dewey noticed he smelled of bay rum cologne. "Hello," he said, looking at Dewey, as if he recognized him.

"Hello," said Dewey. "Thanks for squeezing me in."

"No trouble at all," he said. "I like making myself available to students." Dewey sat up straight, much like a small child at dinner with his parents. "So, tell me again what brings you here?"

"Well, I've got this thing in my right eye that looks like a bunch of dots and squiggly lines. And when I look at something, especially if it's in the light, the dots and lines drift past whatever I'm looking at. It distorts things, and it's just a pain."

Dr. Lyman turned off the lights and moved closer to Dewey. "Hold still and let me take a look," he said. He raised an instrument and shined a beam of light in Dewey's right eye.

Dewey could see and feel the beam of light creep into the back of his eye into the thick array of vessels living there. His first thoughts were cancer or a detached retina. Maybe even blindness.

After a few seconds, Dr. Lyman spoke. "It's as I suspected—a floater."

"What's that?" said Dewey, interpreting from Dr. Lyman's tone that it wasn't serious.

"It's when the vitreous in the eye starts to shrink and becomes stringy. The strands can cast tiny shadows on the retina producing what we call a *floater*."

"A floater? Is it deadly?"

"Not usually," said Dr. Lyman, jokingly.

Dewey noticed the once stern, dour-looking face from Poogan's Porch had become animated, if not charming.

"Is there a cure? Does it go away?"

"It's completely benign. You just have to live with it. Some people get to where they hardly notice it."

"But it drives me crazy."

"But you still have almost perfect vision."

"I suppose."

"It will be more noticeable against lighter backgrounds like a blue sky or a white sheet of paper. I don't suspect it will interfere with much—don't worry, you won't go blind."

Dewey looked around, gazing at the sketches in the exam room. One by one the floater coasted over them. He was able to see, but at the same time felt he couldn't see. Not fully, not perfectly, at least. A certain clarity was missing.

"Do you have any questions?" said Dr. Lyman.

"No, guess not," said Dewey. "Again, I really appreciate you seeing me on such short notice."

"You're quite welcome. My nurse will see you out."

Dr. Lyman smiled at Dewey, turned and exited the room.

As Dewey slipped back into the hall headed for the lobby, something inside made him want to stay. He wanted to know more about Dr. Lyman and his sketches. He wanted to know what had brought Dr. Lyman to East Bay Street to such an old but beautiful building. He wanted, ultimately, to know where this man lived.

Within a few minutes, Dewey was back on East Bay Street headed to the dorm and thinking about Dr. Freeport's class. He crossed the intersection at Meeting and Calhoun streets and stepped onto Marion Square's freshly cut grass. Wet clippings stuck to his shoes, as he took in the scents of summer's sad end.

In the distance along King Street, men and women in resort-casual clothes walked with coffee in hand, while students with books gathered in small groups and moved slowly toward campus. A valet in front of the Francis Marion Hotel helped a woman dressed in all white into her car, while a man in denim overalls washed the hotel's large, street-level windows.

Dewey walked across the park, past the Calhoun statue, and crossed King Street, where he fell in behind the small clumps of students headed to campus. Together, they jay walked across Calhoun Street onto St. Philip Street, where just before the Simons Center, a sign caught Dewey's attention. *Campus Tour Guides Wanted: Contact Admissions at Towell Library*, it read.

Dewey recalled the volunteer service project requirement for pledging. This might be a good opportunity, he thought. After all, it was a simple tour that had brought him to the college. A simple tour that had shown him his potential. A simple tour that had now become a journey. Introducing newbies and their parents to the college seemed the least he could do. He decided to visit Towell Library after class. Maybe Lucious would know something about it.

Dewey entered campus through the back of Randolph Hall and followed the wide herringbone brick path to the front of Physician's Auditorium. His pulse raced, as he smelled the vinegary smell of formaldehyde and pictured the white lobby floor with black and brown specks. Science was hard, not like English or history, and it made him feel dumb. He thought about turning around and going back to the dorm. Then he remembered what the man who sold him the computer said: *Just remember, you can always reboot.*

* * *

Dewey had taken a seat in Dr. Freeport's class, when Mary Pate walked in wearing a white tee-shirt with palm trees outlined in rhinestones, blue jeans and a pair of Keds. They had not spoken since her party. He couldn't wait to tell her about the first night of pledge education. He felt things were coming together, but he'd still have to deal with Alex, who just the day before had asked when bids would be delivered. Dewey played dumb, saying he would drop by the Greek Life office and get back to him.

Dr. Freeport walked to the podium in the middle of the pit. He adjusted his bow tie and eyeglasses.

"The second full week of classes has begun," he said. "Congratulations, you're full-fledged college students now."

Dewey thought his words were sweet, innocent and sincere.

"In the last class, we covered Linnaeus' system of classification, and then you were to read chapter two," he said. "It begins with the rather astounding fact that we humans have inhabited this God-given planet for the last 2.5 million years. And only for the last 200,000 years have we looked the way we do today."

Though truly amazed by this fact, Dewey sank low in his seat attempting to hide, having not read the chapter.

Dr. Freeport called on a nearby student who had raised his hand.

"So, where'd our big foreheads go?" the student asked.

"Brow ridge is what I think you mean," said Dr. Freeport. "Scientists think the bigger the brow the more dominant in the social order of the tribe."

"So, like a bad ass?"

"Perhaps. But let's call him a tribal leader. By the way, your name, please?"

"Trey. Trey Fontaine."

Dewey looked behind him. It was Trey—wave rider, beer drinker and, more recently, champion hot dog eater. Dewey noticed he'd gotten his color back and also his big mouth.

"Welcome, Mr. Fontaine. Where are you from?" said Dr. Freeport.

"Jersey." His accent attracted everyone's attention.

"How'd you get down here?"

"Had some friends at Folly Beach. Got tired of the Jersey shore, so I moved here."

"I see," said Dr. Freeport. "Well, I look forward to regular updates from Folly."

"Stoked," said Trey.

With Mary Pate just a few seats away, Dewey tore a piece of paper from his notebook. *Wait for me after class*, he wrote. He motioned to the boy next to him to pass it to Mary Pate. The boy passed her the note, and she opened it. She looked over at Dewey.

"Okay," she mouthed, nodding her head.

Dewey smiled. Being friends with Mary Pate was easy, he thought. She was becoming someone he could trust more and more.

Meanwhile, Dr. Freeport had briefly ducked behind his podium and emerged cradling a human skull in his hands, causing some in the class to gasp.

"In chapter two we also learn about human evolution," said Dr. Freeport. "Not just physical but also intellectual. Man's capacity for language, for example. Even emotion." He held the skull up high for all to see. "Yes, if you're wondering, it's one hundred percent real. It dates to about 60,000 years ago from Africa."

"Totally rad!" said a boy next to Dewey.

"This was somebody once, like you and me," said Dr. Freeport. "He hunted and killed, probably had a family. Maybe, like us, even had dreams."

The skull was brown and dirty, with a protruding forehead. Most of the teeth were missing, and the eyes, large and somewhat square, looked ghostly.

Mary Pate raised her hand. "But God made the earth in six days, not billions of years," she said. "And, by the way, Adam and Eve were the first humans, not that monkey in your hands."

Most students froze in their seats, either embarrassed by or uncomfortable with where the conversation might be headed. They looked at Mary Pate, then back at Dr. Freeport, curious to see what would happen next.

"Ah, yes, the Book of Genesis, Ms. Hackney." Dr. Freeport had quickly glanced at his seating chart to find Mary Pate's name. "Religion and science don't have to conflict."

"But it's God's Word."

"And some of those words are open to interpretation. The Hebrew word 'day,' for example, is *yom*, which can mean a day, two days, or an undetermined number of days, so it's quite possible six days could mean a billion years."

"Huh, is that so?" said Mary Pate. The rhinestones on her shirt seemed dimmer, as she crossed her arms in front of her.

"Yes, and I think it's entirely possible and natural to combine the two," said Dr. Freeport. He smiled at Mary Pate, while looking over top of his big, brown glasses as if, like Trey, he might be searching the horizon for the next big wave. "They call it theocratic evolution, where God is understood to have a hand in creation."

"Well, that's not what we say at SCA." Mary Pate looked around the room, as if trying to garner support.

A few nodded their heads up and down. Most checked their watches or fiddled with their pencils. Dewey heard a boy next to him whisper, "Bullshit."

Dr. Freeport tried diffusing the situation using a saying he'd used since the first day of class. "In any case," he said, smiling at her, "remember to eat your butter beans."

Dewey felt the mood in the room lighten, as Dr. Freeman gently returned the skull to the podium and pointed to a giant map of Africa behind him. He talked about man's exit from the continent, and how he made his way by foot to Western Europe, then to Asia and finally over a land bridge into the Americas.

Dewey marveled at the map and its long, curvy lines showing man's prehistoric travel. What a long way to come. And to know nothing about what was on the other side. Even *if* there was another side. Dewey couldn't help but think about his journey to the college, a journey not quite as far or perilous as prehistoric man, but one nonetheless carrying similar uncertainties. What had they come for?

Dr. Freeport pressed a button on the podium, and the vinyl map retracted into a long, metal sleeve hanging from the ceiling. He straightened his bow tie, gathered a sheaf of papers and exited the room with his signature smile.

Mary Pate waited at the door for Dewey, holding her books against her chest.

"Some speech back there, huh?" said Dewey.

"You mean Dr. Freeport's?" said Mary Pate.

"No, I meant yours."

"Well, you can't bring everyone to the Lord, even smart professors."

"I just have to ask—do you *really* believe in Adam and Eve?"

"Who wants to know?" Mary Pate clutched her books tighter.

"I do." Dewey knew what she was going to say, but he pretended not to.

"Okay, so I do believe it," she said, the rhinestone palm trees on her shirt shimmering.

"That's cool. I'm sure others in the class feel the same."

"Thanks, Dew." Mary Pate smiled and lowered her books.

That she had called him *Dew* was funny, only friends back home called him that.

"So, guess what?" said Dewey. "I went to my first pledge class last night. We learned some frat history and got this cool pledge pin. See?" Dewey thrust his shirt pocket at Mary Pate, where the pin was affixed.

"Fancy," said Mary Pate, unfazed.

"Probably just like Radford's, huh?" Dewey stroked the pin's engraved surface. "Did he ever show you his?"

"No, he didn't."

"How could he not show you his pin? That's the most crucial part. Didn't you ever see him around campus with it?"

"I told you what happened, and why I didn't see him much. I don't know why something that small is such a big deal." Mary Pate's cheeks got red, and she got flustered.

"Are you okay, Mary Pate? I was just kidding about the pin."

"I'm fine, Dewey. Listen, I gotta go."

Mary Pate looked down the hall. Some of the Maybank herd who were also in Dr. Freeport's class were already reaching for cigarettes, as they headed for the door. Mary Pate looked like she'd just as well join them with their cigarette smoke and alcohol breath if it meant getting away from Dewey and his questions.

"But aren't you happy for me?" Dewey flashed the pin again in her direction.

"Yeah, I'm happy, Dew, as long as you're happy. I'm sorry, but, God willing, I have to get to my next class."

Mary Pate walked down the hall, shuffling, pigeon-toed, across the brown-white speckled floor, past the glass casings of blue ribbons and tall trophies.

Dewey felt bad. On the one hand, he'd made it into Kappa House and was on his way to meeting Radford. On the other, he'd just been a jerk to Mary Pate. He'd try to smooth things over later. Maybe then she'd be happy for him. Just maybe.

CHAPTER 14

Dewey exited Physician's Auditorium thinking about Mary Pate and walked the short distance to Towell Library to inquire about the tour guide position. As he heaved open the building's tall, narrow doors, he looked over his shoulder at the front of Randolph Hall. So beautiful, he thought, as he looked through the windows, once again imagining fanciful figures in powdered wigs and breeches smoking porcelain tobacco pipes.

His musings were interrupted, however, when a tall, bony woman with a rich, welcoming voice greeted him.

"Who you looking for, SHU-gah?" she said, peering through very large, pink-rimmed eyeglasses.

"I'm looking for Lucious." Dewey felt small in front of the woman.

"He's running around here somewhere. Those hot little feet just can't sit still."

A voice called out from above.

"Right here, Ms. Tilley," said Lucious from the mezzanine.

Miss Tilley craned her neck upwards but was unable to see him, so it looked like she was talking into the air. "You have a guest, SHU-gah," she said again.

"Okay, send them up," said Lucious.

Dewey walked to a stairway next to the mezzanine. He climbed to the top, where Lucious, wearing a white dress shirt, a maroon silk tie and khakis, greeted him. He looked at Dewey through glasses with thick, brown frames.

"Hey, Lucious, you may not remember me. We met at the freshman mixer." Dewey extended his hand.

"Sure, I remember," said Lucious, rising up out of his chair and taking Dewey's hand. "What brings you to Admissions?"

"Hopefully a job."

"Really?" Lucious raised an eyebrow. "And what would that be exactly?"

"Campus tour guide."

"So, you saw the sign?"

"Yup."

"Okay, let me run and get some paperwork. I'll be right back."

"Sure." Dewey looked down at Ms. Tilley filing papers, her long fingers with gold bejeweled rings running methodically over each piece. He could also see the small office where he'd interviewed the previous spring. The blinds were shut, but he could make out two figures sitting across from one another. Another prospective student, just like he'd been so many months ago. Part of Dewey longed to go back to that magical day when it all happened, when he first saw Angel Boy. If only he could stop and freeze that moment forever.

On a nearby bookcase were Lucious' high school and college diplomas, and a series of books on engineering. There were pictures of a younger Lucious with white men in ties and white women in colorful skirts and pearl necklaces holding drinks. One woman leaned in very close to Lucious like they were the only two in the shot. Dewey noticed how happy they looked.

Lucious was tall and muscular, but there was something else, something that reminded Dewey of himself, a feeling of longing and dissatisfaction.

Lucious returned with the paperwork. "Here you go. The position does require some training, then you can sign up to lead tours." He gestured in the air with his long, dark fingers as if checking things off a list.

"Sounds good," said Dewey.

"By the way, what's the sudden interest?" Lucious leaned over his desk toward Dewey.

"Not an interest exactly. I just pledged Kappa Tau, and we gotta do a service project. Something with the college." Dewey thought about pointing to his pledge pin.

"Kappa Tau, huh? A frat boy?" Lucious pretended like Dewey had a tie on and reached to adjust it.

"I don't know if I'd say that just yet. I'm still a pledge."

"Why Kappa Tau?"

"They seemed pretty cool during rush, and it was the only bid I got." Dewey kept a straight face, strangely fearing Lucious might read his mind about Radford.

"Funny, but I don't see you as a frat boy. I mean, where you're from and stuff might make you an easy in, but you just seem different. Sorry if I'm getting too personal."

"How would you know—you don't know anything about me." Dewey looked miffed.

"Actually, I do, because I have your student file. In fact, I didn't tell you this when I saw you at the freshman mixer, but I'm the one who gave your application the initial okay and recommended admission. So, of course, I saw everything—where you lived, went to school, test scores."

"You're kiddin' me. But I thought *she* was the one who gave me the okay. She's the one I interviewed with." Dewey pointed downstairs to the small office with the blinds shut, where he'd interviewed with a woman with a short wedge haircut wearing an ankle-length dress and turtleneck sweater.

"No, that's Jill." She does informal interviews just to answer basic questions. But you must have said something right for her to kick your application up here, where we make the big decisions. So, congrats."

Lucious handed Dewey a clipboard emblazoned with a giant cougar. "Let's get this paperwork out of the way. It's really quick."

Dewey filled in his name, phone number and campus address. As he returned the clipboard to Lucious, the sweet scent of tea olive floated through an open window. Palm fronds rustled. A cloud dipped low.

"Thanks for the info," said Lucious. "Come back Friday, and we'll have you shadow somebody."

"So, I got the job?" said Dewey.

"Yeah, you got it."

"Cool, thanks. Hey, just curious, how long have you worked here?"

"Feels like forever, but seven years. I'd just gotten back to Charleston after being discharged."

On another bookcase was a big certificate with US Navy written in the center and below it the words *Honorable Discharge.*

"Why'd you come back to Charleston?"

"I'm from here. Went to high school and college here." Lucious looked out the window toward Physician's Auditorium. A big live oak blew in the wind.

"Seems like a pretty cool place to grow up." Dewey imagined the Market, Battery, and beaches.

"Yeah, overall, it was. There's lots to do on the peninsula."

Dewey expected more enthusiasm from Lucious. "I'd love to have grown up here."

"Kids like you always say that." Lucious returned his gaze to his desk. "What I mean is don't be fooled. It's not all moonlight and magnolias."

"What's moonlight and magnolias?"

"It's this belief that everything in these parts is just great. That the past—slaves, aristocrats, plantations—was just hunky-dory."

"How do you mean?"

"It's a myth, a myth that slaves actually liked being slaves, that they were treated well, and it was this big romantic dream. Everyone here believes that, especially rich kids from the North who know nothing."

The sensation of weightlessness that Dewey previously experienced from the tea olive had disappeared.

Traffic in the library had picked up. People noisily moved about opening filing cabinets, answering phones and typing. The tall, narrow front doors creaked with students entering and exiting. A few students leaned against the mezzanine railing, while waiting for their counselor.

"Hey, thanks for seeing me today. I'll have some stuff from Kappa Tau that you'll need to sign in a couple weeks proving I did my service project," said Dewey.

"No problem," said Lucious. "Just make sure you do a good job."

Then a voice came from below. "Lucious, SHU-gah, you have a call from someone over at the Bursar's office. Can you SKEE-daddle down here?" She had cupped the phone and was looking up in Lucious' direction.

"I'll take the call, Miss Tilley. Tell them I'll be right there." Lucious reached across his desk with an open hand. "I have to go. It's been nice talking. See you Friday."

Dewey shook Lucious' hand and walked down the mezzanine steps. He passed the small office where he'd been interviewed and exited through the tall, wooden doors. In the Yard, it was beginning to feel like fall, he noticed. A lone sunbather stretched out on the cistern. Hints of Coppertone here and there.

Then, suddenly, from behind him from the top of the steps of the Library, a voice called out.

"Make sure you come back, SHU-gah. Hear me?"

CHAPTER 15

Dewey had barely opened the door having returned from Towell Library, when he found Alex standing in the common room looking at him. His face was red, his pimples like tiny volcanoes about to blow.

"Why didn't you fucking tell me?" he said.

"What do you mean?" said Dewey, trying to fake it, but he knew precisely what Alex meant.

"They gave out bids last week, didn't they?" Alex raised an empty hand as if something should be in it.

"Who told you?" Dewey's first guess was Mary Pate. Or maybe someone from rush. Maybe someone from Kappa or another frat.

"Oh, I don't know, maybe fucking Greek Life! Did you even call them like you said?" Alex stomped his foot, his white crew socks drooping more and more.

"I just forgot, man, I just forgot," said Dewey, hoping the conversation might end there.

"The same way you forgot to tell me *you* got a bid?" Alex sat down on the couch, rested his elbows on his knees and folded his hands. Tears welled up in his eyes. The truth had leapt quickly and violently like a leopard into the dimly lit room. Dewey knew there was no place to hide.

"Yeah, Alex, I got a bid. It happened last week. And I accepted. You happy now?"

"You did *what?*"

"I accepted a bid from Kappa Tau. Pledging started last night." Dewey pulled out his pledge pin. "See?"

"But I thought we were in this together?"

"We're roommates, Alex," said Dewey, "roommates who rushed together. I can't tell you why they picked me over you. I know you wanted this more than me." He looked at the few remaining juice boxes high on the shelf. Alex had been so generous. "Don't take it personally."

"Fuck you, Dewey, I was counting on this!"

As evening descended, the room was enveloped in a soft haze that rendered objects fuzzy and shapeless. Dewey looked out the window at students lingering in the courtyard. He wished he could be one of them. "I didn't know it was that important to you," he said. "At first you didn't act like it."

"Have you ever felt like an outsider? Ever sat on the sidelines and just watched life go by? Makes you wonder if you're ever going to be part of anything. You worry about how you look, what you wear and what you have. You worry about every little fucking thing."

Dewey knew exactly how Alex felt. "What do you expect me to do, Alex? Go back to the frats and ask them to give you a bid?"

"No. No, I don't. By far you're the nicest person I've met here. Remember our talk that night in the Yard? I'm not saying that makes us best friends, but it does make us more than just roommates."

Dewey remembered their conversation and how they'd laughed about his dad being a priest. And he remembered Frieda's offer of dinner the night of move-in, when his own parents were long gone.

"Did they say why I didn't get a bid?" said Alex, wiping his puffy eyes.

"No reason. I couldn't even begin to guess. Part of me thinks it's just completely random."

"Be honest. I think you know. You knew the first time you walked in here."

"So you're some kind of mind-reader now?" Dewey mocked Alex by squinting his eyes like he was sending Alex a silent message.

"Yeah, and here's what I read," said Alex, "Short, dumpy guy with bad skin who's never gonna get laid."

Dewey felt like he'd had the wind knocked out of him. Alex could read minds—or at least he'd read his. Dewey felt ashamed. He couldn't explain the mean, petty part of himself that made quick, superficial judgments. He couldn't believe he could be this mean—it was like he was a different person.

"What do you want me to say, Alex?"

"Say the truth, Dew, say the truth."

Dewey noticed juice stains had formed on the carpet.

"Hell with you, Dewey Cellars, I'm outta here. Maybe I'll go see Mary Pate. She'll understand."

Alex pulled his socks up, tied his shoes and sprinted out of the room, slamming the door behind him. Dewey heard the thunderous clang of the stairwell door, which reminded him he'd wanted to go see Mary Pate to explain more about pledging. Now Alex would only muddy the waters further.

Dewey looked out through the open window into the courtyard to find some guys throwing a football. "Don't worry about it, dude. Just go long," one of them said aloud.

CHAPTER 16

Next morning, Dewey sat at his desk preparing for Freshman Seminar. The night had passed without event, despite his argument with Alex about the bid. He heard him return late from Mary Pate's and leave early for class.

Before him lay the personality wheel worksheet that DuGow had assigned. The instructions said to circle the characteristics and attributes that best described oneself. The first word Dewey circled was *amiable.* He believed he was genuinely friendly. He liked people, and people liked him. He believed he was kind.

The second word he circled was *determined.* He'd worked hard in high school, getting mostly As and Bs. He'd taken classes like Honors Chemistry. He'd played ice hockey, soccer and wrestled.

The last word he circled was *honest,* which he'd had a harder time doing. He valued honesty and knew right from wrong, but something nagged at him. At times he would exaggerate or manipulate the truth. Sometimes downright lie.

Dewey connected the three words with a straight line, which together pointed to a place on the outer edge of the wheel that read in large print: *Extrovert, Risk-taker, Shapeshifter.* Then the phone rang.

"Hello, may I speak with Mr. Dewey Cellars?" The voice sounded familiar.

"This is *him*," said Dewey.

"You mean, 'This is *he*,'" said the voice.

"Who's this?"

"This is Dr. Lyman."

Dewey straightened up, surprised by his call. "Oh, good morning, sir."

It had been a week since his appointment for the eye floater, and Dewey figured it would be the last time he'd encounter Dr. Lyman, except for the occasional check-up.

"I'm calling to check on the floater."

"Oh, thank you. Seems fine." What a lazy answer, thought Dewey. He tried again. "You were right about it being worse against light backgrounds, but it seems to be less of an issue. I really appreciate all you did."

"Glad to hear," said Dr. Lyman.

Dewey thought this was the end of the conversation, as Dr. Lyman's voice trailed off. Then his voice picked up again. "And how are your courses going?"

"Fine, too." Dewey felt a bit strange, still trying to figure out where the conversation was going. "I was just preparing for Freshman Seminar."

"I certainly didn't mean to keep you."

"No, you're fine. No interruption at all." Dewey was pleased with his response, the first good one all day long, he thought. Older people with stature didn't want to hear words like *cool* and *awesome*.

"Before I let you go, I wanted to extend an invitation for dinner," said Dr. Lyman. "Poogan's hardly seemed any way to welcome you to Charleston."

The invitation took Dewey aback. Just days before Dr. Lyman had denied ever having encountered Dewey. Why the admission now, wondered Dewey.

He felt the air conditioning on the back of his neck from the vent above. The heat from outside seemed to be creeping into the room.

His thoughts drifted to Alex and Mary Pate—he wondered where they were. Maybe class, maybe the library or somewhere downtown. Dewey felt alone.

"Dewey?" said Dr. Lyman.

"Sure," said Dewey, "Sounds good."

"Okay, then, how about Friday?"

Dewey walked around his room, the telephone cord wrapping around a chair leg. He thought about the week ahead. Kappa Tau had a mixer Friday night, and the pledges would have to work. "Can we do Saturday night?" said Dewey.

"That will do. How about six o'clock?" Dr. Lyman's voice had become fainter.

"That's good. Where should we meet?"

"I'll meet you down at the wharf," said Dr. Lyman. "We can walk to dinner from there."

"Okay, cool." Dewey caught himself using the word *cool* again. "I mean, yessir, that will be fine." He cringed and glanced at his watch— ten thirty. Freshman Seminar began in fifteen minutes. He'd have to sprint to Craig. "I'm so sorry, Dr. Lyman, but I have to go."

"Oh, yes, then go. See you Saturday."

"Thanks." Dewey hung up the phone and ran out the door. He hated being late. It just wasn't his personality.

* * *

Dewey was happy to see Dr. DuGow. He smiled at her as he took his seat, leaving behind thoughts of Alex, Mary Pate, Lucious, Dr. Lyman—and even Radford. They'd entered his life with such speed and force that there was little else he could do but hold on.

"Well, here we are again, class," said Dr. DuGow, leaning over the podium and laughing hysterically, as was her habit. Dr. DuGow was funny and zany, thought Dewey, the proverbial crazy aunt who visited once a year. She was quickly becoming his favorite professor. "Okay, where were we?"

"Personality wheel," called out someone in the front row.

"Ah, yes, let's check in with who we are … Or who you are … Or who somebody is," said Dr. DuGow.

The class laughed.

"I'll go," said a girl with blue eyes and tan lines.

"Step right up. Not literally, of course, but you know what I mean. Stand if you want. Or sit. Whatever."

The girl remained seated and lifted her wheel. "I saw myself as *supportive*, *loyal*, and *positive thinking*."

"Some nice attributes there." Dr. DuGow raised her eyebrows, until the whites of her eyes dominated her long, slender face. "Do those traits come from mom or dad?"

"Probably my mom. My dad's an asshole. They divorced when I was in middle school."

An uncomfortable silence rolled over the class.

"I'm so sorry to hear that. You must have a lot of anguish." Dr. DuGow seemed unphased by the girl's choice words, instead making an extra effort to engage her and her pain. "If you'd like to talk or something, I do have office hours."

"No biggie," said the girl, adjusting her camisole straps and folding her arms tightly across her midsection. She looked out the window toward St. Philip Street.

"Would anyone else like to go?" Dr. DuGow surveyed the class for more volunteers, landing her eyes on Dewey. "How about our runner?"

Dewey missed Dr. DuGow's sudden prompting, his thoughts focused instead on the many conflicting feelings he'd had about his personality wheel.

Dr. DuGow spoke again. "Dewey Cellars, the runner—or is it the chaser?"

"Oh, sorry," said Dewey, looking up at Dr. DuGow and reaching for his personality wheel. "Okay, so I chose *amiable, determined* and *honest.*"

"You can't be that good," said a boy in the back row.

"Enough," said Dr. DuGow, eyeballing the boy in the back. She focused on Dewey again. "Those are admirable traits. Where'd those come from?"

"Probably my dad. He's a priest, so it just kinda runs in the blood." Dewey looked up, surprised he didn't wear a more joyful expression.

"Interesting," said Dr. DuGow, "I don't know that I've had many preacher's kids as students. They say you have to watch out for them."

"Promise, what you see is what you get. I'm not much trouble."

"We shall see!" Dr. DuGow laughed, then turned her attention back to the whole class. "Question," she said, "Are we the same person at all times?"

Dewey and his classmates eyed each other suspiciously, as if they were all imposters.

"I think we'd all like to be the same person all the time but that would be hard to do," said a boy wearing a tweed sports coat and jeans.

"Why?" said Dr. DuGow, raising her eyebrows.

"Because we're different depending on who's around. Around my parents I'm one thing but around friends, I'm another."

Dewey knew exactly what the boy meant. Many times, he'd thought how much easier life would be if he could just be the same person everywhere. At school, he felt he was one person; in public and at church he felt he was another. And then there was who he wanted to be, which is where Radford entered. He thought of Alex's library books on horror masks.

The girl with blue eyes and tan lines spoke again. "But with everybody pretending to be someone else, how do we know who we really are?" she said.

"That's the thing about youth," said Dr. DuGow. "When you're young, there are so many things to pick and choose from. So many shiny things to chase."

"Yes, they is," said a black girl in the front row who Dewey had never heard speak. "Yes, they is."

The class got quiet.

"Okay, let's get our reading packets out and turn to the table of contents," said Dr. DuGow.

The class reached down and searched their book bags for their packets. Dewey placed his personality wheel on his desk, but it accidentally slid off and fell face down on the floor. From his angle, he could no longer see who he was.

Frustrated, he retrieved it quickly. It was crumpled, dirty, and had strands of hair on it. "Dammit," he said to himself.

Instead of opening his packet, Dewey looked out the window and imagined walking through the Yard with Radford toward Kappa House. In his daydream, he was sure everyone would wave and call to them, their shadows sometimes overlapping, and Dewey knowing exactly who he was.

CHAPTER 17

It was almost lunchtime when Dewey stepped out of Craig Hall from Dr. DuGow's class. He was hungry, so he decided to walk to Sharky's. Maybe being downtown would help him get his mind off thinking about everyone, including himself.

He headed toward George Street, passing the parking deck, the Sottile theater and a few small shops along the way, before finally reaching the intersection of King and George. Turning right onto King, he could see Sharky's red and white striped awning, and its swirling shark logo. It was on the opposite side of the street that he and Alex had walked up after eating at Poogan's. The sidewalk was narrow, and in some places broken and uneven; small bits of food, chewing gum and trash were caught in its crevices.

Sharky's featured a bar running the full length of one wall and, just beyond, an open window into the kitchen where Dewey watched two men toss pizza dough. Dewey smelled tomato sauce, oregano, and parmesan cheese, which comforted him. Exposed brick walls with small light fixtures dangling overhead made up the main dining area. Tables covered with red-and-white checkered tablecloths boasted small, round salt and pepper shakers and glass bottles of crushed red pepper. Soon, a waitress approached with a menu.

"Welcome to Sharky's," said the girl, who wore her hair up in a messy bun with a red bandana. "What can I get you to drink?"

"Sweet tea," said Dewey, looking at the large, laminated menu.

"Thanks."

"Got it." The girl turned around and disappeared into the kitchen.

Dewey followed her with his eyes, wondering where she was from. Downtown? Mount Pleasant? West Ashley? Tight jeans and a tank top made him think West Ashley or someplace down Highway 17, where strip malls, convenience stores and small neighborhoods with 50s-era homes abounded.

When she returned, Dewey smiled and ordered a small mushroom pizza. He'd taken a seat at a window, where students shuffled by wearing backpacks, and tourists pointed and peered up at buildings with decorative eaves and wrought iron balconies. Whole families sometimes walked by and, occasionally, serious-looking people with sketch pads or books in their hand.

In a nearby booth, Dewey overheard two girls in sundresses eating salad and talking.

"The Windjammer was totally packed last night," said one of them, wearing a white, low-cut blouse.

"How'd you get out there?" said the other, reaching for her gold add-a-bead necklace.

"Chandler had his dad's car, so we met up at Craig and piled in." The girl took a bite of salad, but some of it fell from her mouth onto the side of her plate.

"All the way out to Isle of Palms?" She twisted a finger around her add-a-bead necklace.

"Yeah, it wasn't that bad. We'd all had a couple beers."

"Who played?"

"Local band—Johnny Quest, I think."

"I heard they were good." The girl released the tension on her necklace and reached for her water. "Is Chandler's dad loaded?"

"Seems like it. He's always talking about their place out on Wadmalaw. Sometimes it's a bit much. I mean we all know what he's got."

"Where's this Wadmalaw?" said the girl with the necklace.

"About forty-five minutes from here. Something about an old tea plantation." The girl had scooped up the fallen piece of lettuce with her fork. "How's your salad?"

"Fine, a little too much dressing."

"Sometimes they can't help themselves," said the girl in the low-cut blouse. "I just scrape it off."

"Any hot guys there?"

"A bunch." The girl in the low-cut blouse looked up and smiled.

"Hook up with anyone?"

"Yeah, just this one dude." The girl wiped some dressing off her blouse.

Dewey's pizza finally arrived, the edges slightly burned.

As he bit into the first slice, he pondered what the girls had said. He felt their energy and desire, and wished he could have been in that car rushing out to Wadmalaw. But he knew he was far away from tea plantations and hooking up with girls in gold add-a-beads and low-cut blouses.

Dewey slowly bit into his last slice of pizza which, by now, looked cold and deflated. A red pepper flake burned his tongue. He had come to Sharky's to eat, but now he couldn't help but think Sharky's had somehow eaten him.

CHAPTER 18

Cigarette smoke billowed over the entrance of Maybank. It was Thursday, and the herd moved restlessly. One cigarette after another, moving from one small group to another to hear about the previous night's conquests and weigh options for the upcoming weekend.

Dewey squeezed past them and shuffled up the building's musty stairwell to the third floor and walked into Dr. Berrygood's class. Having read the selection on Keats, unlike the chapter in biology, Dewey felt confident in whatever questions Dr. Berrygood might throw his way. He'd have to concentrate, though, and not get distracted thinking about meeting Mary Pate and Radford after class.

Dr. Berrygood walked briskly into class, set his textbook down and leaned against a desk. He drew his right pointer finger to his upper lip and began stroking it side to side while looking contemplatively out the salt-caked windows toward the dorm. "My church is having a fundraiser to clean up and restore our historic graveyard," he said. "Brownies, cupcakes, baked goods. That kind of thing. Let me know if you're interested in purchasing any, or if you'd just like to help the cause by pulling weeds in the graveyard."

What a peculiar statement, thought Dewey, but Dr. Berrygood had said it so sincerely. It was almost as if he was communicating something else. From the back of the class came a few nervous-sounding chuckles.

Dewey raised his hand. "What kind of church?" he said.

"Anglican," said Dr. Berrygood.

"So, basically Episcopal?" said Dewey.

"Yes, I guess you could say that. Might I ask how you know?"

"England, *Anglicans*. America, *Episcopalians*. An oversimplification, I know. I'm the latter. Trust me, I come by it honestly."

"An Episcopalian in Charleston. Shocking. I'm sure you're smitten with all the churches in town."

"Yeah, no shortage of steeples and wing tips."

"Have you chosen a congregation?"

"Yes, right around the corner." Dewey thought of the handsome couple who sat next to him in the pew the previous Sunday.

"Well, if you're up for pulling weeds, Mr. Cellars, you're welcome to join us at the church this Saturday." Dr. Berrygood wrote the church's address at the bottom corner of the chalkboard.

"Thanks for the invite," said Dewey.

Dr. Berrygood turned around and spoke to the class. "Okay, that time again. Open your texts to page 165 to 'When I Have Fears That I May Cease to Be.' You'll recall we left off with the notion of time. But did Keats leave you with this impression?" Dr. Berrygood's finger stroked his upper lip. "Mr. Fontaine, how about you?"

"Oh, shit," said Trey, as if a grenade had just landed in his lap. "Well, Dr. B., it's like this—see, Keats is dying and still wants to write a whole bunch of stuff."

"Good start, Mr. Fontaine." Dr. Berrygood walked to the far corner of the room near one of the salt-caked windows.

A girl in the front row spoke. "To me, it was a sad poem."

"How so?" said Dr. Berrygood.

"Well, at the end Keats seems to end up alone without any feeling or meaning," said the girl.

"Indeed," said Dr. Berrygood, then pausing. "How *did* Keats die? Anyone?"

"Tuberculosis," said Dewey.

"Correct," said Dr. Berrygood.

"And both his mother and brother died from it," continued Dewey, having read the book's biographical notes on Keats. "His father was trampled by a horse. Death surrounded him."

Dr. Berrygood had worked his way around the room questioning students and returned to the front. "So, how do we make our stamp on life? How will someone know if *you* even existed?"

Dewey looked at the floor, then turned slightly sideways in his seat. Palm fronds beat hard against the salt-caked windows. "It's how we feel we've counted in life," he said. "What we leave behind."

"Good. For Keats, of course, that meant his ideas, his writing, his work," said Dr. Berrygood.

The class looked down in their textbooks, fearing one of them might be called on next.

"Young people today seem so impatient to make their mark," continued Dr. Berrygood. "Though I guess that's been true through the ages." He paused again. "So, how will you leave your mark, Mr. Fontaine?"

"Crushing beers and catching surf," said Trey, smirking.

The class laughed aloud.

Dr. Berrygood, not amused, shook his head and turned in Dewey's direction. "And you, Mr. Cellars?"

"Can't say right now," said Dewey.

In the same way he had balked in Dr. DuGow's class about disclosing Radford, he had done the same here. But maybe there'd be a surprise fire alarm, he thought, and he could blurt it out amid the blaring chirps, as everyone exited the building. Or maybe a storm would suddenly pop up, and amid thunder and lightning he could say what he really wanted. In either scenario he could take it back or say he'd been misheard. But at least it would be out there—that for the moment his destiny, his stamp, lay in Angel Boy.

The room turned cold. The girl in the front row who thought Keats' poem was sad spoke up. "It's not exactly the same," she said, softly, "but at least I'd like to know someone liked me."

"Thoughtful interpretation," said Dr. Berrygood. "Care to expand?"

"Sometimes I just hate who I am. I look in the mirror, and my skin is awful, I don't like my hair or my boobs are too small. I stress about what to wear."

The class livened up, some of them hooting at her confession's graphic nature.

"I mean, no one has it one hundred percent easy. No one's totally perfect," she continued, "but why is it so easy for some and not others?"

In his own way, Dewey knew exactly what she was talking about. He'd felt the same throughout high school and even years before that. In his mind, he was only average, and apparently not even that in the eyes of Stephanie Hollowell back in high school who, when she found out Dewey was going to ask her to the homecoming dance, jammed a note through his yellow locker vent on a Friday afternoon with the words, in big bubble letters, *Not in a Million Years.*

If he'd only had better clothes, more muscle and clearer skin, he thought, then Stephanie might have said *yes.* Might have. And then they would have gone to homecoming, and maybe started going together, eventually meeting at the mall for Applebee's and a movie, then fumbling around in the dark at her house when her parents were away. He would have had it so easy, he thought.

"Mr. Cellars? Mr. Cellars?" Dewey looked up to find Dr. Berrygood standing in front of his desk. The room had almost emptied. "Class dismissed, Mr. Cellars. We seem to have lost you in a daydream."

"Sorry, I got distracted. Is there homework?"

"No, you've got the weekend off." Dr. Berrygood leaned over and straightened the desk next to him. "Hope to see you in the graveyard."

"What?" said Dewey.

"The church fundraiser—remember?"

"Of course, sure, thanks."

Fearing he might miss Mary Pate and Radford, Dewey rushed into the hall, down the stairs and pushed through the Maybank herd who were patting themselves down in search of cigarettes.

* * *

The herringbone brick promenade leading to the rear of Randolph Hall had very little traffic, clearing Dewey's path to the Yard and Lodge, where he and Mary Pate had agreed to meet. His heart began to pound. When he saw her, he ran to her side.

"I got here a little early," she said, standing in the shade of the archway.

"No problem. I was thinking I was going to be late," said Dewey. "Thanks again for setting this up."

"Sure. It'll be good to see Radford again instead of from just across campus."

Dewey nodded while loosening the straps on his backpack. "I meant to ask—do your mother and his mother ever talk or see each other anymore?"

"Sometimes. Christmas and Easter. That sort of thing."

"Too bad, really—from your ancestor who left you all that money so you could go here for free to your mom and aunt getting in that big fight and dividing the family."

The sun was high overhead. Dewey moved backward out of the archway to feel its rays.

"You should see her debutante picture. She wore a big white dress with a beautiful neckline. She could put any of the girls around here to shame." Mary Pate stepped further back into the archway, so the shade covered her almost entirely.

Dewey tried imagining Mary Pate's mom as a debutante. "It must have been tough to be shoved out of the family like that," he said.

"Still hurts her." Mary Pate wrapped one arm across her waist and let the other hang down in front of her showing her blue-purple veins. "In the summertime all mama does is sit on the porch and tend to her bougainvilleas and listen to the cicadas. Sometimes she'll light up a cigarette."

The Yard was getting busier, with students coming from all directions, many of them headed toward the cafeteria for lunch. Dewey searched for Radford among them.

"How's Alex?" said Mary Pate.

"I guess he's fine. Sleeps a lot," said Dewey.

"Did he tell you I dropped by?"

"Yeah. I meant to tell you thanks."

"For what?"

"For dropping by. It was nice." Still no sign of Radford. There was nothing for Dewey to do but wait. "Did you hear about the big storm down in the Caribbean?" he said.

"I heard something about it on the news last week," said Mary Pate. "Why?"

"They say it's getting bigger and heading toward the southeast coast. Do you think it'll be bad?"

A huge flock of red-winged blackbirds from a treetop scattered, spooking everyone.

"Most of the time you just hunker down and let them do their thing—wind, rain, you know," she said.

They both gazed at the cistern. Dewey imagined Radford magically appearing out of nowhere, the same way he had on George Street.

Mary Pate saw Dewey look at his watch. "Honestly, I don't even know if he's really coming or not, Dew. He said he would. Maybe I shouldn't have tried arranging this."

Dewey noticed Mary Pate's expression had gone from expectant to guarded. "Is it like him to no-show?" he said.

"I mean, he probably just forgot, and he's probably off riding his bike somewhere around town. Sometimes he just goes off into his own little world. Maybe we can try again another time." Mary Pate released her arm from around her waist like she wanted to go.

"Okay, if you say so." Dewey cinched the straps to his backpack and gave one last look at the throng of students in the Yard. "So, what do we do now? Head back to the dorm?"

"Maybe we can just hang out together, if you don't have anything else planned." Mary Pate stepped closer to Dewey, so they looked more than just friends. Dewey tried inching away. "I'm really sorry, Dew."

"Me too, but don't worry about it. You tried your best. Another time." Dewey felt disappointed. He'd counted on this moment to get in front of Radford, get his attention, and be someone worth remembering, and now it seemed his chance was gone. Not even the slightest sign of Radford.

In some ways he felt like he and Mary Pate might be part of some elaborate ruse, like Radford might be watching from a window from Towell Library or Randolph Hall. Dewey couldn't resist looking at both buildings hoping he might detect curtains rustling or a window blind askance.

"Okay, let's walk down King Street and check out some shops," said Dewey. "It'll kill some time."

"That would be nice," said Mary Pate. "But do you think I'm dressed for it?"

"You're fine, Mary Pate. Really, you're fine. Okay?"

The two of them trekked out in the soft afternoon light. Across the street a long line had formed outside the cafeteria on George Street, where pretty people with bright smiles in fall fashions came and went.

CHAPTER 19

It had rained all night, leaving city streets puddled and nearly half the Market flooded up to the ankle. It was heavy, tropical rain that pounded the dorm's tin roof. Dewey sat up and looked out into the courtyard. The crepe myrtle blossoms, reduced to pink globules, were drenched in water, the weight of which bent and forced them almost to the ground. The tabby concrete had lost its dusty, beachy glow and now just seemed like wet cardboard.

Alex's bed was empty, and he was nowhere in sight. If he'd left early, Dewey hadn't heard him. His absence was a little strange, however, since Dewey had always known him to sleep late.

He quickly dressed and headed out into the pouring rain wearing a blue Brooks Brothers all-season coat. With an outer shell and bulky insulation for bitter cold, the thick, almost knee-length coat could be modified for spring and fall by unzipping the sleeves, effectively creating a quilted ski vest. Dewey loved the jacket because it was unique, and no one else on campus had one. He felt good sporting it down St. Philip Street past the Simons Center, where he nodded at André the Giant, still plastered to the corner of the smoky pane of glass.

Dewey entered the Yard through an arched entryway on one of the far walls close to the dorm. It provided only momentarily relief from the rain, however, with Dewey quickly re-emerging on the other side onto the herringbone brick path leading to Towell Library.

He thought the Library looked sad in the rain, as it highlighted all the building's imperfections—cracks and chips in the walls, and dark green mold next to the downspouts.

Standing outside on the steps was Ms. Tilley. "Well, hey there, Mr. Dewey," she said, giving him a big hug.

"Hey, Ms. Tilley," said Dewey. Her hug had been a welcome surprise.

"I understand you're here to shadow someone so you can be a tour guide too," said Ms. Tilley. "Lucious called me to tell you he was sorry he couldn't be here to meet you. His mother fell ill last night. Wait here while I go get the sweet, young thang you're scheduled to shadow."

Dewey looked up at the mezzanine, where he'd met with Lucious just a few days before, when it was sunny, and the jasmine scented the air. Then he looked behind him to the small office where he'd first interviewed. Two upholstered chairs, a small coffee table, a desk and book cabinet. Exactly how he remembered it.

"Here she is, Dewey. Here's who you'll shadow today." Ms. Tilley had returned with a girl about his same age, another college student, with red, curly hair. "Meet Liza, Dewey. Liza, this is Dewey."

They greeted one another, with Liza smiling softly. Dewey smiled back. She was beautiful in an earthy way, a girl who didn't care if she showered or not but could still show up beautiful.

Liza gazed beyond Dewey to a dozen or more moms, dads and high schoolers who had come in out of the rain and assembled near the door. "Welcome to the college," she belted. "Sorry for such nasty weather."

With help from Miss Tilley, Liza funneled the group out the front door, with Dewey following close behind.

"We're one of the oldest colleges in America," she said on the way out.

Outside, the rain had gotten heavier, as Liza gathered the group close to the cistern and started her script. With many having deployed their umbrellas, the small, huddled group looked and moved like a big box turtle, every now and then a head or two peeking out to see or hear better.

"Since its construction in the 1820s, Randolph Hall has served as one of the college's main academic buildings," said Liza. "Latin and Greek were required way back then. The building's architecture is mostly Greek Revival."

Liza, whose maroon and white umbrella had a big, leaping cougar on it, directed the group under the building's portico and asked if anyone had questions.

"Hey, what year are you?" said a girl a bit younger than Liza. "And what made you want to go here?"

Liza tipped her umbrella back, so her round, freckled face was in full view. "Pre-med," she said, smirking. "Actually, that's what everybody here says, but it's not true." The big box turtle chuckled. "People come here for lots of reasons. For me, it was just a magical place. How 'bout you, Dew? You're the newbie here."

Liza's question surprised Dewey, and so did her abbreviating his name. He was, after all, just there to observe. All the same, it made him feel good. Before he could get anything out, she tried to clarify things. "Dewey's shadowing me today. He can probably tell you why he decided on the college."

"Well, I was going to say pre-med, but Liza beat me to it," said Dewey, trying to preserve the light mood. The big box turtle faintly chuckled. This time, however, it was more of a groan. Dewey tried thinking of something quick to say.

"I guess it was the weather. I'm from Ohio, and the weather there is always …"

"Shitty," said a youthful-sounding voice in the group.

"I was going to say 'cold,'" said Dewey, homing in on a boy in a blue baseball cap.

"Same thing," said the boy. "I'm from Ohio, too. Weather pretty much sucks." The boy's parents turned their eyes at him to try and shush him.

Liza, her umbrella still tilted back and her freckles keen against the dreary rain, looked at Dewey. "Anything else, Dew?" she said. "Anything else stand out about coming here?"

At first, as he had so many times before when asked what drew him to the college, Dewey hesitated, but this time something inside him seemed to let go.

"Well, I will say it was a tour just like this one that convinced me to come here. Like most things, you see something you like about a place, and you just want to be there. You can't really say why."

He thought back to Dr. DuGow's class and how he'd stopped just short of revealing Radford. Liza looked at Dewey, as if to hurry him along. "It was a boy on a bike who brought me here, a beautiful boy." Dewey couldn't believe what came out of his mouth. The big box turtle remained silent, not sure what to say. Liza looked like she wanted to apologize and start over.

The rain came down harder again, as the tour moved on, with Liza leading the group through the entrance of Randolph Hall, emerging out the back side and eventually walking over to Sotille House, a grand house with gable roofs, turrets, double-tiered porches, stained glass and elaborate spindles. It was painted yellow and surrounded by a wrought-iron fence.

"Does anyone actually live here?" said one of the parents, poking her head out.

"Yes, it's the Honors dorm for girls," said Liza.

Just then, two girls with arms full of books exited Sotille House and walked onto the promenade. They looked rather plain, thought Dewey. Their raincoat hoods pulled up over their heads, they almost looked like nuns, as they scurried across the brick pathway to dodge the rain.

Next, Liza guided the group toward the grassy median between Maybank and the library, an area of boxwoods and bike racks. With the steady rain, the Maybank herd had moved inside, leaving the building's porch empty.

"Lots of general humanities classes take place here," said Liza, pointing her umbrella toward Maybank.

Dewey looked up at Maybank's windows caked with salt. Like New Dorm, Maybank had a stucco exterior. It was much smaller and less daunting than Physician's Auditorium, with small stretches of hallway, and classrooms off to the sides and bathrooms at either end. During class changes, students passed back and forth. He enjoyed these moments, as he brushed shoulders with pretty girls from the Maybank herd.

Liza raised her hand in the air to direct the group's attention to the library. Dewey recalled how he and Dewey had climbed the granite stairs to the library's entrance the week before, and how Alex had checked out the books on horror masks, while Dewey had walked out with Dr. Lyman's address. He peered into the building's front windows hoping he would catch a glimpse of the short, red-headed man at the reference desk. He felt bad about how he and Alex had dismissed him, despite his genuine attempt at kindness.

"The library is home to literally thousands of books and stuff," said Liza, as if searching for more to say. Her words left the big box turtle staring up glassy eyed at the tops of the building's impressive arches, as if something more noteworthy might rain down.

With the sun beginning to poke through, Liza led the group onto a sidewalk adjacent to Calhoun Street and, wrapping around the back side of campus, eventually turned on to St. Philip Street past New Dorm only to stop in front of College Lodge. An old hotel with wraparound balconies and peninsula views in every direction, College Lodge had been converted into a six-story, co-ed dorm.

"Definitely the coolest dorm on campus," said Liza, pointing to the Lodge's first-floor balcony, where a group of students waved.

Gradually, Liza and the group moseyed up St. Philip Street, stopping at Simons Center. "I can't exactly tell you what goes on in there. Something artsy-fartsy."

At the bottom corner of the windowpane, Dewey saw André who, in his mind, looked like he wanted to headbutt someone.

The rain had almost stopped, and with it the momentum of Liza's tour—her pace slowed, and she said less and less with each step, at one point stopping to look at her reflection in a puddle and stomp on it. Eventually, she and the group—their umbrellas mostly folded and looking less and less like the big box turtle of moments ago—had walked almost the entire length of St. Philip Street before turning back on to George Street and entering the Yard through Porter's Lodge.

"Well, that ends our tour," said Liza, as if she had somewhere else to be. "Any questions?"

The group had mostly disbanded, with some already off stretching and talking.

"Feel free to walk around," she said, half smiling at Dewey.

Then she folded her umbrella—collapsing the ferocious image of the big, leaping Cougar—and sauntered off.

CHAPTER 20

Dewey didn't bother going back into the Library to debrief with Ms. Tilley after Liza's tour. She was probably busy filing papers anyway, he thought, craning her long neck over the cabinet to find the next student folder. Instead, he walked to Coming Street on the other side of Sotille House, intending to head back to New Dorm along Calhoun. Coming Street was a long, one-way street running parallel to King, with parking meters and small trees at regular intervals along high, granite curbs. It was a lonely section of campus, thought Dewey, a sort of boundary between college and the real world.

The lower part of Coming Street was home to a few sororities, which Dewey had heard could be ruthless with their pledges. He'd heard one account where a pledge was blind-folded, stripped naked and put in the middle of a room flanked by sisters, each equipped with a Sharpie marker. Each sister took a turn circling the pledge's physical imperfections—too fat here, not toned enough there—until a few weeks later the pledge had a nervous breakdown and had to take a leave of absence. Dewey didn't know whether to believe the story or not.

Walking down Coming, with its hazy diminishing point that was Calhoun Street and its dreamy, yellow-leafed trees, Dewey didn't think it was possible. But, then again, in some unspoken, unseen way crucial to maintaining the balance of beauty on the peninsula, maybe it was. Maybe such sacrifices had to be made—it was the price of beauty.

Dewey stopped at the corner of Coming and Calhoun and watched as a group of teenagers from a nearby high school raced out the front door. Much to his surprise, he spotted Alex walking in his direction wearing blue, knee-length athletic shorts, white running shoes and a green tee-shirt. Dewey flagged him down.

"How's it hangin', Dew?" said Alex, cupping his genitals and smirking.

"Pretty good," said Dewey. "Just got back from observing a tour. How about you?"

"Not so good. I'm headed over to the dean's office. Only two weeks in, and I'm already fucked."

"What do you mean?"

"I'm failing Algebra, and it's not even the hard Algebra."

"Does your dad know?"

"Hell no," said Alex. "You heard him at dinner. He already thinks I'm a slacker."

"Well, at least your mom still loves her little *radish*," said Dewey.

"Fuck you, man." Alex flipped him off.

Both of them laughed.

"So, what's up with the shorts and running shoes?" said Dewey.

"You've inspired me. I'm going to hit the weight room on the way back." Alex sucked in his gut, striking a muscular but awkward pose.

"Good for you." Dewey reached out and took hold of Alex's shoulder and squeezed it. It was doughy and without tone. It was not a shoulder attached to a strong back.

With the sun overhead, it was getting hot, but it would soon cool. It was summer but no longer summer. Leaves on the trees were beginning to turn, and a lonely, desolate feeling was settling in around the city. *Summer* Charleston was giving way to *winter* Charleston which would soon find its residents bundled in fleece jackets and wool sweaters dodging and denying the brisk, bitter air.

"So, where are you off to?" said Alex.

"Back to the dorm for a bit, then over to the Kappa House for a mixer," said Dewey.

There was silence. Alex sighed, let his gut out, and his shoulders slumped.

"Well, I guess I should get going." Dewey cinched his backpack straps and looked up at the traffic light.

"Better lays, better days."

"Thanks."

Alex walked away, then turned around. "Hey, man, wish me luck."

"Good luck, Alex. I'm sure things will be fine. They know who you are and that you belong here."

Alex resumed his course, passing another group of high school students who in their sea of tartan plaid seemed to swallow him whole, making him more anonymous than he already was.

When Dewey got back to the dorm, he flung his backpack on his bed amid a swirl of flannel sheets and a down comforter. He had slept on these sheets back home on humid Sunday evenings when the carillon in the nearby park rang out with the doxology amid fireflies and cicadas. Threadbare in places, they now kept him warm on cooler nights.

It was almost noon. He decided to skip lunch and catch up on some reading, then dinner at the cafeteria and, finally, the Kappa mixer. Dewey was a little anxious not knowing what to expect, but he figured it would be similar to the freshman mixer at the Stern Center.

Dewey knew he would once again have to borrow from Alex's wardrobe. He was ashamed, but he knew his wardrobe just wouldn't cut it for this important event, and he had no way at this point of buying anything new. He thought of the perfectly chiseled mannequin swimming in a sea of fabric at the men's store—if only he could look like that, everything would be just fine.

* * *

The three-story Kappa House stood illuminated against the night, its open windows and bright interior lights clearly visible in the darkness. Lean, athletic figures danced, drank and laughed in the first-floor parlor, where Dewey and the other pledges had sat nervously just a few nights before at the first pledge education meeting. Some of the brothers stood on the front porch with beers in hand. Dewey walked up and greeted them.

"What's up, pledge?" said one of the brothers who had been at the pledge meeting.

"Not much," said Dewey. "I'm here for the mixer. Where do you need me?"

"Just go inside. Someone will tell you what to do."

Dewey nodded and walked into the foyer, where after a few minutes another brother came toward him and spoke.

"Where's your pledge pin?" he said.

Dewey frantically reached for his shirt collar trying to feel for his pin. Nothing. Next, he searched his pants pocket. He found what felt like a small pebble. He recognized its shape and contours and sighed with relief. He pulled it from his pocket and attached it to his shirt collar.

"Make sure you have that on at all times, dickweed. Got it?" said the brother.

"Got it. Thanks," said Dewey. He couldn't help but chuckle under his breath. At least he'd risen above douchebag.

In the middle of the parlor, not far from the mantle above which hung the composite, was a giant keg of beer. A brother in khakis with his shirt sleeves rolled up stood next to it while talking to a girl in a light green sundress and short, brown cardigan sweater.

"Hey, pledge, come here," he said. "Stay here and pour." He handed Dewey the keg pump.

All this way for a keg, thought Dewey. The Greek Life rep, the one who'd given him, Alex and the others a "thumbs up" the night of rush, had made fraternity life sound so romantic. But if it meant getting closer to Radford, then he'd stand and pour beer as long as they told him to. He watched as the brother and the girl in the green sundress disappeared into the crowd.

Dewey noticed the house seemed to have been hastily cleaned like on the first night of rush—a few brothers with bottles of Windex and Lysol in a blitzkrieg of dusting and mopping. Added to this was the cold, dark, dank smell from the crawlspace below, mixed with the scent of hops and barley. The house seemed to have its own vibration, permeating everything from the old, tired couches and chairs to the ornate ceiling and window molding. From where Dewey stood, he could see up the crowded, two-story staircase. A short hallway at the very top of the stairs exited out the back onto a porch and a small brick building. The parlor was heating up with moving bodies, and Dewey was getting thirsty. He reached for a stack of cups and poured a cold beer. He'd barely touched the stuff in high school, only the occasional sip, or a glass of wine, at special occasions.

"Fill 'er up," said a brother who presented his red Solo cup.

"Sure," said Dewey.

"What's your name, pledge?"

"Dewey."

"Where ya from, Dewey?"

"Ohio."

"Goddamn, everybody here's from Ohio." The brother gulped back his beer, then gazed back at Dewey. "Okay, pledge, time for some good ole Kappa trivia. What do the daggers on the pledge pin mean?"

The question caught Dewey off guard, though he was fully aware that he could be approached at any time for this information. Dewey looked down at his pledge pin hoping for some kind of hint.

"It means to guard," said Dewey, still craning his neck down at his pin.

"Guard what?" The brother held out his cup for more beer.

Dewey hadn't read much, if any, of the Kappa pledge handbook, so he guessed.

"The daggers guard the *mind?*"

"Wrong, pledge. I'll give you a second chance."

Dewey thought hard, but it was futile. "I don't know."

The brother laughed. "I'll give you half credit. The daggers are the guardian of youth. Don't forget it. Now more beer."

"Thanks for giving me a break," said Dewey.

Dewey poured him another beer. He felt a wave of relief come over him, as the brother disappeared into the crowd.

As if out of thin air, another red Solo cup appeared as did the scent of ligustrum. The slender, caramel-colored hand that had just proffered the plastic, red cup felt familiar to Dewey. As he looked up and reached for the unknown person's cup, an easy smile of someone who looked like they'd just walked off the beach greeted him—it was Radford.

"Are you a pledge or just some random guy pouring?" said Radford.

"I … I'm a pledge," said Dewey, stuttering and trying to compose himself.

"Oh, good, I've been trying to track as many of you down as I can. I'm Radford Gaillard, head of pledge education. You can call me Rad."

"Good meeting you, Rad. I'm Dewey Cellars. I think we were supposed to have met you at last week's pledge education meeting."

"Yeah, sorry about that. Something came up last-minute. Plus, I'm easily distracted."

Dewey felt bad knowing Radford was probably lying about his whereabouts during the recent pledge education meeting. Nothing, in fact, had come up last-minute, thought Dewey. Instead, Radford had probably escaped, fleeing into the marsh or riding his bike on some lonely city street like Mary Pate had said.

Radford, still waiting for Dewey to fill his cup, leaned into Dewey so he could hear him over the loud music.

"So, what brought you to the college?" he said.

For anyone else, it would have been an easy answer, a sentence at most. But how could Dewey ever begin to explain that the very face opposite him had brought him? How could he ever put it in words?

"Pre-med," said Dewey.

Radford smiled. "I don't believe it. Nobody here knows who they are or what they want to be. They're just talking out their ass. Most people here talk out their ass."

Dewey thought about the girl with brown hair from Hilton Head who he'd overheard at the freshman mixer at the Stern Center. How foolish to have believed her.

"Yeah, I guess you're right. How about you?" said Dewey, well knowing Radford was on scholarship at the college. But in some strange way he wanted to hear Radford tell it. For just a brief moment, Dewey felt like he was finally an insider, like he finally had the upper hand.

"I was away at boarding school and missed the place," said Radford, "so I came back. There's just something about Charleston—how it moves and smells, the beauty of it all, really."

Dewey was taken aback, though he was quite sure he'd hear at least some mention of the Confederate ancestor and the scholarship. Maybe even some mention of Mary Pate.

"Come again?" Radford cupped his ear in Dewey's direction. "It's so loud in here."

"Oh, nothing, I didn't say anything. But I did get a chance to meet your cousin. She's very nice."

"Who?"

The music in the room got louder. More co-eds trailed through the front door.

"Your cousin here at the college, Mary Pate—I met her at move-in." Dewey was almost yelling.

Perplexed, Radford uncupped his ear and stood back. "I don't have a cousin at the college, and no cousins by that name."

Had he misheard Radford? Maybe it was the loud music. He begged Radford's pardon. "I'm sorry, I don't think I heard you. Did you say you *didn't* have a cousin here at the college?"

"Yeah, that's right—it's just me."

Dewey, pale and wide-eyed, looked back at the composite above the mantel, then to the line of people walking into the house. Why would Radford say such a thing? Was Radford mad at Mary Pate? Had the conflict between the families grown so grave that he was denying her existence altogether?

Dewey watched as Radford called out to some people passing by, laughing and raising his cup. He felt things begin to move in slow motion, as he tried looking for clues on Radford's face that might lead to proof of the Confederate ancestor and his relation to Mary Pate. Dewey inspected every groove of Radford's face, hopeful for some expression, imperfection, even battle scar, reminiscent—however impossible—of Antietam, Shiloh or Vicksburg. But, alas, nothing that would show how and from where this young man came to be. It was almost like Radford had dropped out of the sky. One thing was certain, however: Radford was in the club. Deep in. No wonder he came back to Charleston. It was safe here, but it was more than just safety. For Radford, there was no other place to go.

Dewey suddenly felt something cold and foamy on his hand. His attention had drifted from the keg, and beer was spilling everywhere.

"Whoa!" said Radford, fleeing the keg, as if it had exploded.

"I'm so sorry," said Dewey, frantic.

"It's okay. It's easy to get carried away with these things."

At that moment an entourage of co-eds in khaki and white surrounded Radford, as if to steal him away.

"Well, good meeting you, Rad. Guess I'll see you at the next pledge meeting," said Dewey, holding the pump hose up high like a snake.

"Yeah, it'll be a big one. They'll be assigning big brothers. It's a pretty big deal," said Radford, his right hand being tugged at by a beautiful girl with long, blonde hair.

"Great." Dewey sounded let down, in part because his brief exchange with Radford had ended but also because mention of big brother selection made him nervous.

With that, Radford set his plastic cup down near the keg, nodded and smiled, as the colorful, laughing entourage and the girl with long, blonde hair swept him away.

Then, suddenly, from behind Dewey came a voice.

"You're done, pledge." It was the brother in khakis with his shirt sleeves rolled up, the one who had originally assigned him the job of pouring.

"Excuse me?" said Dewey.

"You can go now. Another pledge is coming." The brother pointed to a young man Dewey knew from pledge education who was sporting a vintage hunting vest, complete with shell pockets and a rear game bag. It seemed odd to wear to a fraternity party, thought Dewey, but all the brothers seemed to like it by the way they had remarked on it.

"Can I stick around for a while?" said Dewey.

"You can do whatever the fuck you want, pledge, I don't care. Just hand over the hose." The brawny brother half-wrestled the black snake from Dewey's hand and gave it to the pledge wearing the hunting vest who was sweating profusely.

Dewey stepped back into the crowd and decided to explore the rest of the house, beginning with the second floor. He squeezed by a group of people on the stairs, until he reached a long hallway of bedrooms. Dewey stopped and peered into one of them. It had high ceilings and a window that looked out onto the fraternity house next door. A blue carpet remnant covered half the floor on which lay small piles of shorts, shirts, jeans and a crumpled blazer. The walls were sheet rocked and painted beige. A banner with the Kappa House's crest hung in one corner. A bobblehead figure ripping off his shirt to reveal a Superman shield sat on a desk, smiling and content. A cheap cherry-scented air freshener hung from the fan above.

Dewey heard footsteps and peered down the hall. A brother wearing a KT shirt emerged. At his side a girl with a pixie haircut wearing tight Guess jeans and a scoop-neck tee. When they stopped, she was buttoning her jeans with a look in her eye that nothing had just happened.

"No pledges on the second floor," said the brother. "Let me see your pin."

"Sorry, I was pouring beer downstairs, and they told me to go, so I figured I'd just have a look around." Dewey reached for his shirt collar and pulled on his pledge pin with his thumb.

"Okay, good job." The brother looked at the girl beside him, then spoke to Dewey again. "Name one distinguished alum from this chapter."

"I don't know," said Dewey. "In all honesty, I'm not that far in the pledge book yet."

He was slowly beginning to resent the brother. His attitude. His clothes. His very presence on the old, squeaky hardwood floors that now supported their different weight. Whereas he'd felt an insider just a short while ago with his special knowledge of Radford, he now felt like an outsider again. Envy for the girl opposite him was the only thing he felt.

"No excuses," said the brother. "I'm losing my patience, pledge. Give me a famous alum now."

A few seconds passed, until the brother brusquely offered up the answer himself.

"Remember the name Lyman. Still lives here in town apparently. Has a house loaded with priceless art."

Once again, Dewey couldn't believe what he was hearing. Could it be the Joseph Lyman he'd met at Poogan's Porch? The same Joseph Lyman who'd looked at his eye floater? The same man he was scheduled to have dinner with the next night?

Dr. Lyman mentioned nothing about having been an alum when he and Dewey spoke at Poogan's Porch. And there was no mention when Dewey went to see him at his office. Dr. Lyman had revealed nothing; he had simply blended into his surroundings. Why had he been so mysterious, thought Dewey.

"Better start reading that pledge book," said the brother, looking back over his shoulder at Dewey.

"Yeah, I'll look more into it. Promise." Dewey walked back downstairs to the first floor, where the pledge from Florida, sweating profusely through his hunting vest, still stood pouring beer. He looked over at Dewey and smiled, which made Dewey feel not quite as alone. Dewey, feeling he'd done his pledge duty, headed for the front door.

"Where ya' going, pledge?" said one of the brothers on the porch, as Dewey was leaving.

"Just going around the back to take a smoke," said Dewey.

"But you don't look like you smoke. You're too clean-cut."

"Well, looks can be deceiving." Dewey gave a little laugh, hoping to slide by.

"Yeah, there's a lot of that going around," said the brother, slurring his speech and tipping back his beer. Within minutes, the brother had found another pledge to occupy his time.

Dewey shuffled down the front steps of Kappa House onto the yard and crossed over Wentworth. He looked back at the house. Though generally unimpressed by fraternity life so far, he felt resolved to stick it out if it meant befriending Radford. If he did everything just perfectly, he might even get Radford as a big brother. But he would have to wait, as the carefree, late-night frolicking across the street made Sunday somehow seem years away.

CHAPTER 21

Dewey walked from Wentworth Street onto King Street, as he headed back to the dorm. The sidewalks were busy with kids he knew from the dorm and class and, occasionally, a handful of cadets from the nearby military college. They wore their summer leave uniforms—gray trousers, starched white tops, white service caps and black shoes. They seemed like regular college kids, thought Dewey—laughing and talking loudly, joking with each other—apart from the fact they went to a military college. In fact, Dewey thought they might have actually had it easier than he did, as their uniform made for only one identity—a cadet. None probably suffered the daily anxiety of having to decide what to wear or wondering if one was in or out of fashion.

As he walked by Sharky's, he glanced inside. To his great surprise, he saw Alex and Mary Pate sitting in a booth. Alex must have asked her out. Why hadn't he mentioned it? Dewey paused for a moment near the restaurant's front door and watched. They were seated not far from where Dewey sat for lunch earlier in the week and had overheard the two girls talking about the party at Wadmalaw. Mary Pate wore a yellow, sleeveless blouse with a rhinestone palm tree on it and a jean jacket, her hair in a giant up-do. Alex wore khaki shorts and the same red and blue striped polo shirt that Dewey had secretly borrowed for the first pledge meeting. It was ill-fitting and draped awkwardly over his torso. Hunched over, Dewey thought he looked like an old man.

Dewey watched as Alex spoke, raising his hands and swatting the air. Her hands rested politely on the table. Behind the rhinestone palm tree on her shirt, Dewey noticed the gentle curve of her small breasts. Not a Kiawah girl, but still attractive to him in ways he did not fully understand. She'd put her hand on his knee after all, a moment Dewey had not forgotten. He knew she liked him. But what if she also liked Alex? He felt ashamed to admit he was better than Alex with more to offer. He might have not had the polos, chinos and braided belts, but he did have looks. Dewey watched Alex and Mary Pate for a few more minutes, until a large group of tourists exiting Sharky's made him abandon his lookout post.

But it was for the better, he thought, as watching any more of Alex and Mary Pate made him feel lonely. With New Dorm's roof in sight and thoughts of Saturday's dinner with Dr. Lyman on his mind, Dewey crossed over Calhoun into the courtyard, passing between the rows of wilting crepe myrtles.

* * *

That night, Dewey dreamed he was back on John's Island with Desirée and the revelers. A roaring bonfire burned, and the air was thick with smoke.

"You done returned," said Desirée.

"Yeah," said Dewey. "But where are the others?"

"They run off, but they be back. Never go far from their nature, you know?" Desirée looked out past the green and brown marsh grass, as if trying to find them. Nearby, the two black men in green, knee-high boots wearing khakis and bright red flannel shirts heaved oysters up onto a rusty, metal grate laid across the bonfire.

"Bring your ear close, boy," she said. "De mouth say more than duh heart can feel."

"I'm not sure what you mean." Dewey could see his face reflected in Desirée's blue-green eyes.

"It mean dat your heart is deceivin' you. You chasin' sumpin' deep down ain't right for you. It's a storm brewin', boy."

Desirée circled her hand in the air, summoning the hungry herd of revelers back from the marsh. Dewey recognized their perfect, tan faces from his excursions around town—doctors, lawyers, shop keepers, waitresses and artists.

The bonfire roared. Giant shards of firelight cut across their faces. They looked like the horror masks in the books Alex had checked out of the library. The revelers crept closer and closer, until—in a sequence of events he could not explain—Dewey felt their crushing weight on top of him.

"Dude, wake up, you're having some kind of dream," said Alex, who was tugging hard on his shoulder. "Plus, you're late for class."

Dewey sat up and rubbed his eyes. He felt his heart race. "What time is it?"

"Close to nine."

"Shit. Dr. Freeport."

"Who?"

"First period. He's so nice. I can't be late." Dewey sprinted to the bathroom to get ready.

"Psych! Just kiddin'—it's Saturday."

"Dickhead. Why'd you do that?"

"Just to fuck with you."

Dewey fell back in bed and put a hand on his forehead. "Uncool, Alex. Very uncool."

"Whatever. I thought it was funny. Anyway, I'm headed out. Gotta hit up the library and return these books, then head over to the registrar's for drop/add."

"Why?"

"Remember when I had to go see the dean about my grades?"

"Yeah."

"Well, he recommended I drop Algebra and pick up something in humanities."

"So, what did you get?"

"Human Sexuality."

"You're kidding me?"

"No. Actually it was the only humanities class still open. But, like I always say, 'Later days, better lays.' Meet you for lunch in a little while at Mistral's in the Market?"

"Sure, I think I can pull myself together by then."

"Cool," said Alex, heading out.

Dewey recalled his dream about Desirée, the second one in as many weeks. What did she mean by a deceiving heart and a brewing storm? He didn't feel deceptive. He felt he acted the same with everybody. How would she know anyway?

Then he remembered Alex and Mary Pate at Sharky's. He couldn't believe this hadn't been the first thing out of his mouth upon waking. Hoping to catch Alex, he spun around and yelled into the common room, "Hey, dude, was that you and Mary Pate at Sharky's last night?"

Dewey got no response. Just silence and juice boxes on the shelf. Wiping his eyes again, he looked out the window into the courtyard. A new month, September, had begun. He looked up at the big, dark clouds, fearing what would happen if they all let loose at once.

CHAPTER 22

The note read, *Yacht Club, 7 pm.*

"Thanks," said Dewey to the girl behind the front desk at New Dorm who had handed him the piece of paper on his way to meet Alex for lunch.

"You're welcome," said the girl. "Sorry there's not more. He didn't say much over the phone. Just said Dewey Cellars and to take down this message. Kinda' weird." The girl put her Walkman headphones back on and continued studying.

Dewey walked out the front entrance and looked across St. Philip Street at the Goodie House diner, where a line had formed. Through a side window with green trim, Dewey could see two men—one big, one small—wearing soda jerk hats and white aprons. One took orders at the counter, while the other flipped burgers and hashbrowns. Opposite them was a counter full of students on swivel seats talking and laughing while drinking bottomless cups of coffee from mugs with green banded patterns at the top.

He crossed over Calhoun and headed for the Market. By now, King Street bustled with restaurant brunchers and window shoppers. As Dewey headed further into Lower King past Woolworth's and the Omni, he felt the joy as when he first encountered Angel Boy. The further he walked down King, the freer and easier he felt. The rustling palms, pastel-colored houses—pale blues and seafoam greens luring him toward a bright blue horizon.

Dewey felt someone behind him, bringing his daydreaming to an abrupt end.

"Hey, Dew, saw you from way back there, so I ran to catch up," said Alex, out of breath. "How's it hanging?"

"Pretty good. Just walking down to meet you for lunch. Glad you caught up. How'd drop/add go?"

"No biggie. I was able to get into the class."

"Did you tell your parents?"

"Nope."

"Why don't you just tell your mom? She seems like she'd understand."

"Maybe, but then my dad would find out one way or another, and that would be all-around bad."

Dewey and Alex walked down Market Street alongside the entrance to the Omni, eventually depositing them in front of Market Hall.

"So, how was your workout yesterday?" said Dewey.

"Good. I did back and bis," said Alex.

Dewey looked puzzled. "Back and bis?"

"That's short for back and biceps. The muscle mag I'm reading says do chest and tris one day, back and bis the other." Alex flexed his right bicep.

"What's the weight room look like?"

"It's a hole in the wall. Really small, but not too many people using it."

"Are you trying to get buff?" Dewey looked at Alex, thinking of him wandering around the weight room.

"Not exactly. I just want to get a little bigger and look good like you."

"Thanks, but as far as buff or good-looking, I have a way to go in that department." The coiffed mannequin in the storefront window crossed Dewey's mind.

"Well, all the girls at Mary Pate's little soirée last week thought you were hot."

Dewey opened the door for Alex. The restaurant was dark inside. The hostess seated them near a window. They ordered water, as a waitress handed them giant, laminated menus with red vinyl trim.

"Beats the cafeteria, huh?" said Alex, the menus so big they hid his head from across the table.

"Yeah, it's nice to have a break. I was getting all granola-ed out."

The waitress wore black pants and a white blouse. "*Bonjour*," she said. "May I take your order?"

"French toast for me," said Alex.

"Make it two," said Dewey.

The waitress turned and shuffled away.

Alex rested his elbows on the table. "So how was the mixer?"

"It was okay. I had to work the keg for a while, which I totally fucked up on and spilled beer."

"Bet that sucked? Meet anyone cool?"

"Yeah, a few dudes, but I'm a pledge, and nobody really likes or talks to pledges."

Alex chuckled.

The wooden table they sat at was coated with polyurethane, which, like a microscope, magnified its imperfections—knots, splits, wormholes, and decay.

"But that'll change a bit tomorrow night." Dewey looked out the window onto the Market, where basket weavers, sitting on large, overturned buckets, were beginning their day's work.

"What's tomorrow night?" Alex had the same look in his eyes as he'd had when he asked what rush was.

"We get our big brothers. They mentor us for the semester."

"How do you get one?" Alex leaned across the table.

"I'm not exactly sure. I think they match you with someone who has the same personality."

"Are there any dudes you've seen that you think are a match? Anyone you'd like to be like?"

"A couple dudes seem pretty cool, but when it comes down to it, I think it's pretty random." Dewey knew well who he wanted his big brother to be but feared bringing Radford back up again. "Speaking of matches, what's up with you and Mary Pate?"

"How'd you find out?" Alex straightened up like he'd been accused.

"I saw y'all at Sharky's last night on my way home from Kappa House."

"Well, I finally got the balls to ask her out. I think she had a pretty good time."

Dewey remembered his and Alex's conversation back at the dorm about whether Mary Pate would say *yes* if he did ask her out.

"She asked about you and how y'all had gone to meet her cousin, or something," continued Alex. "Isn't he a Kappa, too?"

Dewey tried hiding his surprise. "Oh, yeah, Radford," he said. "He's a Kappa. I saw him last night. He's from the peninsula, too."

"Peninsula?" Alex raised his eyebrows and leaned back into the booth. "You're starting to talk like you're from here."

"I didn't mean it that way. It's just an expression I've heard locals use." Dewey wondered why would Mary Pate would ever mention her cousin—if he was her cousin at all—to Alex.

"Anyways, she said they were close but then something happened in the family. A disagreement or something."

"That's what she told me, too." Dewey brought his gaze back into the room.

He didn't know exactly how much Alex knew about Mary Pate's story. But not unlike his interaction with Radford at the frat party, Dewey reveled in the fact that he probably knew more than Alex, which made him feel he had power over him.

"I bet Radford's tagging every chic that comes through Porter's Lodge. I betcha he just lays in wait like a lion." Alex raised his hands, made two paws reminiscent of Clyde the Cougar and roared. Some people in a nearby booth looked at him.

"What makes you think that?" Dewey felt like coming to Radford's defense, but he didn't really know the truth about Radford, certainly not over the span of the last twenty-four hours. Maybe he wasn't into girls at all.

"All those pretty boys are like that. They could get any girl they wanted."

"Pretty boys?" Dewey tried pretending he didn't know what Alex was talking about.

"You should know. You're one of them."

"I don't know why you keep saying that, Alex. I've tried to ignore it but it's pissing me off."

"Because since the moment you got here, you've been in this, like, fog or something. I mean, look at you—you could be just like Radford, or whatever the fuck his name is."

That moment the waitress arrived holding two plates of French toast. "*Pour vous, monsieur,*" she said to Alex, handing him a plate. Then the same to Dewey. "Can I get y'all anything else?"

Dewey hoped Alex needed something more, as this would break up their conversation about Radford.

"I don't know why you continue to think of me as one of *them*, Alex," said Dewey. "I'm hardly model material. I mean, look at me. I look like someone's grandfather." Dewey looked down at his dowdy, pleated khakis, which ballooned just below the waist, and his brown LL Bean camp mocs.

"Do you have your student ID with you?" Alex cocked his head.

"Yeah, I got it." Dewey reached for his back pocket.

"Let me see." Alex stretched out his arm across the table.

Dewey handed Alex his ID who then held it up in front of him. In the upper left corner was a small, color headshot of Dewey smiling wearing a crewneck tee-shirt with his high school logo on the pocket.

"Look at yourself, Dew." Alex put a finger on Dewey's picture. "Why can't you see what others see? Blue eyes. Curls. Nice smile. An athlete. You fit right in with them. Now pass the goddamn syrup, and if you tell anyone what I just said, I'll fucking kill you."

Dewey slid the syrup across the polyurethane. "Thanks, but I don't feel that way. I've never felt like one of them."

"Well, you're a lot closer than I am." Alex lowered his head and with his fork swirled his syrup.

"But I want to be closer. I want to be in. I don't want to be just average." Dewey barely got the last sentence out before Alex interrupted.

"Average doesn't require much, Dew. You should try it."

"I don't mean it that way, Alex, you know I don't."

Dewey looked past Alex to a young couple that had walked in. She wore designer jeans with a hole ripped in one knee and a blue sweater draped around her shoulders. He wore khakis, a white Oxford and a waxed field jacket. Dewey tried not looking and sizing them up, but he couldn't resist.

"Well, I hope it works out," said Alex. "What's your plan?"

Dewey felt like an imposter. "I'm just concentrating on pledging for now." He watched Alex gulp down his French toast, a piece of which dropped from his mouth, brushing his chin and splashing onto his plate. "How's your French toast?"

"Good. I like it when they use Texas toast and put a scoop of butter on top. You know what they say about Texas, don't you?"

"No. What?"

"Nothing but steers and queers." Alex tilted his head back and laughed, drawing the attention of a nearby booth. "But seriously, I could just sit here all day and eat, and just daydream. Ya know, you were right—I am beginning to like this place."

A waitress passed by and refilled their water glasses.

"So, whatcha got going on today?" said Alex.

"Study, go for a run then dinner with Dr. Lyman," said Dewey.

"Who?"

"You know, the eye doctor."

"Why you having dinner with him?" Alex lapped up the rest of his syrup with his fork.

"I don't really know. He just called to check on my eye, and we got to talking. Kinda weird, but you know."

"Sure." Alex leaned in again.

"Apparently he's some kind of special Kappa alum."

"How would you know?"

"Well, I didn't, but then a brother quizzing me on Kappa history mentioned him."

"Why is he such a big wig?"

"Didn't say."

"Sounds a little bit fucked up."

"Maybe." Dewey could see Alex still pondering Dr. Lyman's invite. "So, what are you up to today?"

"Well, with the dean up my ass to get my grades up, I'll probably be in Maybank or the library."

"Sorry to hear that." It was another lucky break, thought Dewey, as Alex would again be away from the room, giving him a chance to go through his wardrobe.

"No biggie." Alex docked his fork on his plate.

Dewey motioned to their waitress who shuffled over. "L'addition s'il vous plaît?" he said.

"Oui, monsieur," she responded, smiling and laying the check on the table.

Dewey appreciated Alex's compliments—blue eyes and nice smile—but, as usual, he dismissed them. Something about the compliments angered him. He felt they put him on the same level with Alex, which he felt he was not. Radford didn't need compliments. He didn't need people telling him what he was or wasn't. Dewey wanted the same. He also wanted distance from Alex, for to be with him reminded him of who he really was.

They rose from their booth and headed for the exit. As they did, Alex stopped and pointed to a newspaper on the hostess stand with the headline, *Storm Gathers Momentum in Deep Atlantic.* "Did you hear about this?" said Alex.

"Yeah, the weatherman was talking about it all last week," said Dewey. "I mentioned it to Mary Pate, and she said it was probably nothing to worry about. Just some wind and rain."

"They sure don't have storms like that up in Raleigh." Alex lifted his arms above his head and circled them in the air like a storm.

Dewey laughed. "You don't see 'em much in Ohio, either."

The front-page story was accompanied by an inset map showing the Caribbean covered by huge, swirling clouds. Bright red arrows pointed to the storm's potential paths, one of which brought it ashore just above Charleston.

"Yeah, probably nothing," said Alex, glancing at the newspaper again.

Both of them walked out into the shards of bright light stretching across the Market. It was the busiest Dewey had ever seen it. Squinting, he swore he could almost see Desirée and the revelers off in the cool, bright distance. Then again, maybe it was just his floater.

* * *

Back at the dorm, Alex packed his book bag and headed for the library. Dewey heard the door slam, as he headed for the elevator.

Perfect, he thought, sitting on the edge of his bed looking over at Alex's wardrobe. He felt bad about what he was going to do, but at least with Alex gone and not likely to be back for some time, he could move slowly and without fear. Maybe even enjoy the act of becoming someone else.

He opened the wardrobe to find Alex's clothes piled high. A sock and some underwear tumbled onto the floor. Since his last visit, Dewey observed that Alex had moved his fall clothes to the center of the hanging rack, while pushing his summer clothes to the side. Fall's browns, reds, and oranges replaced summer's cool yellows, pinks, and limes. Seersucker and madris were pushed aside for tweed and camel hair. Dewey reached a hand into the wardrobe's dense collection of cloth and felt his way to a tan, long sleeve moleskin shirt. He yanked it off the rack and threw it on his bed. Next, a pair of blue, thin wale corduroy pants. The combination looked distinctly Lowcountry, he thought, equal doses earthy and preppy. For shoes, he would wear hand-stitched, low cut hiking boots. A brown braided belt to finish it off.

He stepped back from the wardrobe and looked at the lifeless outfit now displayed on his bed. It was wrinkled, with small hills and valleys of moleskin and corduroy throughout, an anxious-looking terrain waiting to be filled by Dewey. Having picked out an outfit, Dewey kicked and stirred the pile of clothes at the bottom of the wardrobe to avoid suspicion like something had gone missing.

Which is what made him think of his parents. The last time he'd spoken to them was weeks ago after their return to Ohio. They must have missed him. Dewey picked up the phone and dialed the area code 513, imagining the call burrowing deep beneath the dorm and emerging onto St. Philip Street, then under the Ashley River, then north on I-75 into Tennessee and Kentucky, finally into the Buckeye

State, where, at the speed of light, the same wires produced a familiar voice.

"Hello?" said Dewey's father.

"Hey, dad." Dewey knew from experience there would be a slight pause, then an initial wave of enthusiasm and devotion followed by talk of serious stuff.

"Oh, Dewey, so good to hear from you! We've missed you more than ever! How's college?"

"Good. Everything's fine. Sorry I haven't been in touch lately. I had a free minute, so I thought I'd call. How's everything there?"

"We're all good around here," said Noah. "School started again for your brother, and your mom and I are catching up on the house. You know, here and there. We ate at *Jay's* last night. How are classes?"

One Saturday each month Noah staked out the dining room to pay bills, which is where Dewey imagined him at that moment. In his mind, Dewey could see small piles of neatly organized bills on the dining room table and a black, alligator leather checkbook sprawled open with the names Noah Cellars and Virginia H. Cellars written in the upper left corner of the checks.

"Classes are good. I like all my professors." Dewey thought about Noah's description of home—housework, car wash, dinner out at *Jay's*— a world he'd once been so much a part of but now felt so far away.

"How's Charleston?" Noah continued. "For such a beautiful city, I'll never understand why it smells so bad."

"That's pluff mud, dad. It's the natural smell of the marsh. It's just a thing."

"Well, somebody should fix that. The city would be more attractive."

Dewey figured he'd try and change the subject. "So, how are things at the church?"

"Fine. Just rolling along. I mean, you've got the same people who complain. They'll always complain."

"Sorry about that. You said mom was doing okay?"

"Yeah, I scheduled her annual physical last week, and the doctor promised me he'd talk to her about her weight. We just have to get that under control."

Dewey had grown up watching his mother struggle with weight and his father always trying to fix it. In the background, Dewey heard paper-shuffling and envelope-stuffing.

"Anything else new, Dew?" said Noah.

"Well, I joined a fraternity."

"You what? What spurred that on?"

"Oh, I don't know. I went through rush with my roommate, and this guy Radford kind of introduced me to this fraternity called Kappa Tau." It was the easiest, safest explanation Dewey could give. How could he ever tell his dad about Radford? If pluff mud was inexplicable to him, Angel Boy most certainly would.

"Ya know, your grandfather was a fraternity man at Ohio State. Maybe you got his genes." Noah chuckled in the way fathers do with their sons when machismo is the subtext.

"I didn't know that." Dewey thought he smelled naugahyde, and it made him feel ill. "Hey, not to switch topics, but I'll probably need a little extra money for dues."

"Budget's kind of tight, but for a fraternity man, we should be able to swing it."

"Thanks."

More paper-shuffling, more envelope-stuffing. Dewey was sure at some point in the conversation he'd become a hand-written reminder on a yellow legal pad.

"I just want you to know how much we love and miss you. It probably won't be till Thanksgiving that we see you. We'll come down to Kiawah," said Noah.

"Miss you guys, too, and Thanksgiving isn't that far off," said Dewey.

"Yeah, you're right." Noah sighed deeply.

"Well, gotta run. Dinner tonight with a friend."

"*Girl*-friend?" Noah chuckled.

"Yes, father—a girl." Dewey wanted to yell through the phone how unsophisticated he thought his father was.

"Okay, son, have fun. Love you."

"Love you."

Dewey hung up the phone, the long-distance connection faint and scratchy like paper crumpling. He laid a hand on the lifeless outfit next to him and tried bringing it to life.

CHAPTER 23

The yacht club was a sprawling, low profile brick compound with arched windows, pillars and a gated entrance overlooking the harbor. Behind the compound was a hundred-foot, wooden dock with big and small sailboats.

It was close to seven o'clock and still light out, though the days were getting shorter, as Dewey patiently waited by the gated entrance for Dr. Lyman. He had sharp stomach pains like those he'd had at the freshman mixer and Physician's Auditorium. He tried breathing deeply while looking out at the cannons at White Point Garden across from where he stood, recalling how during childhood vacations he played on top of them. Then he looked in the direction of The Battery Carriage House, one of the more prominent Battery homes, where he and his family had occasionally stayed. The memories comforted him as did the scent of tea olive now coming from the direction of Rainbow Row. He took another deep breath and waited.

"Dewey," said a voice from behind. It wasn't like when someone called his name at the dorm or in class. The voice was friendly but also parental. Dewey turned to see Dr. Lyman standing just a few feet away wearing khakis, a white Oxford with a green striped repp tie and blue blazer.

"Evening, Dr. Lyman," said Dewey. "I didn't see you coming from that direction."

"Yes, I live just a few blocks away. Not far." Dr. Lyman pointed in the direction of East Bay Street, just beyond the club. "How are you?"

"I'm well. I got your reminder at the dorm. Thank you."

"Of course. Hungry?"

"Yeah, I definitely brought my appetite." Dewey had looked forward to this meal, a welcome break from the cafeteria.

Together, they walked down a narrow sidewalk until they reached the club's main entrance, where suddenly an older, black man in a white shirt and black bow tie appeared and opened the door.

"Good evenin', Dr. LIE-man," he said.

"Good evening, Moses."

Dewey entered into a carpeted, low-lit foyer with a hostess stand and nearby coat closet. A pretty girl wearing a pearl necklace and floral pattern dress, greeted them and, upon seeing Dewey, disappeared into the coat closet.

Dr. Lyman leaned over to Dewey. "You'll need a blazer for the dining room," he whispered.

Dewey cursed himself under his breath. How could he have missed this? After all, *Jay's* back in Ohio had a jacket requirement too, and this place was even fancier.

The hostess quickly reappeared holding a blue blazer that looked about Dewey's size. She helped him put it on, then showed him and Dr. Lyman to a table near a window overlooking the club's dock.

"Sorry to be so underdressed," said Dewey. "I didn't know there was a jacket requirement."

"Well, I probably didn't mention it when we spoke, and they always have a few extra in the closet. Thank goodness for closets— they can hold life's most important things sometimes."

The club's main dining room was large and spacious with a low ceiling and windows that looked out into the harbor. Dinner guests in khaki, linen and silk socialized in groups of four and six at bulky captain's chair-style tables and chairs. Jazz music played in the background.

On one wall was a giant, framed oil painting of a lone sailboat on the high seas. The vessel heeled significantly to one side, its sail billowing in the wind, as it faced an uncertain horizon. On still another wall was a Lowcountry landscape similar to what hung in Dr. Lyman's office. This one led the viewer's eye down a tidal creek, with its twists and turns, and patches of brown, green and blue marsh grass. White tablecloths, fine china, and silverware dressed each table. It was nice to be in a room bigger than his dorm room, thought Dewey, especially one as grand as this.

"So, how's the eye?" asked Dr. Lyman.

"Okay, I guess. It comes and goes like you said it would but it's not any worse." Dewey touched his eye as if to prove everything was alright.

"Oh, good. I know it's frustrating to have your vision obscured by something so trivial."

"Things are pretty clear for the moment. But I guess you never really know how clear things really are."

"I'm sorry—what was that?"

"Oh, nothing. I was just saying how much there was to see around Charleston." Dewey thought about all the things he'd seen and all the people he'd met.

"How are classes?"

"Biology is kind of hard. English is probably my favorite class."

"Is Dr. Freeport still teaching biology?"

"Yes." Dewey looked surprised.

"I had him, too. Of course, back then, he was only a couple years older than I was. Brilliant man."

"So, you knew him?"

"Yes, and lots of people around town did, too. He was born and raised here. A God-fearing man, that's for sure."

"I like him too. He's got a really sweet way of teaching."

"Have you taken one of his exams yet?"

"No, still too early in the semester."

"Well, you might change your mind about him when you see your grade." Dr. Lyman laughed. "And I see you pledged a fraternity."

"Yeah, wasn't really my idea. My roommate kind of got me into it." Dewey had heeded the advice he'd been given at Kappa House the night before and had since affixed his pledge pin to the lapel of the borrowed blazer.

Dewey was quite sure from Dr. Lyman's time as a Kappa that he would recognize the all-seeing eye, daggers, and a calla lily. Surely, he would say something about being a brother. Maybe he could try and bait him.

"So, how long have you lived in Charleston?"

"Going on thirty years or more. I went to college and medical school here, then the Navy, then came back." Dr. Lyman reached for his water.

"What brought you back?"

"I was from a small town in the upstate." Dr. Lyman paused and looked up at the oil painting of the lone sailboat. "Charleston was smaller and more beautiful back then. It was so pretty, it was like a dream. I suppose to new people it still is. "

Another black man in a white shirt and black bow tie approached the table. "How's y'all dis evening? Specials tonight is the stuff flounder, stake ow poorve and feddacheeny. And, ah course, der's alway the buffay. Is you gentlemen ready?"

The man reminded Dewey of the oystermen from his dream.

"Go ahead, Dewey," said Dr. Lyman.

"I'll have the buffet, please." Dewey smiled at the waiter and thanked him.

"And I'll have the steak." Dr. Lyman closed his menu and rested his elbows on the table.

The waiter hobbled away.

"So, when I saw you in the office, I think you said you were from Ohio?"

"Yeah, I was born there, then we moved to Charlotte, but we eventually moved back to Ohio, and that's where I went to high school." Dewey looked like he was playing a squeeze box, expanding and shrinking with his hands the space in front of him trying to sketch out a timeline of his family's early years on the move.

Dr. Lyman looked out the window at the water. "Parts of the Ohio River can be very pretty."

"Yeah, occasionally we'd hang out at the river in high school. We'd sit and look across to Kentucky."

"Have you ever heard of the artist John Banvard? He was a nineteenth century painter. I have one of his panoramas of the Ohio. You're welcome to see it."

Waves lapped against the dock outside.

"That would be cool."

"As I said, I'm right around the corner if you're interested."

"But for now, why don't we head over to the buffet?" he said.

"I thought you ordered *steak*," said Dewey, puzzled.

"I did, but I'll walk up there with you just the same. I'm curious to see what they have."

A piano had taken up playing in the background, as mostly older, tan couples walked carefully through dim light to and from the buffet, husbands gently encouraging their wives along with a hand on the small of the back the way a small child might give a gentle push to a toy sailboat on a pond.

Dewey stood up, buttoned his blazer and waited for Dr. Lyman who also moved slowly and carefully. Together, they shuffled across the burgundy-colored carpet, past the picture of the lone sailboat to the buffet bar with burning, red heat lamps.

The buffet offered baked salmon, prime rib and chicken almondine. Bright green broccoli florets and orange roasted carrots with stems added color to the bar. The great bounty—a far cry from the cafeteria, thought Dewey—sat in large, steel chafing dishes with Sterno cans beneath.

Dr. Lyman went ahead of Dewey, staying to the periphery of the buffet, occasionally darting his head in and out to view its flavorful dishes. This left Dewey standing in line alone holding a large, warm dinner plate emblazoned with the club burgee. Slowly he started down the line, first reaching for the baked salmon and broccoli. Then a scoop of potatoes au gratin and a dinner roll before heading down to the dessert tray for a plate of peach cobbler. He then turned, circling back to where Dr. Lyman stood.

"See anything interesting?" said Dewey, half-joking.

"Plenty, but it all makes me fat," said Dr. Lyman, grinning.

At about this time, Dr. Lyman's steak arrived. The waiter put the plate down. "Y'all enjoy," he said.

Dewey reached for his salad fork and, realizing his error, put it back down and reached for his dinner fork. He'd hoped Dr. Lyman hadn't seen him falter. He sat up straight and ate his food in small bites.

The two of them ate in silence for some time, Dewey feeling more and more content. For the first time since arriving in Charleston, he felt like he was at home. Maybe it was the blazer or maybe it was that he'd come to a place where so few were permitted—a club. Maybe, still, it was being next to someone who was well-dressed, worldly, and interesting. Someone with authority, connections and sophistication. All the things he, and the other men in his family, were not.

Dewey imagined this was the kind of place Radford might frequent. He envisioned him in a far-off corner updating a group of local matriarchs and patriarchs on college life and the health of Kappa House. *How is it being pledge educator?* they might ask. *Are they good boys?* Then everyone at the table would quietly and politely laugh. If, in fact, Dewey did have the good fortune of getting Radford as a big brother, then his mention of dinner at the yacht club would surely work in his favor.

"How was the salmon?" asked Dr. Lyman. The only thing remaining on Dewey's plate was peach cobbler.

"It was excellent. Tender in the middle and a tad crispy on the outside," said Dewey. "How about the steak?"

"It was good. I wouldn't say excellent, but good." Dr. Lyman had a mix of contentment and disappointment in his face. "Are you going to eat that whole peach cobbler?"

Dewey had taken a huge helping off the buffet. "Not at this rate. Would you like some?"

Dr. Lyman scooted his bread plate across the white tablecloth. Dewey took his spoon and shoveled some of the cobbler onto the plate. Dr. Lyman dragged the plate back. "Thank you," he said.

"No problem and thank you for inviting me here," said Dewey. "It's been amazing."

They sat quietly amid the burgundy-colored carpet and sea of tweed and herringbone.

"I wore that same pledge pin once, you know," said Dr. Lyman, regarding Dewey's lapel.

His comment caught Dewey off guard, but he played dumb. "You were a Kappa?"

"Many years ago, yes."

"What was it like back then?" Dewey leaned closer in.

"I'm guessing it's much smaller than what it is now. I've kind of lost track over the years, but back then there were only twenty brothers."

Dewey thought of the composite over Kappa House's mantle. There must have been close to 100 brothers.

"Do you mind if I ask why you joined?" Dewey looked at Dr. Lyman eagerly.

"I knew no one when I arrived at the college, except for a great aunt on Pitt Street who I lived with during my first year here. I wanted to get out and meet people."

"That's cool." Dewey hoped Dr. Lyman would say more so he could find out what great feat put him in the pledge handbook. "Any tips on pledging?"

"Proceed cautiously and don't take anything they say or do too seriously. You're the type that will do just fine."

"Did you have fun at Kappa House?"

"Yes, I'd say I had a good time. But, like everything else, these things pass. They have a life and a death, though I suppose the brotherhood would beg to differ on life's impermanence. People your age think they'll outlive everything. I hear it in my practice all the time."

Dewey had not expected this response. "Well, I'd like to think I know myself a little," he said.

Dewey felt he was getting closer to the truth about Dr. Lyman and Kappa Tau.

"Well, not every man in the fraternity is made of the same stuff."

"What do you mean?"

"Whenever you get a group of young men that age together, something's bound to happen. And not everyone comes away the same."

"Sorry, I'm still not following."

"There was a certain brother—I say brother, but he just barely made it through pledging—and they taunted him relentlessly. Never should have been there in the first place. Just not cut out for fraternity life. Not that he was a bad person. Quite the opposite."

"What happened?"

"He tried to jump."

Nearby, a short woman in a gray skirt knocked over her glass of water, startling everyone. Dr. Lyman looked over his shoulder at the table expecting to find some kind of injury, until someone at the table gave the all-clear.

"You said someone had jumped?" continued Dewey.

"Yes, tried to at least, and from the third floor no less. But I talked him out of it."

"Talked him out of it?" Dewey looked at Dr. Lyman in disbelief. "Why did he want to jump?"

"That's a topic better discussed outside these walls," said Dr. Lyman. "I'm just a few blocks away, and you'd get to see the Banvard. I'd think that would be of interest for someone from Ohio."

"Who?" Dewey, still captivated by thoughts of the jumper, had forgotten about the painting.

"The landscape artist."

"Oh, yeah. Sorry." Dewey had to quickly decide about going over to Dr. Lyman's. They'd just met, and he knew next to nothing about him other than he was a doctor who loved art. But there was the promise of more on the jumper. Was the story even true? "Sure, I guess, but just for a few minutes."

Dewey knew not to try and offer to pay for dinner but not because he lacked generosity. He didn't offer because he knew places like the yacht club had member accounts. Meals weren't paid for with cash, check or credit card. A small slip of paper with a dollar amount simply landed on the table and the guest signed for it, the debt to be settled through a monthly statement sent home. And so it was at the end of this meal where Dr. Lyman pulled from his blazer a fine fountain pen and with his supple palm signed his name on a small piece of paper in perfect cursive.

Then Dewey and Dr. Lyman got up and walked toward the hostess stand in the main entrance, where Dewey briefly stopped to remove the borrowed blazer. As he did, he felt a chill. When he looked down, he'd completely forgotten he was wearing Alex's shirt and pants—it was so foreign he almost didn't recognize himself. Then Moses appeared out of nowhere to open the door. Dr. Lyman and Dewey walked alongside the building in darkness to the small patch of cement in front of the gated entrance. Dewey looked back at the club one last time to find Moses waving at them as if they'd been set free of something, then they turned onto East Bay to go see the Banvard.

CHAPTER 24

Dr. Lyman's house was located near the city's old wharves in a place where fig leaf and wrought iron abounded. Dr. Lyman's two-story, brick house was newer than most other houses and structures around it and featured two balconies overlooking the harbor within sight of the yacht club. The whole way to Dr. Lyman's house, Dewey could smell the pluff mud, which relaxed him. Dr. Lyman pulled a small key chain from his pocket with three, very similar looking keys—one with red tape on it. He opened the door and motioned to Dewey to follow.

The house was quiet, insulated by thick, beige carpet. The walls were painted various shades of light blue and yellow, with the dining room wallpapered in a spray of purple peacocks. Oil landscapes of the Lowcountry at various times of day hung in large, dark wood frames on the wall. In between, fine charcoal etchings of farm life and gentile country folk peppered the wall. One in particular that caught Dewey's attention showed a black man in overalls and straw hat in an open field behind a mule and plow. Another, a portrait, featured a black mammy in her Sunday best wearing a big, ruffled hat with purple crinoline over the front.

Along one wall in a large display case with ball and claw feet was a large silverware chest made of wood, its lid open and contents in full view. At least two dozen sterling silver knives stood vertically against a red, velvet backdrop, each one tucked neatly and securely into a slot. Below the knives, Dewey could see the tops of fork tines and various soup and tea spoons. A bottom drawer beneath it held oyster forks and sugar tongs.

Dewey had seen silverware chests like this one before. A couple of times a year—on the same dining room table where Noah paid bills and stuffed envelopes—Dewey's mother would bring out her silverware chest, inherited from her own mother, to use at Christmas and Easter. Hers seemed similar to Dr. Lyman's, though on the latter's, was a giant brass medallion stamped with the initials *JHL*.

On a shiny butler's table in the living room sat a small Wedgewood vase and a hand-carved jade figurine in the shape of a dragon. A miniature white and blue ceramic heron stood stoically as if waiting for its next catch to appear in the cubby of a nearby series of built-in shelves.

"Please, make yourself comfortable," said Dr. Lyman.

"Thanks," said Dewey. "Great house."

"Not as old as some around here, but that means fewer repairs. My friends who have old houses are forever complaining about having to find someone to do this or that."

Dewey looked out across the street to see a villa-style home in need of paint with an aluminum front door. Not to mention the money.

"Yeah, I can relate. My parents' house is old and drafty. You can feel it when you unlatch the windows after a long, cold winter. They creak, and the paint chips." Dewey mimicked unlatching an old window. "So, tell me more about the guy you saved from jumping."

"First, the Banvard," said Dr. Lyman, pointing to a picture of an old-fashioned paddle boat in fuzzy, yellow light making its way up a river. Two large, tree-covered hills contrasted sharply with the tiny paddle boat that with a white plume from its smokestack chugged and puttered up the river. "It's such a romantic rendering, don't you think?"

"Yes, it is," said Dewey. "Though I have to admit the hills in the background threw me for a minute. Funny what you don't see when it's right in front of you."

Dr. Lyman smiled. "A new perspective on your home state, perhaps."

"Dreamier for sure."

Dr. Lyman chuckled, then his face turned more serious. "The boy who almost jumped was in my pledge class. He had been unusual from the start, and the other boys, brothers, caught on."

"Unusual how?" Dewey moved closer in.

"Unusual good looks." Dr. Lyman paused to look at a painting of a young woman on the wall. "Quite simply, he was pretty."

"If you don't mind my saying, I've seen a lot of pretty people in Charleston." Dewey thought of Alex's remark about how every guy at the college looked like a model.

"Yes, but boys being boys, *pretty* can be interpreted in many ways—weak, effeminate, threatening to the male order."

Male order made Dewey think of Dr. Freeport's class and Linnaeus.

"Some people just possess a particular symmetry, a perfect symmetry," continued Dr. Lyman, "and that symmetry, under certain circumstances, can invite everything from curiosity to criticism."

"I'm guessing your friend invited criticism?" said Dewey.

"Both, actually. Some found him curious and engaging. Some brothers spent more time with him than others. Others called him names, horrible names. So sad, so fragile, so light—like a creature made of papier-mâché."

Dewey looked at a miniature, blue Wedgewood vase on a side table next to the couch. "Why didn't he just quit?"

"Who knows? Maybe he wanted to be someone, maybe someone other than who he was. Maybe he thought being a Kappa would make him so."

"So how did you rescue him, if that's even the right word?"

"Right place, right time. I quite literally talked him off the ledge, as they say, and grabbed him by the arm."

"How close was he?"

"Close enough for the both of us."

"Then what?"

"Some brothers took him to the infirmary, where he spent the night. He tried finishing up pledging, but it just didn't work. He just disappeared after that."

"Well, where'd he go? You had to know where he was from, right?"

"I want to say he was a hometown boy, a local, but it never really came up. He was gone. Someone said they saw him riding his bike down George Street in front of Porter's Lodge months later, but they couldn't be sure."

Dewey looked at the crystal heron figurine on the shelf, then at the etching of the black farm hand in the straw hat behind the plow. He looked pensive almost like he was waiting for the end of the story.

"Anyway," continued Dr. Lyman, "they made more of it than it really was. My part, that is. Gave me the Order of the Brotherhood and put me in the local newspaper."

"So that's why you're so important," muttered Dewey.

"Excuse me?"

"Oh, nothing." Dewey looked at his watch—ten o'clock. "Well, it's getting late. I'd better hit the road." Dewey had heard all he wanted to hear for the moment.

Dr. Lyman rose from his seat. "I've certainly enjoyed your company and hope we can do it again soon. Remember to call the office if that floater gives you any more trouble. Sometimes it can be blinding."

"Sure thing." Dewey looked at the heron again, who himself looked like he was retiring for the night. Then he walked to the side door, with Dr. Lyman following behind. He stepped off the thick, beige carpet onto the brick stairway and on to the cobblestone street. "Thanks again," he said, waving back at Dr. Lyman just like Moses.

* * *

Dewey arrived back at his dorm room to find four trays of juice boxes piled high on the shelf in the common room. They had been replenished, which made Dewey smile. He remembered how Alex's mother had lugged the first trays of shrink-wrapped juice boxes up the stairs at move-in.

Outside it was still dark, and the common room was dimly lit, with only a sliver of light coming from underneath the door to the bedroom he and Alex shared. That sliver of light suddenly widened, however, when a very angry Alex hastily opened the door and looked straight at Dewey. "Why the fuck are you wearing my clothes, dude?" he said.

"Hold on, Alex," said Dewey, looking down at the moleskin shirt and corduroy pants. "I didn't think you'd mind me borrowing a few things from your wardrobe."

"The fact is that you didn't ask, you just took," said Alex, his face red with anger. "Sharing juice boxes is one thing, but clothes is a whole other. Those are *my* clothes in *my* wardrobe. *Comprende?* Plus, it's just weird."

"I know," said Dewey, anxiously. "I'd be mad too, but I really didn't think you'd mind. I mean, we've become friends."

"Really? That's funny because just last week we were more or less just roommates. That we just rushed together was pretty much the extent of it."

"I'm sorry. I didn't mean it that way."

"So, friendship's convenient only if it's convenient for you? That's bullshit. You're nice, Dewey, but I'm beginning to think there's

213

another side to you."

"I said I'm sorry, okay. It won't happen again."

Dewey stared at the stained brown carpet. He felt ashamed, but also angry. To hell with Alex's clothes. Who would ever want to look like him anyway, he thought. If anything, Alex should be thanking him. After all, in some small way, he'd given Alex the chance to live vicariously through him—to see the city and go places he probably never would have, even if, at the end of the day it only amounted to a pile of dirty Oxfords and chinos.

Alex had turned away from his wardrobe and settled down. "Where'd you go, anyway?"

"You don't wanna know."

"What's that mean?" Alex raised his hands in the air.

"It'll just make things worse."

"Fucking try me."

"We went to a yacht club."

"Yacht club. Where?"

"Near The Battery."

"A real yacht club? As in like real yachts?"

The lampposts in the corridor flickered as they came on.

"For some," said Dewey, "but I think for most it's more a social thing."

"I'm beginning to think there's something wrong with you, Dewey. You're here less than a month and you get invited to the yacht club for dinner by someone you hardly know."

"Strange, I know. But, then again, this place is strange," said Dewey. "You said it yourself with all the guys who look like models. The whole place is like a dream. Sometimes I think I see things that aren't there when I'm walking down King. It's funny."

Alex sat at his desk across from Dewey. "It's definitely weird, I'll give you that. Can't say I've seen any mirages or anything, if that's what you mean. But I'll give it to you that the people around here aren't normal. They're just too perfect." Alex stared at the dark screen of Dewey's computer. "Anyway, I can't believe I'm actually asking this, but how'd the clothes do?"

"Best dressed there," said Dewey, hoping this might appease Alex and make him forget the infraction.

"So, what'd you and Dr. Lyman do at the club?"

"We ate and talked. It was a lot better than the cafeteria I can tell you that. Turns out he had Dr. Freeport for biology, too, when he went here. And he was also in a frat."

"Let me guess. Kappa Tau?"

"Yeah. Sorry to disappoint."

"No shit?"

"Yeah, for real. It was way back when the frat only had like twenty guys. I checked it out."

"How so?"

"Long story. Just something I learned at the mixer last night."

"How old is this guy?" Alex furrowed his brow.

"I'd say he's our parents' age, maybe a little younger."

"So, you're saying you went out hob-knobbing in my clothes with some rich dude at the yacht club?"

A car with a loud muffler zoomed by outside.

"No, it wasn't that at all. I promise. Haven't you ever hung out with older adults before?"

"Yeah, but not like *that*." Alex turned around and pretended to do something.

"It wasn't a date. It was just dinner. With an adult. Not like whatever you and Mary Pate got going on at Sharky's last night."

"Fuck you, Dew. You don't know what we have going on."

"I can only imagine."

"And give me back my fuckin' clothes."

Dewey got up and walked to the bathroom, returning a few minutes later with Alex's shirt and pants. "Here, take 'em. It'll never happen again," he said, throwing them on the floor.

Alex swung his wardrobe doors open and threw the pants and shirt on the same pile of clothes that had been there since move-in. He slammed the doors shut and turned around to meet Dewey face-to-face.

"Whoever these people are, this Radford and doctor what's-his-name, and from what Mary Pate's been telling me, you better just slow the hell down because you're burning through this city fast."

"Maybe you're just jealous that I'm actually doing things, unlike you here in this room."

Alex turned and with all his might shoved Dewey back onto his bed, leaving a crater in the sheetrock wall behind him.

"What the hell was that for?" cried Dewey in disbelief. "Are you *trying* to start a fight?"

"Think of it as a warning. You're low down sometimes, Dewey Cellars, low down." Alex grabbed his robe and headed for the shower.

"I hope you know residence life will hear about this." Dewey's threat was drowned out by the sound of running water.

He walked to the common room and sat down. In the hall someone was coming up the stairwell, one heavy step at a time. The elevator chirped.

It was almost midnight. Tomorrow at this time he'd have a big brother, but he'd have to go dressed as himself.

CHAPTER 25

The phone rang early the next morning. Dewey hadn't even risen for church yet. And Alex was still sound asleep.

"Hello?" said Dewey, quietly.

"Hey, Dewey, it's Lucious. Sorry for calling so early on a Sunday."

"Oh, hey, what's up?"

"We need a tour guide Tuesday. I know it's short notice, but could you help us out?"

Dewey's thoughts were still on the yacht club and the crater in the sheetrock from his fight with Alex. "Yeah, I think I can help you. When did you need me?"

"Around three o'clock."

"Yeah, I can do that."

"Thank you. You're really helping us out. We're trying to get as many tours as possible in before the height of hurricane season. Everything you need to know is in the packet I gave you. Would you like Liza to go over things with you again?"

"No, I'm good."

"Okay, then, Miss Tilley will see you at Towell Library at three on Tuesday. Also, and I don't mean for this to come across weird, but would you like a good, home-cooked meal?"

"Sure, I guess," said Dewey.

"Okay, why don't you come over for dinner. Tomorrow night, good?"

"Where?"

"My mom's house over on Rutledge Avenue."

"Yeah, sure, I guess. What time?"

"Let's do five-thirty."

"Cool."

"See you there. Bye."

Dewey slouched against the side of his wardrobe wondering, because it was so early and the world seemed fuzzy, if the call had ever taken place. Or, perhaps, had it just been some dreamy doing of Desirée's?

Church started at ten o'clock, and it was now a little after eight. Dewey decided he would quickly shower, get dressed and eat breakfast at the cafeteria, while studying his pledge book. Then he'd walk down Glebe Street to Grace Church.

Dewey opened the doors to his wardrobe, again reigniting thoughts from the previous night. No more cool clothes, he thought. Nothing more of Alex's. He'd have to wear his own stuff from now on. He reached for the only suit he had—a light green, summer weight poplin from Brooks Brothers that had been his father's. Yet again, someone else's clothes, but at least it was someone whose blood he shared. He set the suit on his bed and crept into the bathroom to shower. Then he slipped the suit on and headed for the elevator, exiting the dorm through the courtyard.

The cafeteria was practically deserted. A flyer from several weeks before announced how it had acquired four golden malted waffle irons. Dewey thought they looked lonely, heavy and clunky. He poured batter onto the hot, honeycomb-pattern surface of one of them, closed the two metal plates and set a timer for two minutes. He walked to another part of the cafeteria to get juice and a bowl of fruit.

Cafeteria staff in aprons, hair nets, and white slip-proof shoes went back and forth from the kitchen into the dining room picking up empty trays, wiping down tables and straightening chairs. Dewey found a table in a newer section of the cafeteria under a large, rectangular skylight in the ceiling. The clouds parted overhead, and the sun shone down. He opened his pledge book and started memorizing important Kappa names, dates and milestones.

Suddenly, he felt someone next to him. "This here your waffle?"

It was one of the dining staff, an older woman with light brown skin with a hair bun and a nametag that read Iris.

"Yes, ma'am, it is," said Dewey, surprised, as if she'd appeared out of thin air. "I guess I forgot about it."

"Well, it almost burnt to a crisp. I swear I grabbed it jus' in time." Iris threw her head back and laughed, as she handed a plate with the waffle to Dewey. The warm plate felt good in his hands.

"You a handsome one. What year you in?" Iris continued.

Dewey blushed. "I'm a freshman. It's my third week."

"Well, welcome to de college just the same."

"Thanks."

Dewey thought Iris' presence felt familiar, and while he was thankful for her and the waffle, deep down he was ready for her to go. After all, he'd come to the cafeteria to study his pledge book, and with the Big Brother ceremony that evening, he feared being asked questions he couldn't answer.

"Where you come from?" Iris' voice rose, then fell.

Dewey chuckled, thinking how strange her question sounded. It wasn't like he was from outer space, not some alien who'd fallen from the sky.

"A small town in the Midwest," responded Dewey.

"That's a long way away." Iris lifted her hand and pointed as if trying to orient herself.

"Yes, ma'am." Dewey flipped a page in his pledge book.

"Well, I bess be leavin' you to your studyin'. Just remember, don't get burned like your waffle." Iris laughed and walked off, collecting a few more trays along the way.

Dewey sat under the skylight trying to memorize more facts about Kappa House and not feel nervous about the ceremony. What if he were chosen by one of those brothers who looked like they'd been picked up curbside from their apartment on the night of rush? Would he want to just quit and walk away? How would it look if he just bailed altogether?

Dewey felt these questions and others fall like rain through the skylight. He thought back to high school, recalling one cold evening in the bleachers at a football game when a popular senior approached him and complimented his clothes. Dewey offered a sincere thanks, but the conversation went no further, as he might have hoped. No, *"Why don't you join us"* invite to a post-game party—nothing. Dewey, even colder than he was before, watched as the senior turned around and walked off looking like the coolest kid in the world.

He looked around the cafeteria. Students were trickling in, some still in pajama bottoms and slippers. It was a far cry from the yacht club, he thought. He wondered about Dr. Lyman. Maybe he was up early, too, reading the Sunday paper on one of his balconies eating grapefruit and an English muffin, his beautiful artwork within arm's reach.

It was getting close to ten o'clock. Through the skylight, clouds gathered. Dewey lifted his tray and headed out with Radford and the Kappas on his mind.

CHAPTER 26

Dewey sat in the same seat at Kappa House as he had the Sunday before. But this time he sat dressed in his own clothes from his own wardrobe. He had chosen a red gingham dress shirt, a pair of Gap jeans, a brown belt, and brown Sebagos. While he anxiously waited for the big brother ceremony to begin, Dewey straightened his shirt to flatten any wrinkles. He looked at the other pledges seated next to him, the majority of whom looked like they'd jumped off the page of a J. Crew catalog. The way they put themselves together seemed both meticulous and spur-of-the-moment. That enviable balance of knowing exactly how to look, while appearing as though it happened accidentally: shirt untucked here, pant cuff rolled there. A sweater slung low across the waist or over the shoulder, a houndstooth barn jacket over the arm. Maybe a key fob with the name of a yacht club, a marine supply, or a silver, monogrammed bottle opener. These pledges would surely find a big brother before him. One might even get Radford.

The smell of stale beer still wafted through the house, despite what cleaning and scouring the brothers had surely attempted after Friday night's mixer. Dewey recalled working the keg that night and how handing off the tap resulted in spilling beer everywhere. Which meant much of the next day brothers stepping and trouncing through the yeasty, sticky mixture, tracking it everywhere. And still another smell at Kappa House now familiar to Dewey: old wood floors in cooler months. Not the smell of wood floors in warmer months because there was a difference; wood floors in the cold were stiff and brittle in their scent.

"Hope y'all had a great time Friday night and an even better weekend," said an unmistakable voice. It was the same voice that had surprised Dewey at the keg. The same voice he had imagined ever since seeing his face on George Street. It was Radford. Angel Boy.

He wore faded denim blue jeans, a white Oxford and a red, cotton sweatshirt with the Greek letters *K* and *T* embroidered on it. He looked like he'd just had a haircut, short on the sides and curly on top with a slight part. His skin was reddish-brown like he'd just come off the beach. Amidst the heavy crown molding, plaster walls, and aging, blown-glass windows, he blended into his surroundings, much like he had on George Street.

"Tonight is an important night in your life as pledges," Radford said. "You get big brothers who will teach and watch over you. In a few minutes we'll call you one by one upstairs, and at the very top you'll meet your big brother. At this point, you'll follow him wherever he takes you."

The pledges looked at one another, some tapping a foot nervously on the floor, others drumming their fingers across their pledge books. Dewey, however, felt more confident than ever. This was the moment he'd been waiting for.

Radford nodded to a brother toward the back, who dimmed the room lights and brought forth two small lit candles in brass votive holders to put on the mantle in front of the composite. The candles cast an eerie glow about the faces pictured directly above, including Radford's, which was featured prominently in the first row, along with the fraternity's other officers. Radford stepped out of the way, and the assistant pledge educator came forward with a list of the pledges' names. "Bonner," he called out.

"Over here," said a boy a few seats over from Dewey. The boy grasped his pledge book, rose to his feet and headed toward the stairs.

The rest of the pledges waited their turn while listening to the sound of creaky stairs, as Bonner ascended them one at a time. Then the creaking ceased, and muffled voices could be heard coming from the top of the stairs.

"Hoffman," the assistant educator called next.

A tall, skinny boy with red hair got up and moved toward the stairs. Dewey recognized him as the pledge from the mixer who wore the vintage hunting vest.

A boy from Mississippi named Truman followed. Like Bonner and Hoffman, he was neatly dressed. Dewey watched Truman walk to the staircase, imagining him in his home state in a waxed hunting jacket and Wellington boots with a rifle and labrador retrievers running about.

"For the second time—Cellars," said the assistant pledge educator, irritated.

"Here I am." Dewey hadn't heard his name the first time, as he'd been daydreaming about waxed jackets and Wellies.

"You're up," said the assistant pledge educator. "But hold just a sec. I've got a question for you. Name one distinguished alum from this chapter."

It almost sounded too good to be true, thought Dewey. Of all the questions. Maybe he'd spoken to the brother that Dewey had run into at the mixer.

"That would be Dr. Lyman," said Dewey intrepidly.

"Doesn't count, pledge, I need a full name." The assistant pledge educator held his clipboard ever tighter.

"Dr. Joseph Hermes Lyman."

"Good. Keep up with that pledge book." The assistant pledge educator nodded and directed Dewey to the staircase.

The stairs looked larger than they did Friday night, he thought. He began climbing them one at a time, producing the same creaky noises as the pledges before. At the top of the stairs, he saw a tall figure with light skin and a sharp, noble-looking nose. It was all he could see for now, the light just barely enough to make out the outline of someone. Dewey strained his eyes for more, while walking further up the stairs until only a few feet separated him from the outline of his would-be big brother.

"Boo!" said the unknown figure holding a small flashlight under his chin, illuminating his lower face like one of Alex's horror masks. "Did I scare you?"

"Yes. I mean, no. Not scare so much as surprise." Dewey responded.

"Works on some pledges but not you, I guess," said the figure. He still hadn't introduced himself, as Dewey climbed the last few stairs to stand beside him. Then the figure turned off the flashlight, his scary face disappearing. "I'm actually not your real big brother—Radford is—but he had to take care of something right quick. Said he'd be back. I'm Dylan."

"Hey, good to meet you." Dewey could not believe his ears. Could Radford *really* be his big brother? His heart beat fast, faster even than when he accepted the bid, faster than at dinner at the yacht club.

Dewey recognized Dylan as the brother who had moments before dimmed the parlor lights and approached the mantle with votive candles.

"How'd you get to the top of the stairs so fast?" asked Dewey.

"There's a back staircase by the kitchen. We barely ever use it except for stuff like this," he said.

"Hmm," responded Dewey, wondering how much more there was to the house. From the outside, there looked to be a third floor and attic but, like the second floor, Dewey assumed these areas were off limits to pledges.

Dylan stopped at the end of the hall and turned right into one of the bedrooms. Dewey followed. It was dark except for a lava lamp on an end table. A huge KT flag hung from the ceiling.

"So, do you like your pledge class?" Dylan had straddled the arm of a ratty, torn loveseat.

"Yeah, they're okay," said Dewey, who'd also taken a seat on the loveseat. He thought of Bonner, Truman and Hoffman and how easily they outdressed him. How hard it was for Dewey to sit next to them— he, a piece of dirty driftwood in the muddy Ohio River; while they, fine sailboats in the shiny, white-capped Charleston harbor.

"Yeah, personally, I think we're the best frat on the row." Dylan had grounded his feet on the floor, his taut thighs draped over one side of the loveseat arm. "Having Radford doesn't hurt, of course. Dudes would kill to have him as a big brother."

Dewey didn't so much as look up. Doing so might give away that same desire that had brought him from Ohio to the college. In the darkness, Dewey felt nauseous and dizzy. He looked out into the hall, catching the occasional glimpse of another brother and pledge walking by.

"For sure," said Dewey, in a way that even he recognized was a little unnatural. "Kappa is number one." Dewey looked up at Dylan. "How'd you first meet Radford, anyway?"

"Same as pretty much everyone—through rush. That was two years ago when he was rush coordinator. Seems like forever ago."

"So Rad's a junior or senior?" Dewey, as before, was trying to do the math in his head.

"Somewhere around there. But, then again, most people here are on the five- or six-year plan."

"What do you mean?"

"Well, nobody here really graduates on time—it's like one big fucking dream no one can wake up from, so nobody really knows what year anybody's in. Shit, I mean for all I know Radford could be here for the rest of his life." Dylan jumped off the loveseat arm, stretched his legs and swung a key fob full of keys on his right index finger.

Dewey dug for more. "What's his major?"

"Pre-med." Dylan laughed and threw his head back.

"Seriously, what is it?"

"Okay, I'm just fucking with you, pledge. I think his major is business administration. He doesn't need a real major anyway. He's going to work in the family business."

"Family business?" Dewey felt like he'd struck gold.

"Yeah, some kind of import-export business down on Cumberland Street."

"His dad's business?" Dewey thought of the girls he'd overheard at Sharky's talking about a boy whose dad owned an old tea plantation.

"Not exactly. But the business dates back a long way, like back to the Civil War."

Of course, thought Dewey, the Civil War ancestor who'd left money for his descendants, among them Radford and Mary Pate, to go to the college for free.

Dylan started up again: "Yeah, Radford is old money. Old Charleston money. Plantations, slaves, cotillions—all that bullshit. But to hear him tell it, you wouldn't think any of that mattered to him. I mean, he still gets in a tux every now and then when he's got to, but he's definitely not going around every weekend looking for a big shindig."

"Lucky guy," said Dewey. "Hey, what's the deal with him anyway?"

Dylan looked confused. "I just told you."

"No, I mean, is he fucked up or something?"

"Who wants to know?"

"The brother who dropped off my bid said he was cool but to

keep some distance."

Dylan rolled his eyes. "That must have been Travis. Dickhead. Needs to keep his fucking mouth shut."

"About what?"

"Well, fuck, I guess I have to tell you, but just keep an eye on the door in case Radford walks in. So, here's the deal. Radford's a legacy."

Dewey inched a little closer to Dylan. "That's cool."

"Yeah, but not when your old man tries to kill himself." Dylan ran a knife hand across his neck.

"Sorry, I don't follow."

"Radford's dad was a pledge when he tried jumping out the third story window here at the house. Lucky for him, another pledge by the name of Lyman saved him. They gave him the highest Kappa award there is, the Order of the Dagger."

Dewey looked out the window at the fraternity house next door. "Why'd he try to jump?"

"Rumor was he was a fag, some kind of pretty boy, and had gotten caught. Kappa doesn't look kindly on that kind of stuff, but I still know guys in this very house who are giving each other head. Total fuckin' hypocrites."

Leaning back into the ragged loveseat, Dewey didn't know how to respond. He thought about what Dr. Lyman had said about the jumper—how his unusual good looks had invited both acceptance as well as rejection. How, then, did Radford fare with his own good looks, thought Dewey. Was he anything like his father? Was he even aware?

"After Lyman saved Radford's dad's life," continued Dylan, "Radford's dad ended up in a mental hospital before coming back to Charleston and knocking up some girl over on Broad Street." Dylan raised his eyebrows, cupped his hand and stretched out his arm. "And, *voilà*, you get Radford."

"Did he know about his dad? How'd he get to Kappa House?" said Dewey.

"That's where Dr. Lyman comes in. He'd kept in touch with Radford's dad who'd skipped town, and asked Lyman to take care of Radford. Mentor him. So when it came time, Lyman got him accepted into Kappa."

"I suppose I'd be a little fucked up too after all that."

"Yeah, he has his moments. Sometimes what he says doesn't come out right. Sometimes he'll just disappear for hours riding his bike or mucking around in the marsh. Anyways, congrats on scoring him as a big brother. He'll be cool to you. See ya' around."

Dylan rose from the loveseat and walked out into the dark hallway, flicking his flashlight on and off while humming a song.

Dewey looked around the room. It was much the same as the one he'd stumbled into accidentally at the mixer—banners and posters of Bob Dylan and Bob Marley on the walls and dirty clothes strewn across the floor. On the side of a steel filing cabinet was a 1988 Bush-Quayle bumper sticker. A bottle of Drakkar Noir sat on a desk, its box still intact with the slogan *Feel the Power* written across the front. Suddenly, Dewey's attention was drawn to the hallway, where a dark figure quickly approached.

"Sorry, man, I had to help the other brothers with something."
It was Radford.

Dewey didn't know whether to believe his excuse or not, recalling how he'd skipped out on Mary Pate and him at Porter's Lodge the previous week, not to mention his recent revelation that he had no cousin at the college.

"Good seeing you again. I think the last time I saw you was at the mixer when I was doing the keg." Dewey kicked himself. *'Doing' the keg?* He'd made a fool of himself, he thought. This wasn't how they said it, but he didn't know any different. He held at bay the sick, dizzy feeling in his stomach.

"Yeah, I remember that. Dewey, right? From Ohio, I think."

"Good memory." Dewey didn't recall mentioning Cincinnati, but maybe Radford had come across it in his rush paperwork. A good omen, perhaps. Maybe Radford had identified him early on, thought Dewey, making their connection even more a matter of fate.

"Glad you could make the mixer the other night, and thanks for pumping the keg. It can be a messy business."

"Yeah, not much experience with that, but I'm learning." Dewey mentally committed to memory *pumping the keg.*

A lamp light in the fraternity house next door shone through the window into the room, allowing Dewey to see Radford more clearly.

"Well, I can teach you that kind of shit." Radford and Dewey both came to sit in the same loveseat that Dylan had straddled. His brown leather Timberland moc-toe boots rested on the worn oriental rug beneath them, leaving a muddy footprint when he lifted his feet. "Oh, and sorry about Dylan."

"What do you mean?" Dewey looked at the long stretch of light shining in from next door. More of Radford's face was beginning to show.

"The big brother thing. Sorry you had to hear it from him. Not exactly the way it works."

"That's cool. I don't know any different anyways. So, what's next?"

Radford fidgeted in the loveseat, leaving more muddy footprints on the rug. "Well, there's a special handbook I give you, and we'll go through it so you know what you need for initiation, if that's what you really want. We'll hang out some here and there. I heard you know your way around town pretty good."

How did he know? thought Dewey. Mary Pate, Alex, and Lucious were the only ones he'd told about his childhood travels to Charleston.

"Yeah, we used to come into town when my family vacationed at Kiawah. I know the major stuff—the Market, The Battery and stuff."

"Well, one thing you're definitely not going to want to miss is Cistern Daze." Radford smiled and fell deeper into the loveseat.

"What's that?" asked Dewey.

"It's a big party held in the Yard at night under the stars," said Radford. "Only certain people get an invite, and you're in luck. You'll hear more about it at the pledge meeting."

"Any other advice?"

Radford chuckled. "Just don't be a poser."

"Poser?"

"Don't be someone you're not. The guys will spot it a mile away."

"Don't worry about that," said Dewey. "With me, what you see is what you get."

Radford rose to his feet and flipped on the lights. The brightness overwhelmed the scant light coming from next door. "About time to head back downstairs and get this shit done."

Dewey followed Radford through the hall downstairs to the parlor through a barrage of tea olive and jasmine.

When they entered the dimly lit parlor, Dewey saw the usual three rows of six chairs. But this time the chairs were paired by big brothers and their respective pledges. Dewey could see nameplates for Bonner, Truman and Hoffman, and their big brothers in the middle row. Dewey, beginning with the back row, scanned for his and Radford's nameplates.

"Sit here," said Radford, guiding Dewey into a front row seat. Dewey sat down and looked behind him to find a nameplate that read *Cellars* in big red letters. And next to Dewey, also in big red letters, the nameplate *Gaillard*. Dewey couldn't believe it. He'd not only befriended Dewey, but he was also now about to take a front row seat with him. He'd made it into the club.

Dylan then reappeared and, passing in front of Dewey and Radford, handed out individual candles to each brother. Radford pulled a lighter from his pocket and lit his candle, as did the rest of the big brothers. Then everyone in the room stood, with Radford turning and speaking to the group.

The job of the big brother is to educate the pledge in the ways and traditions of Kappa Tau. It is this sacred bond on which the fraternity is built and sustained. The big brother should always mentor the pledge with candor and honesty, and always with good intentions. In turn, the pledge should learn and commit to memory the ways of Kappa Tau as revealed by his big brother. The pledge should show loyalty and obedience at all times, as these are qualities of a Kappa Tau brother.

Each brother then turned and shared the flame with his pledge, until all the candles were lit. At that moment, the slide projector clicked on, and the all-seeing eye, daggers and calla lily shone on the wall. Then all the candles went out, and Radford dismissed everyone. The lights came back on, as chair legs scraped against the brittle wood floor.

"That's it," said Radford, putting a hand on Dewey's shoulder. "Let's catch up mid-week, maybe bike around the peninsula or drive out to one of the islands. Maybe we can hook up with some of my friends in town."

"Yeah, sure, thanks," said Dewey. His pulse quickened. Wherever they decided to meet, one thing was true: he was now in the company of Radford Gaillard III, the most important brother at Kappa House and surely one of the most popular people on the peninsula.

CHAPTER 27

Physician's Auditorium was busy as usual for a Monday morning, with mostly upperclassmen packing the lobby before class, some comparing lecture notes and cramming last-minute for tests, while others coasted around zombie-like, heads down, in textbooks the size of dictionaries—marine biology, zoology, and genetics.

Meantime, wide-eyed freshmen scurried about with schedules in hand, including Dewey. And whatever anxiety Dewey may have had about Physician's Auditorium early on, it now seemed eclipsed by anxieties like whether or not Mary Pate and Radford were related.

Could it be that they *weren't* cousins? But why would Mary Pate concoct such an elaborate story? Maybe Radford was just mad at her—bad family blood—and he had denied their relationship just to be mean. But with Radford as his big brother and things at Kappa House heating up, Dewey decided he needed to figure out the truth. He hoped he might be able to catch Mary Pate before class, but as he stood at the door to Dr. Freeport's class and peeked in, he saw that she had already taken a seat. The truth would have to wait.

"Kingdom, phylum, class, order, family, genus, and species," said Dr. Freeport, entering the classroom and stepping up to the lectern. "Or, King Phillip Came Over For Good Spaghetti."

Some familiar with the mnemonic device nodded, while others laughed at its seeming absurdity.

"This is a handy phrase to remember Linnaeus' classification of the natural world based on shared characteristics," continued Dr.

Freeport. "Take, for example, an ordinary drone fly, known by its binomial name *Eristalis Tenax*—*Eristalis* being the genus and *Tenax* being the species. Ultimately, the drone fly is, like us, part of the animal kingdom."

Angelus Puer, thought Dewey, recalling the binomial name he'd amusingly given Angel Boy on the first day of class. He thought about how he had once attempted to sort and classify those closest to him at the college—Alex and Mary Pate, the doctor and Lucious. Based on their recent behavior, Mary Pate and Alex had slipped in their ranking, with the doctor, because of his generosity, having been elevated toward the top. Radford, of course, remained at the top, and Lucious held a place somewhere in the middle.

"So, we're all related to flies?" a boy in the back called out.

"Well, on the surface it may not appear so, but in fact we share many of the same genes. In fact, we share roughly 60% of the same DNA with flies. With mice, 88%. And with zebrafish, 73%. But you'd never think so judging from how we look on the outside. Let that be a lesson in nature."

"What about humans? How much DNA do we share between us?" asked an Asian girl in the front of the room.

"We share 99.9% of the same DNA. Isn't that just remarkable? Just think, genetically speaking, you're practically a carbon copy of the person sitting next to you."

Dewey looked at the boy sitting next to him who looked like he might be a commuter student judging from the giant ring of keys on his belt and his oversized backpack, which would have included all the necessities for a day on campus. How unlike this boy he was, he thought, but, then again, according to Dr. Freeman and modern science, how much *alike* they were. Still, Dewey felt a slight upper hand in the pecking order. Dewey had come to realize over the course of a few short weeks that "commuter" was usually code for financially strapped, unable to afford on-campus housing and, therefore, unable to fully live the college experience—instead, having to drive or, worse yet, be driven, to campus and use the library or cafeteria as home base, until a ride from a parent later in the evening. But Dewey always knew them as some of the nicest kids on campus.

"So, we should all be equals then?" said the Asian girl.

"Well, yes and no—as humans we have a complex social hierarchy, where certain individuals rise in this hierarchy, usually because of exceptional physical or intellectual characteristics. This gives them greater social influence and access to resources."

"What kind of characteristics?"

"Appearance, of course, physical strength, charisma, special skills or knowledge, too."

"What if you don't have any of these or you're different?"

"Well, then, your position in the hierarchy or tribe may be reduced, but humans, like others in the animal kingdom, do have the ability to climb in the hierarchy."

"Is that where *social climber* comes from?" someone asked.

"Well, as a matter of fact, in a certain way it is, but unlike the rest of the animal kingdom, our climb is less about using force and aggression and more about using charm and persuasion."

The students stirred, indicating that the end of class was near.

"Back to our drone fly," said Dr. Freeport. "One more thing I want to show you." In the same way he had produced an ancient human skull from behind his lectern last class, he now produced two enlarged color photos of two flying bugs that looked like bees. "One of these is an imposter. Can you tell which?"

A few students pointed and guessed aloud, with votes on either bug about equal.

Then Dr. Freeport held up the photo in his right hand and pronounced: "Behold, the imposter."

His loud, enthusiastic pronouncement startled Dewey who was still contemplating the commuter student.

"In my right hand the drone fly," continued Dr. Freeport, "and in my left a honeybee. The latter stings, the former doesn't, but if you were a predator, how could you tell? By mimicking the appearance of a honeybee, the drone fly enjoys a certain level of protection not otherwise afforded him."

Dr. Freeport lowered the photos and put them back behind the lectern, and dismissed the class. "Don't get stung, y'all," he said.

Dewey walked to the lobby hoping to intercept Mary Pate before she got out the door. He was just in time, as he saw her coming around the corner near the display case with all the awards and trophies. "Mary Pate," he yelled, over the hustle and bustle of all the biology and pre-med majors.

"Oh, hey, Dew," said Mary Pate. "It's been a while."

"Yeah, I'm trying to remember the last time we were together."

"I think it was out in front of Porter's Lodge. Anyway, how's pledging going?"

"Not bad, actually. And you'll never believe who I got as my big brother." Dewey paused. "Your cousin."

"Radford?" Mary Pate's eyes got big, and her face turned pale, as she stepped back.

"Yes. Can you believe it? Things worked out after all, but I still want to thank you for trying. We've talked a bunch. Pretty cool guy."

"Congrats. I'm glad things worked out," she said, stuttering. "What kinds of things have y'all talked about?"

"Just surface stuff, really—where we're from, how we got to the college. But I already knew that stuff thanks to you. We're supposed to get together this week and do something. I'll be sure to tell him you said, 'Hey.'"

"Sure," said Mary Pate, backing into the display case behind her and rattling one of the trophies that read, *1st Place Genetics.* "Well, I guess I better get over to Craig for my next class."

"Sure. But, hey, before you go, didn't I see you coming out of Kappa House? I was at church across the street and swore I saw you."

"No, I was at SCA over at Buist." Mary Pate stepped forward, so her back wasn't up against the wall.

"That's the strangest thing because she looked exactly like you. But I guess that's that mimicking thing Dr. Freeport talked about, huh—one animal trying to pass as another?"

Mary Pate forced a painful smile, almost like she'd been stung. "Okay, well, gotta go."

Dewey reached out as if to try and stop her. "Hey, wanna go to Cumberland's Friday night?"

"You mean that nightclub?"

"Yeah, this band is playing. Hootie and the Blowfish."

Mary Pate looked down at her red spiral notebook. "Who's that?"

"They're a band from somewhere. Don't really know much about them. Funny name."

"Okay, I guess."

"Great. Meet you in the lobby at eight o'clock Wednesday."

Mary Pate turned, her rhinestones shimmering, and exited Physician's Auditorium and crossed over George Street. Dewey didn't really know why he'd asked her out. But there was something fascinating, almost tantalizing, about her. But she was no Kiawah girl—this, he knew.

* * *

He hadn't forgotten about Lucious' dinner invite. Lucious' boyhood home was on Charleston's east side. It was an older, two-story home with a brick base and white clapboard siding. It sat on a cozy stretch of street lined with palmettos and live oaks. A brick, low rise wall lined the front of the house, which Dewey imagined Lucious' friends and family hanging out on during hot summer evenings long ago. He sensed a feeling of warmth and comfort to the house, as he walked onto the front porch and knocked on the door.

A tall, dark figure opened it. "Glad you made it. Come on in," said Lucious. "How'd you get here?"

"Walked part of it and rode the bus the rest," said Dewey.

"Sometimes I take the bus, too."

Lucious led them into the parlor, which was sparse, except for a few family pictures on the wall, one of them of a man resembling Lucious wearing a beige, three-piece suit. A couch, TV, some end tables and lamps completed the room. Light from the foyer windows reached into the room.

"So, is your mom here?"

"No, she works nights over at the hospital."

"Yeah, I think you mentioned that."

"She works the night shift. Always has. But she always made sure we had a hot meal for dinner."

"So, you have brothers and sisters?"

"One of each. Well, I should say I had. My brother died."

"How?"

"Lungs—pulmonary fibrosis. Awful to watch. He was so young and funny."

Dewey could see through to the kitchen: green Formica countertops, a stained sink and a wood, laminate dinner table on which sat a large, white baking dish.

"Thanks for inviting me," said Dewey.

"Sure." Lucious moved to the kitchen table, where he removed the baking dish lid. "Looks like we're having meatloaf."

"Smells way better than the cafeteria," said Dewey. "Sorry, I didn't mean it like that. You know what I meant."

"Yes, I do," said Lucious, halfway looking up. He reached for some ceramic plates in the cabinet that were chipped and set them down on the table. He cut a piece of meatloaf and put it on Dewey's plate.

"Who's the man in the beige, three-piece in the den?" said Dewey.

"That's my Pops." Lucious cut a piece of meatloaf for himself and put it on his plate.

"Is he here in town?"

"No, Brooklyn, New York."

"What's the story there, if you don't mind me asking?" Dewey stopped and put his fork down.

"Just different expectations about what a relationship should be."

"Like what?"

Lucious wiped his mouth with his napkin and looked toward the ceiling. "Just a bunch of stuff, from money and work to who he hung out with."

"Sorry to hear that," said Dewey, wiping his mouth. He watched the sun set through the kitchen window. It was nice to be in a house and not a dorm. Lucious' house felt lived in, a place full of stories, scuffs, scratches and chipped paint. But lots of love.

"So, how's pledging going?" said Lucious.

"Alright, I guess. Had our first pledge meeting the other night. Lots to memorize. But the guys are pretty cool," said Dewey.

"Yeah, *I … we … the administration* generally hears good things about Greek life. Not really my area, though."

"Were you ever in a frat?" said Dewey.

"No, they didn't have frats. Only battalions, which is probably the closest thing."

Lucious served Dewey another piece of meatloaf, then refilled their tea glasses, which were finely etched with birds and butterflies. "So, why'd you join the Kappas, anyway?" he said.

"It was for my roommate originally. He wanted to rush and for me to go with him for moral support."

"Did y'all get a bid?"

"That's the bad thing. Only I did."

Lucious looked up. "Does he know?"

"Yeah—he knows. He found out in the worst way."

"How's that?" Lucious lifted his napkin to his mouth.

"He checked in with Greek Life, and they must have told him. It'd been like two weeks."

"Well, count your blessings you got in. It can't hurt—the fraternity thing. It gets you places. And you're a good-looking kid."

Dewey appreciated Lucious' compliment, but it felt a little strange considering Lucious was only a handful of years older than he was. Lucious very well could have been his older brother.

Dewey and Lucious finished eating and decided to sit outside on the low-rise wall in front of the house.

"So, is the college a long-term thing?" said Dewey.

"I'm not going anywhere anytime soon, but at some point, after some coursework I'll move along," said Lucious, twirling an oak leaf between his fingers.

"Where to?" said Dewey.

"Hopefully up," said Lucious.

Dewey looked curious. "What do you mean?"

"You know, the whole climb-the-ladder thing."

"Oh," said Dewey, looking at the small stones buried in the cement sidewalk. At one point he thought he saw a shark's tooth.

"You can't tell me that's the first time you've heard *that* expression," said Lucious, straightening his posture.

"No, I've heard it."

Lucious laughed. "That isn't something just for white folks, you know."

"I know. It's just funny …"

"Funny what? Funny hearing it come from a black man?"

"Yeah, I guess."

"Well, I appreciate your honesty." The leaf Lucious had been twirling dropped to the ground.

Everything had darkened but for the porch lights of nearby houses, some of them hanging helplessly naked. Through the windows, Dewey could see TVs glowing, and men and women pass back and forth behind curtain sheers. Dark wood paneling showed in the background, and the light in the room looked orange and dusty. Somewhere around the block collard greens being cooked.

"Hey, I'm curious—and it's okay if you don't answer—but are you dating that nurse in Student Health?" said Dewey. "The one who helped us with Trey?"

Lucious looked surprised. "What makes you think that?"

"Well, I saw she was one of the faces in the pictures behind your desk at work, and I remember how you winked at her when we were leaving."

"I didn't wink."

"Yeah. Yeah, you did."

"Nah, nothing there—couldn't ever be anything there," said Lucious.

"What do you mean?" said Dewey.

"A black dude dating a white girl on campus, let alone Charleston? Get real, ain't happening anytime soon."

"What are you talking about? It's the 90s—you can be anyone and date anyone you want, and nobody cares."

"Then you must be blind, naïve or both," said Lucious. "Like I told you at the office, you Northern kids come down here with all your money chasing shiny things and think everything's so goddamn hunky-dory. You either have *Gone with the Wind* in your head or you think every black you see on the street needs rehab and a hot meal." Lucious picked up another leaf and crushed it in his hands. "My skin's black, and in this town that still means back of the line. Back of the line even for love."

"This isn't fucking 1860, Lucious. Jeezus."

"Not for you."

"Then what are all those pictures at garden parties with all those white women around you? Is that the ladder you're climbing?"

"They're places I just happened to be. Official stuff."

"Well, judging from the look of them, I'd say you want to be with that nurse. You want to be in her world."

"That would be a dream world, Dewey. Listen, we're all looking for our own worlds. Some are just harder to break into than others. Just like I can't believe you came *all* the way here just to go to college. I'm guessing there was something else."

Pre-med, thought Dewey. No—he couldn't possibly do that to Lucious. He didn't deserve it. After all, he'd opened up so freely. "You're right—I came here for somebody."

"Who?" Lucious cocked his head slightly.

"Radford," said Dewey, reluctantly. "I mean, not just him but the others too. Together. All of them. It's hard to explain."

"He left an impression obviously. How'd you find him?"

"I didn't exactly. I just saw him and a few buddies riding bikes on George Street in front of Porter's Lodge last spring. That's the day you and I must have met—remember?"

"I guess that would have been the timeframe. Is he a student? Would I know him?"

"He's a student, but no one really seems to know what year he's in. He's a big mystery, really. Almost a ghost."

"What's his last name?"

"Gaillard."

"Well, he's definitely a Charleston boy, but I don't recall seeing the name Radford Gaillard anywhere in admissions."

Dewey looked up at the stars. "Somehow that doesn't surprise me."

"So why are you so concerned with him?"

"I was just taken by him. His image. His perfection."

"So, you want to be perfect?"

"I suppose, but it's more complex than that."

"Try me."

"You wouldn't understand."

"How do you know?"

"Because you're all set."

"What do you mean by all set?" Lucious looked over at some neighbors who were sitting and talking on their screened porch.

"You just seem to have it all together," said Dewey. "You'd have to be a dummy not to see that."

"But you don't know what I've had to go through to get here. You don't see that part. You see me isolated in time."

Dewey hung his head and scraped the cement with his shoe. "I suppose so."

"You're getting snapshots, Dewey. You're impressed with people like Radford, without knowing anything about them, and you seem to fall in love with them. But you're falling in love with their image, not the real person."

Dewey looked at Lucious, as his floater careened across his dark face. Lucious gently put his hand on Dewey's shoulder. "Something's blocking your view, buddy."

Two cars playing loud music suddenly swooshed by. Dewey could not make out their color—one red, the other maybe orange. Or maybe they were not that at all. Maybe it was just his imagination, he thought. "Well, hey, I still have some things to do tonight, so I better get going.

Thanks for dinner."

"Thanks for coming over."

Dewey got up and headed in the direction of the bus stop.

"Hey, just so you know, there's two buses that run at night. Take the one on the opposite side of the street. It'll get you back where you came from."

CHAPTER 28

It was almost ten o'clock when Dewey walked into the dorm after dinner with Lucious. The lobby was the same as it had been when he left a few hours ago, with the exception of a mysterious figure in a white polo shirt, white linen pants, and white bucks sitting, legs crossed, on the lobby bench. Dewey instantly knew who it was.

"What are you doing here?" said Dewey.

"Get whatever you need and meet me on the curb," said Radford. "We're taking a trip to John's Island."

"Okay, give me a minute." Dewey headed for the elevator. When he reached his room, Alex was nowhere in sight. Dewey grabbed a low-cut pair of chukkas and a light blue sweater from his wardrobe. He briefly glanced in the mirror. For the first time since arriving at the college, he liked what he saw.

Dewey left a note for Alex and walked outside to find Radford sitting in a red Volkswagen Rabbit convertible. "Get in," he said.

Together they headed out across the Ashley River Bridge along Highway 17 into a miles-long stretch of 50s-era strip mall full of hair salons, package stores, pharmacies, and gun and pawn shops. The night was clear and balmy, and the rush of air into the car felt good to Dewey. Sitting next to Radford, their hair blowing wildly, he felt like a celebrity.

Eventually, the salons and pawn shops gave way to salt marshes, roadside vegetable stands and country churches. Dewey had traveled Main Road before when he was a child. Back then, John's Island was remote and swampy, he recalled, a dark tropical jungle full of intrigue, especially for newcomers from the Midwest.

"So, where are we headed?" said Dewey.

"Headed out to your old stomping ground, or at least you said it was—right?" said Radford.

"Kiawah?"

"Yeah, Kiawah. Some friends are meeting up, so I figured we'd go."

"This late?"

"Yeah, it's never too late for them."

Main Road had turned into two lanes. Dewey could see into the cars traveling in the opposite lane, mostly young couples with the occasional family of four. They drove fast, a contrast to the stillness of the natural world around them.

Within the hour they'd arrived at Kiawah's main gate, where security wave them through. A long, winding asphalt road past lush parks and manicured green spaces led to West Beach Village, a cluster of condominiums. Dewey recognized them from his youth, as well as the Jasmine Porch restaurant and the nearby Straw Market. They were long-closed by now and dark, as it was nearly midnight. A small group of black men and women in khaki uniforms sat smoking near a dumpster. Radford cruised to a stop in one of the parking spaces.

"Your friends around here?" said Dewey.

"Relax. They're on the beach," said Radford.

In the distance, Dewey could see an orange glow with embers shooting up. Radford and Dewey found a boardwalk. The ocean was barely visible because of the darkness. Only the sound of waves crashing. The orange glow got bigger as the two of them advanced.

"Radford, I didn't think you were going to make it," said a girl who had walked from the bonfire to greet them.

"Neither did I. Got a beer?" said Radford.

"Who's this with you?" said the girl.

"A pledge. My little brother."

"A Kappa thing?"

"Yeah, something like that."

"Well, aren't you going to introduce us?" she said.

Others had congregated around Radford and Dewey.

"This is Dewey Cellars, y'all," said Radford. "Dewey, this is the club. The club of … of overachievers." The group laughed. "And *that* one is Daphne Limehouse." He pointed at the girl who'd greeted them.

"Overachievers, alright," said a boy in the group. "How many years you been at the college, Radford? Seems like you'll never leave."

The group laughed again, as they headed back to the bonfire.

Dewey sat down a few feet from the fire. He could only see faces, severe looking from the shadows cutting across them. They were handsome faces—handsome as in family money, big houses, maids and nannies, long, leisurely afternoon walks and, somewhere in all that, stories of a fortune lost or a General's saber hanging from a fireplace mantle.

Daphne located Dewey in the darkness and sat next to him.

"Radford tells me you vacationed here," she said.

"Yeah. Guess the last time was my senior year of high school," said Dewey. "It snowed that morning back home, and we flew down and by late afternoon we were riding bikes on the beach. So weird. Like a dream, really."

"And where's home?" said Daphne.

"Ohio," said Dewey. Someone threw more wood on the fire, and the flames grew higher. "So, what part of Charleston you from?"

"Downtown. Chalmers Street. My parents have a place on Wadmalaw too. But I'm out here a lot. This place makes me feel young."

"It's funny," said Dewey, "there weren't a lot of kids my age out here when we visited, but I remember one time I came out on the beach, and there was a bonfire just like this one. Bunch of kids just standing around with wind and embers. That was years ago. Tonight kinda' reminds me of that."

"It was probably us bunch of drunks," said Daphne, laughing and falling back into the sand.

"Probably," said Dewey. They looked at the fire, as shadows danced on their faces. "Hey, can I tell you something even though I hardly know you?"

"Sure," said Daphne.

"I keep having this weird dream of being in a place like this next to a fire with all these people dancing around, people much older than us, and there's this one black woman, Desirée, who's in charge of them or something. Weird, huh?"

"Maybe not."

"How so?"

"The Gullahs around here believe in dream keepers. Someone who helps you not forget your dreams. Maybe a dream keeper visited you." Daphne looked up at the stars.

"Yeah, maybe." Dewey took comfort in Daphne's words, even though he didn't put much stock in them.

"You seem like a deep-thinking kind of guy, Dewey."

"Sometimes."

"Do you have dreams?"

"You don't want to know them."

"Why not?"

"Because they're not mine, and I'm beginning to hate myself for it." Dewey looked down the beach away from Daphne.

"What's that mean?"

"It just means who I want to *be* isn't really who I *am*."

"Are they here?"

"Who here?"

"Who you want to be."

"No, you wouldn't know them. You wouldn't recognize them."

She moved closer to Dewey, locking her arm around his. They stayed like this for a long time, as the others drank and frolicked around the fire.

He looked at the long line of dimly lit condos in the distance where he'd stayed over the years only dreaming of a moment like this.

* * *

Dewey awoke the next morning in the dorm with Rad and his red Rabbit on his mind. The midnight trip to John's Island was further confirmation that Radford had taken a liking to him and would soon bring him further into his inner circle. And more and more Dewey would be like Radford, until people almost mistook them for each other.

Pleased by this development, Dewey decided to walk to The Battery and look out over the harbor. If there was time, he might even visit Dr. Lyman. He crossed Calhoun and began his journey down toward Lower King, peering through wrought iron gates into private gardens and trellised entryways, until he eventually reached The Battery.

Dewey leaned against the rusty seawall rail and looked out onto the water. A motorboat sped by; he watched its frothy wake slam against the wall. On the horizon, a sailboat unfurled its spinnaker. Seagulls flew overhead, occasionally diving for something to eat. The salt air and pluff mud smelled good—how could his dad ever think otherwise? Dewey stood for a few minutes, as traffic, mostly tourists, came and went. He wondered what his parents might be doing at this moment—their worlds so very far apart.

With the sun beginning to set, Dewey decided he'd venture over to Dr. Lyman's house on the wharf. Once past Rainbow Row, Dewey could see the doctor's house with its balconies overlooking the harbor and the garden cherub in the front yard. He climbed the stairs to the front door and knocked. A few seconds passed and, much to Dewey's surprise, he heard footsteps across the carpet and abruptly stop. He heard a deadbolt unlatch and the door creak open—there stood Dr. Lyman in a blue Oxford, khakis, and brown Sebagos, almost the same exact kind as Dewey's. "Well, what an unexpected surprise. Do come in," he said.

Dewey entered, once again noticing the pin-drop silence of the place, almost like a church. "Thank you. I certainly don't mean to intrude. I was just strolling and found myself down this way."

"No intrusion at all. I took a half day at the office, so I've been home for a while."

Dr. Lyman showed Dewey to the parlor, where he offered him a seat in a yellow, tufted wingback decorated with monkeys wearing red vests and hats, and went to get him a glass of water. When he handed him the water, Dewey noticed Dr. Lyman's soft, supple palm.

"Yes, there's lots of strolling on The Battery. And for such a small peninsula, lots of strollers surprisingly get lost. Not too many years ago I happened upon a middle schooler who'd gotten lost, and I had to walk him back to his parents."

Could this have been the stranger who walked him back to the Market so many years ago, thought Dewey, on that hot day when, feeling faint from the sun, he got lost on The Battery? "Yeah, maybe because there's so many side streets in this city. It seems with every turn you're in a different world."

"Yes, it's particularly dense and disorienting in the Market, I guess, especially to outsiders."

Dewey thought about the houses on Lower King and their

wrought iron gates that like tiny sentries guarded against passers-by.

"So, how's college life? And what's the news from Kappa House?" said Dr. Lyman.

"Classes are still going well, and pledging is in full swing. Last weekend we got our big brothers," said Dewey.

"Who's yours?"

"He's actually from here, but he went away to boarding school and came back. His family is a pretty big deal apparently."

"What's his last name?" Dr. Lyman raised an eyebrow and leaned forward in his wingback.

"Gaillard. Radford Gaillard."

Dr. Lyman's eyes widened, as he leaned back into a cloth landscape of mischievous monkeys with red vests and hats. He set his drink down on an end table. Dewey was sure he saw his hand twitch. A bead of sweat had formed just below his hairline.

A few minutes passed. "Sad to say I don't know the family or the boy," said Dr. Lyman.

Dewey thought it was strange that he didn't know the family, considering his familiarity with the city and how long he'd lived there.

Dr. Lyman reclaimed his drink and straightened up in his seat. He looked calmer to Dewey. "Describe him," he said.

"Looks, personality, popularity—he's pretty much got the whole world in the palm of his hand. Definitely top of the pecking order. But you kind of know that the first time you see him."

"And when was that?"

"Back in the spring actually, way before rush, when I was on a campus tour. He and some buddies were bicycling down George Street and ...," Dewey stopped abruptly.

"Go ahead, I'm listening."

"Well, they were biking down George in front of Porter's Lodge. When I saw him, I couldn't take my eyes off him. I just wanted to be like him so bad. Can't explain it. It was like a spell." Dewey leaned toward Dr. Lyman like he was making his case.

"There's a lot that's strange and unexplainable but beautiful, Dewey," said Dr. Lyman.

Dewey sipped some water, as Dr. Lyman and the sketched figures in the room looked to be digesting his confession. He looked up at the Banvard wishing he could be aboard the dreamy paddleboat steaming down the Ohio toward some hazy, sun-raked vanishing point. Dewey spoke cautiously. "Can I ask you something?"

"Ask."

"Did you go back to Kappa House after the jumper incident?"

Dr. Lyman sat back in his wingback and rubbed his chin with his hand. "No, I just kind of fell away. Or maybe the brothers just let me fall away. It was emotional for everyone."

By now, the sun had set, and the parlor had darkened. The sketched figures on the wall all seemed to be looking at Dewey, as if he'd overstayed his welcome. Night was falling, and for at least one sketched figure it was time to put the plough down.

"Well, I guess I better run. Big day tomorrow. Radford and I are biking around town. Maybe we'll stop and say hello."

"Do drop in, if you're able."

"Thanks."

Dewey stepped outside to the sounds of traffic on East Bay and someone calling aloud to a friend getting out of a car. Two middle-schoolers in white polos and jeans tossed a nerf football under gas lamps at the end of the block.

It was perfect out, thought Dewey, and what good fortune to have a friend like Dr. Lyman.

CHAPTER 29

"Meet under the bull and sheep skulls in half an hour," read Radford's note. Already late, Dewey rushed out of New Dorm, grabbed his bike and headed downtown to the front of Market Hall. The afternoon sky was bright blue, one of the coolest days of the semester yet.

When Dewey saw him, Radford was wearing a white Oxford shirt, yellow wool sweater with thick, blue stripes, khakis that fell just above the ankle and white tennis shoes, the kind made for walking sailboat decks. Dewey waited for a break in traffic before crossing busy Meeting Street and, while waiting, watched Radford who clearly stood out among the crowd. Against the ancient grandeur of Market Hall, Radford looked at home, a part of the facade. As Dewey crossed the street, he spied Mistral's restaurant. He thought of Alex and the big fight they'd had, and how they hadn't yet reconciled. Maybe he could try and be a better friend to him, he thought. After all, they'd got along at the start, and Dewey really liked his family, especially Frieda. But that would have to wait, as Dewey looked left and right, then crossed the street and rolled up next to Radford.

"Thanks for meeting me. Sorry for the last-minute notice," said Radford. "Pretty fall day, huh?" He looked up at the sky, and when he brought his gaze down, a chilly breeze blew past them.

"Yeah, beautiful out," said Dewey. "It really got cool."

"Yeah, September's always kind of potluck around here, never know what you're gonna get. Hot one minute, cold the next. Just like the people." Radford pulled a pair of aviator sunglasses from his pants pocket and put them on. "I thought we'd head out along The Battery and just kind of work our way around the city. Just hang out. Maybe stop and get something to eat or drink."

"Sure, sounds good."

Dewey and Radford took off for the end of the Market, before taking a right onto East Bay Street. With Radford a couple bike lengths ahead, Dewey noticed how effortlessly he pedaled, and how he rode in the middle of the street, unfazed by the traffic, as if encapsulated in his own little bubble. As they came up on the foot of Broad Street, he rode with no hands for the span of Rainbow Row.

Dewey realized how close he was to Dr. Lyman's house. He felt compelled to stop and say hello and introduce Radford, but Radford was riding so steadily and carefree that Dewey didn't think it was right to interrupt him. Where High and Low Battery met, Radford jumped the granite curb and came to a stop, eventually steadying his bike and casually propping his foot up on the seawall handrail. Dewey did the same.

"So, you like Charleston?" said Radford.

"Yeah, a lot," said Dewey. "How about you?"

"Yeah, but sometimes I feel like I've been here forever—except for my time at boarding school. Do you ever feel that way?" Radford folded his arms and looked out over the harbor in the direction of Ft. Sumter.

"What way?" Dewey spotted a massive container ship with a foreign flag exiting the harbor.

"That if you were in a different place you'd be a different person." Radford looked in the direction of the yacht club.

"Well, I guess that goes without saying. I mean we're all products of our environment, like it or not, so, yeah, you'd probably be someone different in a different place." Dewey looked closely at the container ship and could make out small figures walking on the bow.

"Do you think we can ever escape who we are and be someone else?" Radford kicked the handrail with his foot; flakes of rust fell to the ground.

Dewey moved his foot off the handrail, set both feet on the ground and leaned over his handlebars. "I'm guessing you'd have to try real hard, but still you may not be who you want to be."

A group of tourists in a horse drawn carriage passed by. A large woman with candy apple red lipstick and a shirt with *Myrtle Beach* written across it waved at them.

"C'mon, let's go," said Radford, pushing himself off the handrail.

Together they rode down the rest of Murray Boulevard and, once past the Coast Guard Station, turned onto Tradd Street, a narrow one-way road beset with crepe myrtles, live oaks, and Mercedes-Benzes.

Dewey watched as shade from the trees rolled over Radford's face, almost camouflaging it, before full sun claimed it again.

"So, got any questions?" said Radford, who'd gone back to riding with no hands.

"What's initiation like? I mean, if I make it that far."

"It's held at the house, of course, and usually takes about three to four hours. You're blindfolded for most of it. We ask you some questions, and you take a bunch of oaths."

"How do you know if you pass?"

"You mean, if you're in or not?"

"Yeah."

"They put you in this special room with a bunch of other pledges who've made it, and your big brother un-blindfolds you, shakes your hand and congratulates you. That kind of stuff. It's not as big a deal as you think. For now, I think I'd just concentrate on Cistern Daze."

"Yeah, you said something about that. That's where they can kick people out."

"Try not to think of it that way. I mean, as long as you're in this for the right reasons, no one's going to kick you out."

Radford squeezed his handlebars for the cobblestone that lay ahead. Dewey felt a bit like royalty, gliding alongside Radford on a cool, cloudless day past beautiful architecture and creeping fig.

House renovations were ongoing up and down the street, with wood siding being replaced and foundations being shored up. Long 2x4s had been squeezed up under porch roofs for stability. With homes whose crawl spaces were exposed, a damp, dank smell emanated that felt cool on Dewey's skin like under the arch at the Lodge. Not unlike the homes on Lower King, in whose direction they were headed, most Tradd Street homes had small, manicured yards full of hardy perennials and blooming annuals protected by a wrought iron fence or privacy wall.

Occasionally, the road narrowed and then widened, intersected at points by a flurry of side streets—Ashley Avenue, Legare, and Limehouse streets. The sky overhead remained sunny and blue, with occasional contrails from jets high above.

"Let's swing over to King and head back to the house," said Radford.

"Okay," said Dewey.

They turned on to Lower King, Dewey's favorite part of town, but the street and its row of neat, tidy houses near The Battery now seemed less romantic. Whereas before he hadn't noticed their imperfections—peeling paint, chipped or broken masonry, sagging shutters—they now stood out like Mary Pate's shiny rhinestones.

Still riding side by side, Dewey and Radford passed a yellow, three-story house with pale blue shutters. A thirty-something woman in Nantucket red clam diggers, a white button-down blouse and a pearl necklace was sweeping the steps. She looked through blonde tortoise shell eyeglasses with hints of cream and pink on the stems.

"Well, hey, Radford," she yelled, looking in Dewey's direction. At this point, Radford had moved ahead of Dewey and hadn't heard the woman call out. The canopy of trees had gotten fuller and thicker, and clouds passed in front of the sun, darkening the street. The woman started up again. "Well, aren't you gonna swing over this way and say, 'Hey?'" Her glasses had inched down her nose, revealing high cheekbones and a buttery complexion.

Obliging her request, Dewey changed course, gradually steering in her direction and stopping at the curb in front of her. A huge leafy crepe myrtle with lots of shade formed a canopy over them. "Hey," he said to the unknown woman.

"How's the sweetest, handsomest boy in Charleston?" she said, leaning on her broom. "How about your mutha'? I saw her with your daddy at the club just the uh-thu night."

"I'm good, everybody's good," said Dewey, who by now realized she had mistaken him for Radford. His pulse quickened and he could smell the ligustrum. What luck, he thought, that he'd actually, finally get to *be* Radford, even if for just a few minutes.

"Now, where are you in life? Still up at that boarding school or are you back home?" She had moved slightly closer to Dewey, as the shade from the canopy above rolled over his face.

"Back home," said Dewey, doing his best to affect Radford's aristocratic accent.

"It's just so hard to keep up with you Gill-yards. And y'all look so much alike—you're pretty. Pretty people. Can't for the life of me figure out if it's the beauty or craziness that attracts everyone. Maybe a little of both, don't you think?" She slowly swept a section of sidewalk, almost as if she was painting.

Dewey heard the rattle of a bike chain. Looking behind him through the shade, he saw two feet land on the pavement, and a bike come to a stop. Radford had circled back around for him.

"Hey, Ms. Rutledge," said Radford, giving Dewey a dirty look.

Ms. Rutledge looked confused. "Wait a minute—Radford?" She looked at Radford, then at Dewey, then back at Radford whose face had come into the full sun. "Well, then, who's *he*?" She pointed at Dewey, who had come out from under the shade of the crepe myrtles.

"Oh, you wouldn't know him," said Radford, "really, he's *nobody*. Nobody you would ever know."

Dewey felt his heart sink, as he retreated back into the shade. Why would Radford ever say such a thing? He was his big brother, after all—mentor, encourager, protector.

"You still playing around with those boys?" said Ms. Rutledge, affectionately.

"Yeah, still hanging around the frat house, I guess. Some things never change." Radford looked over at Dewey, as if queuing something up. "Dewey, I give to you Miss Claire Theodosia Rutledge."

"Well, now, I don't know which one of you to believe," she said, amused, her hands resting on top of the broomstick. "I swear it was you Radford I was just talking to. Sometimes you boys just seem all the same."

"Believe him," said Dewey, looking and nodding at Radford. "I don't know what got into me. I'm definitely not Radford. Sorry."

"Don't be," she said. "All sorts of things like that go on around here. It's the heat and humidity, you know. People don't see things right."

Ashamed, Dewey looked down at the ground, his floater passing in front of Claire's face.

Claire dipped her head to meet Radford's eyes. "Believe it or not, Dewey, I used to babysit this boy. That's until the boy got too big."

"You just don't give up, do you, Claire?" said Radford. "We were just out riding around."

"You just love that bike, don't you, Rad, even as a child you did.

Zipping up and down this very street like you were trying to get anywhere fast." Claire resumed her sweeping. "Did Rad ever tell you about the pluff mud man?"

"C'mon, Claire, don't do that."

"How do you know? It's not a bad story," she said. "It's downright cute."

Radford biked around in small circles to stretch his legs, while Claire began her story.

"Well, as you may or may not know, Radford loves the marsh. Every chance he got he'd be down there in the marsh flats just below Lockwood. So, one day he comes riding his bike to this very house, where I babysat him every summer, and he says he needs me down in the park. So, I rush down there with him and see this big snowman made of mud. Can you believe it? I don't know how he dragged that much mud out of the marsh and got it to the park, but it was the funniest-looking thing ev-uh. One of his early artworks, I tell you." Claire laughed so hard she nearly dropped the broom.

"Okay, I think we can leave it there, Claire," said Radford, spiraling his bike back to the curb.

"Did you like that story, Dewey? Wasn't it just *dee*-vine?"

"Yes, ma'am, really funny," said Dewey straight-faced, not wanting to anger or embarrass Radford any further.

"Well, we better start heading back to campus," said Radford.

Claire smiled at Radford and gave the step directly below her a giant sweep, kicking up dust, sand and leaves. Dewey watched as the dust got caught in an eddy of fuzzy sunlight and drifted to the ground.

"Nice meeting you, Dew," said Claire, dipping her head and eyes like with Radford. "Good luck being a little brother."

"Thanks, it was nice meeting you, too," said Dewey, trying to avoid her eyes.

"See ya', Rad," said Claire, smiling one last time.

"Bye," said Radford, pushing off the curb. Dewey pushed off, too. Together they rode back to the Market under uncertain skies, as Radford waved to people, while Dewey trailed behind.

* * *

When they returned to Market Hall, Radford violently turned his bike around and came at Dewey fiercely, almost like a different person.

"I don't know what happened back there, Dewey," said Radford, "but it better fucking stop."

"What are you talking about?" said Dewey, sitting as far back on his bike seat as he could.

"Trying to pass yourself off as me. What the hell was that? Total dick move."

"I still don't know what you're talking about."

"The way you coasted up to the curb in front of Claire like that, making her think you were me."

"Sorry. I just heard someone, a woman, call out your name and didn't know what to do," said Dewey. "I was just trying to cover for you—promise."

"I don't need covering for. I'm just fine. I'm who I am." Radford circled Dewey on his bike like a shark. "Imagine if the brothers found this out? You'd be out on your ass, pledge. And Cistern Daze would be totally out for you."

Radford stopped circling Dewey, and they met face to face. Radford hadn't changed a bit since that spring day the year before, thought Dewey—still the noble nose, fair complexion and blond curly hair parted to the side. He still smelled of tea olive, moved effortlessly over cobblestone and blended in with Charleston's dusty clapboard and palm fronds. Dewey was impressed with how much Radford had stayed the same. He would have at least expected some small imperfection—a wrinkle, a sunspot, just something—to show he'd aged, but nothing.

He could only wonder what Radford thought looking back at *him*. Did he think any part of Charleston's beauty had seeped into his blood that would make him more attractive? Or, in Radford's eyes, was Dewey that which he himself believed to be—ordinary and unremarkable just like the gray, cloudy Midwestern state that bore him?

"Are you gonna tell them, the brothers?" said Dewey.

Radford looked beyond Dewey into the late afternoon haze. "Probably not."

Dewey felt relief but also anger, which he resolved with a single question that he knew, like the thrust of a dagger, would pain Radford.

"Mind if I ask you something?" said Dewey.

"Go ahead," said Radford.

"How'd you get into Kappa?"

"That's a long, fucked-up story. I'm a legacy—sort of. My dad was a Kappa, until he tried jumping out a third story window. At least that's what they said. His fraternity brother, Joe, saved him. They sent my dad away or something, but what he didn't know was he'd gotten some girl pregnant. She wasn't from the peninsula. Anyway, she had me and gave me over to my dad's parents. I went away to boarding school, came back and that's when Dr. Joe took over."

"Doctor Joe?" said Dewey, both curious and startled.

"He's a doctor, a real one—Joe Lyman," said Radford. "Big-wig eye doctor here in town. I see him sometimes when he drops by the house."

"So, he's the one that got you into Kappa House?"

"Yeah. I still see him but not much."

Radford's *doctor* just had to be Dewey's *doctor*—or at least the one, the only one, he knew: Dr. Joseph Lyman. But why would Dr. Lyman have denied knowing anyone by the name Radford Gaillard so vigorously?

Radford put his foot on a pedal. "Is that all?"

"What?" said Dewey.

"All your questions." Radford, less agitated, turned his head and looked down Market Street toward the Custom House. In the distance, a cruise ship's smokestack puffed angrily.

"Yeah, sorry, didn't mean to pry," said Dewey.

Radford pointed his noble nose in the air, swept back his blond hair and pedaled off, disappearing like a ghost into the distance.

CHAPTER 30

"So, here's how the sausage is made," said Kappa's assistant pledge educator, or the APE, as the brothers called him. He had just begun his weekly pledge meeting update, with Dewey and the other pledges, including Bonner, Truman, and Hoffman, seated in the parlor the same way as the Sunday before. Dewey nervously felt for his pledge pin on his collar and held his pledge book tightly in his grip, pages visibly dog-eared.

"Think of dues as your membership fee, basically," continued the APE, explaining the fraternity's membership obligations. "You pay them at the beginning of each semester. Your big brother should have already mentioned this."

The APE looked at his notes, then back at the pledges. "Okay, another thing, from time to time you're going to need to hop on down to one of downtown's department stores and rent a tux for formals, unless you already have one. And one of these is coming up fast, Cistern Daze. And what is Cistern Daze, Brother Dave?" The APE handed the question off to a nearby brother.

"Cistern Daze is a big party in the Yard that's coming up in two weeks. It's where all the hot people party, and y'all are invited. We call it getting 'dazed.' Get it?"

"Where is it and how do we get in?" said Hoffman.

Brother Dave oriented himself and pointed toward campus. "You know where Porter's Lodge is on George Street across from the cafeteria—right? It's that great big arch with the inscription *Know*

Thyself?"

Hoffman nodded.

"Well, that's the place. You actually have to pass through the gate to get into Cistern Daze. Just be there in your tux by eight o'clock, and one of us will let you in," said Brother Dave.

"How about girls?" said Bonner.

"They'll be more tail up on that cistern than you can shake a stick at," said Brother Dave.

Dewey remembered Radford mentioning Cistern Daze. He'd known people in his youth who owned tuxedos, but he didn't.

"Thank you, Brother Dave, and on that note, I'd like to open the floor up to questions," said the APE.

"How much are dues, exactly?" asked the pledge who'd worn the vintage hunting vest to the pledge mixer.

"About $500 a semester," said the APE.

"Not bad," said the pledge with the vintage hunting vest.

Dewey gulped. Five hundred dollars. Not once, but twice a year. The dollars began piling up in his head.

The APE scanned the group for any final questions before making one final announcement. "Hey, I need y'all to listen up. Residence Life sent out this memo to all the frats and sororities a couple of hours ago. Some bullshit about a hurricane they think's headed this way. Supposed to be big. They even got a name for it—Hugo. Just be on the lookout, okay?"

* * *

Traffic around the Yard was beginning to wind down, when Dewey arrived to give the Tuesday tour for Lucious. Two students with backpacks walked out of the front of Randolph Hall, as another handful of students sat or laid atop the grassy Cistern catching the day's last rays.

Dewey opened the door to Towell Library and saw Ms. Tilley at her desk hunting and pecking away at her typewriter. When she saw Dewey, she walked over and gave him a big hug.

"How are you, dear heart?" she said. "Lucious tells me today's your big day—your first solo tour."

"Yes, indeed," said Dewey. "I'm really excited." He looked up at the mezzanine hoping to see Lucious and did, but just barely, as he was at his desk on the phone. He also looked behind him to the small office where he'd first interviewed. The door was open, but no one was in it.

"Well, your tour group is all ready to go." Ms. Tilley pointed to a handful of parents and students at the far end of the library. She walked Dewey down and introduced him. "Hey, y'all, I'd like to introduce Dewey Cellars, your tour guide. He's a freshman from Ohio majoring in pre-med."

Dewey laughed.

"Thank you, Ms. Tilley. Yes, my name's Dewey, and I'm a freshman. I guess we can begin the tour right here in Towell Library which dates back to 1856 and served as the college's main library until 1972. Today it serves as the Office of Admissions." Dewey looked over at Ms. Tilley who smiled and waved goodbye like she was saying goodbye to a son.

Dewey led the group outside into the afternoon light. "This is called Cistern Yard," said Dewey. "The cistern in front of you, constructed in 1857, was built to catch rainwater falling off the roof of Randolph Hall. Now it's all filled in, of course, and people come just to hang out."

The group maneuvered around the cistern into Randolph Hall, where Dewey explained how the structure had been the college's first classroom building. In his imagination, he hoped a gathering of esteemed gentlemen wearing powdered wigs and breeches while smoking small, porcelain tobacco pipes might be there to greet the group but, alas, no.

He generally followed the tour route that Liza, his mentor, had established, starting at the cistern and heading to Maybank, crossing over St. Philip Street to New Dorm past College Lodge and the Simons Center before heading back to Towell Library.

At New Dorm, Dewey gathered the group in the courtyard and pointed out his fourth-floor room. "Right up there is my room. The dorm just opened last month, so everything's new. You get a bed, desk, and wardrobe."

A kid in the group raised his hand, as loud traffic sped by on Calhoun. "Do you like your roommate?"

"Sure, he's a really good guy. I mean, we have our differences, but I think we've adapted to each other." Dewey looked at the dorm wall near the side entrance, where he and Alex had crouched down and talked, and watched the room lights go out. He thought about the bid envelope, Kappa House and Radford. So much had happened in such a short time.

As the tour progressed, Dewey offered more facts and figures, until the group reached the Simons Center. In the long, smoky windows, a series of life size figures made of wire struck various poses in the act of becoming, with the last in the series transforming into a giant butterfly. Dewey let the group wander up to the windows. Meanwhile, he went in search of André the Giant, eventually finding his palm-size friend still stuck to the bottom of the same windowpane. The image gave him great relief, as it made him feel like an insider. Whoever put André here, they were on to something big.

Crossing over St. Philip Street, Dewey led the group back to the Yard to the steps of Towell Library. When he turned around to conclude the tour, the group looked at him strangely, as if something had happened to Dewey's appearance.

"What was your name again?" asked one of the parents.

"Dewey. Dewey Cellars from Ohio."

"Thank you for the tour, Dewey Cellars from Ohio. I'm sure you're going to make a great doctor."

The group then disbanded, and Dewey walked back into Towell Library. Only a few more tours, he thought, and he'd have his Kappa volunteer hours completed.

* * *

Dewey answered the phone to find Noah on the other end. He envisioned him at home on the back porch with the cordless phone and a big glass of sweet tea. Noah had picked up a love for sweet tea when they lived in Charlotte, and from there he'd brewed it in a big clay pitcher using a teaspoon to stir in the sugar. Still, despite the sugar, it always seemed to turn bitter.

"Hey, Dad, how are you?" said Dewey.

"Fine, son, glad you answered," said Noah. "How's the weather?"

"Good. Almost feels like fall but not yet."

"Yes, it's always nice when seasons begin to change. Must feel like a different kind of change down there than up here." Noah paused to take a sip of sweet tea.

"Yeah, it does feel different. Something about being on the coast and not having so many trees overhead makes everything just more intense. I know since I've been down here I've felt more intense."

"Well, you've had so much on your plate in just a few short weeks," said Noah. "New classes, the fraternity. How are your friends? Especially your roommate—what's his name?"

"Alex, Dad," he said. "His name is Alex."

"Now, did we meet him?

"No, you and mom headed out before I could make an introduction. His parents asked about you, and I said they could meet you next time."

"Yes, next time for sure," said Noah. "Hey, I called because I need to talk to you about something."

"Sure, okay."

"Things have gotten tighter since we last spoke, and, well, it looks like we're not going to be able to help you financially beyond room, board, and books."

"So, no help with Kappa House?"

Dewey could hear Noah slap his glass of tea down on a coaster.

"Yes, unfortunately, that's right, son, I'm sorry."

"But, Dad, this is big stuff. I've got a big brother and everything. I'm full in, and we've got a big event coming up." Dewey paused. "What happened?"

"We just had some additional expenses come up that we weren't expecting, son. Your mother and I are so, so sorry."

Dewey felt his stomach turn. "I can't believe this. Not now."

"I'm sorry, son, but that's the way it is."

"And you can't pull some of mom's money?" said Dewey.

"No, it's all tied up in her trust," said Noah. "We can't touch it."

"This sucks! Why are you telling me this now, just as things are going my way?"

"Sorry, son, that's just where we are."

If Dewey heard *Sorry, son* one more time, he was going to scream.

"Sorry for shouting, Dad," he said. "I'll figure it out. Tell everybody I said hello."

Dewey hung up the phone, went into the common room and reached for a juice box. The thought of Noah drinking sweet tea made him feel bitter. He would have to think hard on where to get the money.

Just as he was about to get up, the phone rang again. "Fuck," he said to himself, "if it's Dad, I'm going to be pissed." He took a moment. "Hello?"

"Is Dewey there?"

"Yeah, this is him."

"Hey, this is Brother Dave from Kappa House."

"Oh, hey."

"Hey, man," said Brother Dave, "I just want to bring you up to speed on Cistern Daze. It's going to be at nine o'clock on Thursday the twenty-first. About a week and a half away, so I need your money. Remember it's formal so be in a tux. Someone will let you in at the gate. And don't forget your pledge pin."

"Cool, thanks."

"Yeah, bye."

Dewey hung up, leaned back in his chair and sighed. Through the open window he heard two people walk by. Would life be any easier if he was one of them? If he hadn't begun this big chase in the first place? And was it even worth it? He thought he was in with Radford, then the bike incident with Claire Rutledge. Would he even make it into Kappa House?

But right now, he needed to think about how he'd pay for it. With it being just two weeks away, getting a job was probably not realistic. While the thought horrified him, did he have anything he could sell or pawn? The Hartmann luggage? The Dior Dopp kit? His computer? None would probably bring the amount he needed.

But what about a chest of 18th century silver forks, knives, and spoons like Dr. Lyman's? He was ashamed of the very thought, but on occasion he'd seen his mother sell family possessions and heirlooms for quick cash.

But why did it have to be Dr. Lyman? He'd been so nice, treating his eye floater, inviting him into his home, hosting him at the yacht club. What was happening to him that he would steal to get what he wanted? It would be easy, though, Dewey having once seen Dr.

Lyman reach for a spare key under a statue of a cherub in the front yard. Looking out into the corridor, he imagined the brass-hinged silver chest with the medallion bearing the initials *JHL*. He could almost see its design in the tabby concrete.

He reached for a phone book, thumbed to the entry *pawn shop* and dialed the first number he found.

CHAPTER 31

It wasn't so much the knock at the door as it was the scent accompanying it that made Dewey get up from the couch while watching the evening update on the approaching hurricane. He opened the door and, much to his surprise, found Frieda, Stuart, and the waft of leafy greens.

"Hey, Dewey—surprise, surprise, huh?" said Frieda, inching into the doorway. "And, of course, you remember Stuart, right?"

"Oh, hey," said Dewey. "What are y'all doing here? Something wrong?"

"Not exactly. Well, not that we know of," said Frieda.

"We were supposed to meet Alex in the Market for dinner, and he never showed," said Stuart, leaning against the door jamb.

"Why don't y'all come in first?" said Dewey, stepping aside.

"Thanks," said Frieda.

Their presence made Dewey think of move-in—the perfect brown nubby carpet, the light, sweet smell of Elmer's glue from the wardrobe and Alex's possessions piled in a corner.

"Well, Dewey," said Frieda, "the dean's office sent a letter telling us that Alex is on probation. His grades—apparently they're not where they're supposed to be, and since he wasn't the strongest student coming in, the school is worried about him." She paused. "Did he mention anything to you?"

"He mentioned he was dropping Algebra because he was failing, but I didn't think it was serious being it was so early in the semester," said Dewey.

"It's just like him not to say anything," said Stuart, bringing his hand down like a gavel. "I just don't know what he's thinking. This happens over and over."

"He sure puts up with a lot. I mean, no offense." Dewey felt courageous for saying this, as he would've never spoken this way to his own parents. He felt he owed Alex.

"What do you mean?" said Frieda.

"He's had a hard time fitting in," said Dewey.

"But he said he went to a fraternity party and then some party here at the dorm," said Frieda.

"Yeah, we both did," said Dewey.

"He's gotten everything he's wanted," said Stuart.

Dewey thought of Alex's wardrobe full of colorful, expensive clothes, and how envious he was when he first saw them.

"Not everything," said Frieda.

"Almost," said Stuart.

"I'm sure he'll turn up," said Dewey. "He's smart."

"Smart, alright," said Stuart, rolling his eyes.

"You're so positive, Dewey," said Frieda. "It's nice to have real people in the world. Alex needs friends like you."

"Thank you, but I haven't really done anything." Dewey felt ashamed for lying to Alex about the fraternity, borrowing his clothes without permission and thinking such ugly things about him. Frieda and Stuart got up and headed for the door. In Dewey's mind, she still looked like a sweet potato, and he a stalk of celery.

"Please tell him to call us if you see him," she said.

"Sure." Dewey let them out and watched them walk down the hall hoping, in time, they might find their little radish.

***

Signs of Mary Pate preceded her, as shimmering rhinestones played on the dorm's lobby floor. Dewey had taken the elevator down to meet her to go to Cumberland's, as they'd previously arranged.

"You look nice," said Dewey, offering her the crook of his arm.

"So do you. I like that shirt," she said.

It was a slightly threadbare hand-me-down from his father. Not exactly as he would have wished, but wearing the shirt made him feel he'd gotten back at least some small part of himself lost to Alex's wardrobe. They walked down Calhoun Street past Marion Square and took a right on Meeting Street, until they got to Cumberland Street and the bar. Music blared, as Dewey and Mary Pate quickly joined the long line at the door. Night had fallen quick and early, reminding Dewey that the seasons were changing; move-in now seemed such a distant memory to him. The line slinked along, until eventually Mary Pate and Dewey entered the club, with its low light, and smell of hops and cigarette smoke. He recognized the band and its blond, gyrating front man from the Stern Center's freshman mixer.

"Want something to drink?" said Dewey.

"They'll probably card us," said Mary Pate. "Better make it Cokes."

Dewey wondered how Mary Pate would know such a phrase— *they'll probably card us*. She seemed like someone who would abstain from alcohol. Nonetheless, he elbowed his way to the bar. "Two Cokes," he said, as the bartender reached for a soda gun and two red Solo cups.

"No ID, huh?" said the bartender.

"Nah. Just here for the atmosphere," said Dewey.

"That your girl over there?" He pointed to Mary Pate.

"Just a friend."

"For now," said the bartender with a sly wink. "Listen, if y'all want something stronger, no problem. Just come to me, and I'll hook y'all up."

"What do I owe you?" he said.

"On the house. Don't worry about it."

Dewey returned to Mary Pate. "Here," he said, delivering the dark, carbonated beverages. He noticed how her knee length black skirt fit snug around her hips. He noticed her breasts, small and flat against her chest. He noticed how good her hair smelled.

"Thanks," said Mary Pate.

Soon they waded onto the dance floor, where other co-eds—some in clunky, white gym shoes and fake polos, others in linen shirts and fleece anoraks—hopped and shuffled, arms aloft, lost in the rhythm of the night. Mary Pate swayed her hips and squatted low. Dewey inched closer to her, breathing in her vanilla-scented perfume. He could see her panty lines, spaghetti-thin seams outlining her hind flesh that eventually slipped between her legs past the soft private mound of warm, downy folds that Dewey knew, from the stash of *Playboys* he'd found wrapped in a garbage bag back home, could inspire both love and hate. Maybe he'd wanted Mary Pate all along—her twang, her rhinestones, her simple-mindedness. He liked her most because she knew who she was, and he didn't have to be someone he wasn't in front of her. And he knew she would like, maybe even love him whereas the Kiawah girls never would. No matter how perfect or beautiful he tried to be, he would never have a place at the bonfire.

"Having fun?" shouted Mary Pate, her rhinestones flashing brightly on his shirt. They had moved to the edge of the dance floor. Mary Pate grabbed her Coke at the table.

"Sure," said Dewey above the din. "You?"

"Yeah." Mary Pate sipped her Coke. "Who'd you say those guys were?"

"The Archetypes."

"What's it mean?"

"It means the one original one. The first of something."

Mary Pate looked up at the stage. "Sounds made up," she said.

"People do that—they make things up."

"Yes, they do." Dewey looked down at the floor at the sticky spills.

"More to drink?" said Mary Pate.

"Yeah, I guess," said Dewey.

He watched as Mary Pate walked to the bar and lifted a finger. The bartender reached for something on the shelf and mixed it with the Cokes. Mary Pate carried the drinks back to Dewey. "You'll like this," she said.

The crowd on the dance floor had condensed into a giant ball. Dewey thought he recognized some of them from the Maybank herd. One of them, a tall, lanky girl with chestnut brown hair, danced in the center like a whirling dervish.

"I don't know what you put in this, but it feels good," said Dewey, holding his drink up.

"It gets better," said Mary Pate.

They moved back onto the dance floor and penetrated the giant ball, until they were inseparable from the rest. Here, with his head feeling fuzzy and the room spinning, Dewey felt himself let go, if only briefly, of his desire for proportion, beauty, and perfection. He let go of Linnaeus and the storefront mannequin. He even let go of Radford.

"C'mon, Dew, let's go, it's getting to be too much," said Mary Pate, dragging him away from the throbbing mass. "Let's go back to the dorm."

"Yeah, Okay," said Dewey.

It was midnight when they returned to the dorm, and Dewey's dizziness had worn off. The boy who had delivered pizza to Mary Pate's the week before waited for someone at the front desk, while a black girl in pajamas and slippers mashed a button on a vending machine.

"Come up," said Mary Pate.

"Okay, but just for a minute," said Dewey.

The elevator chirped, as Mary Pate and Dewey got off on the third floor. Her room was dark, except for the light coming in from the courtyard.

"Sit," she said, lowering herself onto the couch in the common room. "Listen, I'm not like the girls you want. I'll never be one of those tanned girls from a tropical island. Do you know the ones I'm talking about?"

Dewey looked into the darkness. He admired Mary Pate's honesty. They were a lot alike, he thought—both creatures outside their natural habitats trying not to get eaten. Maybe being with Marty Pate was just the natural order of things, he thought.

"Don't say anything more," said Dewey. "Just stop." He took her by the hand, led her to the bedroom and pulled her close. She struggled like prey that's been caught and glad for it. He traced her panty line with his hand, stopping occasionally to shape a gentle spiral on her ass, before thrusting his hips into the mound below her waist. She grabbed him and threw her head back, so he could kiss her neck, her breath faltering at times. Soon naked, they tumbled into bed.

For the rest of the night, Dewey tried mimicking what he'd seen and read in the stash of *Playboys*. Here, he hoped, according to Dr. Freeman's lecture, he might prove more a honeybee than a drone fly.

CHAPTER 32

Dewey walked to Kappa House to take a break from the dorm. As he stepped onto the porch, the faces of all the people he'd met since coming to Charleston flashed before him—Alex, Mary Pate, Lucious, Dr. Lyman, and of course, Radford. Amazing Radford, handsome Radford, world-in-the-palm-of-his-hand Radford. In only a few short weeks he'd not only met him but ended up his little brother. Still, Dewey felt a part of him was still back in the bleak, gray Midwest.

As he walked into the house, he saw Dylan in the parlor sitting on a sofa.

"Hey, what's up?" said Dewey.

"Not much. Hadn't seen you since the last pledge meeting," said Dylan.

"Been busy with class."

"Hey, I heard you and Rad went biking around town."

"Yeah. It was alright. Showed me some places I hadn't been."

"See anyone you know?" Dylan picked up a Coke can next to him on the floor and spit in it. "Want any?"

"Thanks, but I don't dip."

"That's cool. So, did you meet anyone?"

"Yeah, I met Radford's babysitter from a long time ago."

"Creepy, huh?" said Dylan, a big bulge bouncing in his lower right lip.

"You've met her then," said Dewey, his voice rising.

"No, just heard about her. Another one of Rad's crazy friends."

"Why do you say that?"

"Because they're all crazy. All those kids he surrounds himself with. Bat-shit crazy." Dylan spit in the can again.

Dewey took a seat on a folding chair across from Dylan. Maybe Claire was crazy, he thought. How she seemed to have appeared out of nowhere and the breathy, enchanting way she spoke. Even the way she swept the sidewalk—broad, sweeping semi-circles, one after the other, as if she was creating some kind of mandala.

Suddenly there was movement outside not far from where they sat.

"Hold just a sec," said Dylan. "I'll be right back."

Dewey followed Dylan with his eyes as he got up and headed for the porch, where some of the brothers had congregated. Something was happening out in front of the row.

"Once you go black, you never go back!" yelled one of the brothers.

"Hey, hey," said another brother, trying to get the brother's attention.

Curious about the commotion, Dewey got up and joined the brothers on the porch. Peering out over the railing, he saw, much to his surprise, Lucious and the nurse from student health walking by. Dewey surmised from his own experience a few weeks before that they'd been walking past frat row when one of the brothers saw and took aim at them.

Dylan, the most senior of the group, was trying to quiet the brothers—the big bulge in his lower right lip bobbing up and down as he spoke. Dewey headed toward the corner of the porch, as if to take cover. He looked directly at Lucious, then at the nurse from Student Health. He recalled how she had smiled and winked at Lucious when she transferred Trey's care back to him. Dewey stared at Lucious's chocolate-colored skin, skin he was sure had sailed from

Africa. He thought of how he and Lucious had parted with a handshake just a few nights before. And now Lucious held the hand of a woman who could have well been his oppressor in a different time.

"Screw you, white boys," shouted Lucious from the sidewalk. His date stepped closer to him and whispered something.

"Get on down the road, Oreo," said one of the brothers.

Dylan looked at him. "Y'all get the hell back in the house. Every one of y'all."

"But we're just having a little fun."

"Get back in the goddamn house—now!"

Dewey stepped away from the corner of the porch into the light. Lucious looked in his direction. He tried dodging his stare, but it was too late—Lucious had seen him.

Dylan grabbed the Coke can and sat back down on the couch. "Sorry about that, dude. To be honest, I don't know what to think of that, the way things are changing these days. I just got a problem with them doing it out on the porch like that. It could be anybody, ya' know?"

Dewey looked down at the floor. It was hard looking back up. "Then you have a problem with blacks and whites together?" said Dewey.

"Most down here do," said Dylan, "but like I told you I don't know what to think."

"But why?"

"I don't know—everybody has their own reason. Some just make one up. I mean, half those boys out there are Yankees. What do they fucking know?"

"And you know better?"

"Listen, Dewey—it's Dewey, right?—there's a pecking order in life. Everyone knows that. If you don't know that, then you ought to."

Kingdom, phylum, class, order, family, genus, species, thought Dewey.

"Well, dude, I got to head on over to Maybank for English," said Dylan, spitting in the can. "That Hemingway sure went through some shit, didn't he? Then blows his head off all at the end. Just when you think you know someone."

Dewey shifted back and forth in his seat. "Yeah, just when you think you know."

Dylan stepped off the porch and crossed Wentworth Street, as a driver sped by and honked his horn. "Fucker," he yelled.

CHAPTER 33

The way to Dr. Lyman's house had almost become ingrained in Dewey's mind by now—down King, left at The Battery onto East Bay past the yacht club, finally onto Boyce's Wharf. This day was no different, except this visit was of a different and sinister nature: to secure the silver chest. It was mid-morning, and Dewey knew Dr. Lyman would be at work. The weather was cool and rainy. Whitecaps in the harbor crashed against one another mightily.

Dewey slowly approached Dr. Lyman's house and crept into the front garden. He reached for the cherub, taking it by the wings and tilting the knee-high creature back into some nearby boxwoods. There lay the key like a lost treasure. Setting the cherub upright again, Dewey noticed that its chiseled, weathered eyes looked sad and confused. He unlocked the front door and walked in.

Silence prevailed. From where Dewey stood in the foyer, he could see everything was in its place—the blue Wedgewood, the jade figurines, and the white and gray ceramic heron. He walked across the plush beige carpet and fine orientals. He pulled the heavy, khaki curtains back and peeked through the blinds to see the dilapidated, villa-style house with the prefabricated door across the way. He even opened the refrigerator door: a half gallon of milk, a bottle of white wine, a six pack of Coke, cheese, some vegetables, and a box of chocolates. Dewey went to one of the bookcases and rolled his fingers along the spines of the books: *Mellowed by Time*, *A History of the Lowcountry*, and *The Complete Works of Shakespeare*. The charcoal etching on the wall of a black man in overalls and a straw hat seemed to mind his own business, undisturbed by Dewey's intrusion.

He felt oddly at home in Dr. Lyman's house, despite having entered without the doctor's consent. Somehow, he'd explain it. Or, just maybe, he would never see Dr. Lyman again.

Dewey made way to the highboy and opened its glass doors. He pulled the silver chest off the shelf and placed it on a nearby ottoman, running his fingers down the sides of it from back to front, whereupon he opened it. Expertly polished, the forks, knives and spoons commanded the room's attention. Dewey felt like a king. He lifted the chest off the ottoman and headed toward the front door. He looked over his shoulder a final time. In Dewey's eyes, the sketched figures on the walls seemed to look betrayed and disappointed, and the Banvard landscape less dreamy, like there'd been a flood and everything had been washed away.

As he stepped outside, a strong gust of wind hit him in the face. He felt like he'd been slapped. Meanwhile, the whitecaps continued battling, as storm clouds swirled above.

* * *

The search for a pawn shop had led Dewey to a mostly gray, industrial area north of Charleston littered with warehouses, strip malls, and factory smokestacks. In the middle of it all was a pawn shop, which touted itself as the region's largest, with all kinds of items for sale—surf boards, guns, lawn mowers and, of course, silver and gold jewelry.

How far from the hazy views and gentle breezes of The Battery, he thought. Never did he think he'd end up here doing what he was about to do.

Once inside, Dewey passed by the long glass counter running the length of one wall containing shiny watches, rings and other jewelry for sale. The rest of the shop was composed of gray metal shelves for storing larger items. Above, fluorescent lights buzzed as narrow bands of light bounced off the smooth concrete floor.

"What can I do for you?" said a man behind the counter in his twenties wearing blue jeans, black boots, and a black polo shirt. If Dewey had seen him on campus, he wouldn't have thought twice, but because he worked here, Dewey was automatically suspicious.

"Yeah, I wanted to know if you take silverware—forks, knives, spoons."

"Yeah, we deal in that. Whaddya have?"

"It's a silver chest. A very old one." Dewey pointed to the chest, which, because it was heavy, he had placed on the floor at his side.

"Is it clean?" said the man.

"What do you mean '"clean?"' said Dewey confused.

"I mean is it stolen?" A few seconds passed before the man started up again. "Look, don't worry about it. You don't look like someone who would steal. You're the honest type."

Dewey looked down at the smooth cement floor and thought of the brown nubby carpet back at the dorm. This was a harder, tougher surface, and he could feel his feet beginning to hurt. He reached down, grabbed the chest and hauled it up, smacking the counter and rattling the rings, watches and heavy chain bracelets below.

In the mirror behind the counter, Dewey could see reflected the brass medallion with the initials *JHL*. The very top of the medallion— a sort of downward arc—looked like a frown.

The man behind the counter opened the chest to find several red, velvet-lined cutlery trays containing highly polished forks, knives, and spoons. The man inspected them, picking up various utensils for a closer look.

"Definitely high quality," he said, running his finger across a knife's edge.

"Yeah, a lot of history here," said Dewey.

"What's that?"

"I just meant that it's really old."

"Did you mention where you got it?"

"It's a relative's," said Dewey. "A dead one."

"I can give you $500 for the whole thing," said the man.

"That's it?" said Dewey, expecting at least twice that.

"I might be able to go a little higher if I talk to my boss but not much." The man hovered over the chest with both hands like it was already his. "I mean, whether you wanna sell it or not is up to you. It just matters if at the end of the day you can part with it."

Dewey hesitated. He thought of Dr. Lyman and how kind he'd been. How he'd fed Dewey and spent time with him. Befriended him. Confided in him. Dewey hesitated once more. "Okay, I'll take it."

The man slowly and gently closed the top of the chest, and pushed it aside. A foul, musty odor from the back storeroom washed over them. Dewey glanced outside. The street had darkened from clouds passing overhead. He felt the worst he'd felt since coming to Charleston. In some ways he wanted to go back to Ohio.

The man returned to the counter with some paperwork and $500 in cash. "All I need is your signature, and that'll do it."

"Here you go," said Dewey, staring at the palm of his hand and thinking of Dr. Lyman's fine pens.

"Be sure to tell all your college friends we're up here," said the man, who had a giant diamond ring tattooed on his arm. "Like you, we'll give 'em the deal of a lifetime."

CHAPTER 34

With his back to the cistern, Dewey had just finished giving a tour when he saw Mary Pate from the corner of his eye. He had not seen or been with her since Cumberland's. As the tour group disbanded and spread out across the Yard, Dewey looked over at her. He'd almost come to regard her as a zoo attraction, exotic in her rhinestones and up-do.

"Passing through?" he yelled out.

She came to stand beside him. "Actually, I'm headed to the cafeteria," she said. "I figured you would have called by now or at least come over."

Dewey looked over at the cafeteria, then back at Mary Pate. "I meant to, but Saturday I had this pledge thing."

"How's that going, anyway?"

"Pretty good, as long as you do what they say. I was with Radford the other day biking downtown."

"How is he?" Mary Pate didn't flinch.

"He's good."

Mary Pate looked around at the people in the Yard. "How'd your tour go today?"

"Okay. There was a kid from Ohio, so that was cool."

"What kinds of things do you say?"

"General history of the place. Important dates, people. Some stats thrown in. I'm really just doing it to check the box for the Kappa volunteer requirement."

"Do you tell the truth?"

"What?"

"When you walk them around campus, do you tell them the truth?"

"I guess," said Dewey.

"So, are you going to tell *me* the truth? I mean, you remember Cumberland's, right?"

"I remember." A couple holding hands walked by. She was short with red, curly hair; he was tall with brown hair and green eyes. Dewey recognized them from the Kappa mixer. He wondered if they knew Radford, then turned his attention back to Mary Pate. "The truth is I just don't think we'd work."

"We worked the other night, didn't we?"

"That was different."

"So that was nothing?" Mary Pate clutched her books tighter.

"No."

"No, what?"

"No, that wasn't nothing."

Dewey heard someone exit Towell Library behind him. He glanced over his shoulder to see Lucious with his briefcase headed to a nearby bike rack. He scowled at Dewey, hopped on his bike and disappeared under the arch.

"Someone you know?" said Mary Pate, "another one of your butt buddies?"

"Stop, Mary Pate. Fucking stop. He's a good guy."

"You'd probably date *him* before you would me." Mary Pate lunged at Dewey.

"Since we're on the topic of truth, tell me the truth about you and Radford—the real truth." Dewey crossed his arms.

"I told you the story. Our mothers are sisters which makes us cousins."

"Well, I've got a different version because Radford told me he doesn't know anything about you. Said he was here alone—no family."

"He's a liar. Lied since he was a child. Ask anyone in the family." Mary Pate peered off into the distance. A tear rolled down her cheek. "So, I made it all up, okay? There's no Confederate general and no family feud. I made it up that night because I wanted you to like me and think I was important."

"I actually believed you," said Dewey.

"You'd have believed anything that night, Dewey. So wound up about Radford. It was like something possessed you. I could've told you anything and you would have believed it."

Dewey looked around the Yard. A group of students picnicked in a corner. A boy in a tie-dye shirt played with a hacky sack. A professor walked into Randolph Hall.

"So where does that leave us now?"

"Nowhere."

"You're a poser, Dewey Cellars, and some day you'll see that. You're gonna be in the gutter." Mary Pate marched off toward the cafeteria.

Dewey looked around, hoping no one had seen their exchange. As he sighed and looked up at the sky, his floater appeared. He retreated to Randolph Hall, where he hoped the lack of light might help him see better.

CHAPTER 35

Dewey and the other pledges had been called to Kappa House on short notice. When he got there, he could see Bonner, Truman, and Hoffman standing on the porch. Dewey joined them as they all piled into the parlor.

"Alright, pledges, have a seat," said Brother Dave. "This is a special meeting to collect any last dues and fees and answer any questions about Friday's Cistern Daze."

Bonner raised his hand. "Will a regular suit do? I heard you had to wear a tux."

"It's gotta be a tux," said Brother Dave.

Hoffman raised his hand next. "I don't mean to sound disrespectful, but remind me one more time what this event's all about?"

"Fair enough," said Brother Dave. "First, this is a Greek Life event, so it would look pretty lame if we weren't there. Second, it lets us see you in action. Some of you are gonna get drunk, puke your brains out and fuck this up. The rest of y'all will behave like Kappa men and do this right. I'd be lying if we didn't take this under consideration for initiation."

"Can I be in the first group?" said Bonner, as laughter erupted from every corner of the parlor.

Brother Dave gave Bonner a dirty look. "Finally, while I got y'all here, let me ask how y'all are doing with your big brothers." Brother Dave's eyes landed on Dewey. "You go first."

The request caught Dewey off guard. "It's going good. We've been hanging out some and I'm learning a lot."

Brother Dave interrupted. "Tell me again who's your big brother?"

"Radford," said Dewey.

"That's right," said Brother Dave, "You're the buckeye kid."

"Sorry?"

"Buckeye as in Ohio." Brother Dave had stepped closer toward the pledges.

"Oh, right, yeah," said Dewey.

"Are you yourself tonight, Dewey? You seem a little out there."

"No, I'm fine."

"Okay, then, just one more point of business. I'll be at the door in the next few minutes collecting money for those of y'all who still owe."

Bonner, Truman and Hoffman all got up and headed out the door, each of them depositing a check in Brother Dave's sweetgrass basket. Dewey followed behind with $500 in cash.

"Whoa, pledge" said Brother Dave, putting a hand on Dewey's shoulder, briefly detaining him. "Where'd you get that kind of dough?"

"From somebody very generous who doesn't even know it yet," said Dewey.

Then Dewey walked out of the house and headed for Sharky's.

CHAPTER 36

Public safety officers were stapling yellow flyers to the lobby walls at the dorm as Dewey walked in. One of them, Caesar, he remembered from move-in. Dewey approached him. "Excuse me, what's with all the flyers?" he said.

"It's just a pre-caw-shun," said Caesar, who reminded Dewey of Irene from the cafeteria.

"Precaution?" said Dewey.

"Yassir, a storm pre-caw-shun. They's a storm way out in the Atlantic called Hugo. May head this way. Just wanna make sure y'all's alright."

Dewey recalled the newspaper headline from Mistral's. "Thank you, Caesar," he said. "It is Caesar, isn't it?"

"Yassir, it is."

"My name's Dewey. I remember you from move-in."

"Yeah, I been at the college a good while." He raised an eyebrow at Dewey. "If you don't mind me askin', how old are you?"

"Eighteen."

"That's what I was fixin' to say. So, when you was born, I already been doin' this job about ten years. Kinda strange to think about, almost like we traveled through time together or somethin'. Chaz-tun will do that to you. Well, nice meetin' you."

Dewey rode the elevator up to his room and opened the door. The phone rang. "Hello?"

"Yes, I'm looking for Dewey—Dewey Cellars," said a woman on

the other end.

"This is Dewey."

"Mr. Cellars, this is Lyman Ophthalmology," said the woman. Dewey remembered Dr. Lyman's secretary, a middle-aged woman in a white blouse and gray skirt. "Dr. Lyman has you down for an appointment Monday at eleven thirty. This is just a reminder."

Dewey froze, and the receiver nearly fell out of his hand. "I'm not sure I can make that."

"It won't take long. No procedures. Just wants to check the floater and make sure you're seeing things clearly."

"I'm not sure—I mean, about the appointment, not the part about whether I'm seeing clearly or not because I am." Dewey sat still in his chair, as if trying to hide from the voice.

"Well, he does have after-hours appointments but they're at his residence?"

"Okay," said Dewey, unaware Dr. Lyman had a home office. "I guess I can. What time?"

"Let's do six o'clock on Monday. Do you need his address?" said the woman.

"Sure, I'll take it." Dewey pretended to grab a pen and paper.

"Okay, then, you're all set. He'll see you at six on Monday at his residence."

"Okay, thanks," said Dewey. He set the phone down, but not before his wrist got tangled in the long, coiled cord. Why would Dr. Lyman's office reach out so unexpectedly, he thought? Why the option of seeing him at his home? Did Dr. Lyman suspect Dewey of anything? Maybe he was just being paranoid. The anxiety began to mount. He looked out the window into the bright, blue sky—his floater appeared bigger and more squiggly, full of arcs and angles that again blurred his vision.

Just a few weeks before, Dewey felt his intention had been so clear—find and befriend Radford, and let the natural order of things unfold.

Dewey looked down into the courtyard, where two pigeons had landed. Their feathers were black and gray along the body and tail, while a latticework of green and purple feathers near the neck shimmered iridescently. The two small birds pecked the ground repeatedly for crumbs and seeds. One puffed out his chest aggressively and stepped ahead, while the other trailed behind trying to do the same but failing.

In a lecture on the development of avians, Dr. Freeport had referred to pigeons by their Linnean name, *Columba livia*, Dewey recalled. They strutted everywhere around campus bobbing their heads, which Dr. Freeport explained was an attempt to stabilize their vision in order to get a clearer view of their surroundings.

He'd also said pigeons mated for life but would occasionally engage members of the same sex when the flock was unstable or a bird was having difficulty finding its place. Dewey looked out at the pigeons again. Did one simply like and admire the other, or were they love birds? What if one refused the other? What would the flock think? At the moment, Dewey had no answers. He looked one final time and found that the birds had slipped under summer's last remaining crepe myrtle blossoms, hiding in the shadows, heads down as if somehow ashamed, until they could no longer be seen.

The traffic on Calhoun Street beyond the courtyard reminded Dewey that he still needed a tuxedo for Cistern Daze. Downtown would be a good place to start, and it would also give him a chance to visit Lower King and The Battery.

The city was sluggish. Such were Friday afternoons in Charleston, as if the city were exhausted from all the week's pageantry and mania, driven by dappled sunlight, towering cloud stacks and intoxicating flora. This kingdom by the sea, home to beauties like the Yard's grande dame, needed, quite simply, a breather.

After a few minutes of walking, Dewey was in front of the antique store and haberdashery that he and Alex had passed on the way back from Poogan's the night of move-in. "Ceramic Dalmations and tufted wingbacks," he said to himself, items that seemed to have alienated Alex, the latter having preferred La-Z-Boys with leg rests and cup holders instead. Where was Alex, he thought, feeling a little remorseful. It had been days since Frieda and Stuart had visited to say he was missing.

When he passed the haberdashery, Dewey spied the mannequin, still perfectly chiseled and looking out over the horizon. A short blue windbreaker had replaced the Burberry trench coat; jeans changed out for trousers; and a gray turtleneck swapped for a cable knit sweater.

Dewey opened the door to the store and walked into the sea of poplin, corduroy, and merino wool that he'd seen weeks ago. Displayed on a large wooden table were all the accoutrements of a gentleman—blazer buttons, tie clips and brass belt buckles.

"If it isn't Dewey Cellars," said a familiar voice. "My little brother. My very likeness." The voice came from the direction of the mannequin, as if, just maybe, it was the mannequin talking. It wasn't the mannequin, however, but the lean, blond figure standing next to it.

Dewey turned to find Radford leaning on one side of the mannequin. "What are you doing here?"

"I work here," said Radford, looking around as if to demonstrate his familiarity with the place.

"No way?" Dewey didn't think Radford worked at all. He just assumed he lived off family money, like Dylan had said.

"Yeah, the shop's owned by a distant cousin. I started working here in the summers."

"Cool place," said Dewey, still reeling from Radford's sudden appearance.

"Yeah, I guess so, and the best part is the company." Radford jokingly swung his arm around the mannequin.

Radford and the plastic figure next to him were practically twins, thought Dewey. Same eyes, nose and hair. Same carefree gaze on the horizon. Dewey almost had a hard time differentiating them.

"So, let me guess, you're here for a tux for Cistern Daze?" said Radford.

"Yeah," said Dewey, trying not to call attention to himself among the other shoppers because of his dated, ill-fitting clothes.

"Over here."

Radford and Dewey waded through the sea of fabric to a wall with a long line of tuxedos.

"All made in England," said Radford. "I'd suggest the traditional tux. Nothing too fancy or showy. That's what I've got."

"Okay," said Dewey, running his hand over its velvet lapel and admiring its softness.

"They start at $800," said Radford, grinning.

"You must be kidding? That suit is $800?"

"It's not just any suit, Dew." Radford rested his arm against the metal rack.

"What's wrong?"

"I don't have that kind of money," said Dewey, cursing Noah under his breath.

Just then, an older man in a blue blazer walked into the store. He reminded Dewey of the man he sat next to at church—tall, tan, no socks. He wandered around the store and picked out a pair of wool trousers and several Oxfords. Dewey envied the ease in which he shopped, not once looking at the price tag.

"What if I bought it for you, and you paid me back?" said Radford out of the blue.

"I can't let you do that," said Dewey, incredulous.

"Yeah, let me help. I'm your big brother after all."

How could Radford have such a change of heart after practically denying his existence just the day before? Was he toying with him? Was this some kind of manipulative tactic? Nonetheless, he felt his friendship renewed by Radford's generosity and accepted his offer.

"I'll pay you back, I swear," said Dewey.

"I know you will," said Radford.

The man in the blue blazer had checked out at the counter and was headed for the door, the smell of sandalwood trailing in his wake. Radford retreated to the back of the store to put Dewey's tuxedo in a hanging bag. He returned minutes later, resuming his place next to the mannequin. "Here," he said.

"Thanks, I owe you big," said Dewey, his wrist bent and weighed down by the tux. With the hanging bag draped over his shoulder, he smiled and exited onto Lower King, when suddenly someone in the direction of the nearby pharmacy called his name.

"Dewey, over here," they shouted.

"Who would ever know me down here?" thought Dewey. "After all, I'm nobody.

CHAPTER 37

Saturday morning Dewey went for a run along The Battery. It was cool outside, and the sky was clear. He watched as a cargo ship exited the harbor. With only a few days until Cistern Daze, he pictured the gates to Porter's Lodge opening wide and the Yard, elegantly lit with small lights on the limbs of live oaks, unfolding before him. A dance floor over the cistern would be erected to support banquet tables full of food and drink, and a band.

Bonner, Hoffman, and Tanner would all be there, as well as the rest of Kappa House. And in the center of the dance floor, like a royal court, Radford and his entourage. Dewey imagined standing shoulder to shoulder with him, not unlike how Radford stood shoulder to shoulder with the mannequin.

Before long, he was almost to Dr. Lyman's house. In the aftermath of the theft, he just couldn't resist getting a glimpse of it. Dewey, half naked but for a shirt, shorts and running shoes, took up a position behind a bush and parking meter, fearful he might be seen. From where he crouched, the windows against the backdrop of the white-capped harbor looked like battened down hatches. He could see the garden and the cherub statue, and the second-story balcony. Was he there, wondered Dewey. If so, where in the house was he? What was he doing? Was he looking at his display case and the cold, empty space between the books and porcelain figurines? Dewey could only guess, and though he still felt bad for what he'd done, he could feel himself less weighed down by it. After a few minutes, Dewey swiftly moved on, sprinting the rest of the block to avoid any possibility of detection.

The city's stench was particularly strong this day, as southwesterly winds had ushered in a warm front baking the pluff mud. The odor followed Dewey up Market Street to the Omni's main entrance. The doorman and valet carried on together, as Dewey breathed deep and wiped his forehead. Pushing open the hotel's heavy revolving doors, Dewey walked past the various shops and boutiques and came to sit in a plush yellow chair near the hotel's grand staircase. A couple in matching blue sweatshirts walked by with coffee. Behind him, hotel guests delicately scarfed back eggs, bacon, and grapefruit in an open-air dining room with a grand piano and Venetian glass vases. Light jazz played in the background.

Dewey felt good sitting in the warmth created by his run and listening to the beat of his heart. He looked at his reflection on the white granite tile floor below. He moved his legs back and forth and lifted both arms. Not perfect, he thought, but good enough. That's when he felt someone behind him. It was someone petite with thin arms and legs wearing a skirt and blouse. The mysterious figure was a warm, almost familiar, presence and smelled like magnolia. Dewey looked up to find Iris, the cafeteria worker.

"If you're looking for waffles, they're over there," she said.

Dewey looked up at Iris, surprised to see her at the hotel. She wore a white, starched short sleeve shirt and khaki blouse with an apron. Her hair was pulled back into a bun.

"Iris, what are you doing here?" he said.

"I work here on weekends," said Iris, "and saw you sitting here and thought I'd say hello."

"That's nice of you. I haven't been to the cafeteria much lately."

"I know. I hasn't seen much of you but I do catch a glimpse of you here and there from the cafeteria window when you're over in the Yard."

"You do?" said Dewey, surprised.

"A handsome, kind thing like you?" Iris smiled. "You sure spend a lot of time over in the Yard. What's there for you?"

Dewey tried thinking of the best way to explain things. "You wouldn't understand."

"Nuthin' in this town surprises me anymore. It's a place unto its own."

"Well, let me put it this way. Have you ever wanted to be someone else?"

Iris looked down at her shadow. "Sho have. Wanted to be rich white women on The Battery. Wanted to be someone who works in a big, important building downtown. Wanted to be back out on the island next to a big fire under the stars listening to the oysters sing."

"Well, I want to be like Radford," said Dewey, well-knowing this meant absolutely nothing to her. He said it loudly enough that a passer-by looked over at him. "And in a couple days I will. I mean, I'll be right beside him on stage at Cistern Daze."

"Why you tryin' to be like him? He just a pretty boy ridin' his bike around."

"Wait, you know him?"

"Yes, I knows him and those other three boys he rides with."

"But how?" Dewey raised his head higher, so he was almost eye level with Iris.

"Honey, when you work here as long as I do, you gets to know everyone sooner or later."

"Well, what do you think?"

"I think, why would you ever wants to be him?" Iris took a seat next to Dewey. "Look behind you at that mirror."

"Why?"

"Because I want you to look into it."

Dewey looked behind him into an antique gilded mirror near the registration desk. "But I can't," said Dewey.

"Yes, you can! Look!"

Dewey saw his reflection—square shoulders, curly hair and a symmetrical face.

"There ain't nothing wrong with *that* face that I can seez," said Iris.

Dewey looked back at the mirror again, hoping to see only perfection staring back. It was not there. "Goddammit, goddammit," he said under his breath.

When he turned around, Iris was gone.

CHAPTER 38

His watch read five thirty. It would take Dewey at least thirty minutes to walk to Dr. Lyman's for his follow-up appointment. He dragged his feet across the lobby floor, which had lost its original shine, and exited the dorm into a setting sun that painted the skyline pink and red.

The harbor was unusually calm, almost eerie. In the distance he could just barely see the Cooper River Bridge, one of only a few ways off the peninsula. Part of Dewey wanted to be on that bridge driving away from all that was happening–Radford, rush, the silver chest. A block from Dr. Lyman's house, a strong wind hit him in the face, taking his breath away. He passed the cherub statue in Dr. Lyman's front yard which he noticed had been repositioned since his last visit; instead of facing the harbor, it now pointed toward the house, so no passer-by could see its face.

A lump formed in Dewey's throat, as he knocked on the door. Light footsteps approached. The doorknob turned.

"Hello, Dewey," said Dr. Lyman. "Hardly heard you. I was wondering who was creeping around out here. Welcome to the home office."

"Hey, Dr. Lyman, I appreciate you seeing me after hours," said Dewey.

"Of course, come in."

Dewey noticed his tone was mild. Maybe he didn't suspect anything at all.

Together they walked into the parlor. Dewey looked at the sketched figures on the wall. They seemed to have resumed their labor but not as vigorously as before. In fact, some almost looked lifeless. The Banvard was still dreamy, thought Dewey, but it looked like it was straining hard to hold its position amid the current.

"I'm sorry for bringing you all the way here, but my schedule was full," said Dr. Lyman.

"No problem," said Dewey. "I think I may have mentioned I love getting down this way. One of my favorite places in town, really."

"Well, I just wanted to see how the floater was doing. Is it still bothering you?" Dr. Lyman squinted as if trying to examine Dewey's eye from across the room.

"Yeah, it's still a distraction. The only time I don't see it is when I'm in the dark, which isn't a whole lot. In fact, I'm just trying to forget it."

Dewey watched anxiously as Dr. Lyman got up and walked to a secretary in the corner of the room next to the display case. He reached into one of the drawers and pulled out an ophthalmoscope. He turned it on and held the shiny, wand-like device up to Dewey's right eye. "Hold still," he said.

Dr. Lyman and Dewey were almost nose to nose. Dewey could feel the device's narrow band of light strike the back of his eye. "What do you see?" he said.

"I see this," said Dr. Lyman, mysteriously, almost magically. Dewey backed away from the ophthalmoscope and saw that Dr. Lyman had produced a small silver spoon in his hand. Dewey couldn't believe his eyes—an apparition, perhaps, or, at the very least, a distortion from the floater. "What's that in your hand?" he said, seeking clarity.

"A silver spoon," said Dr. Lyman. "I found it on the rug like it had been dropped."

"Is this part of the appointment?"

"Only when the patient is a thief."

"Thief?"

"Yes, and, in your case, a thief in the night, it seems."

"I'm no thief. I was borrowing the chest. I was going to get it back to you. I promise."

"Why'd you need it in the first place?"

"Dues."

"I suspected as much. I'm sure things like these can be pressing on a clergy salary. A fraternity suddenly becomes a luxury." Dr. Lyman had returned to his seat, laying the ophthalmoscope in his lap.

"How did you know it was me?"

"Because the young man at the pawn shop also works estate sales downtown on weekends. We've done business together for years, so when he saw the chest with my initials on it, he knew exactly whose it was, along with your description."

Blue jeans, black boots, and a giant diamond ring tattoo—Dewey distinctly remembered him. How he'd ever be connected with those attributes to estate sales, let alone Dr. Lyman, he did not know. "So I'm supposing he brought it right back?"

"Right back. A rare species to be so young and so loyal."

Dewey knew to offer an apology and say nothing more. But something spilled over. "I'm not some goddamn country rube, ya know."

"I'm not calling you one," said Dr. Lyman.

The gentile country folk in the charcoal etchings above Dr. Lyman's head looked like they were trying to find cover.

"Don't think I don't know your clothes, your cars, where you go on weekends. I may not come with money for dues but I come with more than you might think," said Dewey.

"You're a hard one to classify, Dewey Cellars," said Dr. Lyman.

"You're an impersonator, trying to be someone you're not, which can have devastating effects."

"I know who I am."

"Then I won't try to enlighten you."

Angry, Dewey got up and looked around the room like he'd forgotten why he came. He walked to the door, as Dr. Lyman followed behind, the scent of his bay rum cologne filling the foyer.

"Sorry for everything," said Dewey, brusquely. "The only thing you've been to me since I got here is nice. Everybody's been nice, everyone except for me."

"Here, before you go, take this." Dr. Lyman handed Dewey a white, heavy cardstock envelope containing the silver spoon from earlier.

"What's this?" said Dewey.

"It was forged here in Charleston, melted down and shaped into its true form. You can get something for it, I'm sure."

"But I don't understand?"

"In time, you will. Just remember, the heat around here changes everything."

The once pink and red sky was now pitch black; the cherub in the front yard looked like it had fallen from the lightly etched clouds above. Dewey took the envelope and spoon, its outline raised and visible through the card stock, and started down the street past the same two middle-schoolers who'd been playing football in the street on his previous visit.

"Hey, wanna play?" one of them called out to Dewey, as he walked by. "You look like you could be a high school football star."

CHAPTER 39

An envelope lay under the door when Dewey got back from breakfast, but this one wasn't crisp, not like the ones from Kappa House he got weeks ago about the bid and pledging. Instead of white, it was cream-colored and sun-damaged around the edges like it had been left out somewhere in the sun, neglected, for a long time. He read it.

Dew,
  Call me. Okay?
    Sincerely, Mary Pate

He fell back on his bed and rested the note on his chest and looked up at the ceiling. What did she want? What more was there to say than what had been said in the Yard just a few days before? Instead of calling, he decided to go see her.

Dewey took the stairwell to the third floor and walked to Mary Pate's room. He hesitated before knocking, afraid of what he might find on the other side. How different this particular knock might sound—hollow, meaningless, maybe even spiteful—compared to just a few weeks ago when he and Alex knocked as eager party guests. Nonetheless, he lifted his hand, clenched his fist and rapped on the door.

"Oh, hey," said Mary Pate, opening the door, her head peeking out as if she did not know who was on the other side.

"Got your note. Can I come in?" said Dewey.

"Sure," she said.

Mary Pate wore an oversized white tee-shirt and blue, baggy shorts. Her hair was undone. Dewey noticed how small she looked and how slowly she moved, like she might have banged her knee or sprained an ankle. They sat together in the common room.

"I didn't see you in biology class this morning?" she said.

"Yeah, I slept in," said Dewey. "I've been really tired lately. What did y'all cover?"

"We finished up classification, we're moving on to animal reproduction." Dewey peered into Mary Pate's bedroom at her family photo. They all looked different now that Dewey knew the truth. Her mother—her hair in a low bun and still fiercely proud—bore no relation to Radford's family after all. A bad imitation. He had thought differently of her before. She had been higher up in the hierarchy. Now all he could concentrate on was her father and his chipped tooth. Of both parents, Mary Pate seemed to favor him the most.

"That's funny," she said.

"What?" said Dewey.

"Animal reproduction. I mean, I could probably teach that. Cows, pigs, chickens. I've seen life come out of all of 'em."

"What's it like?" Dewey scrunched his face like he was uncomfortable.

"Not as bad as you'd think. There's blood and everything, especially with the larger animals, but you forget all that because something beautiful is going on."

"Are you with them the whole time?"

"Well, in the beginning they'll want to be alone and then they take shelter and then you know the birth is close, so you try to be there till the end, when they're scared the most."

Mary Pate reached across the couch and straightened a pillow shaped like a barn cat.

"Your note said you wanted to talk." Dewey leaned closer into her.

"I want you to know I'm sorry. I didn't mean to say you'd end up in the gutter," said Mary Pate. "I just don't know why you wanted me and now you don't. Or maybe you just wanted me in that one way? Is it because I'm not beautiful like those girls outside the cafeteria with their preppy jackets and plantations?"

"They don't have plantations, Mary Pate," said Dewey. "Jee-zus Christ, you sound crazy."

"Well, somebody in the family does. They wouldn't look like that if they didn't."

"Look like what?"

"Money does that. It does something to your face. Makes it all perfect. Pretty. But it can turn you into something you're not."

Dewey could not deny what she'd said. He'd observed and felt the same in his years of coming to Charleston—it was a place and people with a mountain of wealth, privilege and luck amassed over generations from having acquired great swaths of land, sometimes by force, for the cultivation of rice and cotton for transatlantic passage for enormous profit. It was the construction of a Lowcountry mansion filled with slaves and fine silver and, for men to the manner born, the taking, collecting, for a wife a colonial dame of some means who would bare progeny in a backwoods fiefdom until that progeny's progeny, with Roman features, smooth complexions and important social connections, barreled down that great big mountain like a landslide onto King, Tradd or Broad streets ending in a pool of privilege and preppy fleece.

"You're pretty—okay? I said it," said Dewey, raising his voice. "And I like you."

"But not pretty like you and Radford and the cafeteria girls," said

Mary Pate. "Not that kind."

"Why would you ever group us like that?"

"Because y'all are so much alike."

"I only wish."

"What?"

"I said, I only wish. And you know who you're like? Alex! You're stupid like him. You're a hick. You wouldn't understand why I'm here anyways."

"Exactly why are you here?"

"Maybe because I don't like who I am. I don't like my face, my clothes, or even the way I walk. I don't like any of me, goddamn it. So, when I first saw Radford, I knew who I wanted to be. I knew if I just got close enough, things would change. I'd no longer be at the bottom of the pack."

"It probably didn't help I lied about him and I being related." Mary Pate had scooted further down the couch away from Dewey who had raised his voice at her.

"Not at all," said Dewey. "I never understood why you did it."

"Same reason you're doing it," said Mary Pate.

"What do you mean?"

"For someone reaching for the top of the totem pole, you're sure dense. When I first saw you on the elevator, I wanted to be next to you. I knew if I did, then I wouldn't be a hick anymore. You were pretty, you were polished. Don't you see? Everyone's chasing someone because they're running from themselves."

"I'm not running from myself, Mary Pate, I'm just running to something better," said Dewey.

"Isn't it the same thing, Dewey?

"But I can see the top rung, Mary Pate. I'm so close. Cistern Daze is almost here. I'll be like Radford. He said it himself when I got my tux." Suddenly, Dewey got up and stomped off toward the door.

"Don't run, Dewey. Please." Mary Pate grabbed him by the arm like someone begging.

"Get off me." Dewey broke her grip and pushed her back on the couch.

"Don't, Dewey, you'll hurt it," shrieked Mary Pate, clutching her belly.

Dewey looked at Mary Pate with wide open eyes. "Hurt what?"

"You know what."

"How the hell am I supposed to read you're fucking mind?"

"Here in the room after Cumberland's."

"But it was hardly anything." Dewey raised his arms in the air in frustration, before coming back to her.

"It was just enough, Dewey. But you won't have to worry."

"You're kidding me, right?" Dewey looked at her belly, speckled with rhinestones.

"No," she said. "I wouldn't lie about something like this. But you don't have to worry. Pretty people can just leave stuff behind because they think they're above it all. Not like us little urchins on the ground."

"You can be such a bitch, Mary Pate."

"Nobody would ever say that right now."

"I'm not nobody. I'm not. I'm somebody in Charleston."

"No, you're not. Faker!"

Dewey slammed the door behind him. He quickly descended the stairs back to his room, stumbling at one point. He thought he could still faintly hear Mary Pate—"Faker! Faker! Dewey Cellars from Ohio with his daddy's used clothes is nothing but a faker!

CHAPTER 40

Dewey awoke the next morning with Mary Pate on his mind. Was she just faking being pregnant? Could it really be his? After all, they'd only done it once. Maybe it was someone in SCA. Or maybe it was some other guy. If true, how would Virginia and Noah ever take the news? He walked to the common room. He felt strange being in the room alone without Alex. No juice boxes, a brown nubby carpet with countless spills and stains, a window that now seemed to push away the light. Dewey recalled that his last interaction with Alex had been as he set out for dinner at the cafeteria. "Better days, better lays," he'd said.

The phone rang, interrupting Dewey's train of thought. "Hello?" he said.

"Hey, Dewey, it's Lucious."

"Oh, hey, what's up?" said Dewey, his pulse quickening as he recalled the insult that had been hurled by the brother on the front porch of Kappa House.

"I have that paperwork you needed signing off on for your volunteer hours."

"I almost forgot," said Dewey. "I need that before Friday."

"Oh, right, Cistern Daze. They're starting to put the scaffolding up in the Yard. Hey, instead of meeting me in Towell Library, meet me tonight on Lower King at the big yellow house, the one with black shutters and the fountain shaped like an urn. It's a garden party. I can get you in. Just ask for me at the gate."

Dewey considered Lucious' offer. It meant one less meal at the cafeteria, and, after all, he'd be on his cherished Lower King Street. "Okay, cool," he said, "See you there."

He hung up the phone, fell back on his bed and thought about Mary Pate. How awful he'd been to her. Maybe she was just bluffing. How could she prove it was his anyway? He imagined having to marry her and cringed. Raising some hick child with her in some small, podunk town outside Charleston would kill him, he thought.

To escape it all, he drifted off to sleep, soon to be transported in his mind out to John's Island, back to the small peninsula with a bonfire where revelers danced, black men in red waders crabbed and a figure named Desirée orchestrated it all.

"I seez you come back," she said, issuing a warm but mischievous grin.

"I had to come back," said Dewey. "I only wish I could stay."

"Why do you say that?" Desirée's long skirt tangled in the bonfire's billowing smoke.

"Because here you stay beautiful forever. Nothing ever seems to change."

"No room for you here, Dewey Cellars," she said. "Too early."

"For what?" said Dewey.

"For finding out da truth about beauty. See, folks here cain't believe beauty ain't forever. They wants to hold onto it. They come out here hoping mother nature can gives it back to 'em."

"That can't be true," said Dewey. "Radford looks timeless. No one seems to know how long he's been here. He's always been beautiful and always will be."

Desirée lifted her arm and pointed toward the tip of the peninsula, where the marsh grass began to rustle, as if a great herd were stampeding forth. Dewey turned to look and at the head of this herd—shards of firelight playing on his face almost disfiguring it—

was Radford.

Dewey shrieked in horror. "But how can that be? Never in a million years would I think he'd be out here."

"But he is and has been forever. He at the college way before you. Been waiting on you for a long, long time. He almost an appa-ri-SHUN."

Dewey watched in disbelief as Radford danced around the fire, raising his arms wildly in the air. Dewey's face felt warm, so he backed away. Further and further he walked until Radford and Desirée became like embers on the horizon.

* * *

He awoke with his hand across his forehead as if protecting his face from the sun. He had slept for hours, and it was now night. A few rays of light from the lamppost in the courtyard shone through the window. "Shit," said Dewey, "the garden party."

Dewey sprang out of bed and opened not his but Alex's wardrobe. It was empty, empty in a sad way, he thought. No polo shirts, chinos or braided belts. No rugbys, repp ties or fancy loafers. And, above all else, no color. Only brown particle board with dried glue dripping down from the corners. He turned to his own wardrobe and, without looking, reached into it and felt for pants and a shirt. He pulled them out, the plastic cheap hangars falling to the bottom of the wardrobe, which no longer smelled like pine and Elmer's glue but instead was stale and musty. He put on a pair of blue poplin pants and a white Oxford shirt stained with ketchup.

When the elevator doors opened, Dewey could see Calhoun Street. Cars swooshed by in bursts of color—red, blue, and green. This time, he didn't care who was in them, not even Radford. He crossed Calhoun and began his journey down King to get to Lucious. Cistern Daze was now just hours away, and he began to feel the excitement. He would be in the Yard up on the platform next to Radford in practically no time at all.

As he passed the Omni, he noticed the balconies were barren of the petite mannequins that had been there weeks before, as the green awnings flapped in the wind, which had picked up in the past few hours. Meanwhile, further down, the dalmatian in the antique store window looked forever vigilante, continuing his watch over an English manor that may or may not have been. Then there was the haberdashery, home to the mannequin that had occupied Dewey's mind since the beginning, the same one Radford had stood next to and leaned on the previous day when he and Dewey picked out a tuxedo. For Dewey, the mannequin had come alive in that moment, made incarnate by the timeless Radford for whom everything seemed eternal, exquisite, and effortless.

Dewey recognized Lucious from behind by his broad shoulders and narrow waist—he was not wearing his characteristic maroon polo but rather a collared shirt, blue blazer, pressed khakis, and dark brown loafers. With a drink in his hand, he was talking with a small group of women wearing floral jumpers and seersucker skirts. He would speak, and they would laugh, with the laughter coming in waves like cicadas at night wheezing one moment and not the next. Except for his dark skin, Lucious could have been one of them, or one of the church parishioners—tall, slim, sockless.

"Is Lucious here?" said Dewey, calling out to a woman in a floral jumper who stood behind a wrought iron gate in front of the yellow antebellum mansion on whose porch Lucious stood.

"Sure," she said. "He's right over there. Gimme a sec." The woman turned and grabbed Lucious' attention. He looked at her and Dewey before starting down the porch steps and meeting both of them at the gate entrance. The girl who had summoned him disappeared into a mix of nearby crepe myrtles and hibiscus flowers.

She looked a little like Claire on Tradd Street, thought Dewey.

"Thanks for taking the long hike up here, Dew," said Lucious. "I mean, thanks for meeting me up this way."

"No problem," said Dewey, moving closer to the gate almost like he was waiting for Lucious to swing it open.

"I have your volunteer paperwork."

Dewey watched Lucious slip his hand into the breast pocket of his blazer. "Thanks," he said, retrieving the paperwork from Lucious. "Can I come in now?"

"It's a private party, but I suppose," said Lucious, his hand in the wrought iron. He opened the gate and just as quickly closed it, the action of which produced a giant clanging noise inviting stares from nearby party guests. "Well, after that ugly stunt you and your brothers pulled the other day, I'm not sure I should open this gate at all."

"It wasn't me," said Dewey.

"You were still on the porch—you simply hid. Why? I thought we were cool, as much as our being friends could be."

"We are cool, Lucious, but Kappa's changed things." Dewey stepped away from the gate.

A gust of wind went by carrying the smell of pluff mud. Down the way Dewey could see The Battery—whitecaps beating hard against the seawall, with waves coming up over it.

"Is it really them, Dewey, or is it you? Because I don't think you're one of them. Deep down I know you know that, too."

"Thanks for your fucking concern, but I'm okay. At least I'm not some white wannabe social climber." On the porch some guests with bleached-white teeth and over-sized smiles gathered for a photo.

Lucious lowered his glass and pointed at Dewey. "Whatever you're after here, it's drawn you in like a magnet. It's captured you. You'll never let it go, and you'll be stuck here forever, just like the rest of them."

"No, I won't. I'm just a regular college kid. I'll be outta here in four years and get on with my life." Dewey glared at Lucious across the gate. "And how about you—at one of these uppity garden parties trying to play the part. You're just looking to get another photo of pretty people for behind your desk. We're not that different, Lucious. We're just on opposite sides of the fence."

"You're chasing a ghost, Dewey. You're never going to be like that boy you're chasing, not in a million years," said Lucious.

"You don't know what you're talking about. I'm closer than you think, and tomorrow I'll be even closer when Cistern Daze happens. We'll be on that platform together, and people will think we're practically twins. Just this afternoon he gave me a tuxedo to wear for nothing, for free, probably the same one he's got. That should tell you something."

"It tells me coincidence, Dewey. A coincidence. He was just trying to sell you a suit and maybe he felt sorry for you, and that's why he gave it to you for free."

"That's not it." Dewey grabbed the opening of the gate from Lucious' hand, swung it open, then slammed it shut with all his might. It clanged loudly. Lucious tried to distract from the situation, but he could not hide or cloak the image of a black man on the inside and a white man on the outside. Dewey turned and walked off, away from his favorite part of town.

"Dewey, come back, I'll let you in," said Lucious. "You don't have to be anybody you're not."

CHAPTER 41

The lobby at New Dorm was unusually quiet, as Dewey walked in after having stopped at Sharky's to grab dinner and cool down from his interaction with Lucious.

"Where is everybody?" he said to the girl working the front desk.

"It's the storm," she said. "Can't you read the posters? It's made everyone kinda batty."

"Yeah, I've seen them. Guess I didn't really pay any attention." Dewey ran a hand down the side of his face and sighed. "So, is it coming or not?"

"The storm?"

"Yeah, the storm," said Dewey impatiently.

"They say it is. I don't know much about that kind of thing because I'm from Ohio. We just have tornadoes."

"Yeah, me too."

"Me too, what?"

"I'm from Ohio, too."

"Small world," she said, laughing. "I thought we kinda looked alike."

Dewey thought about where the girl might be from in Ohio. She looked preppy, but Dewey couldn't tell if that was just the clothes she was wearing. Maybe she was work-study, he thought, since he'd seen her there before since move-in. He wondered if she had a boyfriend. Wondered how she'd do up against the Kiawah girls. Dewey walked toward the elevator.

"Hey, before I forget, a guy came in here looking for you. Said he was with your fraternity, but I didn't believe him, so I didn't let him up. He's over in the study carrels." The girl pointed to a glass-enclosed room with desks and chairs in the corner of the lobby.

"Thanks. Did he say who he was?"

"I think it was Darren or maybe Dylan—yeah, I think it was Dylan."

Dewey's eyes grew big. What could he want, he thought. Had he done something wrong? Had something gone wrong in pledging? What could it be? For a second, he wanted to run, but instead he opened the door to find Dylan sitting at one of the carrels with his feet up reading a surfing magazine.

"Hey, dude," he said. Dylan reached for a handshake.

"Hey," said Dewey, taking his hand.

Dylan brought his feet down off the desk and set them on the floor. "Feel free to take a seat, if you want."

"Thanks." Dewey pulled a chair up across from Dylan.

"So, I guess you probably know why I'm here," said Dylan.

"Not real sure, actually."

"You sure you don't know?"

"Yeah, pretty sure." Dewey looked like he was preparing to duck something.

"I've just got to collect your volunteer hours. But I had you going, didn't I? Fuck, yeah, I did."

"Yeah, I guess you did." Dewey reached in his back pocket and retrieved the paperwork Lucious had given him just a few hours before. "Here."

Dylan took the paperwork, glanced at it and folded it up into a small square and stuffed it in his pocket. "What was it again you did for your volunteer job?"

"I gave campus tours for prospective students," said Dewey.

"How'd that go?" said Dylan.

"It was okay. Kind of awkward at times with everyone looking at you waiting to say something. Sometimes I felt like I wasn't myself. That I was trying to be something else. But they still seemed to believe me."

Dylan looked out into the lobby and crossed his arms. "By the way, I heard you got a tux from Radford. Classic and timeless—just like Rad."

"Yeah, he was really cool to do that." Dewey still wondered why Radford gave it to him for free. "I don't know if I could have afforded it."

Dylan chuckled. "Yeah, he's good for that. Once he bought all the kegs for one of our parties. Just laid it out on the table and bought 'em. Had them delivered right to the house. Too bad we don't see him as much as we'd like—he's always off in the marsh, they say."

"Yeah, we went for a bike ride last week and he seemed to know his way around. He knows so many people." Dewey thought about Claire and the snowman.

"Mostly locals from what I can tell," said Dylan. "It's like he's always known them. Speaking of Rad, he just wanted me to check on you and the other pledges about Cistern Daze. You ready?"

"Yeah, I think so. I mean, I've done everything. I think I'm right for it. I mean, the whole frat thing."

"Yeah, that's what your friend said." Dylan pointed up to indicate the floors above.

"Who?" said Dewey, curious.

"Some girl who lives below you, or that's what she said. She said she knew you. We turned her away at first, but she came back to the house a couple Sundays ago, so we let her in. She chatted you up— said we had the perfect guy."

Dewey thought about Mary Pate and how he'd seen her coming

out of Kappa House a few weeks ago after church. He looked out beyond the study carrel. The lobby, now full of yellow storm posters, seemed outdated. The large, rectangular planter in the middle was overgrown with big, leafy plants that drooped. The large, tinted case windows facing St. Philip Street looked foreboding. "What exactly did she say?"

"I told you numb-nuts—she said you were a good guy but I'm starting to think different. Anyway, that chick was, like, especially weird. A religious freak. But that didn't keep her from doing the old bone dance. I told myself not to but I couldn't resist. We were in the sack before I knew it. Sorry if you were bird-dogging her.

"But, anyway, my main reason for coming is just to make sure you're still coming Friday night and to give you your ticket, despite what this fucking hurricane does." Dylan pointed to the posters on the wall and laughed.

Mary Pate retreated from Dewey's mind. "Yeah, I'll be there. Wouldn't miss it." Dewey paused. "Let me ask—will Radford be there?"

"Should be. I mean, yeah, he's your big brother. But who really knows?"

Just then a poster fell to the ground.

"Well, anyway, I gotta go. They've got the platforms up in the Yard and we need to start setting up. See you day after tomorrow."

"Sure, day after tomorrow." Dylan got up from his chair and exited the room. On the way out, he grabbed a poster off the wall and made a paper plane. He threw it at the girl behind the desk who tried batting it away.

"Jerk," she said.

CHAPTER 42

When Dewey reached his room, he looked out the window into the courtyard. Through the darkness he could see that it had begun to rain, and the wind had picked up. The pink globules of the crepe myrtles were almost bare, the cool temperatures having halted their growth reducing them to fists of small, twiggy stems. The tabby concrete had lost its dusty, beachy glow and now just seemed like wet cardboard. Motorists across the way drove slowly up and down Calhoun like there might be an accident somewhere.

Dewey sat at his desk and looked at the computer screen in front of him. For the most part, it had gone unused. He'd flipped the switch only a handful of times to type small assignments, the fan whirring and the small, orange numbers and characters blinking. The big assignments had not come as he thought they would, nothing of substance. He felt he owed Noah and Virginia an apology for the big expense.

When the phone rang, Dewey was reluctant to get it. Last time he answered it he ended up in Dr. Lyman's parlor fretting about the silver chest. In his defiance, instead of picking up the receiver, he grabbed the cord, gave it a tug and fished it in. "Hello," he said.

"Dewey?" said a familiar voice on the other end.

"Frieda?" responded Dewey.

"Yeah, it's me," she said. "Stuart and I are still in town. Have you seen or heard from Alex?"

"No. No, I haven't." Dewey's face got flush, and he began to worry.

"We haven't either, and we've been everywhere."

"Have you contacted the college? I know somebody in public safety."

"Yes, we contacted them the first day. They said since nobody had seen him on campus that it was out of their control. But we did hear a rumor from the girl who sits at the front desk there in the lobby that he had mentioned something about Atlanta."

Dewey didn't recall Alex saying anything about Atlanta in all the time they'd been together. "That's strange. Why Atlanta? Is there family there?"

"No, we don't know anyone, and we're worried sick about it."

"Well, as you saw, his things are all still here. I mean, I'm sure there are a few things missing, but he would have packed pretty light to go that far."

"You're probably right." Frieda sighed.

Dewey could feel Stuart's presence in the background—his mind racing about where his son had gone and how he could get him back.

"I can't believe this is happening," said Dewey. "There was no indication."

"Did anything happen between you boys? He seemed so down last time we spoke. I know the whole fraternity thing didn't work out the way he wanted."

"Nothing that I know of. I mean, we teased back and forth but nothing big. Seemed to get along with the folks he knew."

Dewey recalled Mary Pate's party, Alex's desire for more muscle and, of course, his failing Algebra grade. These would be enough to dissuade anybody from staying at the college.

"Well, I'll let you be and I don't plan on continuing to bother you. This isn't your problem."

In his mind Dewey could see Stuart crossing his arms in the

background leaning up against the pay phone. "No, you're not bothering me at all. I mean, we lived together for the past month. I'm going to miss him. If you hear from him, let me know."

"I'll be sure to."

"Hey, what do you want me to do with all his stuff, his clothes?"

"We'll probably be by at some point but meanwhile feel free to borrow whatever you want."

CHAPTER 43

Around midnight on September 21, 1989, Hurricane Hugo made landfall near Charleston as a Category 4 storm with 140 mph winds and a 12-foot storm surge.

The wind around the Yard had picked up, the canopy of live oaks twisting, turning and thrashing. And the rain squalls from earlier in the morning had become more intense. The storm warning flyers in the lobby had been right—Hugo was coming.

Still, Dewey headed out for Cistern Daze, which, he learned, was still on. He felt for the ticket in his pocket and pulled it out. In the center was a line drawing of the Yard. Overlayed upon it was the Kappa crest. "Admit One, Thursday, Sept. 21,1989" it read. Printed on heavy card stock, it felt crisp in his hand like the notes that, over weeks, had been tucked under his door.

With his tuxedo on, Dewey was eager to see his reflection in the long, smoky windows of Simons Center, as he walked to the Yard. Upon passing the first window pane, he noticed his forward lean and gait. He tried pulling his shoulders back and standing up straighter. Then he faced the window head-on. He noticed his face looked fuller. Too many waffles at the cafeteria, he thought. But the extra weight didn't bother him. He ran a hand through his curly hair—it had gotten fuller, too. He turned his back to the window and looked over his shoulder. He could see the contour of the muscle that now helped shape his tuxedo jacket. In the lower corner of the pane, he spotted André, his big, vacuous eyes still bidding onlookers and passersby to obey. But in this case, Dewey could have sworn he saw him smile.

321

When Dewey had finally made it to the last pane, he was ready—he straightened his shirt, tugged on his shirt cuffs, and buttoned his jacket.

As Dewey traveled the short distance between the dorm and the Yard, heavy rain began falling, blurring the shape of things. Gusty winds bent nearby palm trees and live oaks that wrapped around the Yard. Overhead, Dewey could see slivers of blue sky in between swirling, dark clouds. Dewey noticed that the air was plain and odorless. His black, pleated pants were now almost completely soaked. His suit coat wasn't much better, as he sloshed through the pools of water in his dress shoes.

He looked up, and to his surprise, he saw Caesar headed toward him. He wore a long, yellow slicker, black knee-high rubber boots, and a plastic cover over his brimmed hat. His hand shielded his face from the wind and rain.

"What you doin' out here in this storm, Mr. Dewey?" he said, yelling over the commotion of the storm. "We done locked down campus and told you students to git home. Hurricane Hugo's started early."

"But Mary Pate told me it would be nothing," Dewey responded. "Besides, I have to get to Cistern Daze. It's tonight, you know."

Baffled, Caesar looked at Dewey as if he'd heard him wrong, as if the wind and rain might have twisted his words.

"Sorry, I don't know any Mary Pete, and I'm not sure what she told you about no weather, but this here's a hurricane."

"It's Mary *Pate*, with an A," said Dewey, frantically. "I'm sure you've seen her. Maybe you saw us together in the Yard a few weeks ago. Remember? We were waiting on Radford who never came."

"Don't know no Radford, either," said Caesar. "And all the college's events is cancelled until further notice. No Cistern Stars tonight. No, suh."

"Cistern *Daze*, goddamit," said Dewey, repeating it twice.

"Yes, suh, *Stars*."

Caesar's face had become less distinguishable, with whipping wind and rain filling in parts of his face.

"I'm sure it's still on. I'm sure," Dewey persisted. "It's just around the corner. I'm sure they're just finishing up getting ready. Dylan should be there. Look, here's my ticket."

Dewey pulled his ticket from his coat pocket and showed it to Caesar. The driving rain pelted it, chipping away at the drawing of the Yard. Dewey watched as it nearly disintegrated before him.

"I ain't gonna ask for your student I.D., son. Ain't no time for that. Nobody cares who you are. You ain't in no special club."

Dewey looked around at the buildings and streets that he had called home for the past month. They looked plain and lifeless—no André, no herringbone, no salt-caked windows, no sun-bathed views.

"But I'm telling you, Cistern Daze is real," said Dewey, "And it's tonight. Radford is real."

"Everybody got they own reality, Mr. Dewey, and they have to suffer the consequences, I suppose. Now I ain't gonna tell you 'gain to get somewhere with cover." Caesar grabbed the brim of his hat, and, leaning forward, side-stepped Dewey and headed toward College Lodge.

Dewey put his coat up over his head to guard against the driving wind and rain and crossed over St. Philip Street. He was certain he heard music coming from the Yard. Or was it the organ at Grace? Or the band from freshman mixer at the Stern Center? He put his palm on part of the wall encircling the Yard. It was still warm from earlier in the day, when the sun's rays beat down on it before the clouds came and the weather began to deteriorate.

The corner of St. Philip and George streets was dingy and gray, the rain landing hard on the brick sidewalk and bouncing back in the air like so many bouncy balls. A far cry from that spring day a year ago when pleasant sunlight shone through the palm fronds in the wisteria and ligustrum-scented air, and Radford crossed Dewey's line of vision for the first time.

Nearby, a lone cafeteria worker still in her khaki kitchen uniform and a droopy apron stood waiting for the city bus. Soaked to the bone, she clutched her purse like a life vest.

"Is that you, Desirée?" Dewey called out to the unknown woman.

She barely turned her head, the heavy downpour almost blinding. A bus suddenly pulled up on the street in front of her, splashing water high above the curb onto her legs. A sign on the front window read, *Evacuation Bus.* Its doors opened briefly, and suddenly she was gone, as if she'd been teleported.

Dewey turned his attention to the cafeteria and the leafy, rain-soaked foliage out in front that now lashed furiously at the building's entrance, where Dewey, Mary Pate, and Alex had waited with dozens of others to have their meal cards scanned. The plants' broad leaves bending sounded like sheet metal wobbling; thunder began to roar in the background. Inside, the cafeteria was dark, except for a trickle of light coming through the skylight.

He turned toward Porter's Lodge. It looked like an ancient ruin, its ruddy complexion punctuated by dark green shutters. Its iron gate was closed, and its steep, triangular roof looked severe and foreboding. Dewey crossed George Street, certain he'd see something, some evidence, however small, of Cistern Daze. He clenched the gate with both hands and leaned on it, hoping it would open, but it was locked.

Through the gate he could see the cistern rising up in the middle of things, and—even amid the wind and rain—he could see its short, bright green grass. He thought he could make out a wood platform atop the cistern and people dancing. And directly behind, on

Randolph Hall's spacious front porch, long banquet tables covered in white cloth. Tiki torches lit the brick pathways on which Dewey was sure he could see people walking. Strands of tiny lights on nearby live oaks made for a starry canopy. Under the arch, he noticed the air smelled dank, musty, and potent, with occasional hints of pluff mud and sewage. It was as if all the scents, smells, and odors of Charleston had conspired in defiance of a storm that was about to try and wash it clean.

A strong gust of wind overtook George Street, sending loose trash tumbling everywhere. Dewey reached for the gate to steady himself, when he spied, within arm's reach, a small, cream-colored envelope taped to the inside of the arch. The envelope was damp with big splotches of rain and marked with the Kappa crest. And in big capital letters DEWEY CELLARS. Desperately, he grabbed and opened it. *Know Thyself*, it read in cursive.

The letter was unsigned, and Dewey didn't recognize the handwriting. He looked through the gate and no Radford. But through a window of Randolph Hall, Dewey was certain he spied the slightest rustle of a curtain and what he swore was someone with high, chiseled cheekbones, an aquiline nose and curly hair parted at the side. Overhead, lightning cracked, and thunder rumbled. It became harder to see the cistern. Both Randolph Hall and Towell Library, with their red-brown stucco, looked like mud-draped mirages. He looked down toward the end of George Street, and it, too, was barely visible from the pummeling rain. A few tree branches from the oak trees had fallen, blocking the middle of George Street. In his tux, which weighed him down from the weight of the water, Dewey shrank to his knees, his hands sliding down the wet, slick bars of the gate. He felt trapped by nature.

He looked across the street to try and find the beautiful club of co-eds he'd seen the previous spring. Maybe they could help him. He imagined girls in flowing sundresses wearing sandals or Birkenstocks, maybe a wool fleece tied around the waist. Light, auburn or blonde hair, gently sloping noses and buttery complexions. Tan frat boys in white Oxfords and khaki Bermudas.

The storm was getting worse. Dewey couldn't see the cafeteria across the street. At that moment, he felt a hand on his shoulder. The stranger was faceless in the darkness and heavy rain, and smelled of bay rum cologne. Dewey rose to his feet, at which point the stranger pulled him close and, bringing him under an umbrella, whisked him away up George onto King.

The mysterious figure who'd come to his rescue was, in the blinding wind and rain, still unknown to Dewey, who had since pulled his suit jacket up high for more protection from the elements—a pledge pin the only thing now visible on his person. They dashed off to Lower King.

Amid falling palm fronds and water flooding the city streets, Dewey wondered if the ceramic Dalmatian was howling and if the blue and white bone china plates with flower motifs might crash to the ground. As for the mannequin? When he spotted him lying on his side through the storefront window, naked and knocked down, he looked dead. On his face no bright smile or even half-smile, as had been the case so many weeks before, just a sad frown and empty eyes that peered out onto a stormy horizon.

Finally, Dewey and the mysterious figure stopped in front of an old yellow mansion within view of The Battery.

"Over here," said the figure, opening a wrought iron gate and hoisting open a heavy, wooden door in the ground with stairs. "We'll ride the storm out here. It's the lowest point. It's safe. Into the cellar, Dewey, into the cellar."

ACKNOWLEDGMENTS

To Mom, Dad, and Jon, and our wonderful life together. To Kiki for the gift of aesthetics. To Vic for the many gifts from the pulpit. To Jon Paulding for his generosity. To Denny for pipe smoke and history. To James for room and board, fabulous art, and Gerber daisies. To Charles for wicker chairs, afternoon ponderings, and lily pads. To Tom for home alarms. To Nan, Annette, Larry, Caroline, and Dennis—your classrooms changed my life. To Honoré and the tea-colored Edisto. To Rob and Francis—you were there. To the Pitt, and plenty of sherry. To Julie P. for always picking up where we left off. To Scott, Audrey, and Jeffrey for helping save me. To Miss Dian for being Miss Diane. To John and Ursula for always asking. To Gre for good advice, always. To Dave, Nathan, and Rick for safe shel in the Woodshed. To Tim and David, and their platform transformation. To Frank and Rhonda who kindly kept after me. to all those I haven't mentioned—in the Holy City and beyond— have helped me find the club within.

ABOUT THE AUTHOR

David W. Frederiksen is a writer and girl dad who lives in Wilmington, North Carolina, with his wife and three daughters. He enjoys jazz and yoga, and tries not to take himself too seriously.